SOULS

ADRIFT

SOULS

ADRIFT

A Novel of Supernatural Suspense

Max MacCaigh

SOULS SERIES: BOOK I

ALVINA AVANTE

A Note to the Reader

Our formatter has set this book in 14-point Times New Roman font. Neither too big nor too small, this size is considered the optimum for reader eye comfort, readability and enjoyment.

Thank you

https://maxmaccaigh.com

For John and Dorothy

Great Lakes Bulk Cargo Steamship
"Laker" Configuration c. 1873

TABLE OF CONTENTS

ONE

Chicago, 1873

She had crammed everything into the steamer trunk—the only one she had left. It didn't amount to much anymore. What little she had managed to hang onto was stuffed in there like a dead person's personal effects: clothing, jewelry, some coins—every last pathetic bit of it.

Everything else she had brought with her to America was gone.

She could imagine them now, the aunties back in Sussex, tongues wagging and heads shaking over tea. Clucking hens. The comments: *How did she end up like that?* Then: *We expected so much more of her.* And finally: *We warned her, didn't we? We tried to tell her.*

Now, wouldn't they just *love* to find out they had been right all along?

Bankrupt.

Broke.

Those two horrid words summed up the brutal truth of her present circumstances. The bleak reality they conveyed was more than enough to convince Miss Maribeth Eaton it was time to leave. Chicago might be calling itself the "Phoenix City" because it would rise from its ashes, but that couldn't happen soon enough for her.

It had seemed like such a good idea at the time—a perfect plan…

Maybe too perfect.

She would never forget the article in the *Times* of London from six months earlier: *"Come to Chicago and make a million in our city's rebirth,"* the city's mayor had promised. Too good to be true, many surely thought, but…it seemed like the perfect opportunity for her. It all made sense, and her plan was sound in many respects. She had learned a great deal about her family's factories over the years, and now Chicago needed people with talents and insight such as hers to rebuild its industries.

Since the age of eight, she had tagged along whenever her father visited the family's many factories. She loved them, and loved the attention she got from the workers. The textile factories were second homes to her, and their workers her second family. They were so kind to her, and lavished her with attention—frequently bringing little gifts for her, or craft items they had made at home. She loved the sights, the sounds, the smells, and the activity. Each factory had its own personality, its own feel. They were almost living things, to her.

It looked to be the perfect match but…not to everyone. Family members had warned her not to embark on what they called her "silly American folly." Just take a short vacation, the aunts had advised. Maybe she wouldn't like it there, friends suggested. *Chicago? Why Chicago, of all places?* they asked.

Circumspect by nature, she had almost decided to listen to them all and *not* take the leap. Ultimately, though, she took that leap when a widespread family rumor became devastating fact—a younger cousin—a *male* cousin—not Maribeth—was chosen to take over the Sussex Best textile factories when her father—great grandson of the founder—retired.

Within twenty-four hours, she and eight Louis Vuitton steamer trunks—containing her full wardrobe and other prized possessions—were aboard White Star Lines' SS *Oceanic* bound for America.

Now, six months later, four thousand miles from home, in a foreign country and nearly broke, where she had no support, and with her hopes of success now dashed, she knew it was time to give up the dream.

Bankruptcy happened to other people—never to an Eaton. Until now. Once this got out—and it surely would—she'd never shake free of it. Marked for life, an object of scorn and pity. Her life story would be reduced to a wretched footnote in the family history.

I can't leave this city soon enough, she thought.

"Only the one trunk this time, miss? That's all? Just making sure," the mover asked, stopping in front of her and lifting his cap to wipe his forehead with a handkerchief.

She replied with a simple nod.

She knew the mover as Mr. Goode—*Leviticus T. Goode,* according to the sign on his wagon that was still mostly legible, nicely rendered in gold leaf at one time but peeling away, its glittering days long gone. He and his young helper had her trunk on a two-wheeled dolly. Noticing how sweat glistened on his cheeks and neck, she wondered whether his question was just an excuse to rest and catch his breath. She wouldn't have minded if it were—he was a hard worker and, overall, a very nice man. A good-humored older fellow, he was the same one who had delivered her eight trunks six months earlier. He was careful with her belongings, and she appreciated that. She hired him again, partly because of his attention to detail and partly because he was so kind to his horse.

His question made sense, though. No doubt, he remembered handling multiple trunks the last time. A lady moving out of a two-thousand-square-foot luxurious apartment with just a single trunk? Even though the place was furnished, he clearly seemed to find it odd. Which it was.

She smiled at him without elaborating, preferring to spare the details. Her nod was all he was going to get. There was no need to explain. And she wouldn't have done that, anyway. Why spill the whole sad story and invite pity? Still, some people were observant enough to take one look and figure it out anyway.

Che sfortunata might have been his reaction had this been Italy—unlucky woman. People there seemed to feel quite free to express their opinion of you to your face. You and your situation. But this wasn't Livorno, and it wasn't Florence; nor was it the tiny English village where her ancestors had lived for generations, knew everyone's secrets, and felt quite free to spread them around. It wasn't small-town America either, where everybody knew everybody else and there were endless eloquently-stated inquiries: *Where you outta? Who's your folks? What brung you here?* and so forth. No. This was Chicago. Where people figured if you wanted them to know your business, you'd tell them. Which was just the way she liked it.

Her failures were her business. Nobody else's.

She watched as they tied the trunk down on the wagon. She would see it next on board the ship. Seeing that one trunk on the wagon all by itself reminded her again how much she had lost and how desperate she had become. *At least I still have those things*, she thought, as she watched the old fellow walk around the wagon making sure the freight was secure.

She took one last look at the nearby homes, enjoying the sight of them, but sad just the same, fully aware that she would never return. They were all big and beautiful, most of them built for men who had made their fortunes in railroads, cattle, or the maritime trade. Some of them had been kept up, but many weren't, owing to some of those fortunes having been lost in financial panics or the many bankruptcies that followed the fire.

Mr. Goode tipped his cap. Maribeth made a friendly wave in response, then watched as he stepped aboard his wagon and prepared to leave.

She managed to hold back tears as she stood at the front gate taking one last look at what had been her home for the past six months. Red brick construction and built for a railroad mogul, it was in the French Second Empire style with a mansard roof edged with iron cresting and topped with a stunning octagonal tower. Quoins at the corners and arched windows. Lovely pavilions too. Inside, the best furniture and decor money could buy, much of it imported from Italy and France. Persian carpets. Jade sculptures from Hong Kong and a silver service from St. Petersburg, Russia.

The railroad man raised his family here, but he went broke after twenty years and sold the place. The next owner converted it to apartments. Maribeth's was on the first floor. How she loved it here. It was supposed to be her forever home, and she hated having to move out. It was breaking her heart, but she had no choice.

Pale clouds tumbled across a darkening gray sky, hurrying off to anywhere else but here, encouraged by a damp, chilly breeze from out of the south. Maribeth was glad she brought along a wool blanket for the ride, and hoped wrapping herself in its cozy warmth would lift her spirits.

The time had come for the sound she'd been dreading all day. The sound the gate latch was going to make when she let it fall for the last time. The beautiful black wrought iron gate that she loved so much. With all its intricate swirls. That last, sad *clink*. Regret welled up inside her, and she felt as though she should apologize to this place for leaving it. Not only had she failed her family and herself, but she had also failed this lovely home too.

As she swung the gate, a hinge emitted a rusty squeak. It sounded plaintive, as though it were pleading with her to reconsider. With the gate against its stop, she took the latch between thumb and forefinger… and let it fall. It was the end of her life here in this lovely home, and that quiet metallic sound finished her time in Chicago too.

The freight wagon was now gone but her carriage driver was still at the curb waiting patiently for her to board. Pausing a moment before she accepted his helping hand to step up, she handed him a slip of paper on which she had written her destination. She hoped he would accept the note without comment, but…

He held it up, brows knitted, a puzzled look on his face. Held it at arm's length, then closer, letting his eyes adjust. "You're sure about this? That's a rotten, busted up old cargo wharf," he said, in much too loud a voice. "You sure this is where you want to go, miss?"

She nodded, preferring not to discuss in public why her destination was an abandoned old wharf in a rough and disreputable part of town rather than a respectable passenger terminal. He could have just accepted her note quietly but since he had not, his question just floated in the air between them for a few awkward moments.

Eventually he slid the note into his vest pocket. She hoped he had finally understood her nod was a signal that she didn't want to announce to everyone within earshot that she was about to travel on a cargo ship rather than one of the much more luxurious passenger steamers of the day. Even his simple question seemed laden with his awareness of how far she had fallen. Her total failure. Or was she just imagining things again?

People seemed to think she did that a lot.

It made her wonder sometimes what was real and what wasn't.

Then again, maybe her failure was actually that apparent. Yes, how could it not be? To everyone who saw her. The entire city had to know by now that she'd arrived a rich girl but was now leaving nearly penniless. Obviously, there was something about the way she looked or carried herself now that beamed out her failure like a lighthouse. Emblazoning the sky with her desperation for all the world to see.

Not that it mattered much anymore though—it was just days ago when she finally gave up on Chicago in her heart and decided to take flight. Oddly, no sooner had she made that decision than the job offer—which she accepted with great relief—came from the school in Buffalo.

Maybe once she started working at the school and began earning a wage that terrifying word—*bankruptcy*—

would stop bouncing around inside her head and keeping her awake at night.

So at least that worry might soon fade.

But another one remained. And that one told her she had to leave this city. Right away. Something was about to happen and she knew it.

She stepped aboard the carriage. There was no time to waste.

Maribeth's driver hated having to come this way. It was hard on the carriage and frightened his horse.

No place for a lady.

The turn was coming up.

Don't make no sense what she wants to do. Where she wants to go.

He would've just as soon said to hell with the money and let her find another driver, but he'd been waiting there already when she gave him the slip of paper. *Whaddaya gonna do?* A fare was a fare after all, and paying customers were hard to come by anymore. The depression was hitting the city in a bad way. Seemed nobody had spending money these days.

The old fellow leaned forward, groaning a bit as he pulled on a rein. His horse drew to the right, swinging the carriage into a narrow street first of boarded-up little shops and vacant homes, and then…

A barren, charred wasteland. Stretching as far as the eye could see.

Never gonna forget this sight, long as I live.

Whatever had been there was gone now.

Destroyed. All of it.

Everything had burned away; only silence remained.

It was odd—eerie, even.

Broken building walls leaned at crazy angles like erupted tombstones. Blackened structures, with their scorched window openings looking like hollow, gouged-out eye sockets gazing emptily. A stone fireplace and chimney stood in the middle of bare blackened ground. Three stories tall. A lone guardian out there with nothing left to guard. Nothing else nearby, no trace of the home it had once served nor of the family it once kept warm.

No human life along here anymore.

The horse made a snort and darted to the left.

"It's okay, Fancy," the driver said.

But the creature snorted again as though unconvinced, tossed its head and high-stepped. It was getting spooked.

"Now, now, baby. C'mon, Fancy. C'mon now girl. It's okay," he said, calmly trying to keep his tone of voice from revealing the rising sense of unease he was feeling as well, entering this burned-out stretch.

The mare settled down.

The carriage wheels rolled, silent in the dirt but crunching over debris every few feet. The driver let the horse go slower, hoping she'd calm down some more. It seemed fitting, anyway, because he was loath to violate the tragic path of destruction they were passing through. It looked as though the gates of hell had been flung open along this stretch. Blackened shells of structures, heap after heap of debris piled up along both sides as far as the eye could see.

Nothing lived here anymore.

Even the smells of smoke and ash were long gone. What had once been businesses, shops, homes, small feedlots for cattle…

All gone.

This went on for nearly three miles.

After a while, they passed a hand-hewn fence, just branches and twigs woven together. A thin red maple sapling sawed down elsewhere, dragged here and tossed up, served as its top rail. Most of the maple's foliage had turned red and yellow-orange now. Pretty fall colors. The rest of its leaves were still green and bright, twisting happily in the late afternoon breeze, thinking they were still alive.

The simple fence surrounded a patch of cultivated land. A woman and a man were out there in that small field, bent over, harvesting what bit of produce they had managed to grow on that fire-baked ground.

Starting their lives over. From nothing.

She was in long sleeves, wearing an apron, skirt hem caked with mud. Over her arm, a wicker basket. On her feet, oversized work boots, probably men's, also fouled with mud.

He was in muddy bib overalls, shirtless and barefoot, dragging a brown burlap sack.

He spun around and looked up as the carriage passed.

Beneath his wide-brimmed straw hat…

Only shade.

Where there should have been a face.

Maribeth thought how going broke was bad enough, as the carriage rattled slowly through the burn zone. But that sort of danger could be calculated. Expressed on a ledger. You could take a pencil and draw a big X or circle a date and say yes, that's when things started going wrong, when it all stopped making sense.

If only that were all she had to worry about, but unfortunately there was something else.

The other thing.

That one wasn't written on a page or expressed in numbers. There was no way to apprehend or capture it. No way to measure it, and it was impossible to identify even though she knew it was around. She had no idea what it was but had a feeling it was coming… no, she *knew* it was coming. It was stealthy though, like what wakes you from a sound sleep at night—that thing that falls silent as soon as you hear it. Because it knows you're listening. That soft scrape or quiet rattle that you end up telling yourself you had not really heard, but which sends your heart racing anyway. You ask yourself, *did I just hear that?* Then you throw back the bedcovers and walk quickly to the door to check the latch and bolt. You don't know what made the noise, but you know one thing for sure: It doesn't *belong*. Then to the window to peer out from between the curtains. Even though you know the usual sounds of your dwelling and that this is not one of them, you tell yourself it's nothing.

Until seconds later when you hear it again.

At that moment, you realize it's not your imagination and that something is really there, and that the little voice inside you—the one whose only role is to protect—is alerting you. You know you're being warned.

The warning she got was about more than a little rattle at night, though.

That first time…

She would never forget it.

It happened as she approached a sidewalk café downtown next to the river, not quite three weeks ago. She liked the place with its European-style umbrellas and so did her friend Gloria, who was, in fact, her only friend. Gloria was enjoyable to be around because she was so thrilled to be here in Chicago, and her enthusiasm was contagious. In a few weeks she would return to Tuscany where her family owned a winery. Maribeth had visited that region with her own parents in her youth, and she loved exchanging memories with Gloria about central Italy's architecture, people, and weather. They enjoyed each other's company very much.

The café was the only one like it that she knew of in Chicago. A riverside haven that reminded her of strolling along the Arno near the Ponte Vecchio. A bit of Florence here in burly, broad-shouldered, tough-talking Chicago.

Maribeth turned the last corner and saw the café. The place was crowded but fortunately Gloria had already found a seat at their usual table. She was holding a menu and talking to a waiter and had not yet noticed her approaching. Maribeth was so happy to see her friend again after these few weeks and couldn't help but smile. It always gave her such peace of mind to relax and spend time talking with Gloria. Sharing her troubles.

She was so happy she wanted to shout—instead, she doubled over in pain.

Sudden and sharp from her right side just above her hip. She looked down, expecting to see something sticking out of her. A knife? Or had she been shot? Or struck by something? But no. No knife. No blood. Nothing.

Feeling dizzy, she reached for a lamppost.

And the pain went away.

Left her as quickly as it had come.

Her face felt tingly—hot and cold at the same time—and she struggled to catch her breath.

A passing gentleman stopped and asked if she was all right.

She nodded. "Yes, I think so."

No more pain now.

Gone.

He took a step back. "You're sure?"

She managed a weak smile and thanked him for his concern, then placed her hand on her forehead, took a deep breath, and stood up straight. Stepped away from the lamppost. Felt better now…almost normal. Maribeth looked around. She felt a little embarrassed and a little worried at the same time. The kind man had walked on. There was nobody nearby now, and she hadn't drawn attention from anyone else.

She seemed to be okay.

Took another deep breath.

She continued walking toward the café and Gloria… only a little slower now than before.

The two friends saw each other from a distance, and as Maribeth approached, they smiled and waved at the same time. Gloria had such a beautiful smile. Maribeth wanted so much to see her friend again because it had been nearly a month since they were last together. She was happy that

Gloria had found a seat at their usual table. It was the one beneath the blue umbrella they liked, the one with a gold *fleur de lis* on each panel.

Gloria began to speak, but she was slightly out of earshot. Although Maribeth saw her lips move, she couldn't hear what her friend was saying. She was only a dozen steps away at that point and would hear Gloria soon enough, but leaned a little toward her as she walked, struggling to hear.

Maribeth would later recall what she failed to notice at that moment—a shadow. On the umbrella. A shadow from above that grew quickly from the sun overhead and became a flash of movement and a sickening crash as the umbrella flattened.

The table seemed to explode, and all four chairs flew away as if from a bomb blast, just as panicked diners screamed and scampered and dived away from their own tables, dishes and glasses shattering on the sidewalk.

Restaurant staff rushed over, then just as quickly backed away, looking horrified when they saw—among table pieces and shredded umbrella scraps—what remained of Gloria, struck down by a man who had just hurled himself out of a fifth-floor window.

Maribeth dashed over to help her friend, but a waiter stepped in front of her and gripped her arm. "Miss, please. She's beyond saving.... Can't you see?"

"No! Let go of me!" she shouted, yanking her arm away from him. Then she fell to her knees next to Gloria and began picking away the debris that covered her. She was bleeding from the forehead and was missing most of a leg, eyes wide open and full of fear.

"Don't move. I'll get you out," Maribeth said, leaning in close, patting Gloria's cheek. As she pulled pieces of the table away, two other diners and a waiter came over to help. Soon it became clear that Gloria's leg was only folded beneath her, and still attached.

"Do you feel any pain? All I see is a cut on your forehead."

Gloria shook her head and began to cry.

"Don't worry, honey. Just keep still…. We'll get you out of there."

Gloria nodded.

Maribeth stood up to help others clear away debris, grateful that her friend had only been struck by fragments, but then realized the man had fallen directly onto the chair she would have been sitting in. He was badly mangled, and an arm was missing, now somewhere among the debris. Blood pooled all around him. Had Maribeth not paused when she felt the sudden inexplicable pain in her side, she would have arrived a minute sooner and been seated in that same chair—her usual spot.

She would have been killed for sure.

For several days following the tragedy, Maribeth told herself it was just a freak occurrence. A narrow escape that was, although however tragic and heartbreaking, a once-in-a-lifetime stroke of good luck for both her and Gloria. Only days after the event, her friend was able to take a train back east to New York, where she would board an ocean liner on her way back to Italy and her family.

However, Maribeth realized soon enough that it wasn't a once-in-a-lifetime event after all, because an echo of it, another *close call* as the Americans would say, took place a week later.

Just as the second noise at night tells you something is definitely not right, this echo told her what was going on was not simple happenstance. Not a coincidence, but possibly the start of something—the second link in a chain of events to come. A *pattern?* This event told her that whatever was going on, whatever was happening, it wasn't her imagination this time. No, it was *real.* Something was warning her, and she'd better pay attention.

This time, it was a man standing on a street corner as she was about to step off and cross. "Well, well, take a look at you," he remarked. "If you ain't some jammy bit of jam." He looked her up and down, ogling her curves with a peculiar grin as he uttered this impertinent remark in a London accent. She bristled at the rudeness of the fellow. And how could he have known she was English? Impossible. Thousands of miles from London, and this was someone she had never seen before. That question, his accent, how he was dressed, and the look of him startled her and made her stop for a second before she stepped off the curb and into the street.

And in that same second a runaway team of horses raced past, the wheels of their wagon scraping the edge of the very curb on which she stood, iron rims throwing sparks as the wagon hurtled by, its breeze ruffling her skirt and its teamster leaning back in his seat hollering and yelping and tugging on the reins as he struggled to control his panicked horses.

She turned around.

No one was nearby. And the Englishman was gone—nowhere to be seen, now.

She realized that in fact, he hadn't simply walked away…

Standing alone on that street corner with nobody else nearby, she knew at once that it wasn't that he was gone.

It was that… he hadn't been there at all.

Maribeth was not normally one to be moved by impulse, guided by omens, nor steered by superstition. Still, something was telling her it was getting dangerous here, and that for her own safety she needed to leave Chicago.

From now on, she'd give her full attention to this… *something.*

Whatever it was.

And there was more, still. Another troubling thing was taking place, a very peculiar thing, indeed. A puzzling dream in which she was inside a building that housed city offices, or perhaps it was the interior of a train station. She had this dream not just once but every night for two weeks: Ahead of her walked a young blond-haired girl along with her parents. Maribeth was right behind them when the girl turned her head, looked over her shoulder and began staring at her. Parents and girl turned a corner, then suddenly the mother was gone. Only the father remained, still walking, still holding his little girl by the hand. The girl continued to stare at Maribeth as she and her father walked. Then they turned another corner. When Maribeth rounded this last corner, the father was gone. The little blonde girl was alone, still walking, still staring over her shoulder, eyes locked with Maribeth's.

Out of the burn zone and onto cobblestones. Lining the street ahead and leading down to the water was a long row of buildings somehow spared from the flames. A chilly wind off Lake Michigan lifted dust and the stench of decay and decomposition into the air. Something dead lay nearby. Miss Maribeth Eaton brought her white-gloved hands to her face, covering her nose and mouth against the smell.

Raucous yelling screeched from sailors' saloons. Shells of once-thriving warehouses lined one side of the street, and the stink of turpentine and Carolina tar spilled out of ramshackle ships' chandleries and into the dilapidated neighborhood. Empty freight wagons were everywhere. Their horses were idle, heads lowered; their teamsters lounged nearby, hopeful, desperate for freight to haul somewhere. Anywhere. Doorways harbored the sleeping, drunk, or dead. Empty bottles and broken glass lay scattered up and down the street, and the chilly October breeze swirled trash up into the air. Idlers were everywhere—some arguing, others fighting. One man lay splayed out and motionless, face down on the cobbles. Four men stood over him, one of them rifling through his pockets, the other three staring hungrily at Maribeth, their heads turning as her carriage passed.

Her driver jabbed his finger at something far ahead. "There she is!" he shouted. There was immense relief in his voice.

Maribeth leaned forward to hear him over the street noise and the metallic rattle of iron carriage rims on cobblestones. She squinted, barely making it out…

A steamship.

He grinned, shaking the reins. "Almost there," he declared. "Last chance to turn back."

But she couldn't turn back.

No. Not safe here anymore.

The carriage wheels rolled hard onto a patch of cobblestones; the driver yanked on the reins and shouted a command, and his horse stopped in its tracks.

Maribeth's seat wobbled, nearly throwing her onto the floor.

"Sorry, miss. Rough cobbles. Didn't see that one coming."

"This seat's loose. I'm holding on for dear life back here."

"My apologies," he said. "Been meaning to take care of that. I'll slow down for you, miss. Bring her up to a slow walk and let it go at that. Ain't but a few minutes from the ship anyway." He shook the reins and clicked his tongue at the horse to get it moving again; then with a jolt, he straightened up and looked to his left.

Wheels clattered on stone right next to them as a black blur of a carriage shot past, its fast-moving horse high-stepping over the cobbles. Breathing hard and trailing plumes of gray breath, the creature kicked up a cloud of dust and the black canvas cover flapped in the wind the carriage made as it raced toward the distant steamship.

Miss Eaton coughed, as she waved away the dust. "*Good gracious*, what's his hurry?"

"Couldn't tell you," the driver said.

"That poor horse. Oh, dear."

"Coming up on a slow freight wagon just ahead. On its way to the ship too, I reckon. That oughta be Mr. Goode with your steamer trunk. We'll just ease up and stay behind him, if that's all right with you. Take our time. Long as you're not in a hurry, that is."

"By all means, feel free to slow down. *Please.*"

He shook his head. "Elegant, beautiful lady on her way to a dirty old cargo ship. I guess I seen everything now. You think you're ready for this?"

"Oh, yes, absolutely," she replied, even though she was scared to death.

A tall, lean gentleman passenger lifted a gold watch from his vest pocket as he stepped out of the black carriage and onto the old gouged-up wooden wharf. After consulting his watch, he looked down to make sure he wouldn't step on a dry-rotted place where his foot might punch through. He wore a black wool frock coat—unbuttoned—over a dark gray three-piece suit, sported a black bowler on his head, and clutched a leather satchel in his left hand.

Looking at the sky, he took note of the cloud types and wind direction and what they might portend for the weather. He lifted a few silver coins from a pocket and held them out for the driver.

"You sure, Captain? That's twice the usual fare, sir."

"You made good time, and you were right there waiting for me at the train station. I appreciated that."

The driver tapped the brim of his brown derby. "Well now, thank you very much. Generous of you, sir. A little extra ain't never expected but never refused neither, I like to say. That's my saying. Much appreciated. Handsome suit, by the way. Very nice tailoring."

The captain held open the jacket to reveal its black silk lining with subtle embroidered swirls of red and gold. "Augustus Meredith of Portsmouth, England. Had it a few years now."

"Ahh, would you look at that," said the driver. "Yes, made to last, sir. Made to last. Ageless, you ask me. Never out of style. Can't beat that; no, you can't. Beautiful work. Exceptional, in fact. No, I always say a gentleman can't go wrong with a look like that."

With a smile, the captain turned and began walking away.

"And thanks again, sir," the driver shouted after him. "Have a good voyage. Next time you're at the rail station, Captain, you just ask for Tippy Miner. They all know me there. Tippy Miner like the coal mines. Or Tippy Speed. They call me that too. Either one. Tippy Miner or Tippy Speed. I answer to both."

The captain gave the chatty driver a goodbye wave. Crossing the wharf, he approached the 740-ton wooden-hulled propeller steamship *Eli Greaves*, then came to an abrupt halt.

He ran an experienced eye up at her smokestack, then at her deck gear—the masts, booms, and winches. Frowning as though puzzled or troubled by a distant memory, he scanned the deckhouses, then along the hull.

It wasn't the profile that concerned him. It was a familiar one—pilothouse forward, engine spaces aft, long cargo deck in between. A configuration that enabled what they'd started calling *ore boats* or *lakers* to line up alongside the chutes at coal and iron-ore docks for faster, more efficient loading.

No. It was something else. Something didn't look right, yet what exactly…he couldn't quite put his finger on it. And he didn't like it when things bothered him in that way. For several moments he stood there, trying to make sense of what he was seeing. After one last look around, he shook his head, then started up the gangway.

A tall man stepped forward to greet him. Six foot three, the captain guessed. Mid-thirties. Brick-red hair, thick and unruly but trimmed above the shoulder. Beard carefully cropped, its color matching the hair on his head, together framing a well-tanned face with penetrating gray eyes.

At first glance, the captain thought he looked bookish. Something of a cultivated look about him. Being broad of shoulder, however, and having thick, well-muscled forearms belied a scholarly countenance, as did the long scar that began at his throat and ran the entire length of his jawline to just beneath his left ear. There was also a small bare patch crossing his right eyebrow where he had another scar.

It was easy enough to see—the man had been in some battles and weathered a few storms in his life.

The captain paused at the end of the gangway. "Permission to come aboard?"

"Yes, sir. Of course." The fellow extended his hand. "Welcome aboard. Captain McBride, I presume."

McBride nodded. They shook hands.

"Good to meet you, Captain. I'm Atticus Miles, your first mate. Pleasant trip from Milwaukee, sir?"

"Not bad, thank you." The captain brushed dust from his coat sleeve. "There's pretty good train service these days and even more improvements to come. Something to look forward to. I just learned today they're going to change the name of the expanded line to the Chicago, Milwaukee, and Saint Paul."

"I've heard that too, sir."

"More good news for our fire-ravaged Chicago, and maybe not the last, eh?"

Miles nodded. "She's had a tough time. Better days to come, we should hope."

The captain pointed toward the cargo deck. "Tell me, Mr. Miles, since when has this ship berthed here in Chicago? Do you know? What I'm seeing here—the cargo deck, her lines, the hull, masts, deckhouses. Location of the deck gear, too. It all looks so familiar to me. But then strangely not. I've known of the *Eli Greaves* for quite some time. She's sailed out of Milwaukee since as far back as I can remember. Saw her come and go for years. But this ship doesn't look like the *Greaves* I'm familiar with. Not at all."

Miles nodded slowly as he gazed across the cargo deck. "I'm told the present owner moved her two years ago. Patched the hull in a few places, had the hatches and houses painted, made up these new hatch covers, and—"

"No, I just don't see it," McBride said. "Hull repairs are easy to spot. But if it's got the dry dock surveyor's stamp of approval and it stays together, that'll be that."

"Yes, sir."

"Let them fix it; we'll sail it."

"Comes down to that, doesn't it, Captain."

"The work was nicely done though. I'll say that much."

Miles nodded. "Yep, they put some effort into it, didn't they? You can tell. Decent job overall."

"She wasn't dry-docked in Milwaukee to my knowledge. Where'd that take place? Do you know?"

Miles shook his head. "Never heard a thing about that. No, couldn't tell you."

"Anyway, reservations aside, the sailing part, that's where I come in, Mate Miles, being now in the employ of the current owner. And he's a man who knows his steamboats, or so I gather. I have no reason to believe otherwise. Saint Louis fellow, name of Street. Joshua H. Street II. Perhaps you've already met him."

"Haven't had the pleasure, Captain."

"Shipping family, going back years. He's new to Great Lakes ships though. Mississippi rivercraft mostly."

A freight rig's wheels rumbled across the wharf. Wooden timbers creaked and groaned underneath as it approached.

It stopped alongside the *Eli Greaves*.

Miles liked the wagon right away. It was a handsome green Schuttler model and bore the name *Leviticus T. Goode Co., Freighters* in large, cursive letters in gold leaf.

The wagon's glowing green paint was glossy even though the clean and well-polished surface had signs of wear. The wagon was certainly long past new, but the owner took good care of it and must have been proud of it. He clearly wanted it to last.

The teamster was an older man with a thick mop of white hair. Probably the wagon owner. He leaned back, pulled up on the reins, made a click with his tongue, and the horse stopped.

The freight handler was just a boy, barely eight or nine years old, with a dirty face. His long-sleeved white shirt was several sizes too big for him. Big cigar clamped in his teeth even at his age. A duckbill newsboy cap was pulled down low over one eye, a length of frayed rope over one shoulder served as suspenders. He hopped down and dashed to the back end of the wagon. He was barefoot, and his skinny knees poked through holes in his baggy wool trousers. He unhooked the tailboard, and it swung down with a clatter and a cloud of dust.

The old teamster stepped down slowly and with apparent physical discomfort. He gave his horse an affectionate pat on the shoulder, then a quick hug around the neck and a scratch while whispering into its ear. When the fellow tapped his coat pocket, the horse nudged it with its muzzle. The old man whispered again, then removed a treat from the pocket and held it in the flat of his hand. The horse took this from him in a manner that was surprisingly gentle; it nodded, then swung its muzzle over to touch him on the cheek.

The first mate couldn't help but smile.

The teamster gave his friend a quick rub about the ears, whispered to it once again, then went around to help the boy unload the freight. The two of them hefted the captain's trunk onto a two-wheeled dolly, then pushed it onto the gangway and up to the ship.

"To the forward deckhouse, gentlemen. Captain's cabin," Miles said. "And take it right inside, please."

As man and boy maneuvered the captain's trunk forward, Miles took out his pipe, filled it with tobacco, and lit it up. A fragrant gray cloud enveloped him, but did not linger owing to the early evening breeze.

What did linger, though, at least for some moments, was his feeling of optimism now that Captain McBride had arrived. Miles had heard good things about the man and hoped his arrival meant his own luck was about to turn.

Too long without a job this time, he was eager for the ship to get underway. This would be his first employment since July except for a few weeks of pick-and-shovel work inside the burn zone. Things were getting a little better since the fire, but slowly. The Great Chicago Fire, they were calling it now. It was a well-earned title: Three hundred souls estimated lost, thousands more missing and unaccounted for, and seventeen thousand buildings reduced to rubble and ash.

As if all that hadn't been enough to bring the city and its surviving residents to ruin, the recent failure of banker Jay Cooke & Company made a happy ending to the tragedy even less likely. The city was struggling through a depression. Most rebuilding projects were now on hold, and that was the last thing Chicago needed.

At least McBride was on board now. Miles could give the other mates the go-ahead to prepare for getting underway in the morning, and the engineers could light off the boiler and start building steam. He was relieved and hoped nothing would delay their departure. Casting off on this voyage would result in two or three weeks of pay at least, maybe even a month or more. Not a lot, but better than nothing. And this was no time to be choosy.

McBride hadn't gone inside yet. He seemed to enjoy being out on deck observing the goings-on. A good sign maybe—a clue that he was unlike some skippers who'd disappear into their cabin the first chance they got and only come out when they had to. Nor was McBride said to be meddlesome, hovering over every single operation and driving the mates crazy. He appeared to be a calm fellow, just standing there looking around, hands clasped behind his back. Not the nervous type, fortunately. All that kind ever did was create more stress. McBride had aged well despite being etched with wrinkles about the eyes from a reputed forty years at sea. He'd been a mariner since the age of ten, and there'd never been an unkind word uttered about him so far as Atticus knew.

He had earned his excellent reputation, and with his breadth of experience, he had nothing to prove. That was clear in how he handled himself. On the one hand, he carried himself with confidence, but on the other hand, his demeanor was understated, almost to the point of modesty.

A covered carriage pulled onto the wharf and glided slowly toward the ship. It was a beautiful thing—bright white canvas cover, glossy black bodywork with red-and-gold trim, wheels with golden spokes that glittered as the carriage rolled.

It stopped just ahead of the Schuttler wagon.

"The lady arrives," Captain McBride said, standing up straighter, adjusting his collar and hat, then checking his cuffs.

The carriage driver stepped down onto the wharf, then spun around smartly, clicking his heels as though he were presenting himself for a military review.

The man was in his sixties at least, decades too old for such soldierly pretensions. He stood at a modified version of parade rest, facing his carriage while holding one hand at the small of his back, fingers together, palm stiff and straight, or at least as straight as he could manage with that left hand of his clearly twisted by arthritis.

Holding the other hand extended toward the cover opening, arm held out sword-straight, he awaited his passenger.

Who had yet to appear.

Miles wondered if the fellow took his job as seriously as he seemed to or if the display was merely to earn him a bigger tip. Anything that looked the least bit military seemed to him superfluous and extravagant, absent a war. His own Civil War skirmishes and battles and their attendant horrors were years behind him now, and things military—the rigid posture, the accouterments—that had fascinated him in his youth no longer did so. Seeing your fellow soldiers shot and slashed to pieces as well as picturesque fields and idyllic rolling meadows soaked with blood and heaped with the dead and dying would do that to you.

He took his pipe in hand, pursed his lips and blew ash from the bowl. Stepping to the rail, he leaned out over the side and was about to spit.

Then he saw her.

Peeking out from behind the white canvas side flap, she extended her hand and accepted the driver's grip. Then he helped her down the step and onto the wharf.

The shape of her. Impossible to ignore. A lovely, rounded curve of hip, tiny waist, and the rest? How would he put it? The word *abundant* came to mind. She wore a full, floor-length cinnamon-brown skirt with a ruffled coral blouse, the high collar revealing her elegant, slim neck. Clothing purposefully chosen for traveling, Miles reckoned. He didn't know the names of ladies' outfits, but on her it was remarkable, call it whatever the hell you want.

Miles stepped back from the rail, unable to take his eyes from her. Not only was she stunning, but she looked more out of place here than anyone he'd seen yet. He found it astonishing that she had survived the carriage ride through the neighborhood unmolested.

She appeared to shiver, then took the blanket she wore and drew it even tighter over her shoulders, gathering it around her neck. She looked toward the steamship. Seeing Miles staring in her direction, she nodded to him, flashing a beautiful, bright smile.

He nodded in mute response.

The carriage driver followed her to the ship, then stood by as she gathered her skirts, lifting them a bit while stepping onto the gangway. Lifting them a bit more than she needed to, in fact, providing Miles with a glimpse of a slender ankle and fine, shapely calf. She looked up and caught him staring at that pretty leg. He averted his eyes just as she smirked a little. Or appeared to, anyway.

He stood at the top of the gangway, ready to assist her. As she approached, Miles couldn't take his eyes from her face, such was its perfection. Her eyes: almond-shaped, light brown, ringed with a touch of gray, with a slight upward slant. Shimmering like gemstones, imparting to her European features an exotic look. Her exquisitely shaped lips, full and etched so perfectly in a pale vermilion.

He caught his breath and absently brushed tobacco ash from his cuffs, then reached out to ease her step down onto the deck. "Welcome aboard, miss. First Mate Miles at y…your service," he stammered, realizing he still had the pipe clamped in his teeth.

He removed it with his free hand.

"Thank you, officer. Maribeth Eaton," she replied in a distinct and refined English accent. There was a youthful air about her. She wore a tiny and jaunty, rid-ribboned straw hat, and her medium-brown hair in back spilled out in ringlets down to her shoulders. She took his hand in both of hers and hopped onto the deck. Then she took a deep breath of cool lake air while glancing around. "How exciting. My first time on a cargo ship."

The fragrance of flowers surrounded her.

Miles was slow to reply. Everything about her had taken him by surprise. His mind was a whirlwind; it groped for words. He always had something to say no matter the situation, but right now, he didn't. She tilted her head inquisitively, patiently awaiting his response, beaming her intoxicating smile.

"We're ha…happy to have you on board, Miss Eaton. And I'm pleased to meet you. Pleasant ride here, I hope."

"Oh yes, this kind gentleman took great care navigating the bumps and didn't bang me around too much."

The grizzled driver nodded, touching the brim of his cap.

"Thank you, sir," Miles said. "The freighters will handle the lady's trunk." He handed a couple of silver coins to the driver. The fellow studied them briefly, then shoved them in his pocket, tapped his cap brim again, and walked back down the gangway.

Miles looked toward the captain, who had stepped aside for the moment. "Sir?" he said, tilting his head toward the lovely new arrival.

The captain nodded and gestured to let Miles know he should attend to the passenger first.

"Miss Eaton," said Miles, "if you'll come with me, I'll show you to your cabin. It's in the foredeck, just beneath the pilothouse, in the passageway along with the captain's cabin and my own."

"That will be wonderful, Mr. Miles. You're so kind. Golly, you certainly are a tall fellow, aren't you? I'm up on my tiptoes trying to look into your eyes."

As the two of them made their way forward, Miss Eaton explained that she'd been in America for just six months, had applied for several positions, but found nothing suitable in Chicago. "I'm not much of a city girl, Mr. Miles, despite all appearances. But I'm not sure I'm cut out for life on the prairie either. Not yet, anyway. So now I'm headed to Buffalo. There's a school administrator's job waiting for me there. A new chapter in my life," she said cheerfully.

"That's very nice. How exciting for you."

Maribeth nodded. "Mm-hmm, yes."

As they approached the forward deckhouse, he caught her fragrance again. With the elegant lilt to her voice sounding so musical to his ears and in that wonderfully polished English accent, hearing her speak was like listening to a song performed in an idyllic floral garden.

The passage where they walked was narrow. They were side by side between the ship's rail and the cargo hatches. So close to each other that with every step Miss Eaton took, her dress brushed against Miles's leg, sending his heart racing.

He studied her from the corner of his eye, entranced by the exquisite and effortless grace with which she moved— at least what he imagined of her under that skirt—and how she swung her arms back and forth with such confidence as she walked. He noted how her jewellike eyes darted around the ship, expressing her endless curiosity.

"Was that a Southern American accent I heard, Mr. Miles?"

"Yes, Miss Maribeth," he replied in that uniquely Southern fashion that pairs a respectful address with first-name intimacy. "Tennessee born and bred," he added in the exaggerated drawl he normally saved for tourists.

She lifted her chin and smiled, evidently pleased with herself. "I'm learning your American accents little by little."

Arriving at her cabin, Miles explained that the *Greaves* would sail at first light with one stop in Ohio to fill the coal bunker and drop off two passengers before continuing to Buffalo. "Ought to take us four days."

"That's what I've been told. It's perfect. Leaves me a bit of free time before my appointment at the school."

Miles opened her cabin door.

It was a medium-size cabin with a full bed along the forward wall—the one to their right—a dresser straight ahead on the hull wall, and a desk with a reading lamp and small chair against the wall to the left.

"It's splendid. Looks so nice and cozy. And so fresh here. And my very own porthole! Curtains, too. I love it." Removing her gloves, she spun around and looked directly at him. "You're very kind, and I hesitate to impose, but I have a request."

"Of course. Anything, Miss Eaton."

"If you could stop by from time to time and check up on me, that would give me great comfort. And would you mind calling me Maribeth? Miss Eaton is so formal."

Those shimmering eyes, the fragrance of her. And right now, standing so close, nearly touching. Her chest lifting as she took a breath, awaiting his reply. What sane man could say no to such a request?

"Uh, as you wish. With pleasure, certainly. Ye…yes, I can do that."

"And how shall I address you, Mr. First Mate Miles? Does maritime law forbid me from using your given name?" She said that with a teasing smile.

"Oh yes, of course it does. I mean, *no*. Yes, of course you can use it. I mean, *may* use it. Please call me Atticus."

"In that case, I shall indeed," she intoned with mock formality. "Atticus it is, then."

She reached out, and Atticus gladly took her soft, warm hand. He enjoyed the feel of her bare hand wrapped inside his own as he gave it a gentle shake.

He wished he could look at her face forever and never have to let go of her.

She looked into his eyes and smiled. Those lovely lips were the most beautiful thing he had ever seen. Tilting her head slightly, she seemed poised to speak.

A screech from outside.

Squealing.

Somebody running.

Atticus spun around. "I'm sorry, Maribeth. Excuse me, please."

He ran down the passageway and out onto the deck.

Captain McBride couldn't believe his eyes.

Racing to the gangway was the little freight boy, screeching and pointing, looking over toward the wharf.

The old freight man, Mr. Goode, was close behind, walking as quickly as he was able, also pointing.

When the boy reached the bottom of the gangway, he dashed for the freight wagon as fast as his short legs would propel him.

Then McBride saw two men running off with the lady's trunk.

Atticus bolted down the gangway and onto the wharf.

When the thieves realized the trunk was too awkward and heavy, they let it fall to the ground, where it rolled onto its side. Cursing, they threw it upright and flung it open, tossing out clothing and frantically began digging for more valuable things.

The boy was the first to reach them. He tackled one, but the man took such a hard swipe at his forehead that he went flying, his feet leaving the ground. He landed two yards away, hopped back up and threw himself at the other man, only to be knocked down by a dizzying slap to the face.

Atticus barreled into one of them at full speed, knocking the fellow flat onto his back. The thief picked himself up and ran off, but the other was still busy snatching whatever he could from the trunk. Atticus reached him from behind and grabbed his neck in the crook of his arm, then spun around, yanking him off his feet and sending him sprawling across the wharf.

The shocked thief dropped everything and ran zigzagging away, holding his wrenched neck.

McBride had made it over to the scene by then, as had Mr. Goode. Miss Eaton stepped off the gangway and hurried over.

Atticus knelt beside the child, gently cradling his head, whispering to him.

Miss Eaton dropped to her knees alongside the boy. She had recovered his cap from near the gangway and put it in his hands. Gently placing her palm against the youngster's cheek, she turned tearfully to Atticus. "Will he be all right?" she asked in a wavering voice.

When the young lad lifted his head and grinned, she had her answer.

She smiled, relieved. "You're one very brave boy."

Atticus nodded. "He sure is."

"Thank you, miss," the freckle-faced child said. "And thanks, mister."

The captain and the freight man both murmured agreement, as they nodded their heads. Both had great sadness in their eyes.

"No, don't get up yet," said Miss Eaton. "It's okay. Just stay there a minute. What's your name?"

"Name's Frankie, miss," he announced with great dignity. *"Frankie Knight!"*

McBride had to turn away, sad at hearing the child state his name so proudly, all the while with his ragged clothing, dirty face, and filthy bare feet. The captain rubbed his eyes with the heel of his palm. "Where do you live, son?"

"He don't live nowhere," the freight man said. "Mostly he don't, anyway. He stay with his grammy sometimes, though."

"You got folks?" McBride asked, nearly whispering. "A mom and dad?"

"Naw, sir. They dead."

"Brothers? Sisters?"

The boy shook his head and shrugged with a bashful smile.

"They was all lost in the fire, sir," the freight man said quietly and with reverence. "Took them all, what I been told. He been all by hisself past coupla years. My missus, she'll make up a plate for him when she able. But we ain't got much, neither." He pointed to Atticus. "Lookit him, Frankie. He a redhead just like you. Big, strong feller. Maybe you grow up to be big and strong too."

The boy grinned broadly, his face lighting up.

Miss Eaton looked up at the captain, squeezing her face tight as her eyes filled with tears. She softly patted the boy's cheek again, then stood up and walked over to where her belongings lay scattered.

Several minutes later, having picked up her things and returned them to the trunk, she spoke to Captain McBride. "Sir, do you know any booking agents personally? Or anyone else with whom you've done business?"

"As a matter of fact, yes."

She wiped away a tear. "Or someone who can see to it this child is fed and clothed properly and make sure he has a roof over his head?" She reached out. In her hand, she held two twenty-dollar double-eagle gold coins. "Were it not for our brave little Frankie, the robbers would have made off with these and everything else."

"My wife's sister is a widow with a young son," McBride said. "Not too much older than Frankie here. She lives in Milwaukee too. I'll have a telegram sent to her later today. I think she'll be glad to take care of him for a while. And thank you for your kindness and generosity. You can be sure my wife and daughters will also make looking after Frankie a special project of theirs from now on."

Minutes later, McBride and Atticus again stood near the gangway.

"You handled that like a genuine hero, Mr. Miles."

"Thanks, Cap. But Frankie, he's the hero. Had it not been for his sharp eye…"

McBride nodded. "Brave lad."

"I had a boy about his age," Miles said. "And I'm proud of Frankie; he protected Miss Eaton's things."

"That he did, yes. I'm proud of him too. And she seemed to take it all pretty well."

Atticus nodded. "Yeah, she did, didn't she? I'll stop by in a few minutes to make sure she's recovered everything. Looked like it was all there, she said."

"That's a relief. So, we were talking about this ship's name. The more I think about it, the stranger it seems. I don't know about you, but I don't care for it when things leave me puzzled. When things don't line up, I wonder why. This is of no slight concern to me, as you may well imagine. The *Eli Greaves* I knew was an older ship than this one."

"I've been told they rebuilt her."

McBride shrugged. "Well, perhaps. But you can see it as easily as I can, Mate Miles, when a ship's had hull planking replaced, things like that. It stands out. And I see nothing of that sort. I say this is a newer ship."

"I'll give you that, sir. Yes, I know what you're saying."

McBride shrugged. "I must say she looks seaworthy, though."

Atticus nodded, and spoke with his pipe clenched in his teeth. "I was aboard much of last year, and she gave us no trouble to speak of. Performed well enough."

McBride shivered a little, then rubbed his palms together. "Well, there we have it. I'll take that as a vote of confidence. So, reservations and doubts aside, here we are. We've come aboard to ply our trade, have we not? And we've a job to do."

"Yes, sir."

"All right, then. I'll be in my cabin, and please have the ship's log brought to me. We sail for the Straits of Mackinac at first light."

"Yes, of course. I'll bring—"

"Is the chief engineer aboard?"

"Yep. Yes, sir, he is."

"I requested the most recent boiler survey if there is one, or at least the last boiler inspection report."

"I left the inspection report on your desk."

"Excellent. And one more thing. We have a carpenter, I hope. I'll need a frame made for a portrait I want to have mounted."

"Oh, sure. Owen Diggs, a deckhand. He can do that. I'll have him come to check, see what he can do for you."

McBride took a few steps, then spun around. "And Mr. Miles…?"

"Sir?"

"What we've just discussed. About this ship. It's best this sort of talk goes no further than the two of us, hmm?"

"Of course, Captain."

"It's one thing if you or I have misgivings, even suspicions, but our passengers needn't learn of this. Why excite their fears and darkest imaginings? We've no need of that."

"Oh. No, sir."

"Why give them cause to conjure up foolish phantasms? That's my way of thinking."

"Of course. Couldn't agree more."

"We are of like mind, then."

Atticus nodded. "Yes, entirely."

"Good man," the captain said, shivering again. He lifted his coat collar, pulled it tight around his neck, then rubbed his hands together once more. "Well…that's all for now. You know where to find me. And thank you again for how you handled things on the wharf."

Early that evening, deckhand Jefry Walks was on the foredeck with a mop and a bucket of water, giving it a swab-down. He was full of anticipation and excitement. He knew these feelings well; he had them before every trip.

He had finally decided two years earlier to see the world beyond the tribal lands of his Osage Nation. He soon realized he was well suited to this work. This life. Shipboard life. Ever since boyhood, he had wanted to go exploring. Now in his mid-twenties, he knew his decision had been the right one. There'd be no better time to live out his dream. Life aboard ship, moving across the lake waters, watching them pass by and seeing different ports, different people. It was all pure delight to him. It gave him the greatest satisfaction and enjoyment to see this big, beautiful country. America, he had always been told, was never the same from one time to the next. It was always changing.

When he was a little boy, the missionaries had told him about many other Osage who had traveled to the outside world, and those people were his inspiration. Some Osage chiefs had even traveled to France way back in the 1700s, and he often thought about the beautiful and courageous Mi-Ho'n-Ga, or Sacred Sun, who had traveled to France and elsewhere in Europe in 1827. A portrait of her, he was told, had even been on display in Washington, DC. Again and again, as a child, he begged the missionaries to tell him their Sacred Sun story. They retold the story often, and he'd always sit quietly and listen. He savored every word the black-robed Jesuits spoke, relishing the astounding word-pictures they created of the world beyond his tribe's homelands. Beyond even America.

It made him so proud to think of Sacred Sun. He was proud of her and proud of the Osage Nation as a whole—the Children of the Middle Waters. He hoped that someday he'd have the chance to elevate himself. To make them all proud of him, to make them remember him. Maybe one day, they would talk about his travels in their stories and sing his name in their songs.

The sun was about to go down, and Jefry walked backward as he swabbed around the pilothouse. In a minute, he'd empty his bucket of dirty water over the side, then retreat to his bunk and get some rest before his upcoming watch at four in the morning. Later in the day, he'd stand the second dogwatch around suppertime.

He was thinking about the tasty supper he'd enjoyed today—nice and tender roasted beef with mashed potatoes and gravy, along with green peas and hot, fresh-baked bread with lots of butter—when a feminine voice spoke up from behind him. "Shall I move?"

Jefry turned around and saw her. He'd already been told there was a lady passenger on board. He wasn't sure what she meant or what he ought to say in response.

She waited patiently, seeming to expect a reply, but Jefry remained silent.

"Didn't mean to startle you," she said. "If I'm in your way, I can move."

"No, miss, um… you don't need to. It's all right."

"You're sure?" she asked with a friendly smile. "Didn't want to miss this last bit of sunlight." Then she knitted her brows. "Please don't think me rude, but I must ask. Are you from a foreign country?" Then she quickly added: "What I mean is… oh gosh, how ignorant am I. *I'm* the one from a foreign country. *Ha!* It's only that you look… golly, how stupid I must sound."

"No, miss, not at all. I am Osage."

She nodded as though she understood, but then looked puzzled and shook her head.

"The Osage Nation, I mean. They are my people, my tribe."

"Oh. Well, that explains things, doesn't it?" She reached out to him to shake hands. "Maribeth Eaton."

"I'm pleased to meet you, Miss Eaton. My name is Jefry Walks. I've been working just now, and I'm sort of…" He held out his hands to show they were too dirty for a handshake.

"Oh, nonsense," she replied, taking his hand firmly and giving it a hearty shake. "I grew up on a big estate and farm. Did some fieldwork myself. Sheep, cows, goats. Can't let a little honest, earthy dirt come between friends, now can we?" She thought for a moment. "Walks, you say. I'm not sure I've heard that surname before. Walker, of course, but never Walks."

"It's the name the missionaries gave me. I am a Christian now. My Osage name is Walks-on-Smoke."

"Oh, that is so beautiful. In my mind's eye, I see you walking on smoke, or maybe clouds. Splendid, splendid image. How marvelous that is."

"Our chief named me; he did it in this ceremony that they perform. He told my father and mother what my name means, and they repeated it to me as a child many times. They said it means that I walk between, that I am midway between. That I am at the same time both in this world and in the spirit world."

Maribeth stared at him in silent amazement.

"But the missionaries, they'd have none of that. They told me that's not who I am anymore. So they left me with Walks and added the Jefry. They even spelled *Jefry* funny," he added. "At least, I think they did. Not like how you English folks spell it. With a *G*, I guess. *G-e-o-f-f*, I think, yes? Maybe 'cause those missionaries were French Jesuits. I dunno.

"But they were good to us. And anyway, I still know my name—my real name. I have my white people name and my Osage name. Among my own people, I have no first and last name. I am just Walks-on-Smoke. That's it."

He stopped talking and looked down at his mop and bucket. With his head lowered, his long, shimmering jet-black hair spread across his back and spilled over his shoulders, partly concealing his face. "Forgive me, miss. Sometimes I talk too much."

"Not at all. I could listen to you for hours. You don't need to stop. So how should I address you? Do you prefer Jefry?"

"That's fine, and thanks for asking. Either way is okay."

"Well, perhaps you know that many of our European surnames had their origins in what people did for work or where they lived. A Collier had something to do with coal, while Walker was someone who fashioned cloth. Um, and Chapman meant a merchant or a trader of some sort. And my name, Eaton, that meant your home was near a river or a body of water."

"Then you'll feel right at home on our steamboat, Miss Eaton," Jefry replied with a big smile, tossing his hair over his shoulder.

Maribeth smiled as well. "Yes, I sure hope so."

He tilted his head a little to the side, then leaned toward her and looked straight into her eyes. "Miss Eaton, in that carriage earlier today, you were in grave danger. It surrounded you. Coming through that neighborhood."

She gasped and put her hand to her throat. "How'd you know that?"

"I'm sorry, miss. I shouldn't have said that. It's not my place."

She shook her head. "No, it's okay. You're correct, but how did you know?"

"I didn't mean to startle you. I spoke before thinking."

"It's all right."

"Sometimes it'll just... it'll come to me. And I see things—"

"Everything okay up there?" A voice from down on the cargo deck. Atticus was at the bottom of the stairs.

"Just giving it the final touches here, Mate Miles."

Maribeth waved.

"That's good, Jefry. I came to let you know we'll cast off during your watch in the morning."

"Yes, sir. Okay. About time to go below and get some rest anyway."

For several moments, nobody spoke. Then Maribeth broke the silence. "Well, a little rest sounds like just the ticket right now. So I bid you good evening, gentlemen."

Captain McBride stood at the foot of his bed, admiring the newly framed oil painting over the headboard. "Yes, it's perfect. More than I expected. Very nice work indeed. A dear friend of my wife painted that, and she'd be proud to see her work displayed here."

"Thank you, sir." Diggs shifted from one foot to the other. "Anything else you need done, Captain?"

"No, thanks, Diggs. You do good work, and you're fast." McBride reached into his pocket and took out some silver coins.

Diggs shook his head. "No, Captain, I couldn't."

"Nonsense. This isn't part of your job. It's an extra service you've just provided. A personal favor, if you will."

Diggs shook his head again.

"No, no. Please. I must pay you," McBride said, jingling the coins in his hand.

"Well, if you insist, sir."

McBride nodded. "You've earned it, son."

Diggs took the coins and shoved them in his pocket.

Then McBride faced the wall over his desk and spread his arms wide. "Now, here on this wall, I can't figure it out for the life of me. They've got this enormous frame, or what looks like one, but nothing in it."

The carpenter walked over to it and leaned in for a closer look. "You think it's a frame, sir? It's mounted flush to the wall, not hung. Looks like spruce. Maybe molding of some sort?"

Diggs picked at one corner with a fingernail. A chip came loose. He took it in his hand, examined it, and then set it on the desk. "What the heck? I guess it's… I mean, well, I guess it's a frame after all. Isn't it? But look here inside the painted part. See where that chip come out?"

"There's color," McBride said. "Some gray here, and it's got some yellow and black too, doesn't it."

"Yes, sir. Something pretty big underneath looks like."

"Well, how about that? Been painted over. Big mural but painted over. If that isn't the damnedest cabin wall I've ever seen. And it's huge. Now, why the devil would somebody do such a thing?"

Chief Engineer Melvin Murrick had a problem. Not a big problem, though, he reasoned, quick to set his mind at ease. Surely it wouldn't amount to much of anything. No, certainly not this late in the shipping season. There was no cause for concern. In fact, the shipowner, Mr. Street, had assured him of that two weeks prior to this trip.

Upon his initial inspection of the *Eli Greaves*'s boiler, Murrick had noticed cracks in a few of the many hundreds of rivets that held the boiler's metal plates together. After that discovery, Murrick undertook a careful examination of the steam pressure vessel but found no other indications of stress. No cracking, no fractures, no bending, bulging, or dislocation anywhere else on the boiler.

Just as Murrick was about to bring this to the attention of the owner on his recent visit, Street himself broached the subject. Mr. Joshua Street II was already sitting at the table when Murrick entered the officers' dining room on that day. A man in his late fifties, Street wore a well-tailored light gray suit. His hat, a medium-gray bowler, lay before him on the table.

No other crew or officers had yet arrived on board.

Street rose and extended his hand. As the two men shook hands, the more reserved and introverted Chief Murrick couldn't help but notice Mr. Street's confident manner and his broad smile. He had the bearing of a man accustomed to being around people and having things done his way.

"It's a pleasure to meet you, Chief Murrick."

"Likewise, sir."

Street gestured toward the table. "Please do me the honor of being my guest. Have a seat."

Murrick sat facing the table, hands clasped and resting on the mahogany surface. He glanced down at the front of his light blue work shirt, giving it a quick check. A wisp of thread hung out from under a button. When he noticed a new black oil spot on the left cuff, he crossed his arms to conceal it, then shifted uncomfortably.

Street was at the end of the table, sitting sideways to it, lounging in his chair with legs crossed. He took a box of Diamond safety matches from his pocket, withdrew a wooden match, and struck the flame. Several moments passed while he lit his pipe, took a few puffs, then finally exhaled a plume of blue-gray smoke. He stared at the cloud as it rose slowly to the ceiling. "Are you a smoking man, sir?"

"Just an occasional cigar," Murrick replied.

"Nothing wrong with that, for sure. I have enjoyed many a fine Presidente and, as a matter of fact, I had the exquisite good fortune to enjoy a Toro Parejo on the balcony of a hotel one mild Havana evening many years ago." He hauled himself up straight. "And do you know what?" he added, pointing directly at the chief. "I can remember the taste of that cigar, even to this very day." He grinned and raised his hand as though about to testify in court or swear his allegiance to something. "True story!" he said with a hearty laugh, then slapped the table with the palm of his hand.

Murrick jumped.

Street held out his pipe, admiring it. "But I must say, I like the feel of a fine pipe in my hand and being able to gaze upon a nicely handcrafted briar burl. The beauty of that, the craftsmanship—nay, the artistry—it focuses the mind is what it does. And I like to say there is nothing like a good smoke to open the mind to meditation and deep thought."

"Yes, sir, I can see where—"

"Pipe smoking and, to some extent, cigar smoking as well—these, sir, are the contemplative man's addictions. Would you not agree?"

"I like how you put that, Mr. Str—"

"And you being an engineer, and let us say a technical man, a scientific man, you appreciate the value of contemplation, of holding a thing up like a jewel and turning it, observing and evaluating its facets. Its characteristics, one might say, hmm?"

Murrick nodded slowly, silently observing facets and characteristics all right—but those of Street himself. One in particular stood out: the man loved the sound of his own voice.

Street leaned forward in his chair, closed his eyes, and nodded while raising his arm and shaking his forefinger, as though arriving at a eureka moment. "I see it, Chief Murrick," he began. "Yes, I do. I see it. You and I... we are precisely the same. Pre—cise—ly. Yes, of course we have different... roles." He said that last word with a change of pitch and a wave of the hand fanning away any real significance to those differences. "But despite different roles, you and I want the same thing." He gripped his hands together to express unity of purpose. "Our goal, our overarching desire—yours and mine—they're both the same.

"You may wonder what I'm referring to. What could that possibly be?" Street leaned forward and looked the chief straight in the eye. "Just the simplest and most honorable thing there is, sir. Each one of us wants to put a few dollars in his pocket, get back home safe, and give his loving family the good life they deserve." As he said that, he held out both hands. "It's that simple, is it not? Am I right, Chief?"

Before Murrick could reply, Street answered his own question. "We both know I'm right. Our goal is simple—get home safe and provide as best we can for our families. That's it." He crossed his arms and leaned back, relaxing into his chair. "You know it and I know it. You're a family man; I'm a family man."

Murrick was nodding.

"We each do what a man needs to do—must do, Chief Murrick."

The chief continued to nod.

"But alas, I have a problem. No, matter of fact, not even a problem. I'll call it more of… an inconsistency. An error of omission, if you will. Unfortunately, it puts me on the horns of a dilemma. My last chief, Blake by name, found a crack—the tiniest of cracks—in one of the boiler rivets. Well, in a few rivets, to be precise. Call them hairline cracks, even…" Street leaned forward again and looked squarely at Chief Murrick. "The way you're nodding. You know about those, don't you? So, you've seen them too."

"Yes, sir, I have."

"Mr. Melvin Murrick," Street said, looking astonished. He reached over to shake hands. "*Bravo*, sir. *Bravo*. You have just demonstrated your attention to detail, the prime characteristic of a skilled engineer. My God, but I'm impressed."

"Thank you, Mr. Street." The owner's awareness of the defects took Murrick by surprise. "I noticed them and was going to bring it up."

"Blake told me about this back in April. Are you acquainted with the fellow?"

"No, sir."

Street let out a breath and smiled, but the smile faded in an instant, and the look on his face turned annoyed. "Well, he warned me that these cracks—these tiny little cracks—could be a problem. With that in mind, I told him to run the engine at fewer revolutions, just a few, a little less speed for what remained of the season, and less steam pressure as well, of course. You'll come to realize I am inclined to be *over*cautious, you see, rather than the other way around."

"I understand, sir. And how has that plan worked out?"

"Pretty well. Until several days ago when this damned…, when this Blake fellow refused to sign the boiler inspection report this time. *Flat out refused.* And, as I've said, Chief Murrick, that leaves me on the horns of a dilemma right now, having to ponder and evaluate this sudden change in circumstances. I say to myself, 'I know how I'd proceed, but how will Chief Engineer Murrick proceed?'"

"Regarding what, sir? The report?"

Street nodded and withdrew a folded document from the inside pocket of his suit jacket, then threw it across the table and crossed his arms again.

Murrick picked it up. "The most recent boiler inspection report. Unsigned."

Street nodded deeply. "And without a signature, my insurer pulls my policy. No insurance means no cargo gets released and nothing gets loaded. And, much as I despise the expression, I'll be dead in the water. And you'll be out of a job."

Murrick glanced at the report again.

"How long have you been ashore this time, Chief?"

Murrick shook his head, took a deep breath, and blew it out. "Too long. Everything's been so slow to pick up since the fire." He shook his head again. "I need this job, Mr. Street, but if I sign off on that boiler without mentioning it has cracked rivets, I—"

"Christmas is coming, Chief. And I daresay I'm not the only one on the horns of a dilemma. You face a choice as well, but not such a difficult one, it seems to me. On the one hand, you can ignore what are surely the most harmless and tiniest little hairline cracks, and you finish out the season aboard this ship and provide a lovely Christmas for your fine family.

"Or you can put me, and yourself, out of business for the rest of the year. Because you and I both know the insurance man will insist on repairs being made, which will take us well into November. Then, it's winter freeze-up, and there goes our shipping season. And there goes your Christmas.

"And Chief, he is coming aboard *tomorrow*, so I need an answer. I need to know where you stand on this, and I need to know *now*."

Street placed his hand on the hat, then pushed it slowly across the table, to where it was directly in front of Chief Murrick. "What is discussed at this table is between the two of us, Melvin. And with a simple stroke of a pen, what's beneath this hat becomes yours: A year's wages, and then some. On top of your usual pay. Now, think about the nice Christmas that'll provide."

Murrick sat silently, deep in contemplation.

Street waited several moments, then reached over and slowly lifted the hat, then set it back down in front of himself again. "Twenty-dollar double-eagle gold coins. Thirty of 'em."

He placed a pen in front of the chief.

Chief Murrick straightened up in his chair and looked down at the stack of gleaming gold coins, then at the document again. He was silent for the better part of a minute. "Part of me wants to, sir, but…"

Street shifted impatiently in his chair but remained silent.

"If only I could have a little more time."

"There is *no more time*," Street said, nearly shouting. He leaned to one side, reached into his trouser pocket, and withdrew a handful of something, then threw that across the table to Murrick. "Here you go. I've emptied my pockets for you now. Gold and silver. Yours for the taking. You want to break me? *Fine*, you've broken me. But this ship *must sail*."

Chief Murrick was no fool. He knew this was just a tactic. Just a shameless, transparent ploy. It surprised him that the shipowner would pull such a dramatic stunt. He had not just plunged the man into bankruptcy. Far from it, but…

But he couldn't take his eyes off the gleaming, beautiful, scattered pile of coins. He wanted so badly to touch them, but he didn't dare. Those coins could be his own in mere moments. They represented freedom from debt, and finally…*finally*…peace of mind. For nearly half a minute, he marveled at their brilliance. He imagined the look of joy on his wife's face when he'd return home and announce to her that—

Street interrupted his reverie, but in a softer voice, now: "With all due respect to your expertise, Chief Murrick, and to your rank and position here…"

The chief waited.

"Your choice now is clear. As is mine," Street announced, staring coldly into Murrick's eyes. "You either sign right now…or you gather your belongings and go ashore."

Murrick looked at the inspection report again.

Then at the pile of coins.

He held out his hand, which trembled as he let it hover over the pen.

Then he picked up the pen and stared at it for a moment.

Finally, slowly, and with reluctance, he reached for the document.

TWO

Breakfast time

Maribeth stood facing the mirror on her cabin door.

Bonnet? Hat? Windy out on deck? Yes, probably. The bonnet, then.

She reached into her trunk and took out her white bonnet with pale blue fringe and tassels and put it on while facing the mirror again, angled it ever so slightly, tied it under her chin, tilted her head to the right, then to the left.

And saw movement behind her.

She spun around.

Nothing.

And nobody was there. The porthole was open slightly, and the curtains fluttered in the breeze.

The movement had been inside the cabin. Right behind her.

She was sure of it.

"This day," a voice said.

She backed up against the door.

A man's voice. Sharp and clear, but not loud. Reverberating, as though spoken through a pipe or a tunnel. It sounded distant, but it was *right here*. Right in the middle of the cabin. Harsh, spoken as a command, it seemed. Giving an order, maybe? Or a warning?

Not from outside either. From in here, just a few feet away.

Here—*inside* the cabin.

Avoiding the center of the cabin and taking a broad, arcing path across the room, she strode quickly over to the porthole and slammed it shut. The curtains fell and hung motionless.

She grabbed her cape, opened the door, and glanced out into the passageway. Nobody out there either. She threw on the cape and stepped outside. "Must have come from out here," she whispered to herself as she walked aft. She stopped, then turned around, and stared back toward the pilothouse.

A crewman was not far behind her, also heading aft. For breakfast, no doubt.

He stopped. "Good morning, miss. Is everything all right?"

He seemed pleasant. Quite young, though.

She shook her head. "I'm not sure. Were people talking up there just a minute ago? When I was in my cabin, I heard a voice."

He twisted his face, seemed puzzled by the question. "If you mean just now… no. It was just me and the relief wheelsman. Now I'm on my way to get some breakfast. Are you sure everything's okay?"

"Yes, I suppose, except that I heard a man talking."

He smiled. "Wasn't us. We hardly talk at all. And even then, only when I have something to report. I'll step away from the wheel, tell him what he needs to know—what course to steer and so forth. And that's all usually. We know there's cabins below, so we keep our voices down.

And it's been a quiet morning. I'm not sure what it might have been, what you just heard. Wish I could help, but…"

"Someone giving an order, maybe? Sounded like it anyway."

He shrugged. "No, nothing like that at all. Deckhands were out here doing the wash down, but that was a good two, three hours ago."

She was still perplexed. "Forgive me. I know you have to eat and then get back to your watch. I'm sorry to have delayed you."

"It's no trouble, miss. Sorry I couldn't be more helpful," he said, then with a wave resumed walking aft.

Maribeth followed him. When she got to the after deckhouse, she did not go directly into the dining room. Instead, she reached out to steady herself against a stanchion for a moment, looking toward the forward deckhouse, still puzzled and uneasy about what had taken place in her cabin.

That voice. Out of nowhere. And "this day." What on earth could that have meant? If anything at all.

Was it just the wind?

No. Definitely not. She'd heard words. Actual words.

Or had she imagined it all?

There were seven at the table in the officers' dining room: Atticus, the third mate, the assistant chief engineer, two junior officers, and two passengers. German, she gathered from what she could make out of their whispered conversation. Maribeth's own chair was just around the corner of the table from the captain's.

A young girl entered the room and sat down next to Maribeth. Silvery-blond hair, bright blue eyes, pale skin as smooth and lustrous as fine china. Maribeth took her to be Scandinavian, guessing she was only eight or nine years old.

Where are her parents? Just as Maribeth had that thought, she recognized this child… it was the little girl from her dream.

As the girl took her seat, Maribeth tried to control her shock and surprise. How was this possible? She leaned toward her, while trying to keep her voice steady. "Hello. Good morning."

The girl lowered her head and turned it slightly in Maribeth's direction. She avoided eye contact but smiled a little and mouthed a silent hello. Then she resumed gazing into her lap, head bowed.

For several seconds, Maribeth looked over at her as inconspicuously as she could, watching her closely. From this angle too, this child next to her was the one from her dream. The same one. Her hair, her eyes, her jawline, the swell of her cheek…

The girl clasped her hands together and placed them on her lap, then turned slightly in Maribeth's direction. Still looking downward, still not making eye contact, she let the corner of her mouth lift in a slight smile.

The captain's chair awaited him. The German man and his wife sat across from Maribeth. At the other end of the table, beneath the porthole on the after wall, was the chief engineer's chair, also empty. Officers who had underway duties or who were on watch were naturally not present, and nonofficers always took their meals in a separate crew messroom. The steward and his assistant hovered nearby, wearing their starched white uniforms with matching aprons and caps.

The diners were expectant, and the table was set. There was a muted conversation between two of the officers. All the others at the table sat in silence, awaiting the ship's new captain.

When the door to the outer deck opened, everyone looked up as the captain entered the dining room.

"Good morning, everyone," he said.

Those seated made like replies.

"*Guten Morgen*," said the German man. His wife remained silent.

The captain strode to his chair and stood behind it. "Thank you for your patience. My name is T.G. McBride, and, as of yesterday, I am the new captain of this propeller steamship, the *Eli Greaves*. I trust that our honored guests have all had a pleasant time aboard our ship so far.

"My crew and I will spare no effort to ensure that our present voyage will be comfortable for you all. Our steward assures me that this morning's breakfast will be a delicious one. As a matter of fact, my officers tell me that the mere descriptions of his creations wake up even the most recalcitrant of appetites, so I will leave those honors to him in a moment."

A quiet chuckle arose from among those seated. The German couple remained sitting up straight and were without expression, although the husband nodded a little, having understood at least some of the captain's speech. The man leaned a little toward his wife and whispered something to her.

"Having arrived just yesterday, I've not had the pleasure of meeting all of you, but I look forward to that. For the time being, though, I hope our gathering here this morning might be the beginning of our mutual acquaintance and fond friendship. I will only add in conclusion that seeing to your comfort and safety is now and always will be our prime responsibility here aboard ship, and accordingly, I encourage you to voice any concerns you may have to my officers or to me."

Having concluded his welcoming speech, Captain McBride took his seat. Maribeth leaned toward him. "Thank you, sir," she whispered. Two officers at the table nodded in agreement.

McBride gestured to the steward and cook that service could begin, and they started moving about the room, refilling coffees and serving food.

A murmur of conversation began.

Maribeth sat in silence. As a guest, she felt that it was not her place to initiate conversation. She glanced toward the young girl, who continued to stare into her lap, not lifting her head even once, not making eye contact with any others, nor even looking around the room.

The young officer two positions to Maribeth's right leaned toward the older officer seated next to him. In a misjudged whisper, clearly louder than he intended, he asked, "What's *recalcitrant*?"

It was all Maribeth could do to keep from laughing. She looked down at her lap and squeezed her face as tight as she could to keep anyone from seeing. Anywhere else, she'd be howling with laughter. Shaking open her table napkin, she dabbed at her eyes as they filled up with tears.

Breakfast consisted of scrambled eggs sprinkled with cheese and chives, bacon strips, corn dodgers, and flapjacks with maple syrup and butter. Baked beans, and toast with butter and jam. Maribeth stared at her plateful of food, deciding where to begin.

"I thought you might enjoy these," the steward whispered, as he slid an additional plate next to her own.

"British-style flapjacks! Ohh, thank you; I've missed these so much. Thank you, thank you. This is so kind of you."

The others at the table looked on, their faces expressing amusement at Maribeth's surprise and delight.

"I've loved these wonderful little crunchy squares since the age of six. They're my absolute favorite. So sweet and tasty." She turned to the steward. "How did you know?"

He smiled and shrugged.

"I could finish them all, but I'll take only one." Maribeth slid one of the squares onto her plate, then held out the flapjack plate for the captain. "Everyone…please. You simply *must* try these."

The captain chuckled and smiled as he took one of the squares, then passed the plate. "What a nice surprise, Paul. This is so kind of you," he said.

Paul nodded, but remained silent.

"Ladies and gentlemen," the captain intoned, extending his hand toward the steward. "I give you Ship's Steward Mr. Paul Akers, flapjacker extraordinaire and the finest cook on the lakes."

Everyone applauded. Akers doffed his cap and made a formal bow. "Thank you, Captain, and thanks everyone. But I can't take all the credit. Couldn't have done it without Second Cook Mr. Willy Squires, here. I hope you'll all enjoy what we've prepared for you."

Following breakfast, Maribeth stepped out onto the deck and stood next to the rail, hoping to speak with the young girl when she came out of the dining room.

Taking a deep breath of lake air, she looked down at the propeller wash splashing like river rapids as it fell away astern. She felt the shaking, the mechanical throbbing from the steam engine below, and it was so thrilling to look at the turbulence from the propeller driving the ship forward. With all forward movement, all progress of any sort, there is always turbulence. Aboard ship and in life. That was the kind of thing she'd always been taught. Struggles propel you forward. Turbulence falls into the past, your troubles fading as you go onward to success, much as a ship will steam into the calmer waters ahead.

That's what they tell you, and you're expected to believe it. To live by it. To carry on. Persevere. No barriers to stop you, and so forth. *Excelsior*. That word. Ever upward, ever onward to excellence, et cetera. She'd heard it all her life. It was a family favorite, for sure. And it had been a school motto too. Sometimes life has other plans for you, though. No Latin word or pithy phrase ever made a hope or a plan or a dream come true. Not by themselves, they didn't. Even their capacity to inspire dwindled once horizons were shortened and dreams had evaporated.

Six months earlier, Maribeth had often stood at the stern of the ship she took from Liverpool to New York. That was back when *excelsior* still meant something to her. Back when her future seemed certain. Bright rather than bleak. By now, though, the Latin brilliance of *excelsior* had dimmed, its shine tarnished.

Robert Burns knew all about life's "best-laid schemes," and the poet was well aware that they didn't apply to mice alone.

Again, she thought about all the beautiful Louis Vuitton steamer trunks she had brought to America. She regretted having to sell nearly all of them and the outfits they contained, but was, at the same time, grateful that Chicago women were so enamored of European fashions that they'd paid a pretty penny for her dresses and jewelry. The fire destroyed so many businesses that fashionable clothing and accessories were in short supply. Selling nearly all her things was no permanent solution for sure. All it did was buy her a little more time. Financial ruin was still ahead, unless something changed for the better. She had no illusions about that. Options and opportunities that seemed endless six months ago were gone now. All but one. And that last one awaited her in Buffalo, of all places.

Atticus appeared and stood next to her. "Did you enjoy breakfast?"

"Oh, yes, and the captain was right. The steward does quite a marvelous job."

"Paul is a popular cook among Great Lakes sailors." Atticus shifted on his feet and looked over the rail. "You handled it well back in there."

Maribeth shook her head, holding her lips tight to conceal a smirk.

"What's recalcitrant?"

She laughed out loud. "*Oh, my gosh.* I almost couldn't stop myself; I would've cackled like an idiot. Did it show?"

Atticus shook his head. "Nobody else noticed. Either that, or they just didn't let on."

Her smile gradually faded, and she turned to him. "I keep thinking about how gentle you were with that little boy yesterday."

He nodded. "I grew up in a poor family. I know what it's like. We didn't have much, but I had a mom and pop, at least."

"Captain McBride's sister-in-law will be a mom to him for a while; she'll look after him. I'll do what little I can to help. Financially, I mean."

"He mentioned that to me. I was glad to hear that, Maribeth. And I have a little money in the bank. I'll help too."

"Let's do that together, shall we?"

"Yes, excellent idea. Let's do that."

"Oh, *goody*. That'll be such fun."

"But how's that going to work? I mean, with you in Buffalo and me sailing all over the lakes."

She shrugged. "Letters, telegrams." Maribeth turned to him and looked up into his eyes. "Mr. First Mate Atticus Miles, I daresay there's a soft side to you; I think there's a wide streak of kindness in you. Tell me more about yourself."

He shrugged. "Not much else to tell. I fought in the war, and now I'm here."

She smiled and shook her head. "Oh, come now. You have more of a story than that. Everyone does."

He didn't respond, seemed lost in his own thoughts as he stared across the lake.

"May *I* tell *you* something?" she asked.

"Of course."

"It was the first thing that came to mind yesterday as I saw you kneeling next to Frankie, making sure he was all right."

He nodded.

"That you tended to him as a father might. You were gentle, and you whispered to him. It occurred to me that it wasn't your first time comforting a hurt child."

Atticus looked away, offering no comment.

"Do you have children?"

"No. I did. But not anymore."

She placed her hand on his wrist. "If you'd rather not talk about it…"

"Not right now. Another time, maybe."

"I understand. I can tell you my story, if you'd like."

"Very much. Yes. What brought you here to America?"

"I guess I came here to prove something to my family… and maybe to myself as well." She looked down at the deck and shook her head. "Let's just say it hasn't gone quite as I'd planned. But now it's looking like things are about to improve."

"I hope so," Atticus said.

She was silent for several seconds, then took a deep breath. "I'm…different…from the other women in my family. They never understood that I was fascinated not by ladies' usual distractions but by industry. Factories. Always have been. I wasn't like my mother, my aunts, or my female cousins.

"When I was little, while Mama and my aunts were having tea and talking about fine fashions, upcoming dinner parties, or the latest scandalous Irish poet or French novelist du jour, I'd be elsewhere in our home, listening to Papa and other gentlemen discussing our family's textile factories.

"They didn't allow me in the room among the men, so I'd hide in the adjoining room and listen through the crack of the door or the grille in the wall as they talked about things that were unfamiliar to me but fascinating nonetheless. I'd hear strange and wondrous new words: *architects, properties, building plans, millwrights, iron beams.* And my head would spin with their talk of sluice gates and waterwheels, drive belts and shafts, gears and pulleys.

"They talked about canal access, shipments of bricks and glass, or iron bolts and bracing, which looms and presses and punches and other machines were delivered and which were on order. And always, but always, endless complaints about Parliament and taxes and bankers—" Maribeth interrupted her speech as she looked away and waved. "Oh, miss?"

The young girl from breakfast had just stepped out of the dining room and onto the deck. She wore old, scuffed shoes and a plain dress that hung loosely, being at least a size too large for her. She stopped and looked over toward Maribeth with a shy smile.

"Excuse me, Atticus. I don't mean to be rude, but I'd like to have a word with this young lady, if you don't mind. I've been wanting to speak with her."

He smiled. "Of course I don't mind. We'll talk later."

Maribeth walked over to the girl and extended her hand. "I was hoping to talk to you, if that's all right."

The girl nodded, shaking Maribeth's hand.

"Maybe you'd care to stand over here by the rail with me. I enjoy looking at the water going by. It's so refreshing to gaze at, such a peaceful thing to see." She took a deep breath. "My name is Maribeth."

"I am glad meeting you," the girl replied a little slowly, seeming unsure of her words. "My name Kristi Joens… I am sorry. This is first time I use…" She took Maribeth by the hand and moved closer to her.

Maribeth had the strangest sensation, hearing the girl speak for the first time. Or had it been the touch of her hand? She was the girl from her dream. Yes, there was no doubt. A dream become real. It felt impossible, yet here she was. It was unreal, yet real, just the same. How could this be?

It was several seconds before Kristi spoke again. "My name come from my papa. Is Joensdatter, but then he hanging himself at the farm in Iowa. I don't know if I can use that name, anymore."

Maribeth resisted a gasp.

This lovely child's father committed suicide?

And now, such bewilderment and heartbreak in those beautiful blue eyes… Then it occurred to Maribeth—the disappearing father in the dream. Of course. *Yes, it all fits.* She looked at Kristi with astonishment, but was suddenly uneasy, even a little frightened. What was going on? *Who is this child? What is she?* "Joensdatter is still your name, honey."

Kristi looked up, surprised. "Real? I can keep it?"

Maribeth nodded. "Yes, *real*. You can have it. It's your name to keep for as long as you want. Forever, if you choose to."

"Okay. It's good."

"But just between you and me, Kristi is fine, honey. We'll just be Kristi and Beth, if that's okay."

"Yes, okay."

Two officers came out of the dining room, talking and laughing, letting the door slam behind them.

Kristi pressed herself against Maribeth and gripped her hand tighter.

Maribeth felt the poor girl shaking. "It's okay, sweetheart. Don't worry; it's all right." She held her closer and brushed a strand of hair out of Kristi's eyes as the child watched the two men walk forward along the cargo deck. "There's nothing to be afraid of."

Maribeth suddenly felt a little ashamed of her doubts about Kristi. She was just a scared little girl, after all. With tragic circumstances thrust upon her. Lost and alone. Even adults would feel out of sorts in a situation as tragic as Kristi's, yet... the dreams... how to account for the dreams?

Behind her, someone cleared his throat noisily. A fellow from the engine spaces, soot blackened from his cap to his boots.

"Sorry?" Maribeth said.

"Excuse me, miss. Just to say it'll soon get really sooty back here. We're gonna blow down the boilers in a coupla minutes."

"Ah, thanks so much. We'll move."

"I have a cabin," Kristi said, not letting go of Maribeth's hand. "Can you... I mean, would you like... or wanting to see it?"

"Yes, I'd love to. And after that, I'll do your hair for you, if you'd like that. Okay?"

The girl's eyes brightened. "Yes, I'd like."

Later that same evening, the shoreline had long disappeared over the horizon. The sun had set; its pinkish glow was slowly being swallowed up by the gathering twilight.

Red sky at night, sailors' delight, Atticus thought.

He was out on deck having a smoke, enjoying this trip so far, and looking forward to the others that he hoped would follow. At this moment, having completed the day's tasks, he was taking a few minutes to enjoy his surroundings.

What he liked best about this time of year were these crisp and chilly October evenings. Smiling as the gentle, fragrant breeze from the southwest meandered across the deck, he imagined for the moment that it was this breeze by itself that powered them downbound toward the lower lakes and Buffalo Port.

He loved the mechanical part, too: the rugged, pulsing sound of the steam engine back aft, the black smoke billowing out of the stack. The intoxicating aromas of burning coal and hot metal, smoke, and oil. The creaking and flexing of the wooden ship and the gurgling of the water slipping along her hull.

Who couldn't love this? What better life can a man have?

He recalled the conversation he'd had with Miss Eaton earlier in the day. She seemed very pleasant and, of course, beautiful. Talking to her wasn't difficult. It was… He couldn't think of a word that fit. Maybe just easy. Or comfortable. She was quiet, seemed sincere, and, of course, he had noticed how she tended to Frankie with such care and thoughtfulness.

Carpenter Diggs joined him. "Nice evening."

Atticus nodded, holding on to his pipe, giving it a puff. "Yep. Good day for a voyage."

"Captain seems a pleasant enough fellow," said Diggs.

"I thought so too. He even recognized this boat. Well, sort of recognized it anyway. When he walked up to it at the wharf, he looked puzzled; it looked familiar, he said, but then again, it didn't. That's just how he put it. Awfully strange thing to say, it seemed to me at the time. Still does. Smart man, though, and it got me to thinking." Atticus was about to say more, but he recalled his agreement with McBride and stopped himself.

He wondered why the captain had such a reaction as he approached this ship. He knew he was coming aboard the *Eli Greaves*, but this ship wasn't what he expected. What could that possibly mean? He was from Milwaukee and probably knew every ship in that port. He could spot any of them a mile away, no doubt. It was puzzling, to say the least.

Diggs gave him a look. "Thinking about what, Mate Miles?"

"Oh, nothing. We just talked about Milwaukee for a minute or two."

"You remember I'm from there, right?" Diggs said. "I got Milwaukee news and shipping articles goin' back years. I keep 'em in an old journal book. All sorts of stuff in there. Someday, when I'm all done shipping, I figure

I'll read it all again. Maybe with my grandchildren. You know, remember the life and all that. Maybe you'd care to have a look, see what's in there."

"Yeah, sure. Sounds interesting," said Atticus.

"Okay, I know you read a lot. You might like it."

"Yeah. Go ahead. Just leave it in my cabin. I'll read it under the lamp later on."

"Okay, Professor."

The first mate couldn't help but smirk, hearing his nickname. He'd worked with Diggs on other vessels over the years. Other sailors considered Atticus well educated, not knowing he'd only completed sixth grade. He enjoyed reading, though, and his shipmates all knew that when he wasn't up on deck, he was somewhere else with his nose in a book.

"Mr. Diggs, you've met all the new men. What do you think?"

The deckhand looked over his shoulder and drew a little closer before he replied, quieter now. "You and me, we shipped together a couple of times before, right? Different boats, different crews, all that."

Atticus nodded.

"Well, since you asked, most of them guys we got seem okay, most of 'em knows what they're doin', and all of them pretty smart and eager. The Frenchman from Canada, Fournier—you know him. He's shipped with us before. Anyway, you know he's good. And there's Willy, the cook; I know him from before, and he's pretty good too. But our barge bosun…"

"Hake?"

"Yeah, Hake. Well, he fought with the Yankees during the war, you know. Don't make him a bad feller or nothing, but scuttlebutt is that afterward, he killed a man and woman over along the Ohio River somewheres. Sliced 'em up pretty good. That's what I heard anyway. Have you seen that Texas toothpick he carries?"

"I have," Atticus replied. "Beautiful knife. Big shiny blade, probably ten inches. Bone handle."

"Uh-huh, well, what I tell you is only what I heard."

"And how'd you hear about this?"

"Not from any of the lads here. But I know a few of them around Chicago used to work the rivers. They say Hake been runnin' ever since the war. Showed up in Baltimore, then after that, he worked around. Sailed out of Charleston down to the islands, and such. Done that a coupla years. Then later along the Mississippi River. Between New Orleans and Saint Lou. Like that. Hoppin' around from place to place."

Atticus shrugged. "You know me. I like to give a man a chance to prove himself one way or the other. Watch and wait, I like to say."

"Yeah, I guess, Mate. Just the way he strikes me is all."

"As far as stories… sailors like to exaggerate, Owen. You know that."

Diggs nodded. "Yeah, I know. Just kind of a shifty guy, all I'm saying. Too quiet. Keeps to himself. Always sharpening that knife of his. You'll see him sharpening, sharpening all the damned time. He'll be bent over, working on it, looking like he's concentrating. Then you'll meet his eyes, and he's looking right at you. Been looking at you, sneaky like, the whole time."

Seated at the desk in his cabin an hour later, Atticus took a handful of articles from Diggs's journal. With the edge of his hand, he swiped across the wrinkled scraps of newspaper to flatten them out. Then he gave the nearby lamp a shake to mix up the lard-and-whale-oil fuel. He put a match to it, and its yellowish glow spread over the pages.

He hunched forward, squinting at the faded text of articles torn from local newspapers. They all concerned maritime operations of one kind or another: ship sailings and arrivals, new dry docks, and other harbor facilities, shipbuilders' notes about projects begun, projects completed. Ships and crews presumed lost.

Maribeth was having a stroll the next morning when she saw Atticus. He was directing three deckhands on some tasks around the cargo deck. He looked up and waved to her as he spoke to the men, then turned his attention back to them.

She passed by and walked farther forward, stopping along the bulwark that was next to the deckhouse. She gazed out across the lake and occasionally cast a sidelong glance back aft to see where Atticus was and what he was doing. Still back there directing his workers.

She wished life was more like being a ship, with movement as its sole purpose. She loved movement and going places. Load up here, drop off there. And repeat and repeat. Very simple. All a ship needed to do was stay afloat, and the engine had to keep running. All very elemental, it seemed. Moving cargo back and forth. That's all. What a marvelous service to be a part of. Could it really be that uncomplicated? Could she invest in a shipping company? Maybe, but it was too late for that, now. She wished she'd had this idea six months ago, back when she still had funds.

She had been on board many ships with her parents, twice even taking the Grand Tour, culminating in a last leg to Italy, and once to Greece. The crew aboard those luxurious ships were respectful and often obsequious. But one never really met a crewman. One might sit at the captain's table, occasionally address a senior officer, or converse with one. But the officers and crew functioned more like pieces on a game board than real people, being there solely for the pleasure and convenience of the ship's passengers.

Her experience here on the *Eli Greaves* was different. This ship and its crew existed to move goods, not to keep wealthy travelers entertained, distracted, full of food and, as often as not, drunk. Even so, she knew this ship's crewmen enjoyed having her aboard. She could tell. All of them—officers and others alike—were always friendly toward her, and always greeted her with courtesy.

Atticus was at Maribeth's door. "Good morning, Maribeth. Sorry I didn't have time to talk earlier. I trust you're having a pleasant day."

"Good morning, Atticus. Please come in. And you may call me Beth if you like."

"Thank you. Yes, I'd like that."

"Atticus is such a wonderful, strong name. Both Greek and Roman, I believe."

"I guess so. My mother saw it in a book. Poetry, I think. Or maybe history, I forget which. I came to ask if everything is to your liking so far. Do you require anything in particular?"

"Thank you for asking. As a matter of fact, yes. That young girl I met yesterday…"

He nodded.

"She showed me her cabin, and oh, my goodness, but it is terrible. It's tiny, and it smells like coal smoke. Oily stuff is in there, and the crewmen next door are noisy and laughing at all hours."

"I know which cabin you mean. The engineers use it for storage. She was a late arrival, so they moved some things out to make room. The captain is her chaperone for this trip, and he did what he could on short notice to find her someplace suitable."

"Atticus, I am so worried about her. She is a delightful but terrified girl. She's orphaned and all by herself, you know. Can we move her into my cabin?"

"Of course. Right away, if you'd like. That's very generous of you, and I'm sure Captain McBride will be pleased to hear that you're willing to look after her."

"It will be my pleasure to take care of her," she said, when something distracted her. Leaning closer, she reached up to Atticus's face. "I've noticed you put your hand up there a lot. Why do you do that?" she asked, gently curling her fingers around his wrist. But upon drawing his hand away from his face, she just as quickly let it go, yanked her arm away, and lurched backward, shaking. "Forgive me. That scar, I see it now. I am so sorry; I'm very sorry."

"No, Beth, you have nothing to be sorry for. You meant no offense. I understand that."

She shook her head. "That was insensitive of me. You are so gracious, and my manners are horrible."

"No, they aren't."

"Good heavens, such a long scar. And you hide it. Why do you do that?"

"Don't know. Just habit. It doesn't look very nice is all."

"Oh, I feel awful."

"No, please don't feel bad."

She came closer to get a better look. Took his collar between thumb and forefinger and opened it just a bit. "Is it painful?"

He chuckled a little and shook his head. "Naw. Didn't feel too good at the time but no pain anymore. Been nine, ten years anyway."

She reached toward his neck with her forefinger. "May I?"

"Sure, if you wish."

"I've never seen such a thing before," she whispered, tracing the entire length of the scar. "On our farm, then later teaching school, I never saw the likes of it. And I was so sheltered, of course, and well protected. I mean, living with my family and… well, I have never…"

"I'm sorry you were alarmed, Beth. It's a souvenir from our War between the States."

"Ah, yes. What you call your Civil War?"

"That's the one."

"Oh my God. So, from a bullet, I imagine?"

He smiled. "A mounted soldier, a Yankee cavalryman. From his sword. Happened at Chickamauga under General Bragg. September 19, back in '63."

"Oh, dear me."

"He was an officer. Lieutenant. It was foggy all around us that morning. Quiet, not much going on. And this lieutenant on horseback came out of nowhere with that saber of his held high and swinging down, making its arc toward my neck. All I had time to do was lean away a bit—but it was just barely enough."

"My God. And what did you do then?"

He shrugged. "I shot 'im. Drew my Griswold, took aim, and just as he's riding off, he turns around to see what he did to me, and I put a round into his upper left side. Then he shakes the reins, sitting up straight as can be. Couple of seconds later, his left arm goes limp, and he drops the reins. Horse slows down and stops."

Beth's eyes were wide, and she seemed about to speak but only shook her head.

"Then he rolled off his horse and hit the ground. And that was that. All over with. Dead. Just that quick."

"What happened then?"

"Well, what I did, I hightailed it over to where he was, first making sure there were no more bluecoats coming. Grabbed his sword and scabbard. Saw a gold chain coming out of his pocket. Nice gold watch at the end of it. Took that, too. It's all pretty much a blank after that, I had lost so much blood. Woke up on a table in a tent two days later."

"You almost died."

"I reckon so. Yeah. That's what they said."

"But thank heaven you survived."

He nodded. "Another soldier picked up the saber and held onto it for me, made sure nobody snatched it. Tennessee lad like me. Rolled it up in his blanket along with the watch. Somebody else got ahold of his horse… nice mount, that was."

"So you were allowed to keep those things?'

"Sure."

"But aren't there laws or something?"

He smiled. "No laws, Beth. It's war. Total chaos, or prett' near. And besides, everybody's always short of everything. And I mean everybody, both sides. So, soldiers grab everything useful off dead fellas soon as they can. Before the bodies get too ripe, I mean. Anything we can use, we take. Boots, buckles, canteens, knives…. Man's dead, so he won't be needing that stuff anymore."

She thought for a moment. "I've been around horses all my life. How did you not hear it coming? Was it quite noisy there?"

"Not then, no. Just us soldiers sitting around in that fog, talking quietly, having a cup of our chicory coffee. Sometimes fog will muffle sound. Or deflect it, maybe. Something like that. I dunno—strangest thing, but nobody heard anything. Maybe the horse was wearing socks."

Beth chirped a laugh and then clapped both hands over her mouth. "*Ha!* Oh, that's so funny. No, I shouldn't laugh," she said, still laughing behind her hands.

"Don't worry about it. It's all in the past now. All that's left is the scar as a reminder, I guess. To think about that stuff now and then."

"Golly Moses, he almost cut your head off."

"I'm sorry to make you think of such a thing."

She waved away that notion. "Oh, no sense being squeamish about that—nooo, no, no, no. Because we English, we know a thing or two about cutting off heads, our Henry VIII being a prime example. And some other creative ways of killing, too, as with his ever-so-charming daughter Mary. Our beloved Bloody Mary, who had over two hundred Protestants burned at the stake."

Beth moved closer, taking hold of his hand once more. "Let's just leave it this way: I'm happy that your timing was better than the unfortunate Yankee lieutenant's."

"Better aim too."

She smiled, still holding his hand. "Do you still have it? What'd you call it? Your Griswold?"

"Griswold and Gunnison—single-action, .36 caliber, black powder, six-shot revolver."

She straightened up, and her eyes went wide. "Well now, sir. My good heavens. Golly, that sounds impressive. What happened to it?"

"Still got it."

"I fired a shotgun back in England," she said. "Double-side-gated over-and-under, and even a Westley Richards cavalry carbine once. That shotgun darn near knocked my shoulder out of joint. Never fired a pistol, though."

"Hell of a gun, that Griswold. Knock a sorry sumbitch clean off his feet."

"Oh my gosh. Promise me you'll let me shoot it someday. Can I? Or I should say may I?"

"Pretty heavy gun, I'm afraid. It's not a lady's gun. And maybe too big for those lovely, fine hands of yours."

She released his hand and took a step back, straightening defiantly. "Okay, Mr. First Mate Atticus Miles...*sir*...Let me retract and rephrase: should I ever...*ever*...find it even remotely *possible* to wrap my delicate, fine little lady's hands around your *big heavy* Griswold and Gunnison single-action, .36 caliber, black powder, six-shot revolver...*then* may I shoot it?"

He almost laughed, but held it in. He tried to say something but had to turn away to keep from laughing out loud.

She had one hand over her mouth, and her eyes were already laughing, already moist with tears. A little noise came from her throat, but not from her mouth yet.

"You left out..." he started, then had to turn away again.

"I beg your pardon.... *What*? I did *what*?" she demanded, yanking at his shirtsleeve. Then she had to cover her mouth again.

He tried once more: "You left out the best part. You forgot."

"No, I didn't."

"Mm-hmm. Yeah, you did."

"No, I *did not forget*. And I'll say it."

He shook his head and started to reply, but she talked right over him.

"*Knock a sorry sumbitch clean off his feet*," she said in that lovely British accent of hers, then burst out laughing.

He laughed too, and those eyes of hers brightened such that they could never, ever, be more beautiful than they were at that moment.

They laughed out loud until they were all out of breath. Then they took another breath and laughed some more.

When they eventually stopped, breathless again, they avoided each other's eyes. They couldn't look at one another yet, or they'd start laughing all over again.

She was smirking, and he was smirking.

And his head was spinning. *God help me; I think I'm in love with her already.*

THREE

"It's nice here," Kristi said, looking around Beth's cabin. "I know this little window. They call it porthole."

Beth smiled. "Correct. Very good."

"Pretty curtain too."

"Yes. It's a very comfortable cabin. Nice and roomy. I think you'll be happy here."

"Mmm, yes, I think so."

"You don't have to hold on to your bag, you know. You can put it on the desk over there if you prefer."

Kristi tilted her head. "Miss Beth, what means *prefer*? I am sorry my English."

"Oh, it's okay; you'll learn. Prefer means what you like better. I might say, do you prefer apples or peaches?"

Kristi looked toward the ceiling and thought for a moment. "I prefer my big sister not leave. I prefer to be with me now."

"Where is your big sister?"

"She move away. She's a few years older. She marries a man and move away."

"Oh, you must miss her."

"I miss a lot, yes." Kristi took Beth by the hand. "I love her so much. We sit and talk. And then at night, we're in same bed. My nana and my mama and papa, they had tiny house, all little rooms, and small beds."

"Hmm, small like this one?"

Kristi smiled. "Oh, this not small. This one bigger. But not real big."

"I see," Beth said.

"We hold hands and look at the ceiling and tell silly stories."

"Silly stories?"

"Mm-hmm. We make up. I tell her one about a goose that cook our breakfast."

Beth chuckled. "Yes, that's pretty silly."

"Uh-huh. Yes, Big Sister think so too. And I make up another one about a crocodile that wear a hat. And a reindeer who sing old Norwegian songs."

Beth kicked off her shoes, slid onto the bed, and put her head on the pillow. "I guess it must be fun sometimes just to tell silly stories."

"Oh, yes. Very much fun."

"Were you sad when your sister left home?"

"Mm-hmm. Yes. Still sad. And about Mama and Papa too."

"Of course you are, honey."

"Do you have sister, Miss Beth?"

"No. But I always wished I had one."

"I can be your little sister. If you want."

"Yes, I'd love that. I used to ask my mother and father if I could please have a little sister. But I remained their only child. And I need a little sister right about now." Beth patted a spot on the bed.

Kristi slid up next to her and held her hand. They both lay there, looking up at the ceiling.

"You know, in Norway we have horse that count with his foot."

"Really?"

Kristi nodded. "Uh-huh."

"Do you have a story about him?"

"No. No story. And we had a goat that pull our egg cart. My papa drives the cart, and we take eggs to houses and sell."

"Oh, my. That might make a very good silly story."

Kristi nodded, knitting her brows as she gave the idea serious consideration. "Yes, I think maybe. But I am sad to think about Papa."

"Of course you are, honey. I didn't mean to—"

"My sister pretty, but you're much prettier."

"It is kind of you to say that. Thank you. Only one pillow. We'll have to share it, okay?"

"It's okay. So, which silly story I can tell?"

"Let's see… I think… the reindeer one."

Minutes later, having finished the story, Kristi sat up. "I'm sleepy now." She slid around and sat on the edge of the bed. "I make up new story for next time."

Maribeth smiled. "Sounds good to me." She swung her legs over just as Kristi took two giant steps and plopped down onto her mattress from the other cabin.

"Honey, come on back here. Please."

Kristi took two bunny hops and flopped onto the bed.

"You'll sleep here now, okay? I'll sleep on the mattress."

"Thank you. I never have such big bed."

"Yes, it's nice. And it's yours now."

"Big Sister Miss Beth?"

"Yes, honey?"

"A man talk to me."

"A *man*? Which man?"

Kristi shrugged.

"Where?"

"In my old cabin."

Beth straightened up. "A man did?"

"Uh-huh. Yes."

"What was he doing in your cabin? Why was he?"

"He's just there."

"Kristi, you're confusing me," Beth said.

"I'm sorry."

"What do you mean, he's just there? Did he have a key?"

"No, he didn't come in. He just—"

Beth shook her head. "Kristi, this makes no sense. I don't underst—"

Kristi wrinkled her face and seemed about to cry. "I don't know, Miss Beth. I don't know why. He is just there. Sometimes they are just there. They just show up. I don't know why they come."

"I'm sorry, honey, but I don't understand any of this. And he talked to you? What did he say? And you said *they*. Who do you mean? Who are *they*?"

"The man, he say, 'This day.'"

Beth's eyes went wide, and she felt chills all over. *The very same words I heard*, she thought. "Why would…? I mean…"

Kristi sniffed, lifted the sleeve of her flannel nightgown, and wiped her eyes with it. "I think he's not nice man."

"What makes you say that? Why do you think he's not nice man… I mean not a nice man?"

Kristi shrugged. "Mean voice. Rough voice. And he say something sounds like purples."

"Purples?"

"Well, maybe not exact. Maybe only sounded like."

"Peoples?"

"No, not that."

"Porpoise? You know, like a dolphin?"

Kristi shook her head. "But almost that word."

"Purpose?"

"Yes, that's it. Or I think so. Purpose, yes."

"That's all he said? 'This day,' and 'purpose?'"

"Yes, then he is gone."

"He just walked out of your cabin?"

Kristi leaned a little toward Beth, looking confused. "They not walk out, Miss Beth. They never walk out."

"What are you talking about?"

"They don't need to."

"Kristi, what are you talk—?"

"He's not real. They're not real."

Beth felt a chill up the back of her neck, and her skin crawled. "Wh… what are you saying?"

"They're real, but not real like us. They're all *Spøkelsa.*"

"What is that? What did you just say?"

"Spøkelsa."

Beth shook her head. "I… I don't know what—"

"It mean ghost. *Spøkelsa* is ghost. That's what they are. They are all ghost."

"Oh, darling, no. I'm sorry, honey. No, there's no such thing as—"

"*Spøkelsa* is everywhere, Miss Beth."

"I… well, some people think—"

"Everywhere."

Beth swallowed hard, closing her eyes. She formed her lips as if about to speak but did not. She was silent for several heartbeats. "And you weren't afraid?" she said finally.

Kristi shook her head. "Nope."

"Most people are afraid of ghosts."

"Not me."

"You've seen them before?"

"Oh, yes. Lots of times."

"Here? On the ship?"

"Not here. He is first one here. But other places. On the Iowa farm, in little towns, on the big ship when Mama and Papa bring me. On a train one day. In the building where is train comes and goes. *Spøkelsa* is everywhere, Big Sister Beth. All over the place. Everywhere I go, I see them."

The chills wouldn't stop. Beth rubbed her arms and kept rubbing them, but warmth wouldn't come.

Captain McBride hadn't slept since leaving his home in Milwaukee a day and a half before. Not a good sleep anyway. An hour here, two hours there. This trip was affecting not only his sleep but his stomach, his moods— even his mental state.

He considered himself a person of consistent moods, not given to extremes of one sort or another. Not generally. But this trip was so far shaping up to be the exception, for he was feeling the limits of his patience more and more since leaving Chicago.

He came nearly thirty minutes early to the officers' dining room for lunchtime. He didn't feel like seeing anyone else or talking to anybody. His intention was to have a quick meal if the steward could manage it on such short notice. If not, some bread and salt pork, and maybe a slice of cheese, would have to suffice. Then he'd return to his cabin.

He didn't expect to have a dining companion, but there she was, already at the table, sipping tea from a cup.

"Good day, Miss Eaton."

"Good day to you, Captain. I know I've barged in here too early, but I woke up from a nice nap thinking of teatime. We Brits and our tea, you know."

"We're always happy to make allowances, miss. You're welcome here anytime."

"I appreciate that, sir. I know how busy the cooks are right now, but they were gracious and kind, despite that."

"The tea is to your liking, I trust."

"Mm-hmm, yes, it's delicious."

"How is our young friend?"

"She's fine, thanks. Having a nap right now."

The captain groaned a little as he lowered himself into his chair.

"Are you feeling all right, sir?"

He shrugged, managing a faint smile. "Nothing a good night's sleep wouldn't cure."

"A nice deep sleep can do wonders."

"This is not an occupation for one who relishes a full sleep every night," McBride added.

"I can only imagine. I know a captain's attention is often required for emergencies of all kinds."

"Constantly," he replied. "Constantly. If only it were just that."

Miss Eaton nodded slowly. "I hope all is well, sir. Here and elsewhere."

He almost said more but thought better of it. Instead, he changed the subject. "Are you from a shipping family?"

She shook her head while dabbing at her lips with a table napkin. "Textiles. My great-grandpapa Henry Eaton started our business in the late 1700s. He owned a dozen sheep, and it all began with an oiled wool sweater that his wife knitted for a Cornwall fisherman. I'm her namesake, incidentally. She was the first Maribeth Eaton; I'm the second. Anyway, we found out only later that the man wasn't a fisherman at all." She drew in closer and whispered, "*Smuggler.* But the sweaters were well made and durable, so they caught on. Fishermen and seafarers still wear them today, a century later.

"From Cherbourg to Goteborg, and from Rotterdam to Reykjavik. That's Papa's favorite line. He says that all the time. Even Norwegians and Danes buy them. Nova Scotia men who fish the Grand Banks, and lobstermen from Maine, too.

"And so on, and so forth, and now we have four factories that make everything from clothing to raw textiles for export worldwide. And four more that make hats, gloves and other things. My father oversees all of them these days. Third generation now."

"Inspiring story. Textiles, apparel. Yes. A fascinating and lucrative field, I am sure."

"We manage to survive."

"Well, better than that, I should hope."

Maribeth only smiled as she took another sip of tea.

"Miss Eaton, forgive me, but I feel I must inquire…well…out of concern, actually."

"Sir?"

"From Chicago and Milwaukee, there are now several steamboats in passenger service to the lower lakes, yet you booked passage on a cargo ship. And I'm sure that I needn't mention the risk that you faced passing through that neighborhood next to our wharf in Chicago."

Beth closed her eyes and nodded slowly. "I prayed coming through there, Captain. Honestly, I prayed. It was terrifying."

"And those robbers… or would-be robbers."

She shook her head. "But for our little Frankie…"

"I have three daughters of my own, Miss Eaton, and I would never have allowed them to be driven through such a dangerous neighborhood. Did the booking agent for your trip not mention that to you? After all, the passenger ship terminals are far safer, more pleasant, and in a better part of town.”

“They mentioned all that, yes. As a matter of fact, they expressed the same concerns as you’re expressing now.”

“Miss, the last thing I want to do is intrude or question your choices, but—”

“I couldn’t afford a passenger ship,” she said abruptly.

“But I… well, I would imagine that—”

“I’ve run out of funds. Almost.”

The steward appeared from the galley as two deck officers entered through the outside door. Greetings followed all around. There was quiet chatter as the men took their seats.

Maribeth and the captain held each other’s gazes as she continued in a whisper. “I’m broke, sir. Or nearly so. What’s in my steamer trunk is the last of it. What I left England with is nearly gone.”

McBride noticed how she gripped the edge of the table to keep from shaking.

“If I ask my parents for more money, they’ll give it to me only on condition that I return to England at once. And of course all of them—the entire family—all of them will know I’ve failed miserably at what they called my silly American folly.”

He nodded slowly, then placed his hand lightly on her wrist. “I have many contacts in Milwau—”

“But sir, I don’t want to go back. Ever. I love this country, and this is where I belong. I know that now.”

“Miss Eaton, I was about to say that I know many people in Milwaukee. I’m sure I could help you find a—” He cursed silently when he saw she was about to cry, that it was all she could do to hold it in. At her sniffle, he rose suddenly, announcing loud enough for the others in the dining room to hear, "Yes, of course, miss, I'd be happy to let you tour the pilothouse. As a matter of fact, we have a few minutes before the lunchtime service begins. What do you say we take a quick trip up there?" He extended his hand.

She took it, and the two of them exited the dining room and began walking forward.

"Captain, I can't thank you enough for this. I am so embarrassed."

He shook his head. "Miss Eaton, I cannot let myself stand by and do nothing while you suffer."

They were walking along the cargo deck, which was good because now she was crying her heart out, and at least out here on deck, nobody else was nearby.

They stopped at the rail and gazed off into the distance. "Let it go. Let it all out. It's okay. Everything will be okay." He removed something from his pocket. "Here, I stole a table napkin for you."

She laughed as she took it, then dabbed at her eyes while laughing and crying at the same time.

Some minutes later, she said quietly, "Thank you. You're very kind."

McBride shrugged and lightly patted her hand, which rested on the rail. "It's the very least I can do. And since it's funds you need, please don't hesitate to ask. At any point. Call it a loan if you wish or a gift from a friend. Whatever suits you."

"Thank you, sir," she whispered.

"Were one of my daughters in a similar fix, I'd hope someone would come along and make such an offer."

She nodded and dabbed her eyes again.

"And despite your circumstances, you showed great kindness and generosity offering funds toward the welfare of our young Frankie."

"And I'd do it again, sir. I've had such advantages, Captain, and that poor boy has had none."

"A noble gesture, Miss Eaton. And I'd say your upbringing had a lot to do with it."

She nodded.

"I'm curious though…"

"About?"

"About this fisherman fellow. What exactly did he smuggle?"

Maribeth smiled. "French brandy."

The captain nodded, impressed. "Now that's what I call precious cargo. The gentleman was a most discerning smuggler, I'd say."

And they both laughed.

"Beth, if you recall, you asked me to check up on you."

"Yes, of course, and you needn't have reminded me. I was wondering if I'd see you again today." She swung her door open wide. "Won't you come in?"

Atticus looked up and down the passageway. "Maybe we could go out on deck. It's a beautiful day out there. Nice, fresh breeze, sunny…"

"I'll be just outside," she said to Kristi as she closed the door.

Out on the windy cargo deck, Beth noticed a three-masted schooner that was passing not far away. It was on a northwesterly tack and heeling well over as it made good progress under billowing sails.

"So pretty," she said.

They stood watching the sailing ship for a minute or two.

"Whoops!" Beth reached for her bonnet in a sudden gust. "Gosh, so windy out here."

Atticus continued watching the ship.

"So, tell me about your school years, Atticus."

"Not much to tell. One-room country schoolhouse in Tennessee; then later, a bigger one after we moved closer to Nashville. I left after sixth grade, though. Most of the children did.

"There was always work to do around the farm. I liked that. And I didn't much like school anyway. I spent my classroom years always staring off, my nose pressed against the glass, so to speak, always looking for something, always finding the outside more fascinating than what went on in the classroom. Wondering what lay beyond. Over the horizon."

Beth moved half a step closer to him.

The wind on Lake Huron had been picking up for several minutes when a westerly gust blew across the deck, swirled around them, and lifted the hem of her skirt. Even though she wore pantalettes, they didn't cover her lovely ankles.

This time, he didn't avert his eyes; he stared at those shapely, beautiful legs—letting his imagination go wild.

After two or three seconds—or more?—she laughed a little, her cheeks a bright pink, then quickly pushed down her skirt. "What lay *beyond*," she said, stretching out the word, her voice trailing off.

"What's that?" He'd forgotten their conversation altogether.

She waited a moment before replying: "Beyond… the horizon, my dear," she whispered. "You were talking about the horizon."

"Yes, the horizon. Yeah, of course."

"Well then, Mr. *Atticus*," she said, with a bit of husky emphasis on his name. "Now you know." She gave a little shrug of her shoulders and tilted her head to one side, looking up at him, directly into his eyes.

He noticed the slight upturn at the edges of her mouth, her pinkish cheeks, and now the way her lips parted as she awaited his reply.

But he couldn't speak. He hesitated. "Wh…why yes, I guess…"

Where are the words? Damn.

He looked away from her and toward the horizon, searching for words, and then they came. "I… I've never thought of it that way, but I guess you're correct, Miss Maribeth. I know what's out there now."

He meant to extend this reply, but words abandoned him again. His surroundings disappeared, and his mind emptied of everything. Everything but her beautiful lips and those perfect eyes of hers. And those lovely legs.

"Of *course* you know." She smiled, then reached out and made a broad sweep toward the lake, the beautiful blue sky, and the white, pillowy clouds that lay so deliciously spread before them. "Because it's all here. Right in front of you. You are so fortunate to be surrounded by all this beauty. And it's Beth, remember?"

"Beg pardon?"

She moved closer and whispered, "It's not Miss Maribeth anymore. I think we're past that now… aren't we? Besides, I love it when you call me Beth." She reached up and touched his face, right next to his mouth. "And I love watching your lips move when you say my name."

Early evening. Second day out of Chicago.

Teddy, the porter, stood next to a bulwark with his tin bucket of scraps from supper.

Fog rested on the surface of Lake Huron like a thick layer of cake frosting. He enjoyed feeling the coolness of it on his face as the ship glided through.

"Lake steam," he whispered.

This was his favorite time of day. The crew had been fed; the dishes were done, pots and pans were on the drying rack. Finally, the day's pace had slowed down. The sun was off to the west and dropping lower, and everything was calm and peaceful.

"Okay now. Customers waiting."

He watched with amusement the single weaving string of seagulls that stretched back, looking like the tail of a kite as they flew alongside, keeping pace with the ship.

"Supper's coming, boys and girls."

The impatient birds squawked back at him, flapping and swooping.

He grabbed a handful. "Here ya go, ya whiny little critters." He laughed as he tossed the first handful of scraps to the swarm of birds.

He couldn't help smiling as he watched them. They were so funny. Adept, but some more so than others. Some were quick enough to catch scraps in midair; the rest of them were too slow, or maybe too old, so they had to plop into the water and fight over the floating morsels. They had a system of their own: The ones at the head of the line would snatch their mouthful, then fly off or just float as they gulped down their food. A minute or two later, they'd be back in line again, then soon alongside for second helpings.

Teddy wiped his brow with his sleeve and was about to head back into the galley to finish cleaning up. He held the bucket over the side and slapped the bottom to knock out the last tidbits. Then he paused for just a moment and looked off toward the Michigan shore.

Another steamer, a passenger boat. It was approaching from aft of the *Greaves*, now off to starboard and pulling nearly alongside, its course and theirs converging fast. Heart pounding, he glanced toward the pilothouse and hoped everybody was wide awake up there.

McBride was watching the passenger steamer, too. He wasn't worried. Not yet anyway.

The *Greaves* had passed the Straits of Mackinac well before dawn, and by now had reached the southernmost tip of Lake Huron. Ahead, there appeared to be nothing but land, an impenetrable wall of trees, but wheelsman Dwight Pauley steered directly toward it anyway, with the ship moving at a good clip.

"It stays pretty well hidden, doesn't it?" McBride said.

"The Saint Clair River, sir? Yes, it sure does," Pauley replied with a nervous chuckle. "Till you're just about right on top of it."

"And not much maneuvering room, even once you're there."

"No, not much, Captain. Must've been a tough approach back in the sailing days."

McBride nodded, as he gripped the brass rail under the window and stared toward the trees. "It was a tough one, all right. The sandbars here are strewn with a hundred years of wrecks."

McBride had already observed that Pauley had a good feel for the rudder. He glanced through the windows along the back wall of the pilothouse and saw Miles, Bosun Hake, Jefry Walks, and the other hands out on deck, hard at work fixing this and that, and sweeping up coal soot. Things seemed well under control.

That gave him some small measure of comfort, but not much. He was feeling quite ill. He had awakened from nightmares two or three times during the night, head pounding, heart racing. And as if his massive headache weren't enough, his stomach was in utter turmoil.

His discomfort made him even more grateful for his excellent crew: Atticus Miles and his deckhands, Pauley himself, and Second Mate Larry MacMillis. As weak as he was feeling, McBride knew he'd be hard pressed to oversee the operation or maintenance of the ship should there be a need to do so.

At least the tea was pleasant, as well as being nice and hot. That was good, because he was feeling chills all over. The hot cup of tea was the one small but pleasurable thing he could concentrate on right now, and it helped take his mind off his pain and discomfort.

When he had awakened earlier, he noticed another piece had fallen off the mural, the biggest one yet, revealing a new patch roughly a square foot in size.

Maybe it was that damned mural that made him feel sick. But could that possibly be? Every rational part of him screamed *no*, yet still the thought persisted.

The mural was exceptionally ugly and distressing. A chaotic rendering of swirls or clouds with some unnamable thing splashed in a ghastly putrescent palette. It was a face, hideously demonic, the likes of which he prayed could never exist in reality. Eyes projected foulness of every kind from a head twisted into a mask of hostility and menace. It was horrid, to say the least. Human, but not human.

Could he trace his illness to that hellish thing? Could a human hand have even created that abomination?

He couldn't imagine why anyone living in the captain's cabin before him would tolerate that hellish, troubling vision being there. Fortunately, somebody with good sense came along and covered it up with a coat of paint—which was now peeling away, unfortunately. He had thrown a bedsheet over it all, but that came undone. He'd have to think of some other way to cover it.

The passenger boat was closing by the second. McBride could even see its helmsman through the other ship's pilothouse windows.

Gripping the wheel, Wheelsman Pauley shot McBride a nervous glance, but at least he held course. The young man had a firm and confident hand, which was good.

"Steady as she goes," McBride said, not so much giving an order as to let him know he was doing fine. So far, at least.

"Steady, aye, sir."

A figure behind the other ship's helmsman paced back and forth, coming to the window twice to look toward the *Greaves*. The steamer's mate, perhaps, but most likely the captain himself.

Such crazy behavior, McBride thought. He knew exactly what the other fellow was doing; he was racing. Downright stupid conduct from that other wheelhouse crew, but specifically the captain.

The other skipper knew the risks as well, for certain, but maybe he just didn't care. He was trying to pass in front of the *Greaves* before the point where it would be too narrow to overtake. McBride was sure of it. There were a few who plied the lakes these days who didn't give a damn about the traditional courtesies, the rules of the seaway, or even safety.

Sign of the times, he thought.

Not like the old days.

Different world now.

The ships were running out of room.

Everybody was in such a big hurry nowadays. This world and all its goings-on had lately become foreign to him. Was all this even worth the bother anymore?

He owned his home, had money set aside. Had a wife and three wonderful daughters who missed him terribly when he was away, and he them. Why was he still out here after forty years? Someday soon, his daughters would be married and raising families of their own, having known their own father as only an occasional guest in their home rather than as a real father. McBride knew where he preferred to be, and it wasn't out here with skippers who put others' lives at risk. Not anymore.

The *Greaves* ripped through the waves faster than the other captain expected. McBride was sure of it because, suddenly, the captain figure was dashing around, back and forth, crisscrossing his pilothouse.

"He's in a panic," he whispered to himself. "Steady… steady…," he said to the wheelsman, calmly and quietly.

Even if the passenger steamer diverted, they might still collide. McBride saw passengers on the outer decks and in the side windows of the steamer, sitting and standing around, talking, relaxing, enjoying the day, unaware of the collision risk that was imminent now.

Something had to be done, and soon.

The *Greaves* had the right of way. The other captain needed to give way. He shouldn't have tried to overtake here, where they were closing in on the sandbars. McBride knew it was a dangerous gambit.

"Bloody, reckless fool," he muttered. "You caused this. I'm holding course."

Seconds later, the plume of black smoke coming from the passenger boat's stack diminished as they cut back speed, and the curling white bow wave became smaller.

The ship leaned considerably as its wheelsman spun the helm hard over, abruptly changing course. Panicked faces pressed against cabin windows, their mouths open in silent screams, while outside passengers grabbed anything within reach and hung on as the steamer passed so close and leaned so far over that its upper-deck railing nearly struck the *Greaves*.

Wheelsman Pauley sighed with relief.

"Good job, lad." McBride exhaled with relief, too, while shaking his head and mumbling. He took the stairs down to his cabin, flopped onto the bed, and was at once fast asleep.

Nightmares, one after another: Turbulent seas, screaming passengers, a reckless captain throwing his steamship into the path of the *Eli Greaves*. A stormy sky full of threatening swirls of black, gray, green, yellow, purple…

And yet more nightmares. They wouldn't stop: A lovely young woman in a ceremonial costume holding a huge knife over her head. Horrified people watching from nearby. The young woman screaming, the onlookers all screaming too, wailing and crying. And then one of a man in this same cabin picking up a revolver, placing the muzzle in his mouth and pulling the trigger.

McBride woke up exhausted. He felt as though he'd been around the world three times while sleeping. He checked his watch. Only thirty minutes of sleep?

This is insanity.

He swung his feet out and sat on the edge of his bed, so sleepy and fatigued that he could barely lift his head, but well aware that if he were to lie down, he'd not be able to sleep again, anyway.

Another big patch had fallen off the mural and lay on the floor. The thick layer of paint that had concealed it—for years, most likely—was coming down all by itself, now. Huge pieces had already peeled off, and big chips lay scattered on the floor. It made quite a mess. Ordinarily, he'd have swept them up, but lately, he felt little motivation to do so.

There was no other choice but to cover up that damned mural; that's all there was to it. Or do something—he wasn't sure what.

He put on his shoes and crunched across the pile of paint chips. He stood before the damned ugly monstrosity and cursed. Reached up to see if he could find a loose place along the molding, or at least a point where he could take hold of it. He ran his fingers across the top, then down the right side, where he found just barely enough of a space— maybe a quarter of an inch—into which he was able to slip his fingertips. He made sure of his grip, tightened it, then pulled at the molding with all his strength, and the entire thing came off in his hand. Nails and all. *"There! Got you!"*

McBride broke the section over his knee and tossed it onto the floor. Feeling suddenly invigorated, he went to work on the top molding. It refused to come off all of a piece, so he snapped off one part of it—which let go with a satisfying *crack!*—then snapped off the rest, now mortally wounded with its splintered end. He threw it onto the floor with commingled feelings of triumph and disgust.

He ran his finger along the edge of the mural, hoping to find a point where he could start peeling it away. But there was no canvas, no edge to discover—the foul thing was painted on the wall itself.

Continuing with the moldings. Breathing heavy, now. Doing this was refreshing and enjoyable. He grabbed the bottom piece, tore it out with hardly any effort at all, and broke it over his knee. The last piece, the left edge, that one took a little more effort, but not much. He ripped it away and tossed it onto the floor, and that was when he saw blood.

Just some drops among the paint chips and pieces of wood he'd broken. Then he noticed a deep gash on his left forearm. Red rivulets raced down his forearm and into his cupped hand, which was immediately full of his own warm blood. In two steps he was next to the bed, shaking the pillowcase free of its pillow with his other hand and wrapping it around his forearm. In moments, the dressing was soaked through, all red and dripping.

The pillowcase wasn't enough. He unsnapped his belt, pulled it out of the belt loops, then put it on his upper arm, looped the end through, yanked it tight, cinching it around his arm just below the bicep. The blood stopped spurting at once, reduced now to a thin rivulet. He threw the sopping wet pillowcase onto the pile of paint chips, reached for the towel bar next to the sink, then wrapped a fresh towel around his forearm. He walked slowly, carefully, across the floor—now slippery with blood—and sat down on the bed.

Sitting there, breathing hard, he made a conscious effort to calm himself down. He assessed things: The floor was a bloody mess, with paint chips and wood scraps all over. There were only a few spots of blood on the bed, though. He'd be able to lie down comfortably later and get back to sleep. He checked the towel—not much blood on it. His breathing and heart rate began to slow down.

He sighed with relief, slouched a bit, lowered his head, relaxed a bit more. As he calmed down, fatigue began to set in, and he was even a little dizzy. He wanted to lie down and sleep, but wouldn't do that before making sure the bleeding was under control. He was getting drowsy, and as his eyelids began to feel heavy, he looked up at the mural. The horrid face was looking down at him. Was he imagining things, or had the mouth of that demonic thing just twisted into the merest suggestion of a smirk?

He looked up at the face and shook his head. "No. This is *my* ship!"

He rose to his feet, picked the bloody pillowcase up off the floor, then searched for wood scraps that still had nails in them. He took off a shoe and used it to pound a nail through the bloody pillowcase so that it partly covered the face. Then another nail, and another. In a minute, the face was entirely covered by the pillowcase; blood dripped from it, ran down the mural and pooled on the floor below it.

Still holding the shoe, he hopped one-footed back to the bed and sat down. From within himself he felt something welling up. It was dark, and it was hot. It was sheer hatred. More than he had ever felt before. He threw the shoe at the mural. It bounced off and ended up on the floor, next to the door.

"Yes, my ship—*my* command, you son of a bitch! *My* ship!"

Chief Murrick was keeping a close watch on the boiler pressure gauges. So far, so good, he thought, as he tapped the gauge glass with his knuckle. On this trip, he'd been keeping the boiler pressure down, and thus both the speed and revolutions.

No one up in the pilothouse seemed to notice—not yet, anyway. Somebody would figure it out, eventually. McBride, maybe, but definitely Miles. If they didn't know he'd reduced speed, they wouldn't figure it into their dead reckoning calculations, and they wouldn't be as far along as they thought.

Questions would come up.

Chief, we should've passed such-and-such light by now. Or: *Why aren't we seeing this or that point yet? What speed did you say we're running at?*

He couldn't keep it a secret forever. He'd have to think of something.

Gerard LeBlanc, fire stoker, and Bob Wilson, boilerman, were doing their jobs and seemed to know that Murrick had cut back on the steam pressure. Neither one appeared too concerned, though. Just as the chief had hoped.

After speaking a few words of encouragement to the men, he took the ladder topside and went straight to his cabin. He made sure to lock the cabin door, then lifted the mattress and picked at the place where he'd sewn it closed earlier, relieved that no one had tampered with it. He patted the underside of the mattress with his palm, and a feeling of immense satisfaction rushed over him. After a half minute of pulling out the thread, he reached in and withdrew a little suede bag. A feeling of joy enveloped him as he felt the smooth, luxurious texture of the suede and held the full weight of it all in his hand. Feeling dizzy already, delightfully dizzy, he let his fingers feel and identify the edges of the coins within. He loosened the rawhide drawstring, then opened the bag and carefully let the coins fall onto his bed. The clinking sound they made gave him a thrill, as it had done a few times already today. He scooped them all up with both hands, closing his eyes as he did so.

"Gold," he whispered, exhaling deeply. He loved hearing himself say that word and feeling the coolness of the coins in his hands. He said it again, this time stretching it out, whispering the word as though it were a timid thing that would fly off once alarmed: "Go-o-o-o-ld."

How perfect and lovely the sound. He could even feel the word pass between his lips, borne by his own breath. The word and the thought were inside him now. Surrounding him, too, filling his cabin.

Slowly, reluctantly, he opened his eyes. With great care, he returned each coin to the suede bag one at a time, again and again enjoying the feeling of the soft suede and the solid coins within.

Beth looked around the pilothouse as Atticus pointed to the man at the ship's wheel.

"Miss Eaton, this is Eugene Guest, wheelsman on my watch. The finest on the lakes, I might add. And Gene, this young lady is her cabin mate Kristi."

Guest grinned, made an exaggerated and comical salute, and stood stiffly at attention.

Kristi giggled, and Beth smiled.

Beth extended her hand, and Guest took it. "I am pleased to meet you, Miss Eaton, and you as well, Miss Kristi."

Kristi smiled bashfully, but did not reply.

"It's our pleasure, Mr. Guest. To be sure, it gives us both great comfort knowing the ship is in your capable hands."

Pipe and cigar smoke in the pilothouse made bluish-gray shafts of the sunlight coming through the windows. Atticus passed into and out of the shafts of light as he walked around, pointing out this and that, giving the two ladies a personal tour of the room.

He explained the purpose of the engine-order telegraph, which sent change-of-speed orders back to an identical unit in the engine room. Then he explained how the steering functioned with cables running the length of the ship, because the wheel was in the pilothouse, while the rudder was all the way aft, pointing out that it was in fact a steam-operated steering engine that actually made the rudder swing back and forth.

Just as Atticus escorted Beth and Kristi outside, someone whistled from back on the cargo deck and motioned to him.

"Looks like I'm being summoned." He held onto his cap to keep it from blowing away in the wind. "I'm sorry,

Beth. Seems they're having a problem. I need to go talk with them, then it's back to my pilothouse watch. Maybe we can continue this tour later on. I hope you don't mind."

"Of course not, Atticus. Duty calls."

He escorted the two of them back down the stairway to the main deck. "Will you be okay then?"

"Oh, certainly," Beth replied. "I'll just stay here for some fresh air."

"I go back inside and read," Kristi said.

Atticus waved and walked aft.

Leaning against the mast that held the ship's crane, Beth closed her eyes, enjoying the scent of lake air. She let her mind drift. It was such a relief that she had finally found work. Having respectable employment would be a good way to establish herself here in America. She already imagined how satisfying it would feel to wire her parents with news that she had found a position at a well-known, elite girls' school. It filled her with hope that someday soon, maybe even in a month or so, she could send a letter to her parents with happy news about her school duties and other activities, without having to reveal how close she came to financial disaster. She knew it would be best that neither they nor anyone else in the family ever learned how close to a catastrophe she'd been.

Hearing footfalls, she opened her eyes. "Oh, hello, Jefry."

"Hello, Miss Eaton. I hope I didn't disturb you." He set down a tool bag beside the steam winch. "Just about to do some maintenance work. I'll try not to make too much noise."

Holding out her hands, she looked down near her feet and around the deck nearby.

"Is everything okay?" Jefry asked.

"Well…I'm not sure. I had both my gloves just a few minutes ago. Now I've only one."

"You're missing the right-hand one; is that correct?"

She glanced around some more. "It appears so. Mr. Miles showed us the pilothouse; then we came down to this deck, and then…" She shrugged.

"May I show you something?"

"Yes, of course," she said.

"I told you I can see things. Do you recall?"

"Yes, and I believed you. Still do."

He took a step closer to her, adjusted his stance, inclined his head, then held out his hands. "Just hold your hands beneath mine. Close but not touching."

"Close, but not touching," she said, amused. "What are we going to do?"

"Maybe this time I can show you. Are you ready?"

"I suppose so," she said, her voice trailing away, skeptical.

"Haven't tried this—not around here, anyway. Goin' to see if I can do it. Let's see if I can find your glove."

"Ahh, so this is a game?" she asked.

"Oh no, miss. No game. No trick. It's real."

Beth held out her hands and closed her eyes. "I feel a little silly doing this, you know…"

"Just wait…you'll see."

"Ohhh, great ethereal glove ghost," she intoned, her voice wavering in mock spookiness. "Glover of the afterworld. Emerge from your glove crypt and deliver my long-lost white glove—right hand, incidentally—or if you can't do that, just find a nice new pair for me." She smirked playfully, opened her eyes a little, and looked at Jefry.

He didn't respond. Eyes closed, face slack now, he took slow, deep breaths. After a minute, his shoulders fell; he slumped, his head hanging lower, now trancelike.

As Beth watched, the look on his face changed again, from relaxed to one of alarm, even fear. He winced. Then he angled his shoulders and opened his mouth in what looked like an exclamation of pain. Yet, he remained silent.

"Are we starting?"

No reply from him.

Again, his face showed excruciating pain, yet not a sound came from him.

"*Jefry!*" Beth cried.

Atticus was still back aft with his men. He heard her and looked up.

Jefry's shoulders rose, as though he were being lifted by the armpits. No one was there, though. Then he moved backward, but it seemed not by his own effort. His legs were not propelling him; only the backs of his boots were touching the deck. One boot came off. It appeared he was being dragged… by no one, by nothing.

Beth screamed.

Atticus had already started walking toward them; he broke into a run, arriving just as something cast Jefry onto the deck with great force.

He lay there motionless; after several seconds, his eyes opened. He twisted his face in pain while struggling to rise enough to support himself on his elbow. He looked around. "What's this? What's going on? What am I doing here?"

Atticus helped him sit up. "You hit the deck pretty hard."

Jefry winced and held his hand to his chest. "Smacked my head, I think. Ow!"

"Let me take a look," Maribeth said. Leaning over and with both hands, she looked through his long hair. "There's no bleeding, but you're bound to have some swelling later."

"Chest pains too now," Jefry said.

"Just stay there," Atticus said. "No need to rush. The winch isn't going anywhere. It can wait. Don't get up just yet; you're apt to be lightheaded anyway."

Maribeth and Atticus remained with him for a few minutes, observing in silence as he moved his shoulders around before turning his head one way, then the other. After a while, he leaned back, took a deep breath, blew it out, and tried to smile.

Maribeth gently placed her hand on his shoulder. "You took quite a spill."

He nodded while lifting himself up. Maribeth took him by the arm, and Atticus dropped the boot in front of him so he could put it back on. Maribeth kept him steady as he slipped his foot back into it.

"I don't know what just happened," Jefry said. "I have no idea."

Beth and Atticus stood in the open doorway of her cabin. "We'll be back soon, Kristi."

The girl smiled and waved, sat on the edge of the bed, smoothed out her dress, and placed a book on her lap.

"She seems happy enough," Atticus said, as they stood at the rail, looking across Lake Erie. The *Eli Greaves* had transited the St. Clair and Detroit Rivers, and was now bound for the coal docks at Hammond, Ohio.

Beth shook her head. "Poor, sweet child. My heart aches for her, it really does."

"Why?"

Her lower lip quivered. "Kristi's parents brought her from Norway. Her mother passed away on the crossing. From what, I don't know. I learned that from Captain McBride. Kristi and her father came the rest of the way together, finally ending up in Iowa. He found work as a farm laborer. After a year doing that, he hanged himself."

"Oh, no."

"Atticus, my heart bleeds for that poor thing."

"Of course."

"Nine years old. I want to help her, but I don't know how."

"Show her every kindness. And be calm with her."

Beth smiled. "You had daughters too, didn't you?"

He looked off into the distance. "Who will she meet in Buffalo? Do you know? Relatives?"

"An agent."

"A *what?* An *agent?*"

"That's what she said."

"That's nonsense; a little girl needs a parent. What's a child need an agent for? And what kind of agent?"

"She doesn't know—I'm sure of it. Maybe she misunderstood something that someone told her."

"I guess that's possible. I'll mention it to the captain to see what he knows."

"Oh yes, please do that, Atticus. Or, I could ask him. Either way, we must find out what we can about this. She might be in danger as soon as she sets foot off this ship. Please, Atticus. It's up to the two of us to protect her. Perhaps he has papers of some sort for her."

"He's her chaperone. I'm sure he has something."

"It's up to us to protect her, the three of us."

"Of course it is. Don't worry. I'll find out more."

"Thank you. Right now, all she has is a man's name on a slip of paper."

"A *man's* name? I don't like the sound of that."

"Neither do I. Whether it's a man or a woman."

"Yes, true. Doesn't make much difference these days, does it? You never know who to trust."

She shook her head. "So, trust no one."

FOUR

Hammond, Ohio

Atticus stood watching as the coaling took place, happy that his job was aboard ship and not here at the coal docks. Coal docks were dirty places. No surprise, that. Not to anyone, landsman, or mariner. Not dirty in the sense of grimy or disgusting dirty, but black. Just black. Everywhere. Coal dust everywhere. On the loading pier, the walkways, in the air, and covering every single member of the wheelbarrow gang that now pushed barrowful after barrowful of soft bituminous—power-generating steam coal—along the wooden walkway, up the loading ramp, onto the *Eli Greaves*, and into its coal bunker.

Each man's overalls looked blacker than black, as did their faces—covered with coal dust except where each man had wiped off sweat. The only things that weren't black were the whites of their eyes and the white-and-black streaks where sweat ran down their cheeks.

Atticus doubted that any of the men pushing wheelbarrows realized they were the final link in a chain of events that began in tropical swamps supposedly millions of years earlier. In this year of 1873, even top geologists were just beginning to understand it. A consensus was developing among many of them that the process may have taken as long as two hundred million years, but they would not know for sure until the geological record itself supplied definitive proof.

If the coal loaders themselves knew about it at all, they were too busy to give much thought to the way in which organic matter takes all those millions of years to go from prehistoric swamp stumps and grasses to become lumps of coal, those familiar chunks of black organic sedimentary rock that power factories and heat schools, pull trains across the prairie, propel ships through the water, and boil the morning's eggs… and which sometimes end up in children's Christmas stockings, too.

Jefry approached Atticus. "Bunker's half-full, Mate. Thought you'd want to know."

"All right, Jefry." He pointed toward a corner of the after deckhouse. "See that coil of rope over there? The way it hangs? It got uncoiled somehow, and now it's unraveled where those men are walking."

"Yeah, we don't want anybody trippin' on that." Jefry dashed off toward the line of wheelbarrow men.

As he passed one of them—a big, beefy fellow—the man leaned toward him and bumped him with his elbow.

Jefry lost his balance and fell, landing hard.

"Oops. Might wanna watch where you're going, Geronimo," the man said with a hateful, crooked smirk. Then he spat on the deck, near Jefry's feet.

Jefry began picking himself up off the deck, but the man crowded him so close that he lost his balance and fell down again.

"Having some trouble there, feller?" The bully loomed over him, now with both fists clenched. "Oh, maybe you thinkin' to do somethin' about that?" Then he looked up to see Atticus standing right in front of him. "Hey, Mate, this little dummy gotta learn how to walk. He just—"

A crushing left hook to the jaw sent the bully staggering. He lost his balance and fell onto his own wheelbarrow, tipping it over and scattering wheelbarrow, man, and coal across the deck.

The man jumped up, brushing coal dust off his face and arms before raising his fists and squaring off against Atticus. "You ain't done with me yet, Red. We got business to take care of, looks like." He reached toward his right side. "How 'bout I give you another scar on the other—"

His words were cut off by a quick edge-of-the-hand strike to the throat, followed by two left jabs to the kidney, then a smashing roundhouse to the gut, followed by another. He ducked and dodged, but with every feint, another explosive punch was there waiting for him, one shock wave after another, from out of nowhere.

Atticus had already noticed the knife sheathed on the man's right hip, but the bully never managed to touch it. The man doubled over, clutching his throat and his midsection, wheezing and gasping for air.

Atticus ordered two others in the wheelbarrow crew to put the bully back in his own wheelbarrow.

"You mean…?" one said, hesitating.

"*This* is what I mean." Atticus elbowed the man aside, then shoved the bully hard, and the fellow landed flat on his back again. Atticus grabbed the wheelbarrow with one hand and flipped it upright. "Now pick up this pile of garbage and put him in there, then get him the hell off my ship."

The two men did as ordered but only after calling over two more loaders to help hoist the big man into his wheelbarrow.

Atticus reached out; Jefry took his hand and got back on his feet. He was shaking his head and smiling. "Nice punches, Mate."

"You gonna be okay, son?"

"Oh yeah. He didn't hurt me." Jefry brushed coal dust off his clothes and looked at the first mate with admiration and amazement.

Then the two of them stood there watching as all four men wheeled their partner, still choking and holding his throat, down the ramp and back ashore.

Beth had heard men shouting and got up out of bed. She went to the deckhouse doorway to see what was going on. Some sort of commotion back aft. Men fighting, and Atticus Miles right in the thick of it. Shouting, pushing people around, punching and punching. All of this as poor Jefry lie on the deck. Then Atticus was shouting at some other men, and then the same poor man whom he'd hit, now choking, holding his own throat, gasping for breath, then finally getting carried back to shore in a filthy coal wheelbarrow.

A *wheelbarrow*?

And poor Jefry lying on the deck.

She couldn't believe her eyes. Atticus hadn't struck him, had he? No, couldn't have. But what just happened? What was going on? All that awful fighting. Had Atticus done something to him?

Outrageous. Awful. No wonder civilized people preferred passenger ships to cargo ships.

These Americans. Good God.

Beth watched until things calmed down. Shaking her head, she stepped back indoors. Captain McBride was in the passageway, having just shut his own cabin door. His arm was wrapped in a rag or towel of some sort, and he looked wearier than ever.

"Good day, Miss Eaton," he said, his voice sounding frail.

"Sir, I have just witnessed some quite atrocious behavior."

He appeared concerned but was having trouble keeping his eyes open. "What is it you're upset about, miss?"

"The loaders back there and your crewmen," she began, then took a moment to catch her breath. "And that first mate of yours. What I just saw with my own eyes was the… the ugliest display of—"

The door opened, and Atticus appeared along with Diggs and Fournier.

"What's going on out there, Mate?"

Atticus shrugged and was about to speak, but first he glanced at Beth. "Nothing out of the ordinary, Cap. Just one of the loaders acting up is all." He looked directly at Beth as he spoke to the captain. "Got pushy with one of my men. Everything's back to normal now, and the bunker's full."

"So everything's under control then?"

"Of course, sir."

Beth gasped, then muttered something that ended with "*…shoot him with your bloody Griswold.*" Then she spun around, stomped back inside her cabin, and slammed the door.

Atticus stood there, not sure what he ought to do, nor fully comprehending what had just taken place. *What's she so angry about?*

He glanced toward the captain, whose arm was all wrapped up for some reason, and who was clearly fatigued. Their eyes met, there was a brief moment of understanding in the gaze they shared, then Captain McBride shook his head, appeared to shrug, then opened his cabin door and went inside. Clearly he was aware something had gone amiss between Atticus and Maribeth…but wanted no part of it, and by his silence and his actions seemed to indicate the less he knew about it, the better.

Behind Atticus, Diggs quietly cleared his throat. Atticus looked toward him, but Diggs lowered his eyes, feigning a sudden interest in something on his right shirtsleeve. Brushed it off, whatever was on the sleeve…if it was anything at all. Fournier took a quiet, careful step toward the door. There were a couple of mumbles between them—no doubt meant to be taken as conversation—along with both of them together moving closer to the door.

"You men," Atticus said, quietly, "You might as well get back to what you were doing."

They didn't need to be told a second time; the two of them burst out through the door and onto the deck, quietly closing the door behind them.

Atticus paused before her cabin door, hand raised, about to knock. After a moment, he rotated the hand so he wouldn't be knocking with all his knuckles. He extended only the forefinger knuckle, and made a quiet knock with that.

Immediately, heavy footfalls thumped inside her cabin, and she threw the door open. She stood there, eyes on fire, then immediately swung the door halfway closed, as though suddenly expecting a battering ram, or someone trying to kick in the door. "Yes," she said, crisply, her face framed by the now narrower door opening, her fingers wrapped around the door and gripping it tight. She had the attitude of a fuse awaiting a lit match.

"You're angry…?" Atticus asked.

"Angry?" she replied, slowly, almost menacingly, in a voice that was at least an octave lower than her normal speaking voice. "Angry is the least of what I am. And don't you dare pretend not to know what this is about."

"I don…I don't know."

She made a loud exclamation of what seemed frustration, or exasperation. "What did you do to him?"

"Who?"

"*Who,* indeed. Do you think I'm blind? Jefry, that's who."

"I don't know what you're talking ab… I did nothing. I didn't do anything to him."

"I saw him on his back, and you were shoving and punching everyone in sight!"

"Everyone in… What are you—?"

"And don't you dare deny it."

"I didn't… That's not what hap—"

"And that other poor man, the one you nearly killed. You'd better hope he survives."

"Nearly ki…*what?*"

She started to say something else, paused, growled again with frustration, then slammed the door shut.

After coaling, the bunker was sealed shut, fires were stoked, and steam brought up. Deckhands hauled docking lines aboard; the *Greaves* maneuvered away from the loading dock and was soon heading along Lake Erie toward Buffalo.

Chief Murrick stood at the aft rail on the second level, staring at the Hammond coal dock as it faded into the darkening grayish blue haze of the shoreline. He shivered a bit in the chilly breeze the ship made as it gathered speed. He was always nervous now whenever they were in port. Didn't matter where. He hated having new people on board. It made no difference why they were there or what they were doing. He couldn't relax until the ship was underway.

But he couldn't relax even then.

He glanced over his shoulder toward his cabin door. Nobody was nearby. He was starving. Hadn't eaten all day, hunger gnawing at him, but by now it was too late. Galley was closed, cooks off for the night. Maybe there was an apple or something in the crew messroom. He could go below and check, but that would mean leaving his cabin unguarded.

No, couldn't do that.

If he stood out here long enough, somebody from engineering would show up. He could ask them to get him an apple. Yes, that's what he'd do.

But that might lead to gossip: *The chief asked you to bring him food, did he? What's he worried about? Doesn't want to leave his cabin, eh? What's he hiding in there?*

No. No, no, no.

That wouldn't work.

Not at all.

The evening chill was getting to him, so he went back inside his cabin and shut the door.

He lifted the mattress and felt underneath, made sure everything was still where it had been.

Yes. Good. Everything just as he'd left it.

He was so hungry.

He slid into bed, curled up, and was soon asleep.

Fournier and Diggs stood next to the rail.

"If you agree we're gonna do this, then we'll do it," Diggs said.

Fournier shrugged and threw out his hands. "I already say I will."

"You better not leave me in the lurch."

"What you talking about?"

"Means last minute you'll back out, or we go there, and you don't say nothing and make me look like an idiot."

"Yeah, yeah, I know what means *in the lurch*. From French anyway so of course I know. *Lourche*. You and me, we here talking, right? It's my idea anyway, huh?"

Diggs shrugged, nodded.

"Okay, so we gonna do this like you say, then. When I say I gonna do something, means I gonna do it."

"Alright, alright. So, who's gonna knock on her door? You or me?"

"Maybe you better," Fournier said.

"Don't matter really," Diggs said. "But okay. I will."

"You sure she's there?"

"Pretty sure. Seen her and the little girl headed there maybe twenty minutes ago. Ain't seen 'em come out."

The two men looked into each other's eyes for a moment. One shrugged, then the other.

"You sure we ain't gonna get in trouble with the mate?"

"Hell, I don't know," said Diggs. "How can I say? No way to know for sure. She takes what we say the wrong way and says something to him and we're in big trouble."

"I know."

"Be easier to just stay out of it," Diggs said.

"Yeah."

"Why go asking for trouble. Right?"

Fournier shrugged, nodded.

"Ain't no business of ours," Diggs said.

Fournier shook his head. "Naah, somebody else business."

They shared another glance.

"Ahhh, shit. What the hell," Diggs said.

Fournier nodded again, then spit on his hands and slicked back his hair. "Yeah, what the hell. I'm ready. You ready?"

"Yeah. Let's go," Diggs said.

They started walking toward the forward deckhouse.

When Beth heard the knock on her door, she was still upset about the fighting, but not yet entirely sure what had actually gone on.

She threw the door open…

Two men stood humbly before her. The same two who'd been in the passageway with Atticus earlier. One of them bareheaded, the other with cap in hand, both of them with clothes still dirty from their day's work. They were both shaking, and looked terrified.

"Yes?" she demanded.

"Miss, we're deckhands. I'm Diggs, and this here is Fournier. We're sorry to bother you, and we know it ain't our place to be here talking to you, but we figured you should know something."

Fournier nodded.

Diggs continued: "That man. He knocked Jefry down."

"What man?"

"The loader, the big bully from back at the coal docks."

She stood there with arms folded.

"He knock Jefry down," Fournier said. "An' our Mate Miles, he protect Jefry."

"I… I'm not sure I understand."

"The coal man call Jefry bad words because he's Indian, then he knock him down."

"Our first mate helped Jefry," Diggs added. "He always helps us. He don't ever pick on nobody. Back even before

Captain McBride, back when we had a bad captain, not a nice man—very mean—Mate Miles always protected us."

"But all that fighting…" she said, her words trailing off.

"Mate didn't start nothing. The coal man was a bully and pushed Jefry down and threatened him."

"He's not a bad man, our mate. He's a good man."

Beth didn't know what to say.

"And nothing changed after what happened a few months ago. Nothing. He didn't change. He still stands up for us every time, even though—"

She shook her head. *"Change?* Why would he…? Months ago? What happened months ago? What changed?"

The two men looked at each other. Then Diggs nodded to Fournier.

"Mate lose his family," Fournier said, his eyes glistening as he started to tear up.

"His family? But—"

"He didn't tell you?"

"No, he never… Not really. We spoke a little about it but…"

"They die when we was away on a trip," Fournier said.

"His whole family," said Diggs. "All four of them. From the cholera, miss."

"Yeah, they did," said Fournier. "It's all true. They die from the cholera. From bad water. All four of them. Little boy and daughter and even the little baby girl. Sweetest, beautifulest little child. And their mama too. All of them."

Diggs twisted his cap. "But that didn't make him mean or nothing. He's still good to us. I mean, it tore his heart out, but he's still good to us."

Fournier nodded. "Yeah. Big sadness in him for all these months, but then you come and he's different. He's different now. We can see it. All us guys on crew. We all see how he change now with you here, miss." He looked toward Diggs, who was nodding in agreement.

"We see him laughing with you. I ain't seen him laugh since maybe a year ago. Yeah, but now he talks with you, and you make him laugh so much."

Beth whispered. "Lost them all. His whole family…lost them *all*…"

"Yes. His whole family. All of them. We ain't lying. It's all true, every word."

"Thank you. Thank you so much," she said to the two men, whispering, her head bowed.

She slowly closed the cabin door, then sat down on the edge of the bed, next to Kristi, who gave her a puzzled look. "I don't know what those men say."

Seconds passed before Beth spoke. "Were you ever wrong about something? Or about someone?"

Kristi squinted and shrugged.

"What I meant is, maybe you thought somebody was not a nice person, but then you find out you're wrong."

"And they are nice person?"

Beth nodded.

"I guess I did that."

"Well, I did that today. And I'm not happy about it. I saw a fight a while ago. Out on deck. And I thought I saw something happen, but I only saw a part of it, and I drew the wrong conclusion."

"Drew the…?"

"I blamed somebody. I blamed the wrong person."

"Blame wrong." Kristi thought for a moment, nodding. "This about Mr. Mate Miles?"

"Yes."

"Mr. Mate move me from the room yesterday. Nice man, I think. He speaks to me very soft. Um, how do you say this?"

"Quietly? Gentle?"

"Yes, I think. Yes. Quietly. He is gentle and quietly."

"Maybe so, yes," Beth said. "I suppose he is. Yes, you may be right, and he's a gentle and quietly man."

"Large man, and not rough."

Beth shrugged. "Yes. Maybe like that, too."

"I think I like Mr. Mate Miles."

Beth took Kristi by the hand. "We'll talk about something else now, okay?"

"Yes, okay."

"Maybe your mama and papa?"

The girl wrinkled up her face and shook her head. "Maybe not, I think."

"That's okay. Some other time then."

"Big Sister Beth?"

"Yes, honey."

"You lived in a church. I saw you."

Beth gave her a puzzled look, then shook her head.

"A red church."

"No, I've never… where'd you get this?"

"I saw you when I was asleep."

"You dreamed I was in a church?"

Kristi nodded. "But not just there; you lived there."

"I've never lived in a church."

"You did. You lived there, Miss Beth. I saw you."

Puzzled, Beth started to reply but had no words.

"There was a steeple on top and lions in front."

Beth was puzzled. "*Lions?* I don't think churches ever have—"

"Two lions. One on each side of the walk."

What Kristi was describing began to clarify in Beth's mind. "Was there a little metal fence around the lions?"

"Yes! And a metal fence around the roof, too."

Beth felt a sudden chill. "Kristi, I think you saw where I lived. It wasn't a church, though. It was a house. Still is. It's red brick. I lived there for six months and moved out two days ago."

"But the steeple on top."

"That's just a tower. Not a steeple. Some styles of houses have those."

"You're sure. And windows with curved tops?"

Beth smiled. "I'm sure. Of course. And the lions are concrete. And yes, it had windows like that. But how on earth could you—"

"Okay, I guess. So you lived there? And not a church?"

"No, not a church," Beth said. "I must have mentioned it to you when we were talking."

Kristi shook her head. "Didn't hear it from you; I saw it."

"Okay, but—"

"I saw it when I left Chicago for Iowa with Papa."

Beth squinted. "But that was… when was that? No, that was more than a year ago."

Kristi nodded. "I guess about that time. No… more. Maybe two years. Before the fire. I remember that… before the big fire. Yes, before all the big buildings burned down."

"I was in England, honey. I was still in England then. You couldn't have seen me at the house. Not then. That was two years ago. I wasn't in Chicago, not even in this country yet."

"I did, though."

"You saw me at the house before I got there?"

"Guess so."

"Maybe you and your papa went by the place in a carriage or wagon and then you saw it again in your dream."

Kristi shrugged.

"Maybe that was it, hmm?"

"Maybe," Kristi said. "But I saw you there. I saw you before I met you. And then I saw you here in the dining room and you were that person."

There was silence between them for a half minute.

"Big Sister Miss Beth?" Kristi said quietly.

"Yes?"

"We can go outside?"

"Of course. Yes, let's go. Let's get out of here and go for a walk."

Kristi walked over to the desk chair, then sat down to put on her shoes.

Maribeth remained seated on the edge of the bed for a few moments, gazing at the girl, recalling her own strange dreams once again, and now trying to comprehend how Kristi was able to see her at home in Chicago more than a year *before* her arrival in this country.

Who are you? she thought…

Who… are you?

It was a cool, clear early evening on Lake Erie. The sun had set, and a suggestion of twilight had spread across the sky. A few gas lamps were already visible along the shoreline. Streetlights.

Beth looked around for Atticus, but did not see him. What would she say to him, anyway? She and Kristi walked aft on the cargo deck, eventually reaching the galley. As they passed it, a man in a white cook's cap smiled and waved. They waved back at him. Beth recognized him from the dining room.

"Nice cooking smells," Kristi said.

"Mmm, yes. Smells good."

"Mm-hmm."

They stopped at the fantail and watched the flag for a moment as it flapped lazily in the gentle breeze.

"America flag," Kristi said. "My papa love America flag."

Beth nodded. "Many people do."

"You are from America?"

"No, I'm from England."

"Oh, okay. I know England. We learn in school. I like England. Norway is friends with her. She have a queen."

"Yes. Do you know her name?"

"Mm-hmm. Is Victoria."

"Very good. Correct."

"We have King Oscar in Norway. England Victoria was only child. So, she had no sister too. Or brother."

The man who had waved came up to them holding two plates. "Would you two lovely ladies care for some cake?"

"Oh yes," Kristi said, taking a plate and fork and diving right in. "Thank you, thank you."

"This is so kind of you," Beth said. "You are Mr. Squires, aren't you?"

"Yes, Miss Eaton. Second Cook Willy Squires at your service. But everybody just calls me Willy or Mister Willy."

"Thank you ever so much, sir. My name is Maribeth, and this is my cabin mate, Kristi. Your job here keeps you very busy it seems."

"I am pleased to meet you both. Yes, it sure does. But I like what I'm doing, and I enjoy talking with the crew, and I especially like meeting new people such as you both."

"Chocolate," Kristi said. "My favorite. Mmm, so good."

Willy smiled. "I'm happy you like it, Miss Kristi."

"Have you been a ship's cook for many years?" Maribeth asked.

"Been about ten years. I was a hotel cook in Detroit before this."

"Why did you leave that job, may I ask?"

He shrugged. "I don't know. Restless, I reckon. Just looking for something different."

"Where did you grow up?"

"Collingwood, Ontario. My parents settled there. We came from London."

"Oh, so you're English?"

"Yes."

"You've lost the accent."

He shrugged. "Never had it, I suppose. I was only three years old when we left. They left Collingwood and moved to Port Huron when I was eight. Then to Toledo, then Detroit a couple of years later."

"So much moving around."

He nodded. "Story of America, I guess, isn't it? I like movement though. Maybe that's what always draws me to ship work. I've left it before, but I always come back. It's nice to look out the window and see something different every time. And I like the fresh air too."

Beth nodded. "The lake air is wonderful, isn't it?"

Willy held out his hand. "I can take the plate if you're done, Miss Kristi."

Beth smiled as Kristi handed him the plate and fork. "She inhaled that cake."

Willy smiled too. "I think that means she liked it."

"It's very kind of you to bring us this treat, Mr. Willy. Thank you so much."

"There's still more cake left if you'd care—"

"Oh no, thank you," Beth said. "It was delicate and so, so tasty, but I—"

Kristi jumped up and down. "Yes, yes, more please."

A glow was spreading across the shoreline far ahead.

The lights of Buffalo, thought Beth. There was something about seeing lights in the distance. She wondered about that. What is it about far-off lights that draws you to them? What makes you want to go there? But when you get there, it's just another place like all others. Another city, another port. Crowds of people rushing around, pushing this way and that. Some of them nice, some others not so nice.

As Beth and Kristi approached their cabin, Kristi took hold of Beth's arm with both hands. "I just make up a story."

"Okay. Are you going to tell me?"

"Yep, but in cabin maybe. Getting cold."

"Yes, honey, I think you're right. Getting a little too cold out here for stories. When did you start saying *yep*? It's slang, you know."

"Slang? What means slang?"

"It's not a proper way to express things. Not a proper way to speak."

Kristi shrugged.

"Where'd you hear it?"

"From you, I think."

Beth smiled. "Okay. Anyway, yes, going to be a wool-blanket night tonight."

"Only one blanket though."

"Yes," Beth said. "You must have it."

"Or maybe I sleep next to you with blanket on top?"

"If you wish, honey."

"Uh-huh. Then we both stay warm."

"You're very thoughtful, aren't you? Okay then, that's what we'll do. So you have a story, do you? What kind? A silly story?"

Kristi shook her head.

"No? Really? Not a silly one this time?"

Kristi shook her head again. "Boyfriend story this time."

"Oh, you have a boyfriend, do you think?"

Kristi shook her head and turned away to hide a sly smile.

"What?" Beth asked. "What is it now?"

"Not my boyfriend. Big Sister Beth boyfriend."

"My boyfriend? What makes you think—?"

"Story tattle 'Mr. Mate Miles, Miss Beth Boyfriend.'"

Beth looked at her. "Tattle? What's *tattle*?"

Kristi looked at Beth, wrinkling her face as though she'd asked a dumb question. "Tattle is story name."

"Oh, you mean the title."

"Is how you say story name? The tie-tell?"

"Yes, sweetie; tie-tell is how we say it."

Kristi shrugged, and her eyes opened wide. "Okay, I learn now. So story tie-tell is Mr. Mate Miles, Miss Beth Boyfriend. Okay?"

"Yep. Okay," Beth replied, smiling as they headed toward their cabin.

FIVE

Port of Buffalo, Commercial Slip

Beth recalled a story she'd once heard from her father: Back around 1804, a Mr. Joseph Ellicott was thinking about circles. And wagon wheels. He thought they made sense.

Especially for Buffalo.

As a manufacturer, her father had many contacts throughout the world. Through one of those, he'd learned a lot about Buffalo and other American cities.

Modern-day Buffalo began taking shape in 1804 when Mr. Ellicott—surveyor and resident agent for the Holland Land Company and Buffalo's primary designer—came up with a concept for the layout of the city that was not only radical but radial: parks and places of community activity at the center with broad streets spreading out like a wagon wheel's spokes from that central hub.

It was not a well-known fact four years later that a survey had begun. Its purpose was to map out the route for a waterway that would connect the Hudson River to Lake Erie. Mr. Ellicott most certainly knew about the survey, though, because he planned and designed accordingly. Nine years later, the excavation and construction of the 363-mile-long Erie Canal began. When the waterway was finally completed in 1825, it was the first major transportation link between East Coast cities and the Great Lakes.

As well as the vast American interior.

And radical, radial Buffalo would be the commercial shipping lynchpin of it all and one of the nation's first "planned cities." Over a brief span of years, it became one of the most important and prosperous cities in America.

Beth and Kristi watched as the ship was unloaded. It was quite something to see. Beth had never visited a shipping district before. Certainly not one as organized as the Port of Buffalo. She had seen nothing quite like this operation. It was a beehive and a wonder to behold.

Nearly all the cargo from eastern ports that was destined for the American interior came through Buffalo. Most of the immigrant people did as well.

"So busy place," Kristi said.

Beth nodded. "Yes, very busy."

The *Greaves* was tied up alongside a wharf where scores of men, more likely hundreds, hustled about, darting among moving wagons and their horses with handcarts of every size and shape and configuration. The fragrance of the place was a port's usual fishy, sea mossy, watery smell combined with coal smoke from ships, the odors of every imaginable sort of cargo—although mostly wheat and oats here at this place—and always the unforgettable bouquet of horse manure on wet wooden wharves.

You breathed it all in, and it became a part of you, and you felt it envelop you in its rough but honest essence. Things coming in, things going out. Noise, motion. Smoke and smells. What could be more natural? Beth thought. What could be more essential?

And the sounds. Tooting of ships' whistles, the sound of horses' hooves and heavy wagons rattling along the wharf, the whirring of steam winches as they drew nets up out of cargo holds. Men shouting commands, people darting this way and that.

The sounds of a growing nation.

Pale puffs of steam everywhere, from winches, steam whistles, and relief valves on one steam apparatus or another, puffs of breath from horses' nostrils as they clopped along the wharf on this clear, chilly day.

Sling nets bulging with boxes and sacks and hanging from ropes came out of the *Greaves*'s cargo hold, then were quickly lowered to the wharf. Almost as soon as they were set down, the now-empty nets were lifted by whirring winches and cables back to the ship. Men with handcarts dashed back and forth from ships to warehouses and from warehouses back to ships. Seen from a distance, they'd have been a constant, moving flow going in and out of the dockside warehouses that lined Commercial Slip's wharf from one end to the other.

Along the other side of this water slip, the same thing was going on—another wharf, more ships, another row of warehouses—a mirror image. Commercial Slip was a busy place, but not a frantic one. It all appeared well orchestrated, everything and everybody in a constant, smooth-flowing stream, all at the same time.

This place and its activity were fascinating to Beth. Just as fascinating as factories had always been, maybe more so. She felt confused and suddenly a little frightened, just now beginning to wonder if taking the job here in Buffalo was what she really wanted to do in this life. Now she had doubts, and it worried her. Had she enjoyed the teaching jobs she'd had in England? Not really. What made her think she'd like a school administrator job over here in America?

All this way, traveling over to Buffalo, quickly going broke, and still no better off than if she'd stayed in Chicago. Twenty-four years old with the best education money could buy and no direction whatsoever. No purpose, no plan. How was it that every notion and belief you once held dear and thought you had firmly grasped could suddenly stop making sense? She was terrified all over again. That should have all been behind her, but the fear and the doubts and the apprehension remained, still haunted her…maybe even stronger now than before.

And although the port was interesting, there were no jobs here for a lady. It would be insane to imagine otherwise. She had to find something though and hoped the school job would end up being the answer. She'd been living life like a perpetual tourist for the past six months, and that needed to change.

When she saw Jefry climbing up a ladder out of a cargo hold not far away, she waved. He waved back and walked toward her, taking a rag from his pocket and wiping his forehead with it. "Morning, Miss Eaton. Nice to see you."

"Good morning, Jefry; it's good to see you as well. This is Kristi. We're sharing my cabin."

"Hello, Kristi. It is nice to meet you."

"Good morning, sir. Is nice to meet you too."

"Are you enjoying your trip?"

"Yes, sir. Thank you."

"Jefry, how are you feeling after your fall?"

He shrugged. "Oh, pretty good, I guess. Got a lump on the back of my head though."

"I've been worried about you. You hit that deck awfully hard."

"Back to normal now, I guess. So, Miss Eaton, you're leaving us, then. Today, is it?"

"Day after tomorrow actually, but yes."

"We've all enjoyed having you here, and I know I'm not the only one who'll miss you."

She reached out, and Jefry took her hand. "It's an honor to have you as a friend, Jefry, and I shall miss you too."

"I'll not forget you, and I will imagine you often in your new life here, at your new job. I'll think about that a lot. And I'll think about *you* a lot."

"Jefry, you're gonna make me cry, aren't you?" She was half teasing and half about to shed tears herself.

His eyes teared up as well. Then he glanced over toward the cargo hatch. "I can't tell you how much meeting you has meant to me, Miss Eaton, but I will remember you always."

When someone nearby whistled, Jefry spun around. "Sorry, gotta work. Not really safe right here. Best you step aside; sling's coming up. And may God bless and protect you. Both of you."

"Jefry?"

"Yes, miss?"

"I keep thinking about what you tried to do. To find the glove, I mean, and what happened to you that day. I still don't understand what went wrong."

"I was hoping you'd found it."

"Never did," Maribeth said with a shake of her head.

"Oh, sorry. I wish I could've helped." He glanced toward the cargo hatch and made a hand signal to a fellow crewman.

"But what hap—?"

Jefry shouted to a crewman and glanced back and forth between the cargo hatch and Beth.

"What I saw happen to you," she said. "I can't figure out what—"

"Please, Miss Eaton. You could get hurt here."

"Of course, Jefry. Sorry, we'll get out of the way."

With that, he went to the hatch opening and watched as a sling full of grain sacks shot up from the depths of the hold. He waved goodbye and dashed over to assist two other deckhands who were minding the steam winch.

Beth took the steps up to the foredeck, then paused at the top for just a moment. She looked back toward where Jefry was, and he was looking in her direction as well. He waved, and she returned the gesture.

"Big Sister?"

"Yes?"

"Are you sad? You look sad."

Beth nodded.

They walked all the way to the very stem of the bow, next to the long, white steering pole, which wheelsmen used to sight-in, to point the ship in the right direction in narrow or congested passages. Just behind them and looming above was the white-painted pilothouse with its row of windows. The eyes of the ship, ever vigilant. And inside the pilothouse, the brain, the know-how, always sure of where it was going and how to get there.

All the way back aft, the engine spaces with their coal-fired boilers, the oily, pumping steam engine, the black smoke from the stack. There lay the heart of the ship.

Beth had eagerly looked forward to her new future here in Buffalo, but now she had doubts. She was sure about some things three days ago, but now she was uncertain about everything.

In a day or so, the ship would move elsewhere in the port, where the last of its cargo would be unloaded, or so she had been told.

After that, tugs would shunt the *Greaves* one last time. There, at the wharf along one of the city's busiest streets, suppliers would provision her for the upcoming leg of the ship's journey to Lake Superior. Beth was told she'd enjoy the provisioning wharf because of all the people who gathered there, promenading in their best outfits whenever the weather was nice. She supposed she'd like that, but she had spent time around prosperous people all her life. Seeing well-attired people of wealth would be nothing new to her. The sight of gaudily dressed gentry parading their riches was something she tired of quickly. Her family had rubbed shoulders with many of the wealthiest people in Europe, but she'd never felt a connection to any of them. And yet she felt strong bonds of kinship with the crew of this humble steamship.

She knew already that she'd miss them all after starting her new life here. She would never forget this voyage and those she'd been fortunate enough to meet. If she was sure about anything, she was sure she'd miss these nice young crewmen so much. And the kind captain, too. And Kristi.

But Kristi most of all.

Beth glanced at her, standing there with both hands on the railing and looking around with great eagerness and curiosity. There was such intelligence and innocence about her, but such awareness, especially for a child. Beth could tell she was taking in all the activity and the surroundings, fascinated by all of it and piecing things together, trying to make sense of what it was all about. Bringing this busy world that surrounded her, this new world, with all its sights and sounds and smells and moving parts, into focus.

So odd it was that just as Maribeth's own world, her own plans, and dreams, seemed to be slipping away from her, Kristi's understanding of the world, her grasp of things, was coming together. Her child's view of life was gradually becoming more enlightened and informed, bit by bit, her grasp of how this big world worked, a process that would end up someday in her own knowledge of who she was and what her place in the world would be.

For just a fleeting moment, a thought came to Beth's mind: she needed Kristi as much as Kristi needed her.

A tugboat's whistle peeped twice, not far away, as it began pulling a loaded barge from a nearby wharf.

Kristi pointed to it.

Beth explained to her what the purpose of a barge was and where this one was likely headed, told her that cargo ships had been arriving and departing from this harbor for years. She pointed to a lone sailing ship moored farther along the slip, noting that commercial transit by sail was becoming outdated since the advent of steam propulsion. Most every other vessel here was a steamship or a barge these days.

She went on to say that most of the cargo and passengers bound for the interior came through Buffalo, from right here at Commercial Slip.

Kristi looked up at her with an expression of such innocent adoration that it took Beth aback. They held each other's gaze for the longest while. Although they said nothing, the silence between them conveyed something real, nonetheless, something unusual, something remarkable, even beautiful.

Beth felt her eyes grow moist. Something within her tugged at that moment, pulled at her. She felt it all over, but mostly deep in the middle of her chest. It was a vortex, pulling her in. She lost all strength against it and, in fact, wanted to give in to it. There was no question about it; there was no doubt. The intensity of it was like nothing she had ever felt before, and it caught her by surprise even as she was loving how it felt, loving what it was doing to her.

She wanted it more than anything.

Kristi placed her hand on one of Beth's where she held the rail, then looked up into Beth's eyes again. This child, looking into her eyes with as deep a gaze as she'd ever had from anyone else in this world.

Beth put both arms around her, holding her tight. Kristi returned the hug.

How can I possibly leave you?

Beth pulled Kristi tighter against her and kissed her on the forehead.

How can I condemn you to this cold city, not knowing what harm might befall you?

They stood at that railing in their shared embrace for several moments. A welcome calmness came over Beth as she held Kristi in her arms.

This was it; this was where the vortex was pulling her. She thought, yes, this is it; this is everything.

This is what matters; this is all that matters.

She was feeling something she had never felt before, but something about it was so… perfect. It was the feeling that everything she had ever needed or wanted was right here, right now, in this moment.

Then it occurred to her: The events in Chicago, the accidents, the way she'd been miraculously saved from certain death—twice. It was about this moment. Yes, it had to be. All of it pointing her toward here, toward right now. That was it; she was sure of it. She could have lost her life twice, but twice she was spared…so that she could be here. She was sure of it now. Something led her to this ship, led her to Kristi, and to this very moment. Her dreams of Kristi with her parents… then without them. Kristi's own dream of her in the Chicago house—even before she left England—before even setting foot in America. All of that, every bit of it, pointed to this moment.

This precise moment was supposed to happen. It was all meant to be.

"What's that, darling? Were you saying something?" Beth asked her softly. "I saw your lips move."

Kristi nodded shyly, hiding her face in the fabric of Maribeth's skirt.

"Sorry, I didn't quite catch it."

"Because I whisper," Kristi said.

"Ahh, okay then. I see. And what was in that little whisper of yours?"

"I… I whisper, 'I love you.'"

"Step lively, gentlemen," Atticus shouted to his deckhands. "Last of the unloading. Let's get on with it. Put your backs into it."

It was the following morning. An Erie Canal tug and barge were now alongside. Two of *Greaves*'s deckhands had thrown the barge's mooring lines over thick iron chocks, and the canallers were tying off on their end. Soon, the loading of thirteen hundred packets of wheat onto the canal barge would begin. Jefry readied the sling and steam winch for the transfer.

Atticus was farther down the deck, standing near the rail, splicing a rope and watching as deckhands repaired a half dozen of the ship's heavy-canvas hatch covers that had become torn. Two other deckhands were painting hatch coamings.

A shout came from the tugboat below. "Hey, topside."

"Yup. Whatcha need?" Atticus replied without turning around, his eyes on his work as he deftly handled his rope splicing fids.

"Who we got up there?"

"Who you looking for?"

"A sorry-ass, redheaded Johnny Reb is who I'm lookin' for. You see one anywhere?"

"Don't know about seeing, but I'm hearing somebody who maybe wants a swift kick in the backside."

"Ah, so it's like that, is it?"

"If that's the way you need it, friend," Atticus replied.

"So, you and what army's gonna give me that whooping?"

"Naw, no army. Just me. One hand tied behind my back." Atticus was putting accent and voice together. Something very familiar about them. He turned around and looked down at the canal boat to see who was talking. "Well, shit fire and save matches! Arthur, is that you?"

"It be me, Attie." The man spread his arms wide. "Thought that looked like you."

He was of medium height, looked solid as a tree trunk with his broad chest, and he had arms like oak logs. Stub of a cigar in his teeth. He flashed a broad smile, wore his black derby cocked way over to one side, and was shirtless and well-tanned in his bib overalls.

"What the Sam Hill you doing on a canal boat? Last I heard, you were working over on the Ohio."

Arthur tossed his cigar stub over the side, spat on the deck, then wiped his lips with the back of his hand. "You know how it goes. Around and about. One thing leads to another."

"How long have you done canal work?"

"Three years now. Damn me, boy, looks like you come up in the world. Never seen you dress this good before. Looks like you done okay for yourself. You a mate up there?"

"For now, yep. First mate here. Hoping to get my master's ticket soon, so we'll see how that goes. Maybe have my own boat next time you see me."

"Happy for you, old son. Always wondered what happened to you. Ain't seen you since Chickamauga."

"Well, you knew I got this little tattoo, right?" Atticus said as he made the throat-cut sign over his scar and a click noise inside his cheek.

"Hell, yes, I knew. Of course. *Everybody* knew. *My God.* And then you took out that Yankee mounted trooper with a single round when he was on the fly. While you was on the ground, nearly bleeding to death. Your guardian angel was ridin' that bullet for sure, son. *Glory to God,* you done become a legend that day, Attie. A *legend!*"

"Well, I don't know about that, but they patched me up okay in a field unit there. Sat around for a week, then back at it for another year. Fought under Longstreet for a bit. Mustered out in sixty-four."

"But by God, did we ever see action, eh?"

Atticus shook his head. "Hard to believe some of that even happened."

"Hard to believe we made it out alive."

"You ever look back on all that?"

Arthur nodded. "A day don't go by I ain't thinkin' about that, old son. Day don't go by."

"Makes you wonder, doesn't it?"

"All the time. All the time."

"Yet here we are."

"Yes, sir. So, Attie, I'm figurin' you for a family man."

Atticus shook his head. "Used to be. How about you?"

"Wife in North Carolina. Like to get her up here so we're closer. Money's real good here in New York State. 'You'll never get me up there in Yankee country,' she says. Drives me crazy sometimes. Couple of kids, boy and girl. Don't get to see much of 'em, though. Them or the missus. Got us a tobacco patch down there, too. Eighty acres. Brother-in-law operates it for me, but I'm busy on the canal nine months of the year and hardly ever get back. Only during winter freeze-up. So, trying for captain, you say?"

"Taking a crack at it," Atticus said. "Pretty soon, I hope. Never get it if I don't try."

"I'll put in a good word for you with the man upstairs. If he's still listening to me. I always liked the way you fought, Attie. Sure missed you after Chickamauga. I hope you get your wish."

"You know how that goes, Arthur. Wish in one hand and shit in the other, see which one fills up first."

Arthur laughed. "Ain't that the truth. Hey, Attie, we're tyin' up along Central Wharf after we're done here. Leaving for Albany late afternoon tomorrow. What do you say me and you take the Canal Street tour tonight? Me and you and my boys here. Teach you how to drink like a canaller."

Following two days of unloading, the *Eli Greaves* was tied up at Central Wharf for provisioning. It was between Erie and Main, and was the final stop for upbound steamships—where they would load provisions for the return trip back up the lakes.

Tomorrow, the *Greaves* would return to the coal docks in Ohio—to take on a full load, this time—for delivery to Duluth, Minnesota, on Lake Superior.

Beth would not be on board, and that gave her no joy at all. She had never met a group of people more kind and polite to her than these crewmen. Not in England and certainly not in Chicago. She looked forward and aft every few seconds, expecting, hoping to see… whom? The only crew present were some deckhands she didn't recognize.

It was early, before the breakfast hour, but she was already standing near the after deckhouse. At her feet was her one remaining Louis Vuitton steamer trunk.

She had dragged it here without help this time. It was lighter than when she brought it aboard because the weight of the outfit she was wearing and all its devices—the steel half hoops, the fastenings, petticoats, ruffles, pleats and gathers, ribbons and braid—all added up. These accouterments had taken up most of the space in the trunk. Now she was wearing most of that weight.

What troubled her most was that Kristi had disappeared early and now was nowhere to be found. She was already gone when Beth woke up, and had even taken her little cloth bag. Beth was already worried about her and had no idea where she'd gone, whether or not she planned to return to the ship, or what she intended to do. She longed to tell Atticus, but would he even want to hear from her? She hadn't seen him for a day or so, neither in the dining room nor elsewhere. She craved to see him, if only for a moment…if only just to explain things…

There'd be no passenger farewell ceremony or anything like that aboard this ship. It wasn't a luxury liner, of course, but it would certainly be nice to say goodbye to someone.

Maybe even…

She spun around when a person appeared nearby. Not anyone she knew. Her heart sank.

Over on the wooden wharf, vendors were getting their stalls ready for the day's customers. Horses clip-clopped along the cobblestone street nearby, pulling freight wagons, milk wagons, coaches of every kind. Even two lovely Concord coaches passed by together, speeding to who knew where. Maybe to places whose names she'd seen on the map—down the lake to Dunkirk or Hamburg or, in the other direction, to Niagara Falls, maybe Tonawanda or Lockport. Or maybe just to drop off people at nearby railway stations.

There was a strong but not unpleasant smell at the ship's berth. The usual fishy, watery port smell, same as at most ports. But here it gave way to the fragrance of sizzling pork sausages from nearby braziers along with those of potatoes being baked and corn being grilled.

The ship was empty, now. Yesterday, crews had transferred the last of its cargo onto barges which would eventually travel the length of the Erie Canal, then down the Hudson River, ending up in New York City. She had heard that even the gentleman from Cleveland, the oil driller, was using the Erie Canal, now. It was said that during the shipping season—when the canal wasn't frozen—barges loaded with barrels of his oil were making regular trips to New York. It was cheaper shipping by canal than by train.

A buggy-for-hire pulled up next to the gangway and stopped. The driver looked in her direction, hoping for a fare.

Maribeth glanced fore and aft, but saw no one.

The driver waited a minute, then stepped down onto the wharf, still looking toward her, watching for a signal. She was due at the school office soon and dared not be late.

But she hoped that someone… She looked around, but still there was no one else on deck.

Where on earth is Kristi?

The driver kept looking toward her, hands on hips, growing impatient.

Someone came around the corner of the deckhouse. Again, someone she didn't know.

The driver shook his head and climbed back aboard his buggy.

"*Sir!*" Beth cried, gesturing to him.

He hopped off his buggy and dashed over to the gangway.

A minute later, Beth and her steamer trunk were aboard the buggy and heading toward the street and into the city proper. With unbearable sadness, she gazed back toward the *Eli Greaves* as it vanished from sight.

Captain McBride was ashore before breakfast, pacing nearby streets, glancing at a scrap of paper that had a druggist's name and address on it. If he couldn't find that one, an apothecary might do. He'd found nothing in the ship's medicine chest that suited his injury, and had to get something though, somewhere; his arm wound was getting uglier by the day and becoming increasingly red. Definitely infected now. More swollen too, and painful to the touch. He feared he was developing a fever.

He checked the address against the street signs he passed: Erie, Prime Street, Franklin, Main, Pearl, Exchange…

He chuckled as he passed Le Couteulx Street. It was a beautiful-sounding name. Despite being rather short, the street had quite a reputation. It was infamous for having more bars and bordellos for its length than any other street in the world at that time. Or at least that's what the canal boatmen bragged. They took a measure of pride in the accolade.

In any compendium of unforgettable and elegant world avenues, despite being melodious to the ear, Le Couteulx would never quite measure up to the Via dei Calzaiuoli of Florence, which McBride had walked years before. Nor could it compare to Paris's Rue Saint-Rustique, but for Buffalo it would just have to do.

Seneca Day and Boarding School for Girls was just over a mile from the shipping and canal district. Beth was enjoying this buggy ride through Buffalo immensely. The farther away from the harbor the buggy traveled, the prettier the city became. Broad boulevards lined with leafy and lovely oak, chestnut, and walnut trees. Beautiful homes of many styles, all of them gorgeous. Birds chirping, flitting from branch to branch, squirrels going about their business, people sitting on park benches chatting, relaxing, reading the day's newspaper.

Beth imagined them reading the *Buffalo Express*, the newspaper partly owned and edited until recently by Mark Twain, himself a steamboat pilot at one time.

So, so wonderful, all of it.

This opportunity was feeling so perfect to her, much to her surprise and delight now. It seemed so auspicious how it was all shaping up, such a pleasant and harmonious convergence of things: steamboats, lots of activity, culture, a fresh environment, this smart, prosperous port city of Buffalo. "It's all coming together," she whispered to herself. *"Everything."*

The driver reined in his horse in front of the Seneca school; Maribeth was breathless with anticipation. The school building was beautiful. Absolutely stunning. Gothic turrets and a spire atop a slate-tiled tower like that of Malvern Saint James in England's leafy Worcestershire, transplanted right here in Buffalo.

She could already imagine herself in her rooms here, bookcases full of the classics, a lovely view of the park across the street. Just as soon as she settled here, she'd manage to locate Kristi somehow… and someday… she could attend this school. The two of them here together. How wonderful that would be.

Beth looked forward to having deep and important talks with her associates, leading their girls—and Kristi—forward to astonishingly bright futures in scholarly pursuits, in the arts, in music, in—

"Ten cents, miss," the driver announced.

Golly, so expensive.

She fished around in her lace-trimmed silk reticule for the right coin—

"You there. Driver!" boomed a voice from nearby. "Get that filthy rig out of here."

The shouting came from a huge, uniformed man standing in the school entrance, waving his hand to shoo away the horse and buggy.

"I've got a passenger. You can't see that?"

"You'll see me give you a slap if you don't get going."

Beth was shaking all over as she grabbed a coin and put it in the driver's hand, only to realize too late that it wasn't silver, but a British gold sovereign.

"Wait!" she cried.

"Move that damned thing," the big, loud man shouted, pounding down the concrete steps toward them.

Who is he? So rude and uncouth.

The driver shook the reins as Maribeth dug for another coin; the horse lurched forward, throwing her back in her seat.

"Driver, no! Wait," she yelled again, trying to alight from the buggy as it moved.

He stopped just long enough for her to jump off before hurtling down the street and out of sight.

And there she stood.

"And who might you be, miss?" the huge man said with a scowl.

"I am Maribeth Eaton," she replied, stressing her surname. "I am here to begin work." Simple and factual, she thought. Polite but firm. She was not about to feel intimidated by this fellow. "I am to see a Mrs.—"

"Wait here."

Before she could get another word out, the man stepped back inside and slammed the door.

"Fascinating. Absolutely fascinating," the druggist shouted as he scrutinized McBride's suppurating wound. Even though he wore thick spectacles, still he used a magnifying glass, his face nearly touching the odorous infection.

McBride could hardly bear to look at the wound. And now this fellow was—

"Sir, are you familiar with the work of Joseph Lister?" the man shouted again, clearly hard of hearing. "Such a revelation! Fine, fine work. Almost on a par with Pasteur's discoveries. His germ theory of putrefaction. You're familiar with that, are you not?" He looked up, peering over his spectacles.

McBride shrugged and shook his head. "Can't say as I am."

The druggist launched into a dissertation on the history of medicine along with something about ancient Egyptians applying plant extracts and molds to treat infections. He prattled on, citing one John Parkinson, things called animalcules, somebody by the name of Van Leeuwenhoek.

Having completed his examination, the druggist began formulating his "cure," dashing back and forth in his starched white jacket with jars and vials and clinking little mixing spoons. Pouring, shaking, and mixing while running around his shop, yelling as he cited studies by this one and that one, on and on and on.

By the time McBride extricated himself from the shop, his ears were ringing, and he had completely forgotten about the pain in his arm. Maybe that was the whole idea, he thought. Maybe that was the cure. A crazy person running back and forth, screaming at you. He made his way back to the ship, clutching a tiny burlap bag with a jar of foul-smelling powder, a little brown cork-stoppered bottle of liquid, and some instructions scribbled on a scrap of paper.

Twenty minutes ticked by; the front door opened again. A woman with a pale, narrow face stepped into the open doorway but stopped there, a severe look about her, scanning Maribeth up and down. Surveying her with a humorless, critical stare from her shaded, deep-socketed eyes. Late fifties. Skeletal face. Hair braided in a tight coil on top of her head, floor-length black dress, well-worn, high-collared white blouse underneath.

"And you are Miss… *Eaton*, I am told," she slowly and precisely intoned, uttering the surname as though it left a sour taste in her mouth.

"Yes, I am. Mrs. Jacquier, I presume," Beth replied enthusiastically as she stepped forward. She mounted the front steps, her hand extended to shake the headmistress's hand, but the lady took a step backward.

Puzzled, Beth stopped halfway up the stairs, letting her hand fall to her side.

"I am Miss Tibbeth. I am headmistress here now. Mrs. Jacquier is no longer employed at Seneca Girls." The woman had a long, bloodless-looking face and too much chin.

"I see. Well, I trust she informed you I was to arrive today, Miss Tibbeth."

"I am aware there had been correspondence," Tibbeth replied in a monotone, but offered no more.

This is like talking to a statue, Beth thought.

The woman inclined her head and clasped her hands in front of her, saying nothing more.

"Well, I… Assuming you read that correspondence, you know I am here to fill the vacant position in administration."

The woman's lips were so thin that she appeared to have no lips at all. They twisted into a specter of a smile. "That position has been filled. And there are no others available."

"But I've… I've come all the way from Chicago…"

No reply, yet the steady, dark gaze and the cold, thin smile remained.

"Miss Tibbeth, when precisely did Mrs. Jacquier's employment here end?"

"Miss Eaton, I needn't disclose every detail of—"

"I received confirmation from Mrs. Jacquier three weeks ago," Beth began, her blood boiling now, "that the position had been reserved for me. Following that, exactly one week before my departure, I wired Mrs. Jacquier, informing her of my travel itinerary. I received nothing to indicate things had changed."

"If that is true, Miss Eaton—"

"*If* meaning exactly what, madam? There's nothing to speculate about here. I sent the telegram. Was it delivered or not?"

"I… um… We—"

"And did you read it or not?"

The black-clad woman's face became even more severe.

"Make yourself clear, Miss Tibbeth. Please. In your own words, you knew there 'had been correspondence.' Be so kind as to tell me when you learned I was leaving Chicago."

Tibbeth was silent. She stood there shaking—looking meaner by the moment.

"You could have saved me the trip. Yet you chose not to," Beth said. "You read my telegram and decided not to respond. Didn't you? And why did—?"

"No one gets special treatment here. *No one.* Neither students nor teachers. No matter the family na—"

Now I get it, Beth thought. "So you did a little digging, did you, miss? A little research on your own? So, this all has to do with my family name, does it?"

"I don't know what you're talk…" the woman began weakly, now realizing she had just given herself away. Her jaw quivered as she glanced from side to side.

"It might have profited you to know," Maribeth began, "that my family is a generous benefactor to several schools and colleges. In England and over here as well. *Very* generous. Seneca Girls Day and Boarding School would most likely have become recipients of my family's largesse. But you couldn't see beyond your own envy and resentment, could you?"

The woman tried to lift her head haughtily again, but she ended up quivering as though having a seizure.

"Miss Tibbeth, what will your governing board have to say once they find out—and I'll make sure they do—that you turned away a candidate who could have meant tens of thousands of additional dollars in the school treasury?"

"It is not the policy of Seneca Girls Day and Boarding to respond to every little—"

A non sequitur now. Getting desperate. Losing the argument, losing her grip.

"Is it not the goal of Seneca Girls to produce educated young ladies of culture and refinement?"

"Of course it is!" Tibbeth spat. "Our girls—"

"And do these characteristics not include good manners?"

"Look around, Miss Eaton," the woman began, spreading her arms to show the impressive architecture towering above them. "There are at present two hundred young ladies in attendance here and forty-four people on staff. Can you possibly comprehend how busy that—?"

"What I *comprehend*—with great clarity—is that by all accounts, and I've heard several, things under Mrs. Jacquier were very much under control. But I guess that's all changed now, hasn't it?"

Miss Tibbeth half turned around as though to walk away, but turned back again and faced Beth.

She went to speak, but Beth continued, "What I see is that you're out of your depth here. And good heavens, what sort of person retreats from a simple, cordial handshake as you just did? What in God's name is the matter with you, woman?"

The cold, thin smile was gone, the long, bloodless face tighter, the bony hands clenched fists. "Under my tutelage," she began in a now-raised voice, pointing a quivering, crooked finger at Beth, "a Seneca girl will be taught that insolence is neither acceptable nor *tolerated*," she snarled, every bit of her visibly shaking.

Insolence, indeed.

You nasty, petty tyrant.

"I see," Beth replied, taking a deep breath. "And what I now understand is that bad manners and incompetence *are* tolerated 'under your tutelage,' as you put it. And that you set the perfect example."

"I will not listen to this!" Tibbeth shouted.

The big, uncouth man returned and took up position beside the trembling headmistress. If either one's intention was to intimidate Maribeth, the attempt had failed miserably.

"I cringe," Beth continued, "to imagine what sorts of young ladies this school will produce under the spell of someone as rude, intolerant, and incompetent as yourself. You are a hateful, twisted harridan… *madam*. And for Heaven's sake, try to scrape together enough pennies to replace that pathetic old rag of an outfit."

Tibbeth moved aside, making way for her bulky colleague to step forward.

"Best that you leave, miss."

"Or what, you damned ape? You'll threaten to slap me too now? Just like you threatened to slap my driver?"

The man turned toward Miss Tibbeth, perhaps for guidance or a cue, not knowing how to respond to a lady who calls his bluff and stands up for herself. Receiving no direction, he turned to address Beth again.

"Miss… please," he began, but Beth was already walking toward the nearby avenue.

Heading back to Central Wharf. Back to the *Eli Greaves,* which she had now come to regard as her home, and its crew, her family.

SIX

She calmed down as she walked. After several blocks, she realized how far it was back to Central Wharf. She kept looking over her shoulder, and eventually a horse trolley came clattering along. She waved it down, climbed aboard, and took a seat. Owing to the low ceiling, she had to remove her hat. While putting down the hat, she remembered her trunk was still on the buggy. She'd completely forgotten about it. *Good heavens*, she thought as she realized everything she owned was in there and now it was on its way to who knows where.

Those horrible, horrible people. What else can possibly go wrong now?

Half an hour later, she was sitting on a bench along the promenade. The *Eli Greaves* was still tied up where it had been. She felt the need to keep it in sight but at the same time wondered what good that could possibly do now. Why wait for the ship? She couldn't take it back to Chicago; she hadn't enough money left for the passage.

It was oddly comforting seeing it, though. Still there, securely moored. Its time-worn and wave-worn hull spoke to her of reliability, of character, of solidity and predictability. Simplicity too. Maybe even loyalty. Basic, good things.

That headmistress, surrounded by such architectural splendor and beauty, all the while wrapped in her supposed veil of culture and high-mindedness. But wicked, envious, and cold. Nasty and deceitful too.

Compared to the polite and courteous crewman aboard the *Eli Greaves*.

And the girls in attendance at the school? She felt such pity for the poor things. How different, those two worlds. How was it that those who fed off adulation and were accorded the most respect and accumulated the most power could be the least deserving of those things?

She had a thought: Would Captain McBride hire her as a ship's cook? Now there was an idea. Oh, what a joyous, free, and simple life that would be! The fresh air, the polite crewmen. The movement, the sights, and sounds…

She was a terrible cook, though. So that might be a problem.

How she missed that tidy cabin of hers right now. She wanted so badly to curl up in that comfy bed and pull the wool blanket over herself and sleep this entire disastrous day into the past.

And where had poor Kristi gone off to, thinking of disasters? Maribeth's heart sank. Her problems were nothing next to the risks Kristi now faced in this heartless city. Beth feared she had gone ashore to find the "agent" person…who could have been anything…a broker who'd throw her into some factory as a slave laborer or onto an orphan train. Or worse, yet: A procurer or brothel keeper, the sort of person who found not only profit but personal satisfaction and excitement in destroying young girls' lives. She shuddered, as she tried to avoid imagining in what other unspeakable ways they might take advantage of a beautiful, helpless little girl.

She recalled the captain's offer of funds. Maybe that was a way out of her predicament. Borrow enough for temporary lodging, at least. But then what? With her money nearly all gone now and no job, no steamer trunk, and no clothing but what she had on. What choice did she have?

I am such a fool.

Why had she placed all her hopes on that one opportunity? So desperate, so idiotic. But as much as she hated herself at that moment, she hated those Seneca school people even more.

She had not wanted to think of Atticus Miles, but now she couldn't help herself. *What's left of that? Nothing. Surely he hates me now.*

She thought of his poor wife and children having all died and hated herself even more.

He had been so sweet with her and kind to Kristi and wonderful toward the little boy.

Why was I so angry with him? How could he not *hate me?*

She cursed herself for her foolishness and horrible judgment and meanness. So quick to judge.

On top of feeling so frustrated, she was suddenly hungry. The smell of frying sausage beckoned. She imagined tasty corn too, butter dripping off it. She was feeling so fragile. Needed to get some food in her or she'd shatter like crystal.

She walked over to the sausage vendor and bought a sausage and two ears of corn. The sausage was on fragrant, thick-crusted bread, and the corn's delightful, buttery aroma made her lightheaded.

She plopped down on a wooden bench to eat.

A minute later, her sandwich and corn were all gone, but she didn't even remember eating any of it. She was that angry and upset. The breadcrumbs and corncobs were right there on her lap, in the oily piece of newspaper the sandwich had been wrapped in. She had wolfed down all that food without tasting it and without enjoying it one bit.

She cursed at herself again and angrily got up from the bench to walk around, then looked down. Great—the left side of her skirt was dirty now. When had that happened? Maybe when she got off the buggy? From the horse trolley? When? How?

Then she remembered her hat. It was gone.

Where is it?

She looked back toward the bench. Had she set it down?

Not there. Somebody stole it?

Had she dropped it? No, she didn't think so, but… then she recalled taking it off in the horse trolley.

Oh, wonderful. Lost that, too, now.

She shook her head and muttered, wandering.

Passing a storefront window, she gazed at her reflection and hardly recognized herself. Disheveled, dirty. She cursed and continued walking.

Her path took her past a crowded café whose tables spilled out onto the sidewalk. One table's occupants were engaged in conversation with a couple nearby. On an insane impulse, Beth snatched two bottles of beer from their table and pelted away down the street before the diners could react.

Astonished drinkers leaped to their feet. She paid no heed to the angry yells even as a white-aproned waiter began walking after her, pointing and shouting.

Heads turned.

He must have realized she was getting away, because he began to run.

She slid into an upward-sloping brick alley, breathless while gulping down the contents of the first bottle. She let the empty slip from her fingertips and onto the bricks.

But the treacherous bottle refused to stay silent. It rolled back down the alley, back toward the main street. Taking its own sweet time. Brick by brick, its glassy, empty note betraying her, its hollow *tink, tink, tink, tink* heralding her larceny for all within earshot as it clattered back down the slope.

Good God. Can't even throw away a bottle right.

Gulping down the second bottle now.

Another shout.

She looked over her shoulder. Apron Man racing up the alley after her, yelling.

Stupid bottle.

She ducked into another alley, skirts flying as she ran. Finishing the second bottle, she threw it against a concrete wall and it shattered.

When that alley turned left, so did she. And promptly collided with a big, dirty metal can. She fell onto the wet pavement. Pushed herself up off the ground, hands now sticky, and continued running. Down that alley to another. Wiping her hands on her dress as she ran. Then another street, and into another dirty alley.

She ran until she was all out of breath and dizzy. Dizzy and dirty. She leaned up against the side of some sort of tradesman's shop. Fortunately, it was shuttered closed for the day.

She tried to calm down and catch her breath.

Dizzy and dirty. Drunk and broke.

What in the hell was she doing? This was crazy.

This is not me. No, this is not me.

Collect yourself, for heaven's sake.

Several minutes later, having caught her breath, she straightened up, recovered her composure, and strode toward the nearest street.

Beth came out onto a wide avenue, both sides lined with shops. Lots of people milling about, though, most heading in the same direction. But for what reason, she couldn't imagine. She walked, and she walked, no longer sure where she was. Then another alley and another street. Gentlemen and ladies gave her strange looks and moved aside as she approached. Two prostitutes in a doorway giggled as she walked by.

Suddenly she was hungry again, so she stopped at another sausage vendor and ordered yet more food.

"You sure? You want even more? I mean, you've had…" The vendor shared a glance with his lady partner.

The woman shrugged. "It's her money," she said, deftly sliding her oversize spatula and flipping eight sausages at the same time. "Long as she has the money, give 'er what she wants."

Beth realized she was at the same vendor as before. She'd made a big circle and was right back where she'd started. Never mind that. She wanted something to eat. "*Yeah*, I'm sure." Beth poured her remaining coins from her silk reticule onto the counter. "I want… er, no. Never mind. No, gimme three. I want three."

After finishing the very last of her three pork-sausage sandwiches, Beth hoisted herself up from the wooden bench and started wandering throughout the area surrounding the wharf, still a little drunk and now feeling stuffed from all the food.

She didn't go far, though. Her sole remaining hope now was not to lose sight of the ship. She knew that. It was her last and only link to what pathetic debris remained of her new American life. Her silly American folly.

Indians and sturgeon.

Princesses and Indians.

People running and voices from dreams, and those voices were close. Footfalls thumped in the passageway just outside Atticus's cabin. He rolled out of bed and threw open the door.

"What the hell's going on?"

Three crewmen were laughing as they pushed one another while hurtling down the passageway toward the main deck and chattering some nonsense about sturgeon, Indians, and princesses.

"*Princess*," somebody shouted. "C'mon, Mate Miles, *hurry.*"

Minutes later, Atticus stumbled out onto the main deck. It was nearly noon, and the sun was sandpaper against his face. Struck sun blind, he waved his hands around for something to hang on to, then lurched toward a stanchion, grabbed it, and hugged it tight to steady himself.

Once his vision adjusted to the sunlight, he realized the entire crew, along with Captain McBride, was right there standing around, observing his struggle and having a good laugh at his expense. He staggered a few feet and lowered himself onto a deck box while stifling a yawn. "Oh God. Coffee please."

McBride gestured to Teddy the porter, then pointed aft. Teddy nodded and ran back toward the galley.

The captain came over and stood next to Atticus. "You going to be okay, Mate?"

"Musta been some powerful shit you was drinkin' last night, Professor," said a crewman.

"Yeah, no wonder he come back shit-faced drunk," said another.

Everyone laughed at that, even Captain McBride.

"Ninety-five bars on Canal Street, and Professor hit every one of 'em," said another with a laugh.

"He say what don't kill him make him stronger," said deckhand Fournier.

Atticus's only reply was to hold his head in his hands and groan. "What's all this about princesses and sturgeon?"

McBride explained that a Protestant missionary had booked passage aboard the *Greaves* for Port Huron, Michigan. Accompanying him would be a beautiful Indian girl whom he would wed upon their arrival at a chapel there.

"So she's really a princess?" Atticus inquired with a grimace. Even speaking made his head hurt. "And he's a missionary?"

McBride shrugged. "I guess so. But I don't know for sure. I figure that's what he is. He didn't say actually, come to think of it. Could be a pastor or something, I suppose, judging by his clothing. Met him a while ago. I haven't seen her yet though. It seems he's got her squirreled away at some hotel."

"So, nobody's seen her?"

"Not yet."

"And what's fish got to do with it?"

"Her band goes fishing for sturgeon in the rapids below the falls at Niagara. Those fish—ten, twelve feet long, some of 'em. Several hundred pounds. This gent says the Indians carry them over their shoulders coming up out of the Niagara Gorge. Takes two men to carry a single fish, and the fish are so long their tails drag on the ground. So now we have two casks full of smoked sturgeon. That's how the fellow paid passage for himself and the girl."

"What do you figure she is?" said a crewman. "Tuscarora? Oneida?"

"They thought you'd know." McBride looked at Atticus. "Everybody says to ask Professor Miles."

"Yeah, I suppose Tuscarora, but I'm damned if I can say for sure. Go ask Jefry, why don't you. The professor doesn't feel well. He won't be holding class today."

McBride smiled, giving the mate a friendly pat on the shoulder.

"Captain?" Miles said, glancing at McBride's swaddled-up arm, which he now had in a sling. "Your arm. Is it going to be all right?"

"Yes, yes, I'm sure it will be. I picked up medication for it a little while ago. Top man here in Buffalo. He made up some potions for me. Don't you worry; it'll be fine."

Beth sat on a bench along the promenade feeling fat, foolish, and drunk.

The *Eli Greaves* was still in sight, but it made no sense to go back to Chicago.

She had come to America excited and full of optimism, hoping and expecting to create an interesting and fulfilling life for herself. But it had all come to naught. All she'd managed to do was waste money. There was nothing here for her anymore, neither in Chicago nor Buffalo. Nowhere.

The moment she'd been dreading had finally arrived: she had no other option now but to wire her parents for money to purchase a return ticket to England. She'd ask Captain McBride to pay for her lodging here in Buffalo until funds arrived.

God bless that man.

In a little while, she'd send a cable to England. Yes, that's what she'd have to do; there was no other choice now. She couldn't even afford a potato. No job. No money. No fresh clothes. No steamer trunk. Nothing. Drunk and filthy, with one coin left. Down to her very last stupid little silver coin.

She looked around and wondered where the nearest telegraph office was. Was it even open? Evening wasn't far off; where would she spend the night?

Her relatives had told her this would happen. They'd been right all along. She'd thought they were just envious of her going to America, but now realized she should have listened to them.

Why am I so stubborn?

Always wanting to have things my way.

And now look.

This was her silly American folly, all right. It would take the rest of her life to live this down. They'd never let her forget her failure, that's for sure.

Never.

She looked down at her dirty skirt again, knowing how awful she looked, but at that moment, she didn't even care anymore.

A shout came from farther down the street. People stopped in their tracks. Heads turned, and Beth noticed the crowd beginning to shift, now moving toward... *what?* She did not know.

Then she saw it: a horse pulling a fine, brand-new covered carriage. Everybody turned to watch it go by; it swung onto the wharf and headed straight for the *Eli Greaves*.

When the crowd moved in that direction, Beth got up and followed them. The carriage stopped right next to the ship, and the most stunning, extraordinary young woman she'd ever seen slowly exited the carriage and stepped sedately onto the wharf.

She was no doubt an Indian of some noble tribe or other. Very tall, with an impressively regal bearing. Shimmering, midnight-black hair cascaded to her waist. She wore fringed leggings under an intricately beaded doeskin dress. Exquisite necklaces and amulets adorned her neck and wrists, glinting in the afternoon sun.

If anything could have made Beth feel more hopeless and worthless than she already did, it was the sight of this magnificent young woman. The Indian woman was so exotic and mysteriously beautiful. Beth watched, consumed with feelings of what she'd had but now lost.

She had nothing now. Nothing.

This tall, slender woman was led to the ship by what looked to be a man of the cloth, black-clad. A preacher? A missionary? Beth stood there and watched as he helped her up the gangway and aboard the steamship.

But what happened next was not what she expected.

Not at all.

Atticus stood at the top of the gangway, feeling a little better, but not by much. Mate MacMillis had offered to take over his duties today until he recovered, and Atticus was grateful for that. Standing there and watching who came aboard was always a simple job, and that's just what he needed right now.

Buffalo was an interesting place. He enjoyed being at the provisioning wharf. There was plenty to see and a lot going on. After a trip across the lakes, it was always interesting to watch regular people ashore doing regular things. It was certainly colorful, from the wagons, buggies, carriages, and coaches with their shiny paint jobs to the well-dressed ladies and gentlemen strolling back and forth along the promenade, all of them eager to see and be seen. This city was a prosperous place that always bustled with activity of all kinds. Street vendors were cooking their food, and the fragrance of it all would have made him hungry any other time; now it just made him feel sicker. Didn't need that; stomach was already threatening to come up and out.

At least his head was clearer now. Atticus reflected on the trip so far while drinking from the mug of hot coffee Teddy had prepared for him. He thought about Beth. Why had she gotten so angry with him at Hammond? He had even stayed away at meals, thinking it best to avoid her. Now that she'd slammed the door in his face, he had no idea how to approach her. How could he patch things up when she wouldn't listen to him or let him know what she was angry about? He knew her anger toward him had something to do with the fight, but what had he done wrong? Nothing. That was the puzzling part. What did she think happened, anyway? He hadn't seen her for a day or so and wondered if she had already left for the school. If she had, then she was gone for good. The thought of that made him very sad.

The crowd shifted, and the sound of excited voices arose from it. The princess had to be close. When a carriage appeared, then swung off the street and onto the provisioning wharf, he knew the moment had arrived. By the time the horse stopped and the driver had stepped down, the entire wharf was already full of onlookers.

Atticus watched as the man he assumed to be the pastor emerged from the carriage. Black-suited, elegant. He looked the part for sure. Nice clothes, whatever he was. The gentleman took the princess by the hand, helped her down the carriage step and onto the wooden wharf. They made their way slowly toward the gangway. The young woman was extraordinary and moved with an effortless grace. Now Atticus understood what everybody was so excited about.

A murmur swelled from the crowd. All those present, surely numbering in the hundreds by now, could finally see her clearly, and they were transfixed by the sight of the tall, stunning beauty.

The man and young woman moved up the gangway, step by careful step.

Atticus wasn't sure what he ought to do once they reached the top of the gangway. What should he say? How do you address a pastor? For a moment, he wished he'd gone to church more often. What do you say to a princess? An Indian princess at that. Was he even allowed to address her? What language did she speak?

When the fellow helped her off the gangway and onto the deck, the princess immediately shifted. Quickly. Just a little at first. It was a twitch maybe, or a shudder, some sudden feeling of discomfort, perhaps. Or so it appeared to Atticus.

Then she brought both hands up and gripped her head and bent at the waist, thrusting her body forward in some sort of paroxysm or convulsion. She tossed her head to the left and right, her long black hair flying around like a whip.

Then she screamed, *"Otshee Monetoo!"* She glanced quickly around the ship in all directions. *"Otsheeee."* She covered her eyes and turned toward the missionary, appearing to plead for help.

He reached out to her, but she spun away and continued to scream. She began running in circles while swinging her hands around her head as though swatting at mosquitoes. *"No go boat,"* she screeched, shaking her head.

The missionary reached for her, pleading, as she dashed around. "No, it's okay, darling. It's okay. Boat okay. Boat good."

"No go boat. No go!" she shouted and then ran to the far rail and turned around. It appeared she was about to lean against it, but instead, she threw herself backward and vanished over the side.

Crewmen rushed over to the rail.

Bosun Hake had kept himself apart from the others, as was his usual habit. He was already standing by the rail when the princess went over. Without hesitation, he took a quick look over the side and then jumped overboard after her.

Jefry Walks did the same.

Atticus ran over to the rail as well, looked down and saw that Hake and Walks were already in the dirty harbor water, swimming toward the girl. Walks put one arm around her and with his other arm began paddling. Hake did likewise on the other side of her. Slowly, they worked their way alongside the ship, heading toward the stern. A crewman tossed a line and let it dangle over the stern in case that might help. Several other crewmen dashed down the gangway and onto the wharf.

Hake and Jefry eventually brought the woman over to a ship painter's wooden raft; then, with help from others, they lifted her up onto the raft and then back onto the wharf. For several minutes, the two heroes stood by patiently as the missionary knelt beside her, speaking calmly to her while gently stroking her wet hair. After a few more minutes, the fellow arose and, with help from Hake and Jefry, got the princess back on her feet. He brushed some bits of harbor debris off her sleeves and straightened up her top garment across the shoulders and adjusted the neckline for her.

Then the three of them walked her along the wharf, back toward the gangway. Her sleek black hair hung dripping over her shoulders. One leather stocking was still up nearly to her knee; the other had fallen, and was now gathered at her ankle.

When the three of them had almost reached the gangway, they paused. The missionary spoke to her quietly for several moments. She nodded. Gently, he stroked her beautiful long hair again. He took hold of both her arms and was clearly saying things meant to soothe her. She nodded again and was quiet, standing before him with head bowed and body slack.

Atticus had never in his life seen the likes of it. And he wasn't alone in that. All along the wharf, onlookers were spellbound. Where minutes earlier there had been merry chatter and amazement and folks milling all about, now there was only awed silence. All eyes were on the girl. Passing carriages and buggies had all stopped, their passengers and their drivers all staring toward the steamship. Street vendors stopped their work and just stood and watched, as did their customers.

It was only after several minutes had passed that the missionary and the girl took the last few steps to the gangway, then started up for the second time. Jefry and Hake each took her by an elbow, and all four of them slowly took careful, measured steps up the gangway.

Atticus drew a deep breath, then let it out with relief, now that the girl seemed okay. She appeared weak, or perhaps in shock from the cold water, but at least she had settled down.

"Thank goodness," he whispered.

He waited at the top end of the gangway to assist in case they needed him, but the young woman was well supported. Her two helpers and the missionary were kind and careful with her. She was in good hands; there was nothing he needed to do.

As the three men and the girl stepped off the gangway, she lifted her head, but only slightly. She looked around, seemed suddenly aware of her surroundings.

Atticus felt something wasn't right.

A second later, she came to life and spun away, shaking free of all three men. She twisted away but at the same moment reached around Hake with a quick screech of effort, then ran halfway across the deck and stopped.

She spun around again.

Held her hand straight up over her head. In her fist she held Bosun Hake's huge knife, its shiny ten-inch blade glinting in the sun.

A gasp went up from the crowd.

The princess was breathing hard, her chest heaving. She gripped the knife's white bone handle with both hands, turned the tip of its blade toward herself, her shoulders lifting and falling with each breath.

"No, darling," pleaded the missionary, hurrying toward her, reaching out. "Please put it down. It's okay. Please put—"

She screeched something in her native language, then once again the same puzzling words she had screamed before throwing herself over the side. "No go boat! *Otshee Monetoo! Otsheee!*" She wailed again.

Then, with a piercing scream that shot up Atticus's spine like a lightning bolt, the girl thrust the long knife into her body, just beneath her left breast. But it only penetrated a little, so with another shriek along with a ragged, throaty groan, she gripped the white bone handle tighter and shoved the blade in as far as she could, deep into her chest.

Her mouth and eyes opened wide, and she stumbled backward, flailing her arms for balance. Then her knees buckled, and she fell onto the deck.

A horrified moan came from the crowd.

The pastor rushed over and dropped to his knees next to her. He held her blood-spattered arms, murmured, kissed her cheek while shaking his head.

"Sweet child," he cried. "Oh, my sweet child. What have you done?" He kissed her face again and again.

A half minute later, the life that had been in her was gone.

It was gone.

A pool of blood began spreading from her lifeless body.

"Oh, Oh, my sweet girl. Please, please come back. Don't go. Please come back. Oh my God. No, no, no." He lifted a limp arm and drew her hand to his lips and kissed it. "Please, God," he wailed. "Please don't take her."

He lay next to the dead princess, placing his cheek against her lifeless one. He wailed and he wept, and he wept, and wept some more.

Silence had fallen over everything. Nothing existed but the dead girl and the missionary.

What had just taken place was so sudden and shocking that onlookers shared confused glances. What they'd just seen—had it really happened, or had it been… *what?* It was a performance of some kind. Had to be. This was entertainment. They were actors, yes? The beautiful Indian girl and the missionary would scramble to their feet and take their bows to delighted gasps of astonishment, along with hearty applause from the audience.

But onlookers realized soon enough it was no performance.

Many ladies fainted, collapsing onto the ground. Others' legs simply gave out, and they plopped hard onto the cobblestone street or the wharf and burst into tears, their gentlemen kneeling next to them, looking puzzled and helpless.

A single long scream arose from the crowd and along with this a terrible shrieking moan from many women and even some men. It was an awful sound and an awful scene. Many of the *Greaves*'s tough crewmen were in tears.

It was a scene of tragedy all around.

Minutes earlier, fashionably dressed ladies wearing their best and carrying parasols had strolled along the promenade accompanied by their gentlemen, every one of them fascinated by the tall, stunningly beautiful princess. Those same ladies and gentlemen were now frozen in this terrible, terrible moment, horror-struck by what they had just seen.

Atticus had never in his life witnessed anything as awful as this. It broke his heart, and he knew other hearts were breaking all around him.

Where moments ago, there was someone—in fact, some*thing* as well, a vision truly exotic and remarkable, of youth and beauty, a vision new and timeless together, both familiar and foreign—now there was only horror and death.

The dead princess lay soaking in her own blood, and beside her was the missionary who, no doubt, in this moment, preferred death to life. His own life meant nothing to him right now. He would eagerly give up his life as well, wishing they would reunite in death, rather than lose her forever.

Atticus could hear him beseeching God, praying to be taken. It shouldn't have happened; it couldn't have.

But it had.

SEVEN

Four hours crawled by. The pastor had accompanied the princess's corpse to the city mortuary; a contingent of Buffalo Police concluded their inquiries; the last of the pressmen headed off to file copy; the crowd eventually dispersed.

Save for a lone ship chandler's wagon making a last-minute delivery, there was nothing going on. The pace of activity on the street had come to a halt as everyone in the waterfront district had gone home for the day. Coaches, buggies, and passing wagons moved at a more leisurely pace, the slower cadence of horses' hooves now declaring there was no need to rush anymore.

The normal chatter of voices—hoots and laughter and loud talk across the wharf and on the street and on the wooden sidewalk—that was all gone. The food vendors' shacks and carts and cookhouses and kiosks were all shuttered for the day.

Maribeth had witnessed everything, had seen it all. She sat on a bench well down the wharf from where all the activity had taken place, desperate to be out of sight of the café so Apron Man wouldn't see her. Sitting, arms crossed, and head bowed, slouched over. She had needed to get away from the ship after the suicide. It was all horrible enough without staying around to witness the body being wrapped up, carried off the ship, and put into a wagon or hearse and transported away.

Her heart had gone out to Atticus, too, as she watched from a distance how he'd controlled events as best he could.

Immediately after the tragic death, Beth took a long walk up and down streets and avenues whose names she didn't bother to note. Walked and thought, weighing her own life's options considering this recent, dramatic twist of fate. The suicide would forever be a pivotal moment, not only for her but for everyone else who'd been there. How could it not be? In the hearts of those who'd seen it, there would be the time before the suicide and the time that followed. It was a life marker, that point at which everything that you had previously done or strived for or worried about was trivial compared to the horrible self-sacrifice the young woman had made.

Returning to the wharf, and gazing toward the *Eli Greaves*, Beth's heart sank once more for the girl and for her panic or whatever had gripped her. She could not imagine what had happened in that poor soul's mind as she took that knife and plunged it into her chest. The terror—or whatever it had been—to say that it was puzzling couldn't capture how incomprehensible it all was.

Weeks ago, Beth had the feeling that something was in motion and that she and everything she knew would soon be challenged by inexplicable events and perplexing times. It was terrifying and exhilarating at the same time. This was about more than her fear of going broke. And somehow, she realized now—some unknown thing told her—that the *Eli Greaves* was a part of it.

What, though?

What was it?

As troubling and as bewildering as it all was, at least in the present moment, in the deepest part of her own soul, there was something different now.

She was different now.

There was a new imperative, and it wanted an answer.

It demanded to know. It was asking her…

What now? What now?

Despite her confusion, she knew one thing for sure. She knew what she had to do. There was, in this moment, one thing that she *must* do—and only one thing—and so she rose from the bench and started walking across the wharf, toward the *Eli Greaves*.

A wagon had just unloaded its crates and bales. Deckhands were sorting through the provisions and going this way and that way, to wherever on board the ship the supplies needed to be stowed. Standing in the middle of the pile of provisions was Atticus, holding several pieces of paper in one hand while checking nearby items.

As Beth approached the gangway, Atticus was not aware of her. She took careful steps, knowing how filthy she was and how awful she looked; but she didn't care. That wasn't important now.

The only important thing was what she had to do.

She stepped off the gangway and headed directly toward him. He was several yards across the deck, facing away from her, but suddenly he looked over his shoulder and toward her. As she got closer to him, he laid down his papers, not taking his eyes away from her. Then he turned slowly and faced her directly as she walked those last few feet, trying to stop the tears from coming.

She reached out for him, and at the same moment, he reached out for her too. When they embraced, she let go of her tears, and while burying her face against his shoulder, she pleaded, "Please don't hate me anymore."

But he loosened his embrace, held her slightly away, looked her in the eyes and said, "I never hated you. How could I possibly hate you? I *love* you."

Half an hour later, Beth and Atticus were standing at the same location along a forward bulwark where they'd previously laughed together and shared happy moments.

Atticus had given his shipping papers and packing lists to Second Mate MacMillis, who was now doing the counting and sorting. He was more than willing to help; he and all the deckhands had better attitudes now, and some appeared to be almost joyful at seeing Mate Atticus and the lady together at last. Holding hands even.

Atticus took Beth by the shoulders and turned her to him. "Keep your eyes on me. Don't look, but there's a man coming this way, and he's looking right at you."

Beth gasped. "Oh no. Oh my God. Is he wearing an apron?"

"Yes. And he's got a policeman with him."

"Hug me again."

Atticus willingly complied.

"Now kiss me," she said. "And don't look at them."

Atticus followed her instructions.

"And keep on kissing me."

And so, he did.

With their lips pressed together, she managed to ask: "Are they still coming?"

"No. They're not coming now," he said between kisses. "They're right here, right next to the ship."

"*Ahoy, you!* On board the steamship," shouted a voice from the wharf below.

Atticus broke away from the kiss and the embrace. "Good day, gentlemen." He noticed the three chevrons on the policeman's coat sleeve. "How may I assist you, Sergeant?"

The sergeant spoke, serious but looking amused at the same time. "Sorry to disturb you right now, sir, but we're searching for a lady who—and I apologize, miss, but you seem to match the description of the lady this gentleman would like to speak to—whom *we* would like to speak to."

"This lady is my wife, Sergeant. I don't understand. How could she have come to your attention?"

"This gentleman is from the café. He recognized her from a while ago when she—when someone matching her appearance—was involved in an incident."

"That's not possible. She's been here on board with me all day. For several days, matter of fact."

Apron Man waved his arms in front of the policeman, his voice carrying, though they couldn't make out his words.

"Just minutes ago, he saw her walking along the wharf," the sergeant said.

"Well, a few minutes ago, yes, but I had sent her off to find some food because the street vendors are gone for the day. Our cooks are busy stocking supplies right now, and my wife's been helping me log in deliveries. So, we're both a little dusty and tired right now. And hungry."

The officer and Apron Man conferred, with the latter making gestures toward Beth with one hand and toward the café with the other, while the officer shrugged and threw out his hands.

"And I take it you're the captain, sir," continued the officer.

"Atticus Miles. First mate."

"If there's any way I could have a word with the shipmaster, Mr. Miles, I'd appreciate that."

"Sergeant, any other time it would be my pleasure to oblige your request, but unfortunately, our captain is bedridden with a serious injury. Presently healing but under heavy medication for a severe infection."

"I'm sorry to hear that, but it wouldn't take more than a minute."

"Sir, I am terribly sorry, but he's in no condition to talk. He lost a lot of blood and has been in and out of consciousness today. Earlier today, we thought we might lose him, but not long ago, he rallied somewhat. In his stead, I am the acting captain of this ship and am happy to help you in any way I can. It's been a difficult and tragic day for us all, as you can well imagine. Many of my crewmen are still badly shaken and unable to perform their normal duties. Which is why my brave wife is helping me."

More gesturing between the officer and Apron Man.

"We are hard-pressed right now, as we are already late to depart. Soon we'll fire up the boiler and get underway.

But until then, I can certainly be on the lookout for the lady you wish to question. Apart from that…"

"Yes, that could help, Mr. Miles. Please let us know if you see anything. Thank you for your time. And good day, sir."

With that, the officer turned, and the two men started back across the wharf.

Once they were out of earshot, Beth gave Atticus a kiss on the cheek. "'Acting captain' is it now?"

He shrugged.

"You're not only my lover, darling Atticus. Now you're my hero as well. I love you, love you, love you!"

"You've just made a liar out of me."

"Mmm, yes, but such an eloquent and convincing liar. My oh my, but you are smooth. You can turn that Tennessee talk on and off, can't you? Whenever you want. No wonder they call you Professor. I think you could talk me into just about anything. And I mean...*anything*," she cooed, moving closer. "But it'll all be worth it in the end, my Tennessee gunslinger. You'll see. Partners in crime now too. How deliciously decadent. You may kiss me again if you'd like."

"You're gonna get me into big trouble yet."

"Am I not worth the trouble, my handsome hero?"

Atticus looked around behind her. "Where's your steamer trunk? And I taste beer on your lips. And where's Kristi?"

"Mm-hmm. I swiped two bottles of beer. And Kristi… She's been gone since daybreak, and I'm worried sick. We must go find her, Atticus."

"You didn't pay for the beer?"

"Nope."

"You *stole* two bottles of beer?"

"Yep. Hence the visit from Apron Man and our friendly local *gendarme*. And as for you, my man of many questions—your eyes are bloodshot, and you smell like a distillery." She brushed something off the front of his shirt, then put her lips against his ear and asked, "Do I misapprehend thee, sir, or has my beautiful Atticus been a *very* bad boy?"

When Beth heard three knocks, then two knocks on her cabin door a little later, she knew it was Atticus because that was their code.

"Come in, dear; I'm not wearing anything," she said, then remained sitting on the bed, wearing a sly smirk.

And clothing.

The door flew open, and Atticus was there in the doorway, looking wide-eyed but then suddenly not so wide-eyed after all. He couldn't help smiling. "You know how to get that door open in a hurry, don't you?"

She was laughing behind her hand while nodding. "I know what you're hoping to see, my dear. But don't worry. Someday soon. Maybe. Provided you behave yourself."

He remained in the doorway.

"Is something wrong? Any word about Kristi?"

He shook his head.

"Darling, we must find her before it's too late. I'm serious."

"We will; we will. I'm working on it."

"Come here, love," she said, patting a spot on the bed. "Come on, sit next to me."

But still he remained in the doorway, now holding both hands behind his back.

"Is everything alright?"

No gesture, no reply.

"Atticus?"

Again—nothing.

"Atticus, please. You're scaring me. Is something wrong?"

He broke into a smile and brought out both hands. In them, he held folded-up fabric.

"What's this?" Beth got up and went to him.

He held out two squares of cloth.

She took one while giving him a puzzled smile, then shook it out. A pair of pin-striped bib overalls. "Oh, I *love* these." She held them up against herself. "And I think they'll fit. Come inside and close the door. I'm going to undress and put these on."

But he stayed in the doorway, still holding the remaining square of fabric.

"Come on now," she said. "What else have you got?"

He took a step backward, out into the passageway. He looked off to his left at something she couldn't see.

"Okay, mister," she said. "What are you hiding?"

She came to the doorway, looked around the frame, and screamed. "My steamer trunk! You've *found it!* Oh, thank God, thank God." She dropped to her knees and threw it open. "It's all still here. Everything. Oh my God. Even the gold. And Mama's jewelry. My brown skirt too." She stood up. "It's all here, Atticus. How'd you do this?"

He began explaining as he carried the trunk into her cabin and set it down next to the bed. From what she had told him earlier, he went to his canaller friends and passed along the information. They knew the buggy driver; he went by the name Top Hat.

Within the hour, Top Hat himself had brought the trunk back to the *Eli Greaves* with sincere apologies. He explained that once he realized it was still strapped to his buggy, he returned to the school, only to get the door slammed in his face. Not wanting to leave such an expensive trunk with strangers, he took it home.

"I doubt that he even opened it," Beth said in amazement.

"Honest man," Atticus said.

"Here, my sweetheart." Beth sat down and patted the bed again for him to sit. She started going through her belongings with relief, having thought they'd been lost forever.

"Not just yet." He opened the door and went back out into the passageway.

"Now what?" Beth asked.

When he showed up at the door again, Kristi was with him.

Beth jumped up and ran to Kristi, taking her into her arms. "Oh, thank God; I was sure we'd lost you for good."

"No, I just send telegram to Nana—my gramma. I tell her I have America big sister now, and then I go for long walk."

"Please don't do that again, Little Sister; we were so worried about you, that you'd been kidnapped and taken to one of those awful… Oh, never mind. I'm just so happy to see you. I love you so much."

"I love you too. Sorry I make you to worry."

"Oh, I almost forgot…" Atticus fished something from his pocket. "Top Hat said to make sure you got this."

"My gold sovereign. I thought that was gone too. Oh, what a dear soul he turned out to be."

Atticus watched her go through her things for a few moments. "What was it I heard you say? Something about not wearing anything?"

She punched his arm, darting her eyes toward Kristi. "Patience, my darling." She wagged her finger at him.

Kristi smirked, covered her mouth, and looked off to the side. Apparently, she knew what they were talking about despite her age.

"And the other piece? A shirt, I presume?"

He nodded, while shaking it out. A man's long-sleeved shirt. "Maybe just a little big for you, but I think the railroad overalls will fit."

"Railroad overalls. The blue pinstripes. I love these." She held them against herself. "Length—not bad, hmm?"

"Looks okay."

"Oh, I wish Papa and Mama could be here to see this." She shook out the shirt and checked the size of it as well. "I'm going to put these on. So, my gunslinger, this is the part when you get up and turn toward the wall. And you can imagine all you like, but don't you dare look. Kristi, make sure he doesn't look."

A minute later, she was in the overalls but had not put on the shirt yet. "What do you think?"

"Delicious."

"And the fit?"

"Looks okay to me."

"Yes, I think so. Maybe just a little loose behind, but otherwise, not too bad at all. Should I wear the shirt in or out?"

"In."

"Good. Tucked in is how I'll wear it then. Until I decide not to. Okay, now I want you to kiss me." She leaned over, taking his head in both her hands. They kissed. "How about my lips? Do they taste better now?"

"Yes, Miss Beth. Delicious. But the beer taste wasn't really all that bad."

She laughed. "Good. I'm happy that – Oh, but Atticus…"

"Yes?"

"Those hands of yours. Please remember that we… Are. Not. Alone here," she said, angling her head toward Kristi. "So tell those hands they're doing a little too much exploring on their own just now."

"All right, I'll tell them. How's this?"

"Mm-hmm. That's better. Thank you. Oh, and there's just one more thing, my love," she said and whispered something in his ear.

"Of course," he said. "How much?"

A minute later, he took a step toward the door. "May I leave, now?"

"Yes, my handsome hero. You may leave."

Glancing at her overalls, he said, "You're not gonna wear those, are you?"

She looked down at them. "Sure, why not? They'll think I'm a farmer. The only person I need to impress now is standing right in front of me."

"A farmer with a British accent," he said, with a laugh. Then he stepped out into the passageway.

As soon as the door was closed, Beth turned to Kristi. "My darling little sister, are you ready? You're coming with me. We're going shopping."

Chief Murrick didn't dare leave his cabin while the ship was in port. Not for meals, and not even to go to the engine room. He didn't dare go anywhere while strangers milled around and lurked about.

In his cabin. That's where he needed to be.

He lifted the curtain on the door and peered out. Almost everybody who had been on the wharf was gone now. There'd been screaming and howling a while ago, but that had nothing to do with him. Now everything was quiet, and that was the way he liked it. Whatever had gone on didn't matter. He was happier now. He didn't trust people. Didn't like people, didn't enjoy being around them and didn't like commotion. Especially now with his treasure to protect. The fewer nosy people around, the better. He'd been worrying about how to get the coins off the ship and safely home, back to his Indiana farm. There were always stories about people getting waylaid along those dusty trails. What he'd have to do, he'd have to buy a pistol. Yes. Something that'd pack a punch. A thirty-six caliber. No, a forty-four. Yes, that would do it. Get their attention for sure. Stop 'em in their tracks.

Okay. Time to worry about that later.

After making sure the door was locked, he lifted the mattress, pulled out the thread, and took out his bag of treasure. He spread the gleaming coins out across the surface of the mattress, taking great care to make sure they were all perfectly aligned. A rectangle; that's what he wanted. But it had to be perfect, he reminded himself, kneeling next to the bed and using his arm as a guide to make straight edges. He was unhappy with the edge though and resolved to find something to make it straighter next time. He had just started arranging the heads in a straight line when there was a knock at his door. He looked up. Somebody's shadow was on the door's curtain.

"Yes? What is it?" he shouted.

"You okay, Chief?"

He knew the voice. The second engineer. He went to the door and unlatched it but opened it only an inch, wedged his foot against the bottom so the door couldn't be shoved in. "Yes, I'm fine, of course."

"It's time to build steam, Chief. Wanted to let you know. We're gonna light off the boiler in a few minutes." The man came closer, putting his face nearly against the door. Peered through the opening as best he could, but the chief blocked his view. "You sure you're okay?"

"Of course I am. Why wouldn't I be?"

A shadow passed across the door curtain.

"Who's with you?"

"Nobody."

"Someone is there with you. Who is it?"

Another shadow on the curtain. Then another.

"Don't lie to me!"

"It's just me here, Chief. You sure you're alright?"

Is he telling the truth? Can't say for sure. What's going on? Is this a trick?

"You haven't been down to eat. They're worried."

"Yes, I know. I… I've been busy. Quite busy."

"Chief Murrick, I can bring up some food if you like."

"No! I mean thank you, but I'm fine. Thank you. And don't worry. I shall be down soon. There are just some things that I must… Just don't worry. I'll be down very soon."

"If you're sure."

"Yes, yes, of course."

The chief closed the door, not even sure if the second engineer had gone away. No matter. The important thing was that his little golden and silvery beauties were all in position now. All there. Right there on the bedsheet. Waiting. Waiting for him. Only for him, all in their neat rows. All his lovely little round soldiers.

"I have such wonderful news." Beth smiled at Atticus and then at Kristi, who was carrying dresses over one arm and two shoeboxes under her other arm.

Kristi looked first at Beth, then at Atticus, back and forth. She seemed eager to smile, but looked unsure. She went over to the bed and put down her items, listening carefully, waiting to hear what Mr. Mate Miles had to say, watching his face, probably wondering how he'd react to Beth's news.

"That's good; that's good," he said. "What's the news?"

"Kristi is staying here. On the ship. She'll stay with us from now on."

"She's not staying in Buffalo? Really?"

Beth nodded.

"Oh, that's great news. We're happy you're going to stay with us, Kristi."

Her face lit up, and she clapped her hands. "Thank you, Mr. Mate Miles."

"Yes, thank you, Mr. Mate Miles," Beth said. "We talked and talked, and then she asked me to take her back to the telegraph office."

"I telegraph my nana in Norway again and tell her I stay with new big sister."

"What's this?"

"It's just what we call each other," Beth said. "I'm Big Sister and she's Little Sister. Right?" She turned to Kristi.

Kristi nodded and smiled. "We tell silly stories at bedtime."

He laughed. "That's great. And you won't go back to Norway?"

Kristi shook her head.

"I'm happy you'll be staying with us."

"Thank you, sir."

"Yes, thank you, sir," Beth said. "Have I told you lately how much I love you?"

He shook his head. "You'll have to remind me."

She gave him a big kiss.

Kristi got up and started toward the door. "I think I just go outside."

Beth gave her a look. "You can stay, honey. It's all right; it's just love talk. You can stay."

"Okay. You are sure?"

"Yes, of course, I'm sure. Come here, sweetie. I was so afraid when I couldn't find you." Beth opened her arms, and they hugged. "I love you so much."

The little girl snuggled close. "I love you, too."

"Show Mr. Miles what we bought today."

Kristi's face brightened as she went over to the bed, laid out two pairs of new shoes and her new book across the bedcover, then held up her two new dresses.

"Very pretty," he said. "All of it."

"She is so happy," Beth said. "Thanks again."

"Don't mention it. My pleasure."

"Yes, Mr. Mate Miles," Kristi said. "Thank you."

"You're welcome. I think you'll be very happy with your new things."

"Mm-hmm, yep. I like 'em. Big Sister help me pick them out." She went over to the door. "You can love talk now; it's okay. I am go read my America book outside."

"I love her so much, Atticus. And making her happy makes me happy."

He smiled. "Of course. I can tell. I enjoy seeing you two together."

"She's the sister I always wished I had. And her big sister married and moved away, so that makes me Big Sister now."

"Big Sister in overalls."

"Yes, in overalls. Takes me back to being on the farm."

"They're not ladies' wear, but they'll be easy to keep clean, I reckon." Atticus sat on the edge of the bed while Beth posed in her railroad overalls.

"They're perfect. Do you like your lady in these?"

"You are stunningly elegant, milady."

She came up so close their faces almost touched, then she looked him straight in the eye and made a kiss sound through pursed lips. "You're a very sweet man, you know." Then she twirled away while looking down at the overalls. "It's fun, dressing just like one of the crew. One of the boys. I should tell you, I always enjoyed working on the farm and getting dirty."

"So, you were a bit of a tomboy."

"Oh, much more than a bit. I'd pull on my wellies at the drop of a hat and go romping among the cows and the sheep and the goats. I was always much happier as a muddy farm girl than a tea-sipping lady." She brushed her hand over a crease in the pant leg. "Where'd you find these overalls, by the way?"

"They've been in the dresser in my cabin. Lying there folded, just the way I brought 'em to you."

"Hmm," she murmured. She felt the fabric and liked it. Then she sat down on the edge of the bed, next to him.

"Must've belonged to the first mate that had my cabin before me."

"We'll dine together for the evening meal today? The three of us?"

"Sure, if you'd like," he said. "Second seating though. There's a couple of things I need to get done first."

"Darling, will you always love me?"

He looked her in the eyes. "What brought that on?"

"I don't know. Just a question. I see how ladies ashore look at you. You are a handsome man, you know. Maybe you'll decide you prefer another."

He shook his head. "I'll love you always. You and only you. Why wouldn't I?"

"Just wondering; that's all. You've known me less than a week, so…"

"You are the most beautiful and fascinating—"

"People change. Maybe you love me now, but—"

He shook his head again.

"Really. I'm asking. How do you know? How can you be so sure? How can anybody know for sure?"

"I just am. I know myself. And I've met no one else like you. There *is* no one else like you. You're so different in lots of ways, and I love them all."

"When did you start loving me?"

"At the gangway that first time. Why are you asking all this?"

She shook her head. "No, that's when you started desiring me."

"No, I felt something. It was…I don't know. More than that, I guess. I… I don't spend time thinking about this stuff like ladies do. Or talking about it. But I felt something. I felt it right away. I guess maybe I thought I could love you. I don't know…"

"Okay." She chuckled. "Remember when you welcomed me aboard?"

He nodded.

"While holding your pipe between your teeth?"

He smiled. "Yeah. A little embarrassing, I guess. Forgot to take it out. Not too high-class a thing, was it?"

She shook her head. "Oh, my darling; you don't know how refreshing that was to see. Refinement and courtly behavior had surrounded me all my life, and there you were, doing your best to be polite."

"I could've done better."

"No, no, sweetheart. It was so charming. You were trying. I can't quite express it. I loved that about you. And I think I started falling in love with you a little bit, beginning right then." She put her arms around him.

"That's good."

"And do you know what else I saw, my dear, gentlemanly Atticus? Just before that. I looked around the carriage curtain and toward the ship. And what did I see but you, just about to spit over the side."

Atticus laughed silently, then shrugged. "But then I saw you."

"Yes! And you didn't spit. You stopped yourself when you saw me."

He nodded.

"And it made me catch my breath. You stopped what you were about to do because of me. In that small way, at that moment, your instinct was to act better, to be better.

So as not to make a poor impression. And I found it so…
charming.”

“No. What? Not spitting?”

She smiled. “Yes, really. It was just a silly little thing,
but it was your first reaction to me, and it was as honest as
could be. And then when I came on board, you were struck
speechless.”

“I was?”

She nodded. “And you stammered.”

“I did?”

She laughed. “You did. And, my dear, it was just about
the most flattering thing I can imagine.”

“What, that I was tongue-tied?”

“Yes.”

“No. Really?”

She nodded again. “And I found that so enchanting.”

He shrugged. “Okay. I guess.”

“But darling, are you sure you love me? I mean really.”

“Yes, I really, really love you. You’re not convinced of
that yet?”

“I am. But despite that, I wonder… I’m just
wondering.”

“Okay, well, I have work that’s gotta be done right
now. We’ll talk later, okay?” He gave her a kiss, then got
to his feet and started toward the door. “I’ll see you at—”

“Atticus?”

“Yes?”

“What’ll I do?”

“What do you mean?”

"I mean, I don't know what to do. What will I do now?"

"Today? What, right this minute?"

She shook her head. "When we get to Chicago. What shall I do?"

"I'm not sure what you mean."

"Nowhere to stay and no way to support myself. That little bit that's in my trunk. It's all I've got. And Kristi won't be able to support herself, not for many years. We must support her, darling. She's all alone here. And then there's Frankie…"

He came back to the bed and sat down again. "I hadn't thought about all that. I don't know. I just figured… I just reckoned you had—"

"What's in my trunk might last me a couple of weeks. And I've nowhere to live, anymore. And I don't know anybody."

He slumped, looked down at the floor. "I never wondered about what your circumstances might be. I just thought…"

"Atticus, darling, I want to tell you something." She took his hand and held it in her lap. "There are some things you need to know about me. My parents are very wealthy. We're one of the wealthiest families in England. Aside from royals, of course. And yes, they supported me by paying for my passage here, but they weren't thrilled about it. They insisted that what I left England with would be the last of it. No support afterward."

Atticus shook his head. "You mean they just—"

"They didn't want me to come here. And although they supported me, their feeling was, and still is, that I belong over there."

He looked into her eyes but said nothing.

"But I belong *here*. In *this* country. I realized that right away. I was sure of it my first week here. This started as a curiosity trip, but right away it became much more. This is my home. I know it now; I feel it here," she said, bringing their hands together tightly against her chest, over her heart.

"And there's something else: it's been just me, alone, all this time. The past six months. And that's not enough anymore. I'm twenty-four, Atticus. I'm not a little girl anymore, and life is short. And I've just found the love of my life—the two loves of my life—and I cannot bear the thought of stepping off this ship in Chicago and never seeing you or Kristi again."

She released her left hand and wiped her eyes with the heel of her palm.

"Beth, look at me. What am I? Sixth-grade education. I work aboard ships. You could have a banker, or a lawyer. Senator maybe."

She shook her head. "But I didn't meet them first, dear. And I thank heaven that I met you instead. Against all odds, I met you. *You.* Not them. And I'm glad. Bankers or lawyers? Good God. Can you imagine the schemes they'd devise to get their hands on my family's money? Or a senator? Even *worse*.

"Darling, I know you now. I know you're honest and kind, and you are a just man, and you're fair with your crew. And you're the sort of man who'll protect me, and you'll protect Kristi too. You'll let nothing bad happen to us. You are fearless, and you are loving. And you're loyal."

"I know you were angry after what happened at the coal docks," he said.

"And never mind that sixth-grade education stuff. You're smarter and wiser than most other men no matter their education or their…" She waved a hand around as she searched for the right word. "their station in life, or their college degrees or any of that. My love, men like you have built empires. Men with your qualities. And yes, I was angry with you after the coal docks, but…

"But the most horribly sad moment of my life was when I left the ship to go to the school, riding away in the buggy this morning without seeing you. And Kristi was gone, too. I had no idea I could ever yearn for someone the way I yearned for you. Yes, I was upset before that, but then after the two…"

He looked straight at her. "The two what?"

"Oh dear," she began, but stopped.

"Tell me, Beth. I won't be upset. Tell me."

She shook her head. "I shouldn't have said—"

"It's all right."

"Two crewmen." She closed her eyes. "They came to my door and told me what happened."

"Which ones?"

She shook her head. "No, I can't take the chance they'll get into trouble. They were humble and so sweet. They were only trying to help, honey. And they explained it all, everything that happened at the coal dock. They made sure I knew you were just protecting Jefry."

"I was."

"See, that's what I mean. You fight for those you care about. You're their commander; you are their Alexander the Great, and they love you. I've met leaders many times in my life, and you have those qualities. Anyway, darling, there's something else too."

He waited.

"They told me about your family." Tears came to her eyes.

He bowed his head. "I wanted to tell you. But I didn't know how or when I was gonna bring it up. But after you left, I figured it didn't matter anyway."

She was still holding both their hands against her, over her heart. "It does matter, though. And I'm glad I heard about that, because the way your men described how you were afterward, that's all I needed to know about you.

"Atticus, there's a big empty space in your heart and in your life, and I wish you'd let me be the person to start filling that back up again, even if just a bit at a time. You need someone, my love, and I want that someone to be me. And I need somebody too, and it must be you."

"I never imagined I'd hear you say—"

She waved away the comment. "Oh, my love, will you please promise me you'll do something for me? Just one more thing. One more little favor is all I ask."

"Of course."

"Promise me, please? You must promise."

"Yes, yes. Okay. I promise. So, what is it?"

"One of these days, someday soon, will you please ask me to marry you?"

He brought her hand up to his lips. "I'll ask you right now: Miss Maribeth Eaton, will you marry me?"

"Oh yes. Yes, I would love to marry you, my darling Atticus. My sweet man. My answer is yes, of course I will."

"C'mon, it's my turn to tell a silly story." Beth slid onto the bed, on top of the covers. Then she patted the place next to her, and Kristi slid in alongside. Looking up at the ceiling, Beth took a long, deep breath, then held Kristi's hand. "Once upon a time a sad and scared princess—"

"That's the tie-tell? 'Sad, Scared Princess'?"

"All right then. Why not? Yeah, I guess that's it. 'Sad, Scared Princess,' that's my story tie-tell. Okay?"

Kristi nodded.

"Really? You're sure? Do I have your permission to continue?"

Kristi smirked at that.

Beth poked her softly in the ribs. "Well, Captain Kristi, which is it? May I finish telling my story now or not?"

Kristi giggled.

"Well-l-l?"

"Ohhh-*kay!*"

Beth laughed. "So, this princess grew up on a nice big farm and had a nice mom and dad. They let her go and watch the cows and sheep and goats. She loved being with the animals because they were always calm and happy when she was around.

"Then, years later, after she got older, she went to fancy schools and learned a lot, and her mom and dad took her on long vacations to France and Italy and to Greece, and she learned a lot more and met many people. She wasn't as happy as she had been years before, with the animals, just because of how people are.

"Most of them were nice, but some were not."

"They were bad people?"

"I don't think so, honey. Just boring people. Or they gossiped about one another, or they were jealous or said mean things. Many were foolish, especially the ones her own age. That's what she thought of them at the time.

"As she got older, she saw a lot of the same people again, most of them boys. Because her mom made her dress up in all sorts of frilly dresses, made her go to fancy balls and cotillions where they'd parade rich young boys from other rich and famous families in front of her.

"They'd say, 'That one, he's so nice, don't you think?' Or 'This other one, his father is in Parliament; he'll be famous someday.' But she didn't know or care what they became, because to her they were all fops, fools, and drunks. Or Oxford snobs. And she—"

"What is this fops and snobs?"

"I'll tell you about all that later. Anyway, this princess, she never liked the way they looked at her. The boys would stare at her in the rudest way. It was…well, maybe you know what I mean."

Kristi wrinkled up her face and nodded.

"And everyone around her, they'd say, 'You need to do this,' or 'You need to do that,' and 'You must get that done before you're twenty-five years old or it'll be too late,' and it all became so frightening. Or they'd say, 'This boy might not seem like much now, but you'll love him someday' and so on and so forth.

"Then one day she moved to a new place and met a different boy, and he wasn't like any of the boys that her parents had brought around. He was strong, and he was kind, and he wasn't foolish. And one day she understood that he really loved her, and she knew then that she loved him too. And when he asked her to marry him, she said…what do you think she said?"

"She say yes!"

"Correct. And so they got married, and she wasn't a sad, scared princess anymore."

"And was happy princess then?"

"Yes, very happy."

"Not sad, not scared?"

"No. Not anymore."

"Big Sister Miss Beth?"

"Yes, honey."

"I am glad you're not sad, scared princess anymore."

EIGHT

Jefry liked Buffalo, but today he was relieved to see the city behind them, fading into the distance, slipping away over the horizon. He was flaking down mooring lines as the *Eli Greaves* steamed down the lake, now headed back to Hammond, to load coal for Duluth.

A part of him was happy that Miss Eaton had not stayed ashore. He always enjoyed seeing her, but now he was concerned for her. He wished there was some way he could protect her. But from what? He had felt something was going to happen, and it had happened with the princess. But was that it? Was that all? There was no way to be sure.

Living and working a great distance from his Osage people, struggling to make his way in the white world, was hard enough. But now an unfamiliar spirit world was making its presence felt. There were forces in play aboard this ship that were beyond his understanding.

He'd gotten powerful forebodings over the past few days. Much worse than anything he had ever felt before.

He was convinced something dark had enveloped the ship. He'd felt the emergence of this dark force in recent days, suspected it might be present, but now he was sure of it. In the past, he often had such feelings about a person or about a place, and usually he was right. This had been happening since his childhood, but it was only since age nine or ten that he realized he was seeing, or maybe sensing, those influences before bad things ever happened.

By now, he knew enough to trust those visions and thoughts and voices. Those echoes from the future. Then a person would do something, or in a certain place something would happen that would confirm his feelings. He had crewed aboard the *Eli Greaves* for just a few months off and on, but had never gotten such feelings as this, not with such intensity. Except for one time though, and that was his vision about the nasty captain. And the warnings in his soul had been correct. That captain was a truly cruel and awful man. But as soon as that captain left the *Greaves* for another ship, the feelings stopped.

This time it was different, and not about one person. It was all-encompassing; it was everywhere on board.

He wanted nothing bad to happen to Miss Eaton. She had been so friendly toward him. Now he knew she was in danger again. Greater danger than before.

But how would it manifest? And when?

Jefry was vaguely familiar with the spirit world that surrounded them, yet its forces were beyond his ability to grasp or fully understand. He did not know what to do. There was a ceremony he could perform, but not here. It might prove fatal to him if he so much as tried it. Around here, this place, this was an Algonquian world, had been so for hundreds of years. His people had once inhabited nearby lands, but that was long, long ago.

His tribe had gained great power where they lived, now much farther south and to the west, but not here. Not in this place. He was as foreign to the forces here as were the white people. In his Osage world, he was a seer, a commander of spirits, but only in the land of his own people, not here. He had no power here.

His cabin mate Nicky came running. "Jefry! Get over here. You gotta see this!" Then the young man dashed halfway across the cargo deck and stopped, waving at Jefry to come look. "Hurry or you're gonna miss it."

Jefry walked quickly over to where his friend stood, pointing toward something in the distance. There was no wind at all, and the lake's surface was calm, so glassy calm that clouds reflected perfectly on the water's surface.

"You see it?"

"See what?" said Jefry.

"There!" Nicky pointed and jabbed his finger toward something on the horizon. *"Right there!"*

Jefry squinted. And yes, there was something. But what he saw made no sense. It was a ship in the distance, coming in their general direction, upside down.

Completely upside down.

"What the heck?"

"Good. You see it now?"

"Yeah, yeah, I see it, but…"

The more he watched it, the less sense it made. The ship was inverted, and it was a steamer, and the black smoke was going downward.

Nicky looked at him with big eyes and a big, boyish smile. "Crazy, right?"

As the two deckhands stood watching the ship, it flattened, spreading out. Just a little at first, then steadily flatter and flatter and widening until it was just a dark line on the horizon, and then it vanished.

Wheelsman Guest joined them. "What're you fellows looking at?" Guest was in his late twenties, a few years older than the two deckhands. He put the last of something he'd been eating in his mouth, then brushed his hands together while still chewing.

Jefry and his cabin mate both pointed toward the horizon while talking excitedly over each other.

"Wha'd you say? It was a *what*?"

"Upside-down ship."

"Oh, okay. And it looked like it was up in the air?"

"Yeah."

"Sure, I've seen 'em; we all have," said Guest dismissively. "Called a mirage. Reflection of a ship over the horizon."

The other two stood open-mouthed.

"Yeah, a captain told me it's when a layer of air is so smooth that stuff reflects off of it. Like a mirror. *Fata Morgana*, he called it. Stick around for a couple of minutes. It'll come up over the horizon. You'll see."

The three men stood there, watching and waiting for the ship to reappear.

"Awfully sad thing about that girl," Guest said.

The other two nodded.

"What was she yelling, Jefry? You were the closest. All I could make out was 'Manitou,' or something like that."

"Yeah, sounded like that to me too," Nicky said.

"Was it Indian words?"

"Not sure. She spoke a kind of Algonquian, I think. Not my language. We have lots of different languages."

Guest shook his head. "Too bad about her. Beautiful girl."

They stood in silence, waiting for the ship to reappear.

Minutes later, Guest spoke up: "Okay, there it is."

"Yeah, that's it. Ain't that something? That's the ship. How about that?"

They watched as the ship crested the horizon fully, then passed abeam of them a quarter mile or so away.

Guest started off. "Okay, wheel watch coming up. See you two later."

A few minutes after that, Nicky walked off too, leaving Jefry by himself, standing there, watching until the ship disappeared over the northeast horizon. He returned to his cabin and sat down on his bunk. He knew exactly what the woman said but hadn't wanted to tell the other two men. The words were not in his language, but he understood them perfectly. They meant "dark spirit" or "evil spirit." *Aashaa Monetoo* was the good spirit, and *Otshee Monetoo* was the dark spirit in the world of the Algonquian tribes. *Otshee* was the master of mischief, creating hardship and making awful things happen and twisting people's minds. Jefry had suspected the ill forebodings he'd received in recent days were from *Otshee*. Now he was sure he'd been right all along.

It was unfortunate that Miss Eaton was not safe at the school in Buffalo because now she was in danger, and so was Kristi. How could he let her know that? What could she do about it anyway, even if she knew? He barely understood this Algonquian world, and the whites understood it not at all. Even the Jesuit missionaries, with all their holy saints, even they had been ignorant of these things. How on earth could he protect Miss Eaton when he had so little power?

It was just before lunch the following day by the time the *Eli Greaves*'s cargo holds were full of coal and the ship was finally underway for the Detroit River, en route to the Sault Sainte Marie lock and Lake Superior. The wind had risen, and the sky was partly cloudy, although farther to the west, it was darker gray.

Ship's Steward Paul Akers watched over the dining room as the officers, minus the captain and chief engineer, sat enjoying their noon meal. He was glad to see them all chatting happily and taking such pleasure in the meal he'd prepared, especially after all the sadness back in Buffalo.

Sturgeon, pan-fried in butter and oil, with sides of mashed potatoes, fresh corn, and green beans with Italian bread. Paul had prepared the potatoes the way he always did, with a bit of cream along with pepper and chives. They always whipped up nicely, and he liked not only the taste of them but how they looked as well. His mashed potatoes were always a big favorite, and most of the officers and men had at least one helping, but usually two and sometimes three.

Steak was also on the menu, and the men could choose either that or the sturgeon or both.

After the main course, he surprised them with peach pie. He'd bought the pies the day before at DeLorenzo's Primo, an Italian bakery on Prime Street in Buffalo, along with sixty loaves of their bread, a local favorite and always a treat for the crew. Although Paul had bought thirty of the pies, he was sure they wouldn't last more than a day. That was okay. Even though all of it was expensive, it was a relief to see the men happier again after the tragic events in Buffalo.

He was as disturbed by the suicide as the rest of the crew, and now, if going a bit overboard on the food budget helped boost ship morale, it would be worth the extra expense. Having worked the lake boats for years, he knew tasty meals always went a long way toward keeping things harmonious aboard ship.

Second Mate Larry MacMillis was the first to finish. Never one for table talk, he was always quick to the door when done. On his way out, he nodded to Steward Akers. "Very nice, Paul. Thank you."

Paul nodded and smiled. He turned around and went back into the galley to see how things were going there. Owen Diggs was done with his meal too and was getting up to leave. Both he and Mate MacMillis had each finished two helpings of the sturgeon.

Second Cook Willy Squires was leaning against the dishwashing sink with a big smile on his face, already knowing what Paul was going to ask. "They liked the fish a lot. It sure was good. Had two helpings myself," he said, patting his belly.

"Just what I needed to hear," Paul said with a smile, then started going over his list of ingredients for the evening meal.

Beth woke to the feeling of someone curling up next to her. She had crawled onto the mattress for a nap. When she opened her eyes, Kristi was right next to her, face inches away, finger to her lips. She came closer.

Beth felt Kristi's warm breath against her ear.

"Man here."

Beth went to move. "What?" she mumbled.

"Shhh, no," Kristi whispered again, a little louder this time, suppressing a giggle. *"Spøkelsa."* She pointed to the bed, then leaned back so Beth could see past her. "You can see him… yes?"

Beth shook her head. "See what? Who?"

Kristi looked over toward the bed, then back at Beth. She shrugged, then smiled. "Still there. He's still there on the bed. You can't see?"

Beth shook her head again. "Can he see us?"

"Nope. Most cannot. Don't know we're here."

"Cold in here now," Beth whispered.

"Uh-huh. Yep. They make it cold."

"Where were you?"

"In the chair. Right there. With my book. He wasn't there; then he's there."

"Have you seen him before?"

Kristi nodded. "Outside, not in here. Others too now."

"Is this the 'purples' man from your cabin before?"

"Not sure."

"How many others?"

"Don't know."

Beth shivered. "My gosh, I'm freezing cold."

"Me too," Kristi whispered, snuggling closer.

Beth kissed her on the cheek, then sat up, grabbed the wool blanket and drew it over Kristi. "How's that? Better?"

Kristi pulled the blanket under her chin and smiled. "Uh-huh. I'm sleepy now too."

"Are you warm enough?" Beth asked, looking over toward the bed.

"Mm-hmm."

"He's not going to eat us, is he?"

Kristi chirped a laugh, clamping a hand over her mouth. Shook her head. "No. Not eat us. Just gonna come and go like the rest of 'em."

"Or make things move around?"

Kristi shrugged. "I don't think so."

"That's good." Beth felt her eyes wanting to close.

Kristi patted the mattress. "C'mon, Miss Beth. Come lie down. Getting chilly."

"Are you sure we're safe?"

"Uh-huh."

Beth flopped back down on the mattress.

Kristi pulled the blanket over them both, then cuddled closer and nestled her head on Beth's shoulder. "Good. Now we sleep," she whispered.

Evening. Third day out of Buffalo

Atticus was in the passageway, about to knock on Beth's cabin door, when he heard a commotion outside. Shouting out on deck and footfalls coming closer.

The deckhouse door flew open.

"Mate, you gotta come quick! It's terrible. It's Mate MacMillis."

Three crewmen led Atticus aft on the cargo deck, the men shouting one after the other. He understood only a little, but made out the words *sick* and *fish.*

"We got him on a deck box," one of them said, pointing.

Rounding the deckhouse, Atticus saw MacMillis not on the box anymore but splayed on the deck, his body thrashing with violent convulsions, bloody vomit bubbling from his mouth. He was deathly pale.

"He's choking! Help me turn him. *Hurry.*"

A deckhand came running. "Diggs and Willy the cook. They got it too."

Maribeth appeared. "Atticus, what can I do?"

"Help those others." He stood up. "Food poisoning. Never seen it this bad. We're turning back to Port Huron. I'll be in the pilothouse."

"I just felt his forehead," somebody shouted. "He's burning up."

"You men. Get everybody up and out on deck," Atticus shouted. "Everybody. C'mon, right now. Gotta find out who's sick and who isn't."

Crewmen brought Diggs and Willy, and Maribeth began tending to them. Atticus spun around and sprinted toward the forward deckhouse, which contained the captain's quarters. Pounded on his cabin door, received no response. Pounded again, shouted: "Captain, Mate Miles. Sir, I'm coming in."

Once inside, he staggered back, overcome by a ghastly stench.

Paint flakes and pieces of wood crunched underfoot. In the dim light, he glimpsed the strange, otherworldly swirls of color painted on the wall—revolting, dark, demonic-looking. A bloody rectangle of fabric in the middle of it, nailed there with wood scraps. Blood tracks down the wall, pooled on the floor.

McBride, sprawled in his bunk, appeared all but dead already, clutching a black, massively swollen arm. Something Atticus had seen in the war. Gangrene. The arm was past saving; it needed to come off…there was no time to lose. McBride groaned weakly, tried to lift his head but gave up and let it fall back onto his sweat-soaked pillow.

There was nothing Atticus could do for the man; he turned to leave. "We're going back to Port Huron, Captain, just so you know. I'll get help for you."

He dashed out of the cabin and up the stairway to the pilothouse. "Bring us about," he ordered. "Steer for Gratiot Light and Port Huron. Sickness aboard. We're going to need help."

Port Huron, Michigan

Beth stood along the rail, watching as white-coated orderlies removed the bodies of Mate Larry MacMillis and Willy Squires. Owen Diggs was carried ashore, still alive, but near death.

It had taken the *Eli Greaves* four hours to make Port Huron and tie up. Too late for Willy and the second mate. MacMillis had died with Port Huron in sight, and Willy passed away just as the first mooring lines were being tossed to men on the schooner that they'd tied up alongside.

Atticus opened the valve to admit steam to the winch, then manned it himself, lifting the two casks of sturgeon while a deckhand swung the boom over the side. They dropped the casks of tainted sturgeon into the river.

Maribeth hooked her arm around his. "You did what you could, darling."

"Captain's still in his cabin," he replied. "Needs his arm amputated or he'll die."

"What will you do?"

"Doctor's on his way. How about the five others?"

"They walked ashore. They'll survive."

"Yeah, good. Couple of days, they'll be ready again. Captain too. He'll be back at it soon enough."

"So, you're sure it was the sturgeon, Atticus?"

"Beyond a doubt. Whoever ate steak had no trouble at all. Even the ones who had only a taste of sturgeon, they'll be okay. Back on board in the morning."

"What else needs to be done? I want to help."

"I've gotta grab a couple of deckhands. Captain's cabin's a mess. Needs a good sweeping and swabbing out."

"I can do that."

"No, I don't want you to. It's an awful scene…it's bloody in there and smells horrible too."

"I helped deliver a calf once. I'm not squeamish."

"It's not that. I don't want you in there at all."

She gave him a puzzled look. "What's so bad?"

"Something horrible on the wall. A mural. Made me sick to my stomach to see it."

"Just a mural?"

"Take my word for it. Believe me. I don't know why it's there or what it means. And there's something bloody nailed to it. You don't want to look at it. Please, Beth. Promise me you won't get curious and go look."

"Okay, I promise."

NINE

Jefry and the deckhand they called Wimmy were at the door to the captain's cabin with mops and brooms.

"I'm getting a bad feeling about this," said Jefry.

"Why? Just another mess. We'll be done in a couple of minutes. Mostly just chips on the floor. Just a sweep-up job, Mate said. C'mon, sooner we start, the sooner we're done."

Neither one expected the overpowering stench, and the pile of chips on the floor struck Wimmy as odd, Captain McBride being so fastidious.

Jefry took a few steps into the room and began choking. He gasped for air and just as he put his hand up to his throat, he was cast onto the pile of paint chips by something unseen.

"Jefry! What the…?"

He tried to get up but was thrown against the far wall, then onto the floor, landing on his back. Then he was hurled back again, nearly to the door, his feet never touching the floor. He slammed into the captain's dresser before falling to the floor again. Wimmy grabbed him by an ankle and tried to pull him back toward the door, but something yanked both of them back into the room; they were both getting dragged. Jefry's arm was disappearing into the floor as though the wooden planks had liquefied.

"*Help!* Somebody!" Wimmy screamed.

Clinging to Jefry's ankle with one hand, Wimmy stretched as best he could, grabbed the doorframe with the other hand but couldn't hold on.

Jefry was reaching out to him and was struggling against whatever was pulling him into the floor.

Wimmy shouted for help again.

Jefry was getting pulled with even greater force. He was disappearing into the floor.

Wimmy's grip was failing.

"What the hell?" Hake's voice from the passageway.

"Help me!" screamed Wimmy. "Grab my ankle! *Get us outta here!*"

Hake braced himself against the doorframe and began pulling Wimmy; after a few seconds, he got him to the doorway. Then the two of them grabbed Jefry by the ankles and hands, pulling him through the doorway and out into the passageway.

"Holy shit, what was that?" said Wimmy.

"I don't know."

"Something was pulling."

"Yeah."

"So—you felt it, right?"

"Yeah. Into the floor. Good God."

"I never felt nothing like that before."

"Me neither."

"Omigod."

Jefry was on his back and now lifted his head. "What's going on?" he asked, trying to turn onto his side.

Hake shook his head. "I don't know. We just got you out of there. Wimmy, look at that. His arm's all red and blistery like it's burned."

"Jefry, what the hell was that?"

The doorway to the deck burst open.

Atticus stood there with Miss Eaton. "What's this?" he said. Miss Eaton saw Jefry on the floor, then gasped and started toward him, but Atticus grabbed her by the arm and held her back. "What happened here?"

"Mate, I don't know," Wimmy said. "Me and Jefry, we just got here to clean up like you told us to, and Jefry got thrown around."

"I did?" Jefry said.

"Soon as you went in. Just a minute ago. Right away, all this happened. In a few seconds, maybe a minute."

Atticus said, "Just got here? What do you mean? Where've you been?"

Wimmy looked confused. "We didn't go nowhere, Mate. We came right here, soon as you told us to. Minute ago, most two or three."

"No, you—" Atticus began.

"You just seen us with our brooms and stuff. Just a minute ago."

"That was an hour ago," said Atticus.

Wimmy shook his head, confused, scared. "Can't be."

"No, son. Longer," Atticus said softly. He pointed to the door to the cargo deck. "You took longer. We watched you and Jefry come through that door an hour ago."

Wimmy shook his head. "But how could…?"

"An hour ago, Wimmy. We got worried about you both."

"Three men short," Atticus said to the third mate. "Crew of twenty-three now. I hate to start out this way, but we can manage. We'll just stretch out the watches from four hours on, eight off to six and six."

The *Eli Greaves* was still at its temporary emergency berth at Port Huron. Still tied up alongside the schooner, not far from Clyde Street. Atticus and the third mate stood at the rail, looking past Dunford's Dry Dock toward the buildings on Quay Street.

"Six on, six off," the third mate said.

"Yeah. It's not the way I like to do things, but the skipper wouldn't have it any other way, missing arm or not. There's no way he'll take the time to hire crew."

"How's he look?"

"Not bad. Surprised me. Tough man. And still stubborn, still a stickler for time, just like I've always heard about him. Wants to get back on schedule soon as possible."

"And all the other lads are back on board," the third mate said.

"Yeah, I know. Not in the best of shape yet. But they'll be right back at it in a day or so."

Underway again on Lake Huron

Several deckhands were sitting and talking under the tarp they'd set up midships along the cargo deck. It was a makeshift canopy they'd gotten permission to erect, a place to be out of the sun and rain and anyone else's earshot, a place to congregate when they were off watch and not working, where they could smoke and gossip and where nobody else could hear them complain.

"Something's not right," said one. "I'm figuring the steward musta had something to do with that bad sturgeon. I mean—"

Several others shouted him down.

"You're crazy," one said. "That preacher brought it aboard. I seen it in the casks. All dried up nice. Looked okay to me. Paul had nothing to do with that fish. Anyway, I been shipping with him since seventy-one. Best damned steward there ever was. How long you been aboard?"

"He come on in Buffalo," another one said.

"That right? You only been here since Buffalo?"

"Yeah."

"Where you outta?"

"Brooklyn."

"Well, lemme tell you something, Brooklyn. Paul works hard to feed this crew, and he's the best. None better on the lakes. Reason I shipped on this boat is mostly because of him."

"Yeah, he feeds us good," one deckhand allowed, with others murmuring agreement.

Brooklyn was shaking his head. "I don't know. I mean, I saw guys with food poisoning before. Had it once myself, but what the hell, to die so quick."

"Yeah," said another. "Helluva thing. And even the second cook too. But why would Paul poison his own cook? Tell me that. Answer that for me."

Much muttering followed, most of it in agreement.

One crewman lifted his head, sniffing. "I smell something. Somebody been drinking? Who's been drinking?"

Everyone shook their heads.

"And who's that crazy-eyes guy always sharpening his knife?" Brooklyn asked.

"That's Bosun Hake. He's bosun whenever we got a barge to tow. When we're pulling a consort, he's on it. Otherwise, he's like the rest of us, just a deckhand."

"He don't talk much," Wimmy said. "But he was the first one in the water when that princess went over the side. First man in."

Many others agreed.

"And Jefry here. You were the second one over, Jefry," one said.

"You and Hake, you save that girl," said Fournier. "Very brave thing."

Brooklyn shrugged. "Lot of damned good that did, saving her. She goes and kills herself anyway. What the hell was all that about? Huh? Can anybody tell me that? And then the food poisoning? What the hell's going on here?"

No reply.

"Tell you one thing," Brooklyn said. "Nothing good ever comes of having a woman aboard. That'll jinx a ship quick as anything."

"Who you talking about?" demanded Fournier.

"That Englishwoman. Who the hell do you think?"

"We refer to her as a lady," Jefry said.

"Damn right," said another. "A fine English lady."

"Almost like royalty," another added.

"Like a duchess or something," someone said to murmurs of agreement.

"So, what's the matter, Brooklyn? How about it? You don't like women on ships? Or, uh, you don't like women at all?"

"Oh, you bet I like 'em," he replied in a lothario-type manner, artificial-sounding. "And about that English…you seen those…?" He held his cupped hands out in front of his chest. "When's the last time you seen a pair like—"

The sentence went unfinished.

Jefry pounced on him, threw him flat onto the deck, then slammed his head on a hatch and punched his shocked face again and again, his gaping mouth instantly bloody and spattering glistening red droplets onto a nearby canvas tarp. Jefry kept it up even as others pulled him away, fists still flying, punching the air.

"You crazy bastard!" Brooklyn sprayed wet words out of wet, bloody lips.

"She's with Mate Miles, friend," said a deckhand. "You show disrespect to her and you're showing disrespect to our first mate."

All the deckhands nodded.

"Damn right," one said.

"You gonna figure out how things are on this boat, Brooklyn," said another. "And you best be quick about it; hurry up and figure things out here, or you ain't gonna last long."

"Maybe end up taking a midnight swim," somebody muttered.

"Mama?" Kristi sat up in bed. She couldn't believe her eyes. "Oh, Mama, you're here," she whispered. "You're *here*." Tilting her head a little, she listened. After a moment, she smiled, then nodded. "Okay."

She watched and listened some more. Nodding again, she swung her legs out.

Miss Beth was sound asleep on the floor mattress.

Kristi tiptoed, barefoot, over to the cabin door and, as quietly as she could, opened it and went out into the passageway. She left the door open, not wanting to make noise closing it.

Mama would want her to be quiet.

It was cold in the passageway, especially being barefooted and with only her flannel nightgown on. She giggled. This was like playing a fun little game. And it was Mama. It was okay. The knob on the big door going outside was hard to turn. And the door was so heavy. Pushing and pushing, then putting her shoulder against it, she finally got it open. Walked out onto the cargo deck, not closing this big door either, instead letting it stay open.

Out on the cargo deck, Mama was there, arms open. Kristi rushed to her, but Mama moved away. Light as a feather…seemed to float away. So beautiful. Arms out still, welcoming her, but then with one hand gesturing, as though to say *come, my darling. Come here. Be with me.*

The door slammed and Kristi turned around. Then it swung open again.

Just the wind doing that, or the movement of the ship.

Turned back around, faced Mama again.

She was farther away now. By the walkway, near the railing. It was dark out, but Mama was glowing and beautiful. It was so wonderful to see her. Did she know about Papa?

Kristi tripped on something and landed on her knees on the cold deck. She looked up and saw Mama still there, so she got back up and walked slower now, more carefully. It was so dark out. Really dark out, so she reached out ahead with her toes, feeling around for anything that might trip her.

The wind blew harder near the rail.

Mama telling her to come, to come and be with her. Her mouth moved; she was saying something, but Kristi couldn't hear what it was. The wind in her ears was getting noisy and making it hard to hear.

Maybe if I go closer.

Yes, that's what she wanted. Telling her to come closer, gesturing with both hands now.

Kristi came all the way over to where she was leaning against the rail.

Mama nodding. Y*es. Yes.*

Farther away.

Out over the water now, in a beautiful flowing gown that waved gently in the wind.

Be with me, my love, my darling. Come, be with me.

Kristi looked down. The moon was over on the other side. She couldn't see anything on this side. It was so black. A moving-water sound just below where she was. Dark water moving down there. A quiet, gentle sound.

So quiet. So peaceful.

Mama gesturing, waving for her to come. She was getting smaller, farther away.

Please don't go again, Mama. Please don't go.

Kristi put one foot on the metal-wire cable between the uprights. It hurt her bare foot. She brought up the other foot and sat on the top wire cable, and then it hurt less. She heard the wind in her ears more now.

The wire was thin, making it hard to balance. And the wind was making her move, too. She swung one leg over and now had one leg out, one leg in.

Now the wind was louder in her ears. Huffing and puffing. And there was a high-pitched noise too, but it wasn't the wind. And it wasn't coming from Mama either. The noise was coming from over to the left, from over by the big door, and there was a moving light along with it. The noise grew louder and louder, and the wind became louder too. Then the noise was next to her, and she knew it was screaming.

Hands and arms went around her, and she was lifted away from the railing.

The screaming stopped, and it was Miss Beth next to her and Mr. Mate Miles, too. Miss Beth held her tight. And then they were both lying on the deck, and Mr. Mate Miles was there right along with them, kneeling next to her, holding a lamp. That's what the light was.

Miss Beth was crying and saying things that didn't make sense. Crying and talking so fast that Kristi couldn't understand. And she wouldn't let go. Still crying. She held her so tight and wouldn't let go.

Kristi looked up, over toward the water. *"She is gone!"*

Beth held on tight as Kristi cried and screamed in her arms and reached toward the railing. She cried like she would never stop.

"They bury my mama in the ocean! They show me Mama's going down under the water! My mama and papa are gone!"

Beth stroked her hair, speaking softly and holding her as tight as she could. "Shh, shh, my darling. I'm here. I've got you. Mama's here now. Mama's right here. I'm here. I've got you, my child. Mama loves you. Mama will never leave you. You're okay. Mama loves you."

Atticus held out his hand, and Beth took it. She sat up, still holding Kristi, and rocked back and forth with Kristi in her arms as Atticus knelt next to them, holding the lantern.

Beth woke up feeling hot and uncomfortable. No light came through the porthole; it was still dark outside. Still nighttime, but she wasn't sure what hour it was. Kristi was next to her on the bed, fast asleep. Breathing softly now.

She'd settled down since a while ago when she was having nightmares. She'd whimpered and kicked in her sleep until Beth woke her and got her to calm down.

It must have gotten very warm out because Beth was sweating.

A storm on its way?

Rising quietly and carefully, she slipped out of bed so as not to disturb Kristi. Beth swung open the porthole, letting in a gentle breeze. The curtains fluttered and the glimmer of the full moon reflected off wave tops, making hundreds of bright white streaks across the lake surface.

So pretty.

She pulled on her shirt and overalls, went out into the passageway, then over to the pilothouse stairway and walked halfway up.

"Psst. Atticus."

He appeared at the top of the stairs.

"It's too hot in the cabin. I'm going to sit outside for a minute. Kristi's okay. I've calmed her down, and she's fast asleep now."

"I'll keep an eye on the passageway from here," he said. "I'll make sure she stays in the cabin."

It was less stuffy outside. Not chilly at all. Odd sort of smell now. Storm coming maybe. The refreshing breeze off the lake made her feel better. And the moon was so lovely. Maybe a few minutes out here would clear her head so she could get back to sleep.

There was a flickering glow back aft. It looked like it was coming from both the galley side and the dining room side. Someone had lit the lamps. A nice cup of tea would be so refreshing… Approaching the galley, she heard the clatter of dishes and the clanking of pots and pans. Passing the screen door, she glanced in and saw the porter hard at work over the dishwashing sink.

She continued around to the fantail. Halfway around, she crept over to the dining room porthole and peered through to see who was at the table. Her view was straight on, down the length of the table. The lamps were all lit and flickering, and it was bright in the dining room. Several men sat at the table, maybe eight or ten of them, none of whom she recognized. They were all clad similarly, some in uniform and some in working clothes. The styles were a little different from what she was used to seeing lately, though. How nice it would be to go in and have a cup of tea, but she didn't want to disturb the meeting or whatever it was they were having.

A man seated near the end of the table turned a quarter way around in his chair, then slowly turned his head and looked straight at her.

Grinning.

It startled her.

He had already begun grinning while turning around, even before he saw her.

She caught her breath and took a step back.

How did he know she was there?

She went around to the starboard side and glanced through another porthole.

Most of the men at the table were deep in conversation.

Grinning Man had turned back around and was already looking in her direction, staring straight at her as though he knew she'd appear at this porthole next. He was still wearing the same grin. She didn't recognize him.

Oddest thing—he was dressed just as she was. Railroad overalls, same long-sleeved tan shirt.

It was quite rude, the way he was staring. Ever since she had developed physically, years before, she had always attracted attention from men. She was accustomed to it by now and was neither offended nor impressed by it.

And certainly not intimidated.

And she really did fancy a nice cup of tea.

She took one last quick glance through the porthole.

Opened the door and went inside.

Into an empty dining room.

Nobody was at the table.

Nobody in the room.

Not a soul.

She spun around. Grinning Man was right behind her. Barely a foot away. She gasped, lashed wildly, slapped him hard across the face.

But her hand struck nothing. Cool air passed between her fingers.

And yet he was still there.

Teddy the porter sensed movement and looked up from his dishwashing.

The lady passenger—Miss Eaton—was at the screen door. Outside looking in, without expression. Staring at him.

Silent.

He was startled. "Oh, hello, Miss Eaton. It's a bit late for you to be out here. Are you okay? May I get you anything?"

No reply.

She stared at him, eyes blank, showing nothing, her long-sleeved shirt fluttering in the breeze.

"Is something wrong?" He put the pan he'd just rinsed on the drying rack, then dried his hands on his apron.

Her eyes remained fixed on him, her head turning as she watched him step over to the screen door. "We've got the crew messroom right here if you'd care to sit. I can fix something if you'd like."

She remained still. Her eyes blank.

"Coffee or tea," he said, nervous now. "It's no trouble really. Or there's fruit here. I can slice up an apple or a peach, maybe."

"The men in the dining room," she said.

He shook his head, confused, wondering what was going on with her. "Dining room? I'm not sure what you're talking about, miss."

"A group of men there."

Teddy smiled uneasily. Was something wrong with her? "Nobody's there. Not since suppertime."

"Having a meeting or something? Just now. They were sitting around the table."

"No, I'm sure there was no one." He swung the door open. "Come inside if you like."

She hesitated a moment, then stepped through. Once inside, she stopped. Crossed her arms as though chilly. Looked up toward where the ceiling met the wall, angled her head slightly as though she saw something up there.

"There's been nobody in the dining room. Not since supper. I would've heard," he said, then looked up toward the ceiling too, wondering what she saw.

She looked him straight in the eyes. Wearing a slight smile. "What's happening here? You must know what's going on."

Teddy didn't know what to say.

Her smile widened, but it was a smile of suspicion, without cordiality, without affinity. "It's *you* doing this. Isn't it. You're doing this."

He took a step back. Away from her.

"They came through here," she said, her smile now gone. "They must have."

He shook his head. "There's been nobody. I been here since suppertime."

"Impossible," she replied.

"The officers come and go through the door over on that side," he said. "They never come through this way."

"Not just now?"

"No. But I'll go take a look if you'd like."

She looked around as though thinking about something. Wondering, trying to decide. Then she seemed to change. Lowered her head, looked toward the floor, remained that way for several seconds. Nodded. Then she lifted her head, and looked straight at him. "I'd be grateful."

Teddy took the short passageway to the dining room. He looked around. He had turned off the lamps hours ago. Now they were lit again. Every one of them. Every single one, their flames quietly flickering. The tablecloth was back on the table, as well. Everything was in place, as though set for a meal.

Back in the galley.

"My God," she said. "The look on your face."

"Miss, they're lit. All of them. The lamps are lit. I can't figure it out. I turned them out just after supper. And thirty minutes ago, I went in there to stack the plates and saucers in the cupboard. The lamps were still out. But they're all lit again now. Plates back on the table, but nobody's been in there. And I didn't put that stuff there. Been in here washing dishes the whole time. I can show you if you'd like," he said.

She took a step back while shaking her head. "What's going on, here? This isn't happening. This can't be happening."

"I'm not lying, Miss Eaton. You should come and take a look at least. I don't know what's going on, either." Teddy took a few steps along the short passageway to the dining room. He stopped, then turned around, reached out, held out his hand for her.

After a moment's hesitation, she took his hand, following him. Entering the dining room, she gasped. "It wasn't like this. When I looked in a few minutes ago. No. It wasn't like this. I saw men around the table, but no tablecloth. And there was no…" She backed up into the passageway, slowly, hand over her mouth. "No, no, no. This isn't happening."

Teddy shook his head. "How could these be on?" He walked around, turning out lamps, one after the other. "I have no idea what's just happened."

"Please come out. We shouldn't be in here."

He looked toward her, about to reply, but could not.

She waved him back. "Let's go. We need to get out of here now."

They left the dining room. "And I'd better get you out of here and back to your cabin. Just give me a second to lock the door."

Back in the crew messroom.

She walked over to the door out to the deck and stopped. Slumped against it, let her head drop to where her chin was against her chest. Placed her hand on her forehead.

"You going to be all right, Miss Eaton?"

She nodded, still with her hand on her forehead. "I'm sorry. Forgive me. I thought maybe you were doing…" She threw out her hands. "Doing something…I don't know…"

"It's okay," he said.

"Am I losing my mind? How could I have suspected you of… I'm so sorry I've troubled you, Mr.—"

"No need for the mister, but thanks anyway. It's just Teddy. I'm nobody special, miss. And it's my pleasure to be of help, but—"

"I shouldn't detain you any longer," she said, reaching for the door.

"Don't go out on deck by yourself. Please, Miss Eaton. Please."

She nodded, thought for a moment, then turned to him, her hand still resting on the doorknob. "What is this? What did we just see?"

"Wish I had the answer, miss. Fact is, I've been wondering about something myself."

She paused, listened carefully.

"Reason I'm up so late. Something woke me up tonight. You sure you don't want to sit?"

She shook her head warily, still appearing puzzled.

"So, I'm fast asleep in my cabin a little while ago. I'm alone in there now, right? Because Willy was my cabin mate."

Beth looked down and shook her head. "I cannot tell you how sad it makes me. I was there, as you know. When they were all sick. And I wish there was something we could have done for Willy. He'd been so kind to Kristi and me. Such a nice man. It is so heartbreaking about him and the second mate. And Mr. Diggs."

"Heartbreaking for everybody," he said. "All of us. I mean about all this stuff going on. First it was the princess and then the food poisoning. It's all so sad." He went silent, closed his eyes for several moments.

Beth waited.

"Anyway, I'm fast asleep. Then somebody's talking in my ear and grabbing me, shaking me by the shoulder. And I wake up in a daze and wonder what's going on: Ship on fire? Sinking? So, I swing my feet out of bed and nobody's there. Nobody in the room but me.

"And that voice. Not a voice I know. Not Willy's. Even as sleepy as I was, I knew it wasn't him. It was… deeper, I guess you'd say. And it said something to me. It said, *'Get out!'* Like that. And that was it. Just *'get out.'* And I'm not sure if I'm saying this right, but… All I can think of is that it was hollow. Sounded hollow. I don't know.

Like from inside a cave. Does that make sense? The voice was hollow. I'm not even sure how to say it, but that's how it seemed to me.

"And so I'm sitting there on the edge of the bed, wondering what's going on. Anyway, Miss Eaton, I know you saw something tonight. Just like I heard something. And what we both saw a minute ago. I'm just as puzzled as you are. I wish I could explain what's going on, but…"

"Thanks ever so much. Thank you for listening to me. And for believing me," she said, again casting a wary glance over toward the passageway to the dining room.

"And there was something else," he said. "On the floor there was wet shoe prints. Well, look outside right now. There's no rain and no spray blowing. Not yet anyway, maybe soon. But this is a couple of hours ago. No rain or nothing. But on my floor there's wet shoe prints. And nobody there.

"Miss, if you're going back to your cabin, please let me escort you. It's no trouble, believe me. And I won't be able to sleep unless I know you've returned to your cabin safely."

"You're so kind, Teddy. I can't tell you how much I'd appreciate that. And I shall address you as Mr. Teddy if you don't mind. Because to me you *are* somebody special."

Teddy lowered his head. "So nice of you to say that."

"Well then… are we ready?"

"Let's go."

As Teddy reached for the outside door, a loud noise came from back in the dining room. Then a crash. And another. Then what sounded like a voice. A screech. A cry.

Human, but not human. The door that he'd locked was making noise. Rattling. Then something thudding against it.

Another screech.

He turned, about to head back toward the dining room.

Beth put her hand on his arm and shook her head. "We must go. Now."

They started out, but paused for a moment as the outside screen door rattled in a sudden gust.

He stepped out. "Uh-oh. Rain's coming. I better batten down the underway door." Another gust nearly pulled the door away from him, and he was pelted with raindrops. "Too late. Looking like we're gonna get soaked." He looked back over his shoulder. "You okay?"

"Yep. Let's go," she said, following him out the doorway and onto the deck. "Goodness, so windy all of a sudden."

They hadn't gone ten feet when someone raced past them, running at a full gallop.

"Hey! watch out!" Teddy shouted. "Be careful, you!"

"Who was that?"

"Don't know. Couldn't tell. Too fast."

The runner turned the corner and disappeared around the deckhouse.

"Why is he running? Something wrong maybe?"

"Could be. We'll take the leeward side forward to your cabin. Maybe not so much spray over there. We'll see what's going on, too. Make sure everything's okay."

Beth shivered, then clutched her shirt collar tight around her throat as she followed Teddy.

He looked over his shoulder, made sure she was right behind him once he'd turned the corner. He reached back, gestured to her, and she took his hand. Keeping her close now, having realized already…

The running man had made no sound.

Eugene was at the wheel. Atticus stood near the pilothouse windows, staring out into the darkness. The charts and dead reckoning plot showed them to be twenty hours out from the light at DeTour Point.

Atticus couldn't help but smile as he thought about Beth. And about them, the two of them, together. Kristi too now, and maybe even Frankie. Just the idea of having a family again filled him with hope. It gave him such a feeling of pride that Beth even considered becoming his wife. And she had even asked him to propose to her. Couldn't help but chuckle at that. Never heard of such a thing before. She was full of surprises, for sure.

Remarkable lady.

What would their lives be like? He couldn't think of that without remembering his late wife and children. He still loved them all so much, would love them all for the rest of his life; then someday they'd all be together again. For now, though, in this life, there were things he'd have to do. For one, he'd have to work faster on getting his shipmaster's ticket. It was the least he could do for Beth's and the children's futures, for their lives and security. He owed everyone that, for sure. Even as he looked out into the darkness of Lake Huron, as he had done hundreds of times before, everything seemed different. The world seemed brighter, full of possibilities. His mind swirled with plans and daydreams.

"What the hell was that?"

Atticus turned toward the wheelsman's voice. He could barely see him in the pilothouse gloom. "You see something, Gene?"

"I think so. Over that way."

Atticus grabbed the twin telescope binoculars and peered into the darkness.

"Mate, you looking ahead?"

"Yeah."

"No, over here. This way, just outside the door, port side."

Atticus walked across the pilothouse and looked out through the door window just as a gust splashed raindrops against it. "It's coming down heavy all of a sudden," he said. He watched for several seconds. "What did you see?"

"A glow. Just a glow. From the corner of my eye. Soon as I turned, it was gone."

Now Atticus had a good view both ahead and toward the steps just outside the door.

"Who'd want to be out in this rain?"

Atticus didn't reply, rather kept looking, both ahead and to the side.

"How long to DeTour, Mate?"

"Twenty hours, according to the plot."

"After we unload, are we getting iron ore for the lower lakes?"

Atticus shook his head. "Not this time. We'll go back to Chicago afterward. Captain needs to recuperate, and we need to hire crew. I've made full turns on the six and six before, and it's too tiring for the men."

"Yeah," Guest said. "It's hard enough to stay awake as it is, sometimes. There! Did you see it?"

Atticus threw open the door. He had to shield his face from the driving rain but glimpsed a figure dressed in dark clothes just then descending the stairs, holding a lamp. Now concerned for the man's safety, Atticus shouted at him, then whistled.

No response.

He leaned back inside. "You okay here for a minute, Gene? I need to see what's going on. And listen for Miss Eaton's cabin door, will you? I don't want Kristi coming out." He went down the outside stairs. Whoever was ahead of him was in a big hurry, not a safe thing in this weather. And on slippery decks. Atticus followed the swaying lamplight, making his way carefully along the deck in the pounding rain and fierce gusts.

Beth and Teddy reached the starboard side just as there was a clatter in the darkness. They turned the corner and saw something lying there.

Slowly, they came closer. A small wooden box had fallen over. Along with something nearby, suspended from a rope… tied to an overhead beam… swaying and twisting in the suddenly fierce wind…

A body.

"Oh God, no!" Beth cried.

Teddy grabbed its feet. "No, no, no!"

Beth braced herself against the wind, also trying to hold on to the body.

It was a crewman, clad in railroad overalls. Despite the wind, the two of them managed to stop the body from swaying so much.

Rain dripped off Teddy's lips and eyebrows. "I got nothing to cut 'im down. Gotta get a knife."

Beth looked up at the hanging person, looked up at the face, and screamed.

It was her own face she saw.

Saw herself dangling by the neck, swinging from the end of the rope.

Atticus had made it to the end of the cargo deck; the lantern wasn't swaying anymore. Whoever was carrying it had stopped. It was sitting on a hatch cover now. By itself, still lit, flickering from the wind. Whoever had carried it was gone. He looked around, wondering where—

A scream.

Had to be Beth. He sprinted toward the sound.

She was on her back, trying to get up, Teddy helping.

And nearby, hanging from a rope, twisting, and spinning in the wind…

"Teddy! My knife!" Atticus shouted as he grabbed the hanging person by the ankles, taking the weight. *"C'mon, cut it."*

Teddy took the knife from its sheath and began sawing at the rope.

Beth sat down against the side of the deckhouse, out of the wind and rain, hugging her knees to her chest.

As Teddy cut, Atticus struggled to hang on to the legs. They felt solid, but there seemed to be no weight to the body.

"Hold 'im still!" Teddy shouted. "He's twisting…I can't…"

"Can you reach the rope?"

"Yeah, I just… Spray's in my eyes, I gotta…"

Atticus felt the coarse fabric of the overalls and the girth of the leg, but when Teddy had cut through, the body just drifted down, settling silently onto the deck. No sound of impact, no thud, or noise of any kind. Even with the howling of the wind and the hammering of the rain, Atticus should've heard a sound. But he had not.

"Who is it?" Teddy said.

Atticus wiped rain from his brow and flicked it off his hand. "I don't know. Never seen him before."

"*Him?*" Beth said, getting to her feet and coming closer for a better look. "It's not a him, it's… Oh, God," she began, before a guttural sound choked off her words.

She dashed to the bulwark and hung her head over the side. Atticus assisted, holding her shoulders, steadying her as she emptied her stomach.

Teddy froze, a corpse on the deck before him, a grin spread across its face.

"What's going on?" Steward Paul appeared, holding a lantern. "I heard a scream. What're you all doing out in this rain?"

Teddy pointed down to the deck before them and was about to speak—about to explain the hanging man and the running man and the dining room lights and now the body— but remained silent when he saw there was nothing there now—nothing on the deck but a wooden box and a piece of cut rope.

"Well?" Paul said, looking down to where Teddy pointed, probably seeing nothing out of the ordinary as he held his collar closed against the rain, then glancing over to where First Mate Miles held on to Miss Eaton as she leaned out over the side, obviously sick to her stomach. "What in the bloody hell is going on here?"

TEN

"You all know how this sounds, right?" Paul said. Beth, Atticus, Kristi, and Teddy were present. The five of them were in the crew messroom following breakfast. "You know what fellas are gonna say. That you're crazy. That we're all crazy. Or making it all up."

No one contradicted him, because it was true.

Atticus said nothing because he had no words. Where to begin? How do you even start explaining it to yourself, let alone others, when you have no idea what's just happened?

"Maybe it's ghosts." Teddy looked around the table. "Right? What you're all describing. Sounds to me like ghosts."

Atticus shook his head. "I never believed in that stuff." His next thought: *There goes any chance of a skipper's ticket.*

"Me neither," Paul said. "Anyway, we start talking about that stuff and people think we've gone crazy."

"But Teddy and I saw it," Beth said. "Yes, I know how people react, but we saw it. And so did Atticus. How can we forget what we've seen?"

"Lots of people believe in that sort of thing," Teddy said. "Tell you what though. You know who really believed it? That girl. The princess. She believed it. She took her own life because of it. Remember what she was saying? Those words she was screaming? *Otshee Monetoo?*"

"I can hear her even now," Beth said. "It gives me the chills."

"She felt it right away," Teddy said. "The moment she stepped aboard. Everybody there saw how she acted. What *was* that? Can anybody tell me? What did she feel? Or put it this way: What did she feel that we could not?"

"So, what then, Teddy?" Paul asked. "That all means something?"

"To the Indians, yeah. Manitou is how we say it; the French voyageurs and the trappers, they learned about it a couple hundred years ago. The Indians call it *Monetoo*, and it means spirit. *Otshee* is the dark spirit. *Aashaa* is their good spirit."

"But why kill herself?"

"Tell you what I think. Just my opinion for what it's worth. I think she took her own life before *Otshee* could seize her soul. She was afraid *Otshee* would escape with it to the dark world."

Paul shook his head. "Silly campfire talk, sounds like. The sort of thing grown-ups tell kids at night to scare them."

"We're new here," Teddy said. "Recent arrivals. This was all their world long before we got here, for hundreds of years… thousands."

"The things we saw tonight we'd have called impossible," Beth said. "Yet they happened. We all saw them. Either we're all suffering from delusions or mass hysteria or something really happened."

"Atticus, you were in the war," Teddy said. "You never heard of restless spirits on the battlefield after a battle or a skirmish?"

"Well, yeah. We all heard about it or saw it ourselves. A man would get killed, then maybe later that night, you'd see him up and walking around, searching. Looking for something. We had this one corporal who bled to death after an arm got shot off. For two days and nights, lead was flying back and forth across that battlefield. We couldn't haul off the corpse. Too dangerous. We had to leave it where it was. Fellas said they saw him get up at night, even with his dead body lying there, that he'd get up and walk around, searching, always searching. They figured he didn't know he was dead and was looking for his arm.

"But we'd all see things like that and just say, 'It's war,' and leave it at that. Never thought any more about it. We got used to things not making sense.

"One afternoon I was talking to another soldier. We were both along the edge of a field, each of us sitting on a rock, just chatting. He was from Alabama, and he was telling me about his family's goats; they raised goats and sold the milk.

"They lived off that. Up until Yankee soldiers stole their goats. Anyway, all the while we were talking, this fella, some of the back of his head was missing. It had got shot away. Bullet must've tore right through his skull. And yet there he was, talking to me normal as could be."

With that, Atticus stood up. "I've got some work to do, folks." He held out his hand. "C'mon, Kristi. Let's get you back to your cabin. You didn't want breakfast. You sure you don't want something now? Or are you okay?"

"I'm okay," she said, taking his hand in both of hers and smiling as she looked up at him.

He gave Beth's shoulder a gentle squeeze, and she stood up too. "Fellas, we can talk about this later." They started toward the door, then Atticus stopped. He was silent for several moments. "There's something I probably ought to bring up. Now's as good a time as any. I've been piecing some things together."

Everyone was silent.

"With all that's happening. So puzzling. The princess, the sturgeon, what happened in the captain's cabin with Jefry. The man with the lantern and all the rest of what happened last night. Think about it, Paul. And Teddy. Think about it for just a second. You've both spent years aboard ship. Have you ever seen so much strange stuff happen? And in such a short time? In what? Seven, eight days. I haven't. Have you?"

Paul and Teddy both shook their heads.

Beth asked, "What are you thinking, Atticus?"

"About what the princess said before she killed herself. The words she used. What Teddy just said. A few years ago, a steamer disappeared while crossing Lake Superior. It was declared lost with all hands. Then a year later, almost to the day, it showed up again. Perfect condition, like nothing ever happened. Lightly grounded along the Canadian side a ways north of the Sault. Seemed to appear out of nowhere. Back from the dead, everybody said at the time. Missing for a year, then suddenly shows up out of nowhere. No damage. Perfect condition but no one on board.

"Two local men found the ship; at least it's assumed they did. Their steam launch was found tied up alongside, but no trace of them was ever found."

"*Le Petite Veronique,*" Teddy said with a shiver. "Little Veronica. Yeah, that was their steam launch, that little boat of theirs. I'll never forget that name. Just gave me a chill. Good God. You're talking about the steamer *Monetoo*. I remember, of course. It was the talk of the lakes for months."

Atticus nodded, then looked straight at Beth. "Others came looking for those missing men after a day or so. They found that steam launch, and went aboard. They said the dining room table was set for a meal—tablecloth, knives, and forks…even the china. All of it still there where it ought to have been. Undisturbed. And the dining room lamps… They were all lit."

Beth took a deep breath, nodded a bit, locked eyes with Atticus, and managed a slight smile. "This was when?" she asked. "How long ago?"

"It was '68," said Teddy. "So, five years."

Atticus nodded. Teddy nodded, too. Atticus smiled at this confirmation of things they'd witnessed the night before.

"My God," Beth said. "But what… I mean, how did…" she began, but trailed off, then was silent.

Atticus continued. "But no crew were ever found, either. No survivors, no bodies, nothing. Yet the ship came back."

"Mate, so, you're saying the princess thought this ship is the *Monetoo*?" Paul said.

"Well, she wouldn't have known about ships. Ships are *our* world, not hers. But I think she felt the presence of an evil spirit. We all saw it, the way she reacted. Maybe that presence is here, no matter what our ship's nameplate says. And that's what she felt."

"You really believe all that?" Paul asked.

Atticus shrugged. "I don't know what to believe. There was talk all around the lakes about the *Monetoo*. They said she was a ghost. That she was cursed. A week after she reappeared, the owner had her towed back to Milwaukee, intending to put her back in service, but that didn't work out. No mariners would sail on her. She couldn't get cargo, and the owner ended up going broke. He came aboard late one night, went into the captain's cabin with a pistol and shot himself. This was a couple of years ago—or two and a half, maybe three. Everybody said the ship got taken out into Lake Michigan afterward and burned to the waterline, then sunk.

"But I'm thinking that's not what really happened; it's just what somebody wanted people to believe. So, of course, what would they do? Tell the newspapers they burned it up and sank it and that now it's on the bottom of the lake, and so that's what everybody believed took place. And probably still do."

Paul shrugged. "All right, but so what? That's got nothing to do with the ship we're on."

"I think it does," said Atticus.

Paul shook his head. "There's no connection."

"I think there is. In fact, I'm sure there is."

"No, I don't see it."

"The nameplate. That's the connection."

"Which? The *Monetoo* nameplate?"

"Yeah. It was found washed up on the Wisconsin side. Door Peninsula. Not far from where I live."

"Okay. So? Ship sinks, you expect some flotsam, some debris. Something. There's always something. Always. I mean… wooden ship, right? Things get dislodged, float to the surface…"

Atticus nodded, smiling. "Exactly. Except this time there wasn't any flotsam. There was nothing else. At least, nothing was ever reported. Near where that nameplate was found, you'd expect there'd be other things. Pieces and parts of this and that. *Always*, like you just said. But there was just the nameplate. All by itself. And you'll never see that unless part of the stern section gets torn off and comes to the surface. Something like that. The nameplate was attached there for years. How's it gonna come undone? It's only going to come undone if somebody takes it off. Which of course, people do. All the time. For a memento. But not this time."

"Somebody took it off," Maribeth said, "because they wanted it to be found."

"Yep," Teddy said. "Had to be that. They wanted it to be found."

Paul shook his head. "There were burn marks on it. The ship burned up."

"Someone could have created those," said Maribeth. "Burned that piece of wood just enough so the name could still be made out."

"Yep. Easily. You could do that over a campfire," Atticus said.

"The *Monetoo* was never sunk," Paul said. "This is what you're saying?"

Atticus shook his head. "The second time, Paul. Just the second time. The first time…nobody disputes that. It sank, then reappeared. Nobody really knows how that happened, but it was lost for a year, then came back. Everybody agrees on that. It reappeared one day, right near where that little steam launch was. The men on that launch, they'd have a story to tell, maybe, but they vanished. Others confirmed the rest—the condition of the ship, the dining room table all set for a meal…all of that. We'll never know what made that happen."

"But the second time…that's what you're talking about," Teddy said.

"Yes," said Atticus.

"Okay, the first time. Alright, then," Paul continued. "Sunk out on Superior the first time. Nobody doubts that. But not the second time. That time, they wanted people to think it was taken out of Milwaukee Harbor and sunk." He looked at Atticus. "Right?"

"Exactly. Somebody *wanted* people to think it was taken out and scuttled. Yeah. You're getting it, Paul. I don't believe it was sunk the second time. Not for a moment. Not anymore. After what I've seen these past few days. I don't believe the *Monetoo* was sunk twice. It was a sound and seaworthy ship by all accounts but most certainly cursed.

"And then you have the *Eli Greaves*, an older ship that had reached the end of its useful life. Not really that old, and not a bad boat. Just badly run, with all those mishaps. No fault of the ship itself. So what do you do? You switch the nameplates and say, 'Well, we rebuilt the *Greaves*, and now she's got a few more years left in her.'"

"Can't do that over a day or two," Paul said.

"No. You can't. Several days, maybe a couple of weeks. People all around Milwaukee Harbor would see that taking place over an extended period.

"So, what you do is hide both ships somewhere, maybe in a quiet little cove. You keep strangers away. Take what you want off the old ship, keep the nameplate, then take this older boat out onto the lake at night. And you've already filled it with rocks, and so you scuttle it.

"*That* is the one they sent to the bottom. The older ship. The *Eli Greaves*. Not the *Monetoo*. Then you work on the other one—the ghost ship *Monetoo*—attach the nameplate off the tired old *Eli Greaves* and make other changes. You paint the stack to match the other ship, then you take off this, add that, switch the masts, move something from here to there, so it looks like the older boat.

"And then—and this part is important—you move her somewhere else and operate out of that new location. Then, after a while, memory fades; people go about their lives. And where the *Greaves* berths in Chicago, no other shipping operations take place. Nobody wants to operate out of there—"

"Horrible neighborhood," Beth said.

"There are no maritime watchers like there always are in a busy port. No little items in the paper, and you come and go as you please. No news about the ship shows up anywhere. And after a while, it's like shifting sands. It's all covered up and forgotten.

"I'll never forget how Captain McBride looked at this ship when he came aboard for the first time, what he said.

'This is not the *Eli Greaves* I know,' or words to that effect. And he can always spot a Milwaukee ship, I'm sure. Well, I have no proof, but… no, the newspaper version is not true."

"I'm getting chills," Paul said. "I'm not sure I like where this is going."

"This ship," Atticus continued, then stopped to collect his thoughts. "I… If I'm correct, this ship we're on. This is not the *Eli Greaves*. That one—the real one—the real *Eli Greaves*, what's left of it, is at the bottom of Lake Michigan. This ship, the one we're on, this is the *Monetoo*. At least that's what I believe."

Maribeth gasped.

"I was afraid you were going to say that," Paul said.

Atticus shrugged. "It would explain a lot."

"The *Eli Greaves* was an older ship," Teddy said. "Similar profile to the *Monetoo*. Not real old, not ancient. Had a spell of bad luck, though. Not a bad boat, but unfortunate, you might say. Poor piloting, for the most part. Ran up on the rocks a couple of times. Fire in the boiler room once. Rammed by another ship once. She'd been through an awful lot. In and out of the dry dock a few times, but never got a bad reputation. But anyway, so there she was, beaten up, falling apart, taking up space on a pier or wharf somewhere, and so you take it out and sink it."

"Exactly," said Atticus. "That's what they'll do. Fill it full of rocks to weigh it down. Anything. Even scrap metal. Then tow it out to where it's deep and there are no witnesses. Just scuttle it. If you were to do that, when would you do it?"

Teddy shook his head. "Not sure I know what you mean."

"I mean the time of day," Atticus said. "When would you do it?"

"Well, first thing in the morning, I guess. Daytime. It's safer that way because your fellows can see everything."

"But what if you don't want anybody to know what you're up to?"

"You'd do it at night."

"What if I told you the *Eli Greaves* was at its pier in Milwaukee Harbor, where it had been tied up for a year or so. Then somebody spotted it being towed out late in the evening, and of course in the morning it was gone. I know about that because the other day I saw it in a notice among Owen Diggs's things. I almost missed it. Just two lines on a little slip of newsprint, nearly faded away. A forgotten old notice from the Harbor News section of a newspaper. From two years ago. Diggs saved a lot of old shipping articles from Milwaukee papers.

"And guess which other ship was there one day and gone the next? Just like the *Greaves*."

"The *Monetoo*," Paul said.

Atticus nodded. "Also taken from Milwaukee Harbor. At night. Within a day or so of the *Greaves*. Here's what I think happened. The real story, not what they told the papers.

"We have two ships, right? One was in poor shape, only because it'd had bad luck. Otherwise a good name. It got taken out and sunk. But they took off what deck gear they wanted and kept the nameplate. I don't know this for a fact, but I'd put money on it."

Paul was nodding. "And the *Monetoo* was altered to look like the older ship."

"Older but with nearly identical lines," Atticus said. "Profile just about the same. So, yes. The newer ship was in good condition but wasn't making any money because nobody would sail on a cursed ship. I think you're getting it. So Joshua Street from Saint Louis, or somebody acting on his behalf, with an assumed name maybe, buys the cursed ship for pennies on the dollar. Or maybe he doesn't buy it at all. Just hauls it off without paying a cent, and people are happy this ghost ship is finally gone.

"Then he changes some things around to make it look more like the *Eli Greaves*—the location of the steam winches, maybe makes the masts look like the other ones, paints the *Monetoo* stack to match the one on the *Greaves*. And so forth. It's got basically the same profile, so most people couldn't tell the difference."

"But McBride could tell," Paul said. "No matter what the nameplate said. So, whoever did all this changing around went and switched the nameplates and tossed the *Monetoo* nameplate out on the lake somewhere, expecting it'd drift ashore and be found, to help convince people it was taken out and scuttled."

"Right, and you have a newer, seaworthy ship with a good name…"

"Except you don't, of course," Maribeth said. "Well, it's a name that hasn't been earned."

"A stolen good name," Atticus said. "You may have a seaworthy vessel, but you have a cursed ship—a ghost—bearing the identity of another. But keeping all its own secrets."

"And so what you have," Beth said, "is a conjurer's switch. A fake, a magician's trick on an enormous scale."

"How could they do that without somebody finding out?" Paul asked. "People around here would notice. Somebody would blab. Or the fellows who did the work, or scuttled the ship, they'd say something."

"Not if they did the work in some hidden place," Teddy said. "And not if the men were from elsewhere and never talked to anybody local. Remember, this ship's owner is a Saint Louis man."

"He would have brought his own people." Paul said.

"And paid them off," Teddy added, looking around the table.

"Or kept them quiet another way," said Maribeth.

Atticus nodded. "Yeah, also possible. Because dead men tell no tales."

Atticus made to leave once again.

Paul was shaking his head. "That's a lot to digest."

"It all fits though," said Teddy. "Right? Wouldn't have believed it. But the way he lays it out…"

"I know I don't feel safe here anymore," Beth said. "Not after what I've seen."

"Please be careful, everyone," Paul said. "It can't hurt to be more cautious. There's not much left of this trip. We can't take it for granted that we're even safe on board here anymore."

Maribeth looked at Atticus. "What shall we do? What *can* we do?"

"Paul, Teddy, me. What choice do we have?" he replied. "All of us. We're under contract. What do we say? 'There's ghosts on board' and tie up somewhere and jump ship?"

"We'd never work again," Paul said.

Atticus looked at Beth.

She shook her head. "I know what you're thinking," she said, looking straight at him. "And the answer is *no....* *No!* Absolutely not. I am not leaving. My place is here with you. Come what may."

Kristi gripped Atticus's hand tighter and looked up at him, fear in her eyes.

"Okay, everybody," he said. "Look—we've made it this far, right? And I think by now we all know what not to do. Or we should know. Don't be out on deck at night, for one thing. And just take normal precautions. We'll unload in Duluth, have a nice easy steam back to Chicago, tie up and leave this ship for good."

"Word might get out, though," Paul said.

Atticus shook his head. "Not from me it won't. Far as I'm concerned, I never brought up any of this stuff. Matter of fact, this conversation never took place. And Teddy, what you said, you were right about how others will react. If anybody connects us with this ghost stuff, we might never work aboard ship again."

"Put this all behind us and shut up about it," Paul said.

"There you go. Just be careful, do our jobs, and keep quiet." Atticus let a smile spread across his face and looked down at Kristi. Then he leaned over and whispered something in her ear, to which she nodded with excitement, then giggled behind her hand.

"Paul and Teddy, we've been good friends. We've worked together quite a few times. When we all walk out of here in a minute, I want it to be on a positive note and with optimism about the future. I have some joyous news that Miss Kristi agrees I should share with you. If Miss Eaton will give her permission, I would like to make an announcement.”

He looked toward Beth.

She smiled, nodding an enthusiastic *yes*.

“Gentlemen, you’re the first to be told about this: Miss Eaton and I are going to be married.”

Paul and Teddy jumped to their feet, cheering and applauding. Kristi squealed, and clapped her hands too. Teddy and Atticus shook hands. Then Teddy extended his hand to Beth. She shook her head and opened her arms to him instead. “I’m afraid a handshake won’t do.” As they embraced, she said, “Mr. Teddy, I am sorry I ever doubted you. I hope you’ll find it in your heart to forgive me. And thank you so much for listening to me.”

“Can I get a hug too?” Paul said.

“I want that whole danged wall torn down,” Captain McBride demanded, nearly shouting.

“All of it, Captain?” Atticus asked.

“Every last evil, demonic splinter of it. Right to the very last paint chip.”

Atticus was amazed at the strength in the captain’s voice. Mere days since losing his arm and he seemed back in fine shape, his bandaged vestige of an arm the only reminder of his troubles.

The two of them stood just outside the pilothouse. The rain had stopped, and the sun was coming up. It promised a clear, mild day as the ship slowly steamed past DeTour, beginning its winding passage up the Saint Marys River on the way to the State Lock at Sault Sainte Marie.

"It's got to be all of it. How're you going to just scrape off the paint? It's even in the grooves. We need saws. Where's Diggs and his tools?"

"He's gone, sir. Back in Port Huron."

"He *left?* He jumped ship?"

"No, sir. He's gone. Died, I mean. From the fish, the sturgeon. Along with Mate MacMillis and Willy."

McBride gripped the handrail and lowered his head. "Oh Lord. My God, Mate. To think that it was me. I was the one who got this all started. I wanted a picture frame made; remember that? Oh, my God. I wondered what was on that other wall, and Diggs pulled off the first chip of what had covered that damned mural."

"Sir, I don't think—"

The captain shook his head, dismissing any notion that he was mistaken. "No, it's all my fault. I let him peel off some of that paint that covered the mural, Mr. Miles. And right away, I felt sick in that room.

"And I was having awful dreams. Terrible nightmares. Even one where I saw that unfortunate Indian princess, and the knife, and even one with a fellow in my cabin with a pistol, who—"

"Captain, there's no simple explanation."

"No, no, no," McBride insisted. "How on earth could I see such things before they occurred? And then what happened to Jefry. Right in that very cabin. Yes, I've already heard about that. It's all the mural. You've seen it, Atticus. Is it horrific or not?"

"It is horrid, I must say. Pretty ugly."

"Well, then. There we are. No, here's what we'll do: You gather four men right away, right now before breakfast, and saw that danged wall into little pieces along with those paint chips, and we'll feed it to the firebox. Feed it to the boilers and send that horror right out the smokestack, and we'll be done with it once and for all."

"Of course, Captain. Sure, if that's what you want. I'll take care of it right away."

"Good. I can bunk elsewhere for a few nights. After unloading, we'll have a leisurely sail back to Chicago. Then we'll all take some well-deserved time off. And now I want to offer my congratulations on your upcoming marriage to that beautiful and spirited young lady."

"Thanks, Cap. I appreciate that."

"Let me know how much time you'll need to take off, and I'll use what influence I have with the shipowner."

Atticus nodded. "And, of course, when we decide on a date for the celebration, you and your family are cordially invited. And the entire crew as well," he added with a big smile.

"Where's it going to be held?"

Atticus shrugged. "Why not Milwaukee?"

The captain threw his head back and laughed. "Oh boy, oh boy—we'll light up that town all right! The owner of Philip Best is a friend of mine; he'll bring in a canal boat full of lager for us. What a time we'll have."

Atticus was happy to see the captain show enthusiasm for something, all things considered.

"And those four men. The ones doing the cabin cleanup. Tell Paul they all get beefsteaks for lunch. As many as they want."

ELEVEN

Gerard LeBlanc threw open the firebox doors to empty the last bucketful of paint chips. His aim was off though, and he missed the opening and smacked the fire door with the bucket; half its contents spilled out.

He grabbed a shovel as fast as he could before Chief Murrick had a chance to get upset again. He'd become so nervous and short-tempered in recent days. The boiler room crews couldn't figure out why he was always so jumpy now, so they just tried to stay out of his way and not get him riled up.

The chief lowered his head and gave him a hard look over his spectacles—a sure sign you were about to get a scolding.

Not today, though.

"Be more careful, Gerry."

"Sorry, Chief." Gerry was relieved not to get yelled at. Maybe the chief knew the men were on edge. He was sure he'd heard about the weird stuff, too. Or maybe it was something else. Nobody could figure out what was bothering him. All they knew was that something was on his mind. The man was different now. Fellows said he hardly left his cabin anymore. Gerry couldn't figure out what it was all about, but something about him was odd.

It was always so much easier doing your job when the chief wasn't right there watching every move you made and making everyone nervous. At least he never stayed around too long before heading back topside.

Boilerman Bob Cuthbertson was minding the gauges, but he remained at his station. Gerry's spill incident wasn't serious, anyway. Gerry looked over, and Bob shook his head and smiled a little. He knew they were both thinking the same thing, and it was about the chief. He knew Bob was more concerned about a feedwater gauge, anyway. It would hang up and show water going into the boiler when it really wasn't. Not a big problem. Just a jiggle of the needle now and then, and after that the flow always steadied out. Bob had no intention of letting the chief know. Why the hell do that when he'd just get angry anyway?

Gerry swept up the last few paint chips, although a bunch of them had slipped through the cracks between the floor pans.

The chief clearly had something on his mind and never wanted to hear about anything that wasn't going perfectly. So, the stokers and boiler tenders all figured it was better to keep him happy by taking care of the minor problems themselves. Keep him thinking things were perfect. Which they were.

Almost.

"Gerry, I been seeing them little things everywhere up on deck," Bob said.

"What things?"

"Those stupid little paint chips."

"Yeah, I know. They're everywhere now—all over the place. Wind blew lots of them out of the buckets when I was bringing 'em back here from the captain's cabin."

Gerry was tense. Bob was tense too, and it seemed so was everyone else on board. By this time, everybody knew what had happened late the night before. The hanging man. And the lamps in the dining room. Teddy made sure everybody who showed up for breakfast that morning learned all about the strange events that had taken place. Everybody knew what had happened to Jefry and Wimmy too, also thanks to Teddy.

Teddy acted out the hanging man event at that morning's breakfast, and it spooked Gerry so much that he'd been terrified as he tossed the fragments of the mural into the firebox. The spill was his fault; he should've been more careful. He'd been too hasty getting rid of the contents of that bucket; that's all there was to it.

Despite the strangeness of the stories, Gerry had no doubt everything had happened just as Teddy had described. If a deckhand described something like that, he'd be more skeptical, figuring it was all just a crewman wanting to tell an entertaining story. But when so many others were a part of it all, Gerry thought, how can you have any doubts?

Once Chief Murrick climbed the ladder and disappeared out of the hatch, Gerry breathed a sigh of relief.

Bob hollered over. "Hey, Gerry. You want to go topside? Take a little break? Maybe get some fresh air? I'll shovel for you."

"Yeah, good. Thanks. I could use that. I'll see if Teddy has any food laid out too. You want anything?"

"Sure, why not? Piece of fruit, maybe."

Reaching the top of the ladder, Gerry stepped over the hatch coaming and onto the deck, liking the cool feel of outside air on his face. Instead of going straight into the crew messroom, he walked past it, back to the fantail, and stared down at the prop wash. Maybe the pretty English lady would be there again, just like the other day when they were about to blow down the boilers.

She would often stroll about the deck, and he knew he wasn't the only one who enjoyed having her on board. He was disappointed but not surprised that she wasn't there that day. She seemed such a happy, friendly person and, of course, was awfully nice to look at. He'd heard about the stupid comment the "Brooklyn" fellow had made about women on board ships. He didn't know anyone else who had such crazy notions. He woke up every day this trip hoping he'd get a chance to see her and say hello or even just nod. Those moments were the nicest part of his day. He was glad Jefry smacked that idiot Brooklyn around; he deserved it.

"Hey, Gerry." It was Teddy, leaning out and holding the galley's screen door open. "I got some leftover cake here. Take it away, will ya? I'll wrap it for you and Bob so I don't have to give it to the seagulls."

A minute later, Gerry was descending the ladder with a big smile on his face and an even bigger yearning for another taste of the chocolate layer cake from the day before.

Captain McBride stood just outside the pilothouse, looking aft as the State Lock at Sault Sainte Marie receded in the distance. Whitefish Point Light was abeam as the *Eli Greaves* steamed out of Whitefish Bay and into Lake Superior.

He had felt relief and satisfaction a minute earlier, watching as the mate on duty swung the engine-order telegraph to full ahead. Now he felt even better as the thick black smoke rose from the stack. One less thing to worry about, he thought as the smoke from coal and the awful mural billowed up into the chilly October sky.

How would his wife and daughters react upon his return home in a few days, minus an arm? He had sent a telegram from Port Huron informing them that, as a result of an injury, his arm had been amputated. He was inclined to be pragmatic about most things and was relieved that he'd lost the left arm rather than the right, but he could just imagine his family's response and knew there would be screaming and wailing and tears no matter which arm was missing.

Atticus, Beth, Jefry, and Wimmy stood together in the narrow passageway.

"Jefry, Wimmy, I don't enjoy having to do this," Atticus said. "But I need to know how it feels to you in there. The men who did the cleaning said they felt nothing odd. The captain wanted the wall torn down, so now it's gone."

Maribeth gently touched Jefry's shoulder. "Are you okay?"

He nodded.

"Everybody ready?"

No one nodded or spoke, nor did either crewman object as the first mate slowly opened the door to McBride's cabin. The room had been swept and swabbed. Gone was the wall displaying the mural. Save for wooden support studs, now there was nothing between the captain's cabin and the adjacent dry storage room. The awful smell was gone too.

Wimmy made his way cautiously into the cabin, holding out his arms, reaching into the corners, waving his hands around the wall studs and making broad sweeping motions like a symphony conductor, or a magician trying to make his rabbit appear. Generally making quite a show of feeling around for invisible entities. He stopped in the middle of the room and shrugged. "Nothing," he announced.

"Jefry?" Atticus said.

"I'm sorry, Mate Miles. I just can't do it."

"That's okay. All right, Wimmy, c'mon. Let's close up this cabin. And thanks to you both."

Jefry turned to Maribeth. "Miss Eaton, the man you saw at the table, the one who was grinning. You said he was wearing railroad overalls and a tan shirt, correct?"

"Uh-huh, yes."

"And that he sat near the end of the table?"

"First mate's place maybe," she said with a shrug.

"My gosh," Atticus said. "And I'm in the first mate's cabin. And your overalls—I took them from that dresser."

"I'm wearing *his clothes!*" Beth shrieked, then dashed out of the room.

"How could I do that?" Atticus said. "That may be the suicide's clothing, and I gave it to her to wear."

A few moments later, Beth's cabin door opened, and the overalls and tan shirt came flying out.

Atticus snatched up the garments and headed for the door. "These are going straight into the firebox."

T.G. McBride put down his fork and pushed his plate away. Dabbed his mouth with a crisp cotton napkin and let it fall to the table. He was aware of being watched by everyone else in the dining room. They were respectful, but no one dared start a conversation with their now one-armed captain.

He took the initiative: "I suppose this'll get easier someday. I'll have to get better at the knife-and-fork business though."

That brought a quiet chuckle of relief. McBride was relieved as well. He'd suspected that recent events had left the crew spooked, unsure of just how their captain would respond to all the tumult and tragedy. Would he be the same? Would he be heartbroken and morose, spending his days sulking in his cabin, or become some sort of one-armed storybook tyrant?

"I have a joke," he said.

Everybody's face lit up.

"How does a one-armed captain tie his shoes?"

Everyone chuckled at once. Maribeth did as well, but no one dared reply.

McBride shrugged. "I don't know either, but I'll let you know when I figure it out."

The table erupted in laughter and applause.

Beth leaned toward him. "Well done, sir," she whispered. *"Well done."*

He thanked her and whispered something in response.

After the meal, Beth joined him along the starboard rail.

He heaved a sigh of relief. "That went as well as expected."

"Come, sir, much better than that. You did magnificently. What's the saying? You had them on the edge of their seats."

McBride smiled. "I had to do something. They were all wondering, trying to figure me out. I've felt it all day."

She nodded. "I sensed it too. Not anymore, though, Captain. You handled that like the leader you are."

"Don't go too far with that kind of talk. Pride goeth before destruction and all of that."

Beth smiled. "And a haughty spirit before a fall."

"Indeed."

"Mmm, Proverbs 16:18," she said. "I knew them all, once upon a time, but…"

McBride nodded. "Life goes on."

"It does. And in the day-to-day, sometimes you end up setting aside some cherished and important things."

For several moments, they stared in silence across the endless expanse of Lake Superior.

"I've often been told about how majestic this lake is," she said. "But nothing can prepare you for the reality. Nothing."

"Étienne Brûlé," Mc Bride said.

She gave him a puzzled look. "I think I've heard that name, but…"

"Born in France, fifteen ninety-two. He came to New France—today's Canada—at age sixteen with Samuel de

Champlain's first group of settlers. Seeing the dreary and hopeless existence they faced in what eventually became Quebec City—malnutrition, starvation, scurvy— he took up with the native tribes and adopted what the French call *ensauvager*."

"The wild life," she said.

"Yes. That's exactly the life he adopted. He aligned himself with the Miq'maq, the Montaignais, and later on, the Algonquin, and the Wyandot Huron. Learned their languages, and their ways. They accepted him. It wasn't a comfortable life, but at that time probably better than life for a poor man in France, and he was even tortured by the Seneca at one point—they were an enemy of the Wyandot—somewhere in what's central New York today. Later, he became a *coureur des bois* for Champlain—a woods runner.

"He didn't live long. Died at age forty. Not many woods runners lived long lives. Hazards of that occupation. One day, on an expedition, he saw the depression in the earth that the glaciers left—perhaps ten thousand years before and which had filled with glacial melt water, and which today contains one tenth of the world's fresh water—this lake that lies before us."

Beth gazed at the endless lake. "Our young and wild Monsieur Étienne Brûlé was the first European to see Lake Superior."

"Exactly," the captain said. "The first one as far as we know, and I like to think the sight of it affected him as it has so many others, even up until the present day. Myself, I went to sea at age ten, and by the time I was about your age, I'd sailed all of the world's oceans, but after one trip on the upper lakes—especially this one—I knew I'd never want to work anywhere but the Great Lakes. There's nothing else like them. Anywhere else in the world. And I've seen the world.

"I wasn't even thirty yet, but I was already feeling that I'd done enough, seen enough, and wanted nothing more than to settle down. So, I found work on the lakes and have never looked back. Well, I've been feeling something like that—again—for several days now. And that's partly why I asked you to meet me out here on deck."

She waited for him to continue.

"I'll let you know of a decision I made just a couple of hours ago. You may share this with Atticus. I have decided that when I step off the ship in Chicago, I won't be coming back. This is to be my last trip. I'm going to retire."

"Congratulations, sir. You've earned your retirement. I can only imagine what comfort that will bring to your wife and daughters."

"I hope so. They'll all want to watch over me like mother hens from now on. Making sure I stay out of trouble."

"Of course. And I have a suggestion if you don't mind."

"Not at all. Please. I'd like to hear it."

"That you wire the bad news to her as soon as we reach Chicago. About your arm, I mean."

"Of course, yes. I know what you're referring to. And I like the way you think. I took care of that before leaving Port Huron. Sent a telegram. Couldn't wait for a response, of course. No time for that. But I let them know I'm okay otherwise. Good spirits, fine fettle, all of that. And they know I'll be back home for good this time."

"The shock will have worn off by the time you make it back."

"Yes, I hope so anyway. Now the second thing: I'd like to know what you think of this idea. Because all of us will part company soon, and after the misfortunes we've seen on this voyage, I thought of something that I'd like to do. Something that'll end the trip happily for us all." He paused for a few moments. "Would you do me the honor of letting me perform the marriage ceremony for you and Atticus?"

"Oh, spectacular! What a wonderful idea." She clapped her hands. "Yes, yes, *of course*."

"Right here on board the ship."

"Perfect, perfect. Oh *yes*."

"And young Kristi, she can be a part of it too."

"That's so thoughtful, sir. Thanks so much. She'll love that."

"Yes, I'm sure she will. Very sad story about her parents, by the way."

"Captain McBride, Atticus and I have decided we'll raise her as our own. And Frankie, too. We hope that'll be okay with…"

"Oh, of course. My sister-in-law knew Frankie would be with her only temporarily. I made that clear at the time. I figured there'd be some sort of solution for him, and was pretty sure something would come up. And it has, hasn't it? I couldn't have imagined anything more perfect, though—you and Atticus. I am so glad you'll make a home for them both. Poor things. So sad. But not sad for long; and you've just given me the best news I've heard in a long time, Miss Eaton. What an ordeal for them both. Now with you and Atticus, all the sadness will fade."

"Yes, sir. I hope to make that happen."

"Well, here's what I'd like to do: Have your wedding in the pilothouse, then maybe with Steward Paul's help, we'll contrive some sort of incident just as the ceremony ends, one that will require the groom's immediate attention back aft. He'll be the only one not in on the secret."

"Oh, what fun!"

"Yes, and we'll all be there, of course, along with whatever crew members aren't on watch. We'll surprise him with a wedding reception in the dining room."

"I'm all for it. Just tell me what I need to do."

"I shall. I'll get to work on it. One last thing: an observation if you don't mind. We may not have another chance to talk like this."

"Of course."

"You and Atticus. You'll do great things together."

"I hope so, sir."

The captain shook his head. "I know so. I see it in the two of you. You will not have a conventional life. You may even have an extraordinary one.

"Here's how I see you two: You're the pilot. The navigator. With your background, you can see the way ahead and how to get there. You have the vision born of your education and having witnessed the breadth of your family's business activities at an early age. You'll see the possibilities and figure things out from there. The where and the how and the when.

"Atticus, he's the boilers and the steam engine; he's the fearless force that'll power you all through everything and anything that gets in your way."

"I tell him he's my soldier, my Tennessee gunslinger."

McBride threw his head back and laughed. "Oh, precisely." He laughed again. "I really like that. Yes, he is, isn't he, and you two are quite the pair, aren't you? And the children, thank you so much for taking them under your wings."

"It'll be a pleasure, sir."

"Now, whenever I see you and Kristi together, it strikes me how you're such a natural pair. Already I think of you as mother and daughter."

Maribeth wiped away a tear. "That's how I see us too," she said. "I love her so much."

"I am so happy about that. It gives me such joy to hear you'll all become a family. Now I'll think of you two—all four of you, actually—as the highlight of this trip…. No, more than that…the capstone of my career."

"Thank you, Captain McBride."

"That first time I saw Kristi, I knew there'd been some tragedy or misfortune. When agents asked me to be her chaperone, I wasn't given any details. Maybe they didn't know much, either. Having those three girls of my own, I can spot it right away. The fear, the sadness… Confusion too, I guess. Lost and alone. That all told me something terrible had happened."

"She'll always be safe with us, sir. Safe and happy."

"Of course she will. And that is a great relief for me. She deserves some joy in this life. You and Atticus will be good for her, and I believe you'll all find happiness. It might be at sea level, or it may be on a mountaintop, but I think you'll find it."

"Mr. Willy, do you see me?"

Kristi was in the crew messroom by herself, sitting on one of the stools that surrounded the mess table. She braced herself when the ship rolled with a wave. A wooden box was attached to the tabletop. In it were coffee cups and dispensers of salt, pepper, and sugar. The ship shuddered briefly as it rolled; cups clinked.

"Can you hear me? I am sorry what happen to you, sir," she said, first looking around the room, then leaning out to where she could see a bit of the galley. "Very sad thing." She leaned some more, listening, tilting her head, then got up and went into the galley.

There were pots and pans in the drying rack; they clanked together as the ship moved.

Kristi looked up and smiled broadly. Looked up toward the corner where the ceiling met the wall. "We are okay, I think. It is a little stormy though. You look sad. Please don't be sad."

She tilted her head, took a step forward, seemed to listen, then nodded, crossed the room, and opened a drawer. "This place? Here?" she said. "Not sure, but I'll look." She rummaged in the drawer, then held up a wooden spoon. "No?"

She put the spoon back and rummaged some more, holding up a pair of scissors next, then a rolling pin. She looked up. Shrugged, shook her head, reached farther back, back to the end of the drawer, then leaned forward and peered inside. She squeaked in surprise, then withdrew her hand. In it was a small suede bag. She clutched it tight but did not open it.

"This? Yes?" she chirped. "Okay, I take it. I take care of it. Thank you, thank you."

Brooklyn unscrewed the cap on his whiskey flask and took a sip. Just a little sip because he had boiler watch in an hour. Didn't want anybody smelling his breath.

All he kept near his bunk was the small flask, which he normally carried inside his boot. He'd fill this from a full bottle that he'd hidden in a nook elsewhere on board.

He put the cap back on and slid the flask under his mattress. While doing that, he saw a few more of those damned paint chips that were everywhere now. Sticking to soles of shoes and getting tracked all over the place. He brushed them into his hand and tossed them into the wastebasket.

Then he went back to bed, hoping for a nice quick nap before watch. He needed one. Hadn't slept well in recent days. Felt sick to his stomach all the time now, too.

"I don't want you out on deck by yourself anymore," Atticus said. "Neither you nor Kristi. Not after everything we talked about with Paul and Teddy. Night or day. All right? And after dark, please don't roam the ship. Just stay here in your cabin."

"Yes, that was my intention already," Beth said.

"Anywhere you need to go, I'll escort you. We'll be aboard just a few more days; then we'll be done with the

Eli Greaves forever. Or whatever its name is. And I'm not comfortable in the first mate's cabin anymore."

"Stay here with us. I'd feel so much better if you would."

"Then I'll bring in my mattress. I can sleep on the floor."

"Oh yes. Wonderful. We'll make room. Yes, do that please. What a grand idea." She leaned a little toward him. "There's something else on your mind, darling."

He looked down for a moment and shook his head, puzzled. "They're saying things about Chief Engineer Murrick."

"Who is? What things?"

"Got this from Paul, but the engineers are saying things." He shrugged. "I don't know. Nothing's real clear. He can be moody, and from what I've heard, he's always been enigmatic and peculiar, but it seems it's more than that."

"He hasn't showed up in the dining room at all."

"No. He hasn't, has he? We've not seen him there. I asked Teddy if he's been eating, and he said yes. But he'll just stop in the galley and take food up to his cabin."

"Is that so odd?"

"Well, no. We've all done it now and again, but this has been going on since Chicago." He shook his head. "I just don't want anything else to go wrong. We're so close to finishing out this trip."

She took his hand, then leaned toward him and gave him a kiss.

Atticus stood up and walked over to the porthole. "Lot of lightning off to the northwest. Weather's on the way."

He started toward the door. "My watch is coming up soon. Let me get my mattress. I'll need to get some sleep, and you and Kristi can settle into bed too."

"Okay, darling."

Once Atticus left the cabin, Beth gave Kristi a look. "What is it, honey? You look like the cat that ate the canary. What's that you've got?"

Kristi held up the suede bag.

"What's in it?"

Kristi shrugged, smirking.

"Does that belong to somebody?"

Kristi nodded. "Mr. Willy."

"No, honey. I don't see how—"

"He gives it to me, shows me where it is."

"Wh…when? When was this?"

"Few minutes ago. He shows me. He is *Spøkelsa* now."

Beth placed her hand on her forehead. *God*, she thought. *Just what I need…more ghosts.* Slowly, she took a deep breath, then exhaled. She nodded. "That's nice, honey. That's very nice."

Kristi opened the bag and shook it over the mattress. Out tumbled a wood carving of a horse, a pocketknife, some silver coins, a gold wedding ring, and a small locket. Beth opened the locket. Inside was a miniature painting of a woman in profile. Also in the bag was a piece of folded-up beeswax paper. She unfolded that to reveal a small piece of newspaper, also folded. She carefully opened that to find a hand-beaded frame made of cloth, inside of which was a tintype photo of Mr. Willy, some years younger, with a lady—presumably his wife—at his side.

Beth's voice wavered. "These were his personal things, his cherished things."

Kristi nodded.

"And I suppose this was his wife." Beth wiped tears from her eyes and put her arm around Kristi. "Oh, honey. This was really his, wasn't it. Oh, my gosh. And he showed you where to find it." Her voice wavered more, and her hands shook. "These were special mementos for him. His cherished memories. He wanted you to have them, didn't he, sweetheart. He wanted you to have them."

Atticus looked up from the chart table when he saw lightning dead ahead but far off. Heavy weather coming for sure. Off the port bow, he saw only darkness, though, and that worried him.

"Gene, we should've seen Copper Harbor Light by now."

"You figure?"

"Yep. Plot works out that way. But over there, off the port bow. Nothing. Not even a distant glow."

"Yeah, you'd think we woulda—"

"The telegraph, what's it at? Still full ahead, right?"

"Yeah, since last watch."

"And I know you haven't changed it."

"No, of course not."

Atticus muttered a curse under his breath. "We're not going as fast as I thought. It's not my plot; I've checked and rechecked my figures. We should be here." He jabbed the chart with his forefinger.

"And we'd see the light by now."

"Yeah," Atticus said, looking out the window and shaking his head. "I knew it. Damn it. I knew it. We've been going slower the whole trip. It hasn't felt right. I just figured I hadn't got the feel of the ship, yet. It didn't show up much on the rivers or the lower lakes. And back on Lake Huron, we had to turn around, so… But out here, it really shows up. No lights to go by for a couple hundred miles. It throws off my speed, for the dead reckoning. Throws it all off. This is no good; we can't be sure where we are."

"Yeah, and with weather coming."

"Exactly. Just what we don't need." He spun around. "I'm going back to the engine room, see if I can find out what's going on. You going to be okay?"

"Sure, Mate."

The windows rattled in their frames.

Atticus opened the door to the stairway. "Look at this. I need to really push it against this wind. We're gonna get something for sure. Are we falling off in this sea? Are we wallowing? How's she steering?"

"I'm having to work her more than usual. Getting a little harder to keep her on course."

"Damn," Atticus said. "Any slower and we'll lose steerageway. Okay, gonna go check with the engineer. I won't be long."

"Be careful out there."

A minute later, Atticus descended the engine room ladder. In the dim light of the room, he saw the reciprocating steam engine's steel piston rod working up and down, to the tune and to the sight of bursts of steam shooting from relief valves. The rich essence of lubricating oil and steam filled the engine room.

As Atticus stepped off at the bottom, the second engineer came over and they shook hands. "Welcome to God's country, Mate Miles," the man shouted, over the mechanical noise.

"Thanks. Nice and warm down here; good place to be on a chilly night."

"How may I help you?"

"What are we doing for speed? My plot's showing us farther west, but I'm not seeing it. We're at full ahead up in the pilothouse, and I see the telly here is set the same. What're you doing for revolutions?"

"Not quite what they ought to be I'm afraid. Been wondering why myself. Just about to go check. Let's go next door to the boiler room and see what's going on. We're wide open here, but I don't feel it cranking like it ought to."

At the ladder, the engineer put his foot on the first rung and stopped. "Maybe that's what it is…"

"What's that?"

The man shook his head. "I'm not sure. Something's different. I've been feeling it all night."

"Feeling what? About the revolutions?"

"Can't say for sure. Different things. Some men have been feeling sick, for one." He shook his head and shrugged, then climbed up the ladder with Atticus following.

When they reached the boiler room, the stoker was leaning on his coal shovel, and the boiler tender was watching the gauges for steam pressure and feedwater. The engineer walked over and talked to him, yelling over the roar of the firebox.

"He says we're not making pressure enough for full ahead."

Atticus shook his head. "But why is—"

The boiler tender waved the engineer back, and they talked for half a minute more.

"He says the chief came down and had the stoker damp the fire."

"Why would he slow us down?" Atticus shouted over the surrounding roar. "This is no good. We need to go faster. Wind's coming. Bigger seas too. At this speed, we're gonna lose steerage and roll."

"I'll have him bring up the fire. We'll have some pretty good pressure then. That'll get the speed up to where you need it."

"Do that. Please. Quick as you can."

"Right away."

Daybreak

"Thanks so much all of you for being here," Beth said to the men. She was in the now-vacant captain's quarters with several crew members, among them Teddy, Paul, Jefry, and Eugene. Deckhands Hake and Fournier were there, too.

"Thank you for being here, Jefry and Gene. I realize you've just gotten off watch and are probably worn out.

Atticus is across the passageway, getting a little sleep. And to the rest of you, thanks as well for agreeing to help me out with this. I know you're all busy too, and I am grateful you're here.

"I'll not take up too much of your time. You all know what this is about, so no need to repeat that. The captain says the ceremony will be symbolic and not official because he doesn't have the authority to perform one legally. But we're going to do it here today because we wanted officers and crew to share this happy moment with us. Who knows where we'll all be in a few weeks' time?

"Captain McBride will be in the pilothouse to perform the ceremony. Gene will be at the wheel. Then, just as we finish up, Jefry will run up to say Atticus is needed back aft immediately, and Paul and the rest of you will have things all set up for the reception, and you'll take it from there."

The ship lurched; those present looked at one another as they reset their stance to keep from falling over. One went to the nearby porthole and looked out. Maribeth opened the door and looked up and down the passageway. "Excuse me for just a moment." She went into her cabin. No Kristi.

Atticus was just waking up.

"Atticus, have you seen—?"

A metallic clatter came from out on deck. He jumped up and went to the porthole. "Uh-oh, looking wild out there. That sky. Tornado green."

"Have you seen Kristi?"

"No. I just woke up."

She ran back to the captain's cabin. "Has *anybody* seen Kristi?"

Atticus showed up in the doorway, still groggy from sleep. "What're y'all doing here?"

"Who's seen her? *Anybody?*" said a now-frantic Beth.

"In the galley," Teddy said. "Fetching a pot of tea for you. She's not back yet?"

Atticus walked to the end of the passageway and threw open the door, then slammed it shut again. "Don't anybody go back aft. It's glare ice everywhere out on deck."

Returning to her cabin, Beth made sure the porthole was shut tight. She looked out again. Windblown ice struck the glass, sounding like bits of gravel. She started toward the cabin door and was suddenly walking uphill. Things crashed somewhere outside. Desk items slid off and onto the floor. The ship stayed over as if to capsize. Beth struggled to make her way to the door but couldn't reach it. When the ship rolled the other way, Beth slipped and was thrown onto her back, slid across the cabin and into the wall.

Men shouted out in the passageway just beyond her door, and she heard them running aft toward the cargo deck.

Atticus threw open the door. "Ice is everywhere out there. Stay in here for now."

"But—*Kristi!*" Beth cried, getting back on her feet, just as he slammed the door shut.

The second engineer pounded on the door to the chief's cabin again and again with no answer. The ship rolled, propelling him against the door. It burst open, and there was the chief. On the floor, on hands and knees, grinning like a madman.

"Thirty," Chief Murrick said triumphantly, holding up a gold coin. He put the coin in a suede bag, then reached for another and put that one in the bag too. "Do you see? They're all still here. I just gotta find 'em; that's all."

"Chief, we're losing the steering engine!"

"Yes, yes. Of course. Steering's important. Now, if you'll just give me a minute…" He scrambled around on hands and knees, looking for more of his scattered coins.

"We can't steer the ship!"

The chief straightened up for a moment, seemed to understand the gravity of the situation. Then he smiled and nodded. "Very well. Carry on." Mumbling, he went back to rounding up his treasure.

Brooklyn was sick and close to throwing up. Surrounding him was a kaleidoscope of a thousand colors.

The second engineer showed up and ran to the gauges, then to the firebox, and screamed at the top of his voice.

Brooklyn looked up. "What?"

"I said we got no pressure. What's the matter with you? You deaf? Where's the stoker?" He pointed to an empty whiskey bottle. "What the hell's that?" Then he cursed as he picked it up, then threw it off to one side. It smashed against an iron brace nearby.

Brooklyn realized his own whiskey flask was on the floor too, right between his feet. He shifted a foot to conceal it. "What's going on?"

The ship rolled violently.

"We're losing it. *You can't feel it?*" The engineer took a wide stance and held on to a nearby pipe. "Where the hell is the stoker?"

"I dunno, but Chief had him damp the fire."

"*Again?* When? Is he crazy? Good God!"

"Maybe twenty minutes ago."

The engineer threw open the firebox door. Nothing but smoldering ash and some glowing embers. No fire at all. He grabbed the shovel. "What the *hell* are you *doing* down here? We got no fire, no steam, no pressure, no revolutions, no nothing. Steering engine's just shut down too."

Frantically he hurled in a few shovels full of coal, then lit an oil rag, held it out in front of him, watched as its flame grew, then he threw it into the firebox and shoveled in more coal on top of it, then slammed the door.

The ship rolled heavily again; tools clanked in their toolboxes.

"We've lost headway, lost steering. And we're in a storm. You can't tell? What the hell's wrong with you?"

Brooklyn had no answer other than to shrug his shoulders and shake his head. He was feeling sicker by the minute, and the engineer standing there yelling at him didn't help.

"Grab the other shovel. Feed that box. *Move!* We gotta make steam."

Brooklyn got to his feet, and everything immediately went sideways. He slammed into a pipe and ended up flat on his face on the metal deck plate.

The engineer came over and offered his hand. Brooklyn took it and stood up again.

Then the man kicked at something on the deck plate, and Brooklyn's flask went spinning across the surface with a metallic clatter. "And you're drunk too?"

Brooklyn felt even sicker now.

"Get shoveling! Come on!"

The engineer cursed and kicked the flask once more, and it spun away out of sight, clattered two or three times, then disappeared, clanging, ricocheting off piping in the surrounding–darkness. "Keep on shoveling and don't stop!" he shouted, then raced up the ladder.

The moment Brooklyn started shoveling, he felt even more sick. Convinced he was about to throw up. But he kept on shoveling, now wondering where the stoker had gone. It was hard to keep his balance, what with the ship rolling so much, and at one point he hurled a shovelful of coal at the firebox but forgot to open the door first, and lumps of coal scattered everywhere.

But the more he shoveled, the more the hungry firebox roared. The dancing yellow flames inside gobbled up every bit of coal as fast as he heaved it in. It was hypnotic, and the louder the fire roared, the more energy it seemed to give him. The draft of the huge fire sucking in the air roared like a tornado, and he felt it pulling on him too. In the firelight, he saw it inhale the coal dust that swirled around every time he swung the shovel, and his shirt ruffled in the breeze it made.

Brooklyn lay face down on the metal deck plate. He lifted his head, realizing he had passed out.

A shout.

Movement off to his right.

The chief. Coming down the ladder.

And fast.

Brooklyn knew even before glancing at the gauges, just by the sound and the smell in the room, that he'd let the boiler run dry, under full fire. He had forgotten to let in the feedwater. If he had been sober, he might have remembered that water expands seventeen hundred times upon conversion to steam. It would have given him pause.

But he was overheated, exhausted, sick. And drunk.

He panicked, surrounded by blistering heat, bright yellow flames, and red-glowing iron. It was so hot in the boiler room that it felt like his body was on fire.

Another shout from the chief.

Sliding down the ladder too fast, the chief lost his footing halfway. His legs got tangled in the ladder rungs, throwing him sideways, slamming him hard onto the iron plating.

Brooklyn stumbled over to the boiler and spun the wheels hard to open fully the cold feedwater and at the same moment saw the chief try but fail to get to his feet, managing only to drag himself closer on crippled legs. Scuffing and dragging himself crablike across the deck plate on his ruined legs, Chief Murrick was waving, shaking his head, shouting, his eyes huge with panic.

No! No! No! his mouth said, but Brooklyn heard no words, only the deafening squeal of escaping steam and the rivets popping off like gunshots, the clattering of piping and the chugging and shuddering of the boiler as it shook the whole room—and the whole ship—until it finally gave up and blew apart.

TWELVE

Day One

The pilothouse windows all blew out; glass shards sprayed across the room, the roof ripped open and folded over. The entire house lifted a few feet, and the ship surged up and down as though striking lake waves.

Beth looked up. The ceiling was gone. Roiling gray sky swirled and lightning flashed overhead where the ceiling had been. Papers and nautical charts lifted off tables and swirled around the room as if by ghostly forces. Men shouted, ran in all directions.

Stunned, Beth took hold of the chart table to steady herself. Her ears were ringing. More shouting. Atticus and Jefry both grabbed her at the same time and yanked her over to the side door.

Jefry ran back inside; Atticus helped her down the iron steps and onto the foredeck, Beth clinging to him. Debris rained down everywhere, clattered all around them, splashed in the water. Atticus pushed her down and threw himself onto her to shield her from the falling wreckage. A chunk of cast iron big as a woodstove landed with a clang six feet away. It shook everything and buried itself into the deck and then just sat there, still red-hot, sizzling, smoking and crackling.

Beth looked aft. The ship ended at the last cargo hatch. Nearly everything beyond that was gone. Only part of one wall of the after deckhouse remained. The stack was gone.

The second level was nowhere to be seen. Gone, and along with it, the entire crew's quarters. What remained of the first level was still there, still attached, somehow, swinging back and forth in the seas. She couldn't tell if the galley and crew messroom were still there or if they were gone, too.

"Atticus, what just hap—?"

"Boiler explosion."

The first patch of the storm seemed to have passed, but ugly skies and tall seas surrounded them still. The ship made cracking and creaking noises as it twisted and flexed in the waves.

Back aft, two crewmen hung on to a remnant of the side rail, making their way along to get to a safer place. One of them held the rail with one hand while reaching out with the other to help his fellow crewman.

Then a third person. Smaller, shorter. By the hair color, Beth knew it was Kristi. Also struggling. Also hanging on, trying to get to a safer place.

The first man reached out once more, stretching toward Kristi, and she reached for his hand just as the entire aft section suddenly rose with a passing wave, followed by a foaming white crest that washed over all of it. What was left of the stern section—the rail, the deckhouse, and what remained of the fantail—tore away, then fell behind, floating free, the two men and Kristi all hanging on. It all floated for a few moments, then slipped beneath the surface. Gone.

Everything and everyone.

Gone.

Atticus got to his feet.

"All she wanted was to get tea for me!" Beth cried.

"I know. C'mon, we need to go. No time. Let's go!" He grabbed her hand and took her down the stairs to the cargo deck. "It's all icy here. Watch your step."

Everyone else who'd been in the pilothouse discussing wedding preparations was there on the cargo deck already. They were strangely quiet, grabbing wood and torn tarps, pallets, ropes, boxes, and casks. Whatever would float. They seemed to know exactly what to do, and did all this while hanging on for dear life, trying to keep from sliding down the icy deck and into the frigid lake.

Jefry came over with an armful of wood and canvas to help Atticus prepare rafts.

"Will help come?" Beth asked.

Jefry shook his head.

"Can't we find her?"

"No," Atticus said. "Impossible. Ship's sinking."

She looked around.

The aft end of the ship was gone, completely gone. Dining room, galley, where the engine and boiler were… all of it gone. The ship ended now at one of the hatches. Even that was already slipping into the lake, the deck slanting as it did so, weighed down by the cargo of coal.

Hake tied pieces together for the captain, who couldn't do much for himself. Eugene was also busy, as were Paul and Fournier and Teddy. They threw things together for one another so quickly she could hardly make sense of it all.

Jefry held out some long pieces of rope to Atticus. He cut them with his knife, and then they were busy tying knots.

From aft there came an ominous grinding. The sinking ship lurched; one by one, the holds surrendered their cargo of coal to the depths. The ship shuddered as water rushed eagerly up the deck.

Atticus and Jefry both shouted something to her and gestured that she should lie down on the raft. They put tarps over her and ropes over that, tightened the ropes, then added more still. While Atticus continued the rope tying, Jefry dropped to his knees next to Maribeth, placed his hand on her forehead, and then with his thumb and forefinger made a cross there.

"The Lord is my shepherd; I shall not want. He maketh me to lie down in green pastures: he leadeth me beside the still waters…"

Someone shouted, and Beth saw Hake and Eugene launch the captain's raft. They had covered him with tarps, and they had him tied down too. He glanced over toward Beth and nodded; she did the same. Hake and Eugene pushed the captain's raft away; each of them prepared another raft, then pushed themselves away from the ship.

More shouting from the remaining men as they finished making their rafts.

"…restoreth my soul: he leadeth me in the paths of righteousness—"

Another cargo hold gave way with a splash.

Jefry shrugged off his thick wool sweater and held it out for Maribeth. "Lift your arms."

"No, you keep it. You have no shirt underneath."

He shook his head and pulled the sweater over her; she pushed her hands through its arms.

He began speaking louder and faster as the ship shifted again, slipping lower and lower into the water.

As Atticus finished tying Beth to her raft, she reached up and took Jefry by the hand. He held her hand in both of his. They didn't need to say anything. He tried to smile, and so did she. He began saying something in a low voice in his native language: *"Ho-wa-gi tha-thi"* but it was drowned out by men shouting and the cargo holds crashing and even louder sounds of the ship flexing as it made its final complaints before settling beneath the surface.

Despite the noise, Jefry continued. Beth watched his lips move as he quietly chanted over her in his language. He said things in Latin too. And then he began reciting silently, but she could see his lips forming the words of his chants and then of the twenty-third Psalm again:

"Through the valley of the shadow of death, I will fear no evil: for thou art with me; thy rod and thy staff they comfort me..."

Lake water was only a couple of yards away. All the cargo hatches had broken off. The air trapped in the forward compartments was all that kept the ship afloat now.

Atticus placed his lips against her ear. "We're all tied together, darling Beth. Remember to cover yourself and stay under the tarps and the rope. Try to stay warm. If it gets freezing, don't go to sleep. We'll both be watching over you." He gave her a kiss, his eyes full of love and terror in equal measure.

When the ship lurched, Jefry nearly lost his balance.

"Time to go, Jefry," Atticus said.

They lifted Beth's raft away and lowered it into the lake, and it floated free. They were both up to their knees in the water. The bow section was steadily going vertical, but quicker now. Atticus gave her raft a push, and she saw them both pay out the rope that connected her with them, and they grew smaller and smaller. Then Jefry got onto his raft, and Atticus shoved it off and then got onto his own raft and shoved it off, too.

They were all floating free now and could do nothing but watch the ship as it settled lower and lower into the cold, deep waters of Lake Superior.

Seconds later, what remained of the ship was pointing straight up. The pilothouse slipped quietly beneath the surface, followed by the ship's bow itself. And then only the long, white steering pole remained, settling lower and lower, until it too was gone.

Turbulence from air bubbles followed. Debris and flotsam bobbed up. It surrounded them in all directions. Wooden framing from the hatches, deck boxes, the dining room table upside down and missing most of its legs, a chair, somebody's trunk, then another one. Small packages everywhere.

Atticus shouted; Jefry threw a piece of broken board to him, and Atticus untied his rope and used the broken board to paddle toward some floating packages. He reached for one and pulled it out of the water. Then he paddled toward another one. The men on the other rafts were paddling and picking things out of the water, too. Jefry hauled in the rope that connected his raft to Beth's, pulling it hand over hand until his raft bumped up against hers.

"Are you okay, miss?" he said.

"I think so."

He pointed toward Atticus. "Had to untie his raft. Couldn't pull us both with him. He's checking for food packages floating around."

Beth nodded.

"He'll find something; try to stay warm."

She nodded again.

He held out something for her. "Here, take this. Put it on." It was his wool cap. "Drink water from the lake. And don't be afraid." He waved and let the rope go slack again. Slowly they drifted apart.

She put on the wool cap, then lay back on the pallet and sighed, thinking they were all lucky it wasn't as stormy anymore.

Beth looked up. She knew she'd slept because now the sun was lower in the sky. There was not a sound to be heard. Not even the wind. Even the waves lapping against the raft had stopped.

She lifted her head some more and propped herself up onto her elbow. Jefry's raft was still attached, and she could see Atticus and one group of three rafts in the distance, but not the third group.

Atticus was still hard at work, paddling with his broken board. But he was farther away than he had been.

There was not as much debris in the water now.

Already it was hard and uncomfortable to lift her head up, and her neck was sore. She couldn't look around for long. This was like being a bug trapped in a cocoon or spider's web. The ropes and tarps were heavy, and her legs were already sore. She could move her feet a little, but not anything above that. Between her ankles and her hips, she couldn't move at all. If only she could turn. But no, that was impossible. She understood it was to keep her from falling off. Still, it was uncomfortable.

She lifted herself from the waist, up onto her elbow. Her hands were free, and she could turn her head this way and that.

All it took to reach the water was to stretch her arm a little, so she only had to cup her hand, then bring the handful of water over and plop it into her mouth. She couldn't hold much in her palm, but three or four scoops, and she'd had a good drink.

Except for this confinement, she was not too miserable. Atticus and Jefry had made sure there was one corner of the tarp loose enough to flip over in the rain, or to block the sun, or against waves.

When will people on shore realize our ship is late? she wondered. *And then how soon will they tell other ships to be on the lookout for us?* Telegrams would go out to shore stations eventually, and lifeboat crews would be on alert. But no one knew where they were and didn't even know yet that the *Eli Greaves* had sunk. Or the *Monetoo*—whatever its real name was. They'd know the ship was somewhere between Sault Sainte Marie and Duluth, but those cities were four hundred miles apart.

It would be days before anybody even thought to search for them. What if it gets cold? Or stormy again?

Exhausted already. She tried to lie flat and relax a bit. She thought about Atticus and lifted her head to see where he was. He'd made it a little closer with a few packages on his raft, and he was paddling toward her and Jefry.

Waking up to the gentle sound of water lapping against the underside of her raft.

Pitch-black out.

Nothing to see across the lake's surface. No moon. Couldn't see Jefry, but assumed he was still close, and that Atticus had tied his own raft to them again. She hoped he had anyway. She felt the slightest bit of breeze against her face and prayed it wasn't blowing Atticus away from her and Jefry. A beautiful canopy of stars was overhead, but at the moment, it didn't give her any feeling of peacefulness.

Listening. Then listening more but hearing nothing save the gentle lapping of the water underneath her. It was such a relaxing sound. So peaceful…

Day Two

From the *Copper Harbor Independent*, Copper Harbor, Michigan.

Boom Heard Out on Superior!

Loud Noise from Lake.

In the hours before publication this morning, many reports have come in, most of them describing an "explosion-type" noise, or that of a meteor strike. The sound was first heard at 11:00 a.m. yesterday in Marquette and Grand Marais, and as far away as lakeside communities in Ontario. Be sure to follow the Independent *for the latest on this emerging Superior Country story.*

Maribeth awoke. She was adrift on a mirror. She would never have imagined a lake could be as perfectly flat as it was right now.

The sky was blue and clear, and it was freezing. Maybe even below freezing, but with the sweater and wool cap on and with the tarp over her, she wasn't chilly at all. Her face was icy cold; so were her feet, but that was all.

She looked over toward Jefry's raft. He was still on it, all covered up. Atticus was nowhere in sight. She tried to lift her head but could not. She could move it to the left or right, but that was all. Couldn't move her arms either. They were under the tarp. She wanted to drink some water but could not. A shiver of fear raced up her spine. Why was she stuck? Why couldn't she move? What did it mean?

Hoped Atticus was all right.

Where are you?

She'd felt enjoyment hours ago that they were almost husband and wife. But now? Would they even survive to get married and spend their lives together? She laid her head back down, so that she was looking toward Jefry's raft. Atticus would show up there first.

She let her eyes close.

When Maribeth opened her eyes again, everything was still the same. Except for one thing: She had to be dreaming because there was the strangest thing on the horizon. It was a ship, and it was coming toward her.

Upside down.

No. Cannot be.

Was she upside down now? No, still on the raft. Water still beneath her. Sky overhead.

But an upside-down ship.

Heading straight toward her. All white and not a propeller ship but a paddle wheeler. A side-wheeler. It had two or three levels. And smoke came out of its stack, but…

The smoke flowed downward.

She had to be dreaming because smoke doesn't…

But how can a ship be upside down?

Was it sinking?

Her raft. Was it sinking?

Was she having visions? Hallucinations?

Couldn't take her eyes off the ship, though.

She lay there in fascination and confusion, unable to look away.

Seconds later, the ship did the strangest thing—it grew wider, stretched wider, and began to flatten. It became so stretched out that in half a minute it was just a white line across the lake's surface.

Then it vanished.

She wondered if Jefry had seen it too but couldn't tell. He was still on his raft, covered by his tarp. No movement, though. A few minutes later, the same ship came up over the horizon. Not a hallucination at all, but real. She realized that she'd seen a reflection of some kind. An actual ship. A real ship, now. Coming toward her— coming toward all of them.

They were found!

Rescue was imminent.

She felt a surge of joy. "Thank you," she whispered. "Thank you."

Somehow, some way, somebody had found out where the *Greaves* survivors were. And now this ship was coming to their rescue.

Now if she could only lift herself up so that she could wave hello back at them when they'd surely wave at her upon approach. She wished Atticus was beside her so that together they could share the joy of this moment.

But no matter; they'd all be together mere minutes from now.

The ship loomed larger and larger. Coming straight at her.

"Thank heaven," she whispered.

She heard the music a moment later. Band music. It had to be coming from the steamer, because there was nothing else in sight. She was so happy and relieved.

They had struck up the band to celebrate finding the survivors.

She hoped they'd have bathtubs aboard the steamer. She wanted to laugh with joy. Yes, of course, they would! Of course they'd have bathtubs! *How wonderful it will be to slip into a nice hot bath.* She closed her eyes and easily imagined even now, adrift upon the icy lake, that she was soaking in the delightful, delicious warmth of a nice, hot, wonderful bathtub. Maybe a candle or two, some fresh flowers. *Do they have flowers on board? Of course! Yes, for sure they do*, she thought, wanting to laugh.

The ship was still heading straight toward her, and she could see one of the enormous paddle wheels spinning. She heard it splashing even over the sound of the music—

and the music was *loud*! What a celebration they were having! Oh, and what stories she and the other survivors will have to tell. All the passengers on this rescue ship will gather 'round to hear their shipwreck stories.

The paddle ship should have slowed down by now, but it hadn't.

It wasn't slowing down at all.

And that huge paddle wheel was heading right toward her.

What was going on? Would they launch a smaller boat to pick them all up? Was that the plan? But why weren't they slowing down, not even one bit? Didn't they know she was in the path of that big paddle wheel? As the wheel came closer, she knew she'd be crushed or killed if they didn't slow down; she tried to see where Jefry's raft was. He was off in the other direction.

She couldn't paddle away to safety because her hands were trapped.

Closer, now.

She struggled against her restraints, but to no avail. If only she could free her arms, she could wave. Maybe then they would see her.

But no, she couldn't move, and the ship continued heading toward her.

She closed her eyes knowing death was coming.

The music boomed louder, and the paddle wheel splashed louder, and just when it was a deafening roar in her ears and she could even feel the spray from the wheel on her face, she opened her eyes and it was right there, towering. Towering above her, right next to her, three stories tall and not five feet away, swirling and slapping and roaring.

Frothy white water flinging from the wheel blades as they spun.

Then passed her by completely.

Blades still spinning, throwing froth every which way.

And not slowing down.

As the sound of the blade wash diminished, she looked up and saw the name of the ship painted on the paddle wheel enclosure: *City of Duluth.*

As the steamer passed by, she saw people out on the deck, laughing and walking around and greeting one another and having a good time as the band played on. On the lowest level, a lady was out on deck and leaning against the rail—not more than twenty feet away—holding what looked like a glass of champagne. A pretty lady. Right there in front of her. Looking out across the water.

Looking toward her.

She wore a nice beige hat, seemed to look toward Beth, seemed to glance at her for just a moment.

I know you see me. Please. You must see me.

"*Please!*" she said weakly, trying to raise her voice but not able to. "*This way. Over here. Can't you see me? Please! I'm here!*"

The woman wore a coat with a fur collar, a medium-blue outfit underneath, and her lips were bright red. And then she looked away from Beth's direction and turned toward the gentleman she was talking to and laughed, continuing the conversation she was having with him.

Beth tried to call out but could not. She still couldn't lift her arm to wave.

And in that moment, with the side-wheel steamer alongside and looming above her but now slipping away, Beth saw its reflection off the tarps that covered her.

Why did they reflect?

Then she realized they were covered with ice. She was encased in ice.

No wonder she couldn't sit up or wave. She was under a layer of ice several inches thick.

Continuing across the lake, its music fading into silence, the ship eventually slipped over the horizon. Beth understood, for the first time, that no one was coming for her.

She would not be rescued.

None of the others would, either.

They would all die out here.

She would die out here.

Day Three

From the *Soo Citizen*, Sault Sainte Marie, Michigan:

LIKE NEW MADRID ALL OVER AGAIN

New Madrid Survivor Compares Boom to 1812 Quake.

From the *Marquette Mirror*, Marquette, Michigan:

WHAT WAS IT?

Lakes Region Residents Puzzled by Loud Noise.

Beth woke up thinking someone was right there, right above her. She opened her eyes and was going to ask them to please go away, but no one was there.

Nothing above her but sky.

And nothing around her but water.

Nothing anywhere.

Someone had been there, though. She knew it. She'd felt the touch on her forehead, heard words being whispered over her. Prayers and Psalms in English and Latin and chants in a strange tongue.

It was terribly, terribly cold out.

She'd never felt such cold before.

She couldn't feel her feet or her face and could barely move her hands.

Jefry's raft. Still there, but he hadn't moved. He was still huddled beneath his tarp.

It grew dark. The prayers and chants continued. The touch and the voice, again and again, whenever she drifted off into sleep. It awakened her during the night. Several times. Sometimes loud and insistent, and she snapped awake in the darkness, only for exhaustion to lure her back to sleep.

She needed a good night's rest. That's what she really needed. Everybody needs that. Why didn't the voice let her sleep? It was so aggravating. It could just stop and leave her alone. Why didn't it? Everything would be okay if only she could get some nice, comfortable, beautiful rest. That would do it. Everything would be okay then. Rest is the answer. Rest is a good thing. Everybody knows that. How did the voice not understand that?

Getting drowsy now.

So drowsy.

Crashing and clattering. Pots and pans dropping on the floor. It shocked and scared her, and she looked all around, but there was only lake around her and the nighttime sky overhead.

No pots. No pans. No sound at all.

Stop it, Jefry.

He was doing it. She knew it. He was coming over here and bothering her and praying and so forth, keeping her awake. Making the pots and pans crash.

And over there having a good sleep for himself.

After bothering me and keeping me awake.

She would holler at him to stop it, but she hadn't the strength to holler or even whisper.

Maybe she was a little bit awake now because she was gazing at all those stars again.

Day Four

From the *Chicago Tribune*:

CHICAGO STEAMSHIP LATE, FEARED LOST

Local Steamship Come to Grief?

The cargo ship *Eli Greaves*, a 740-ton wooden propeller steamer, is over four days out of the State Lock and overdue at Duluth, Minnesota, with her cargo of…

From the *Copper Harbor Independent:*

SHIP DEBRIS SIGHTED ON SUPERIOR

Steamer Sunk on Lake?

A tragic development in the fate of the missing cargo steamship *Eli Greaves*…

Cold water was dripping on her face, and it was keeping her awake, and she didn't want to be awake.

Jefry had finally stopped bothering her so much sometime early that morning, although he had come and whispered to her once or twice.

It was much warmer today already, even though the sun had not yet come up. The sky was getting purplish, so it'd be daylight before too long. It was not raining though, so why was water dripping onto her face? Because she couldn't move her arms, it wasn't so bad that water dripped on her face. Now she only had to tilt her head to have it drip into her mouth. It had a bit of a dusty taste, probably from the tarps, but overall, not bad.

Then it came to her: The water was from the ice melting. It was warmer now. Melting the ice. Maybe after it all melted, she'd be able to pull her arms out from under and move them again. That would be nice. You don't realize how much you like moving around until you can't do it for a few days. What had it been? Two days under the tarp now? Three? She'd lost track. If the ice was melting now, after sunrise it would melt faster.

She lifted her head a little. Some ice crackled and broke off, then slid down onto her neck. *Yikes!* So chilly. After a minute of that, she could angle her head up a little and see more of what was around her. Still nothing but the lake.

Lake and Jefry.

He ought to be up and moving soon.

No sign of Atticus, though.

No ships on the lake, no birds, no debris.

The lake air had a funny smell, like that of bad weather coming. And although there were still a few stars visible overhead, off toward the west, the sky was getting darker; even now, before sunrise, she could see that.

Day Five

From the *Chicago Tribune*:

SEVEN ARE ALIVE!!

Seven from Doomed Ship Found Alive on Rafts

Brave lifeboat station crews pulled seven SURVIVORS from the foundered steamer Eli Greaves from frigid Lake Superior this morning. Among them were Captain T.G. McBride, First Mate Atticus Miles, Steward Paul...

From the *Times*, London, England:

SUSSEX GIRL ADRIFT ON AMERICAN LAKE

Daughter of "Sussex Best" Textile Industrialist Now Missing on Lake Superior.

From the *Copper Harbor Independent*:

IT WAS A BOILER EXPLOSION!

Survivors Confirm Catastrophic Boiler Explosion.

It was a boom heard nearly 200 miles away. Now confirmed by survivors: a boiler explosion. Seven rescued so far. More still adrift on Lake Superior. Storms moving in from the northwest.

"Wake up, sleepyhead," says Mama.

I'll tease her and pretend to be asleep.

"Uppy uppy, little puppy," she says.

That's my favorite. I always laugh out loud when she says that, and I try not to giggle now. She jiggles my shoulder, and I try to keep from smiling.

"What's that you say, Mr. Horsey? You and Miss Foo-Foo and Froggy are lonely? Well, I'm sorry, but our Bethie can't seem to wake up this morning. I'm afraid I must put all of you back in the toy box because—"

"No, don't, Mama. I'm up," Beth shouted and sat up.

But she had not really sat up. She was held down by ropes and tarps. And Mama wasn't there. And although she had tried to shout, no words came.

The sun was up, but it had not yet pierced the gloomy, dark gray sky. Icy waves washed over the raft, but by now the air was much warmer and the ice that had covered the raft was all gone. The sky in one direction was a medium gray above, but below that, from one end of the horizon to the other, it was a dark, rolling carpet of black and dark gray and bluish black. She'd grown up near the English Channel and knew what a squall line looked like. Ships and boats furled their sails ahead of squall lines. Either that or got knocked down.

It really was quite beautiful, but terrifying too. Black and bluish dark gray and rolling and rolling toward her. It was tumbling toward her fast. That meant it would pass quickly. The waves were going from rolling to pointy, and now there were whitecaps. She felt a sudden gust against her face. It was nice and warm but then cold again. Cold and warm together at the same time.

The first blast came a few minutes after sunrise.

The piece of tarp that Atticus and Jefry had left for her was flapping a lot, so she reached out and grabbed it, then pulled it over her head and grasped it as tight as she could. A fierce blast of wind slapped spray at her, and the flap was trying to whip out of her hands, but she held on. She rolled the edge into a sort of handle to grip it better. It kept on tugging and trying to get away, but she held on. She had no strength left, but she held on anyway.

When the raft tilted and a wave washed over it, there was nothing she could do but hold on to that tarp piece. Let go of it, and the whole thing might come off and loosen the ropes. It was dark under the tarp, but she dared not look outside. The raft tilted again, then slid down the side of a wave. Then a hard splash against the raft and another one right after. The wind howled, huffed and puffed, and the tarp slapped crazily in the wind. The raft began twirling at one point, then a hard punch by a chilly splash of water followed by another slide down another wave.

Lightning flashed, and the thunder was immediate. The lightning was everywhere. Not distant, but surrounding her. Flash after flash with thunder booming like army cannons. The hard rain on the tarp felt like a solid thing as it roared down upon the raft. Between the roar of the rain and the roar of the wind, she couldn't tell which was which, but still she held on. That was all she managed to do. She hung on through the roaring and the twirling and the sliding and flashing and booming.

And then there was a lull. She peered out and saw a lighter sky but a thick, dark gray wall of rain, coming fast. The next thing she knew, she was in the middle of it. Tons of water struck like a wagonload of bricks, hammering and roaring, but that passed too, and then the sky was even lighter than before and the wind seemed to abate.

Day Six

Waking up again.

Everything was soaking wet. She was soaking wet too, even beneath the tarps. More water slapped up from underneath than before. Was her raft coming apart? How about Jefry's raft? How was it doing, and how was he doing? She lifted her head and even lifted herself up onto an elbow—something she hadn't been able to do for days—and looked all around.

Jefry and his raft were nowhere in sight.

Beth woke to mechanical sounds. Clicking and clanking and whooshing noises. A steam engine? She lifted her head and looked around. Nothing but darkness. No lantern lights from boats or ships. She listened for a minute or two, but could no longer hear anything beside her own breathing. Total silence surrounded her. Feeling sure she had dreamed the sounds, she dropped off to sleep again.

From the *Daily Globe*, Toronto, Canada:

SUPERIOR STORM SINKS SHIP

Daughter of British Industrialist On Board, Feared Lost.

From the *Times*, London, England:

HOPE WANING FOR SUSSEX GIRL?

Has Stormy and Merciless Lake Superior Claimed Another Victim?

"Please find my daughter," pleads industrialist Henry Eaton III. Textiles titan offers reward for the rescue and safe return of his only child.

From the *Copper Harbor Independent*:

RESCUE EFFORTS SUFFER SETBACK

Squalls Hamper Search Efforts.

Yesterday was frustrating for those searching for English lady Miss Maribeth Eaton of the "Sussex Best" textile empire.

Day Seven

It was dark, and then it was light, and then it was dark again.

Mechanical noises came and went all night long.

She couldn't feel her hands or her feet.

So cold.

She could feel her face, though. Her head and face were wet, and that moisture was turning to ice. It was freezing over her eyes, too. Whenever she opened them, the thin ice covering them came apart a little, and when she blinked, chilly icicles scraped her cheeks.

Day Eight

Those mechanical noises again.

Daytime.

Voices. Men's voices.

Something bumping her raft, then the flap being lifted.

A man's face above, looking down at her. This couldn't be happening.

She wasn't seeing this. No…not possible.

She closed her eyes.

When she opened them again, he was still there.

THIRTEEN

The man looked over his shoulder and shouted to the other one with him. "She's alive! Great God in Heaven, she's alive!" He looked down at her again, now with tears in his eyes. The two of them ripped away tarps and untied knots. They cut the ropes and lifted her off the raft, up and over the gunwales and onto their boat, taking great care to set her down gently.

She was on a small boat, a steam launch, and the two men motored it through mild waters for several minutes, then the boat shook and made a crackly, crunchy noise as they drew its bow up onto a gravelly beach before getting out.

Wings fluttered; gulls called and mewed, now upset that interlopers were nearby.

The men tried to lift her up onto her feet, but having no strength in her legs, she collapsed. They caught her, and together the two of them carried her onto the beach.

It was twilight and the sky was clear, now. Nearby trees made long shadows.

"The blanket. Lay the blanket down for her."

The other one came close and looked her right in the face. "Are you Miss Eaton? Miss Maribeth Eaton?"

Her mind tried to grasp his words. She heard them clearly but they had no meaning to her. She tried to reply, but no sound would come to her lips. She wanted to sleep. That's all she wanted to do.

He brought his face up close again. "Miss, can you blink your eyes? Please blink your eyes for me."

That was something she could do, so she blinked.

That pleased the two men; they smiled at each other.

"You're in Canada, miss." Then, more slowly: "*Can... Ahh... Dah.* You are in Canada. Do you understand me? Nod if you can understand me please."

They were polite to her. *That's nice,* she thought. *I'm glad they're so polite because—*

"Nod your head if you can hear me, miss."

She nodded.

"You're in Ontario, Canada. On land now. You're safe."

"Atticus," she said. Then "Jefry." Or that's what she tried to say. What came out was a rough, scratchy sound, like she was talking through a mouthful of gravel.

"We'll make sure nothing happens to you. You're safe. There's water and nourishment here for you. We're gonna light a fire. We'll make sure you stay warm. You'll be okay now."

Beth looked around, wondering where she was, and how she'd wound up here.

The man was holding her up in a sitting position, making sure she stayed awake.

Getting dark, now. One of them held up a lantern. In its light, she could tell she was missing a shoe. Her ankle was bleeding and her feet were black. Was that dirt? Or gangrene from frostbite? She was soaking wet and chilly.

Gulls still complaining, muttering nearby.

Trees all around.

She tried to move the foot, but the pain made her squeal. Tried it another way.

"What can I do to help you?" the man asked.

She shrugged…couldn't have told him even if she knew. So, she leaned back on her elbow for a moment, but the gravel made it hurt. She drew her knees up and pulled both legs in against her chest, then clasped her hands together around them and hugged them for warmth.

"Is that comfortable for you?" he asked.

She nodded.

"Are you cold?"

She nodded again.

Her dress was ripped and ragged. Meant to be her wedding dress. Filthy now.

She was alive.

Didn't know how she had ended up here nor why she survived. She wasn't the only one left alive, was she? She hoped Atticus was alive. And Jefry. She remembered seeing Kristi go under.

Kristi was gone.

She looked around but couldn't see Jefry's raft anywhere. They had taken her off her raft and brought her here on a boat. She had been on the water, and now she wasn't on the water. Nothing made sense. What was this place? He had a name for it. He called it something. What had he called it?

I am the only one, she thought, then remembered the explosion and wept.

All those people. All those people…

"It's okay, miss," the man said, patting her shoulder. "You're okay; you're safe. We'll make sure you stay warm. Try not to worry."

The fire was crackling now, and it cast a yellow-orange glow that danced among the surrounding trees. It was dark out, but she was feeling the fire's warmth upon her.

Jefry Walks-on-Smoke saved her life. She knew that much. She wasn't sure how, but he knew what to do and what to say. Somehow, some way, he had saved her life by some means that she couldn't understand. In her mind, she could still hear his prayers and chants. Atticus, too. Together, they had saved her.

Where are they?

Then she took a deeper breath and pushed, pushed words out as hard as she could. Tried to speak again, but she could not. Her strength ran out just as the kind man sat down next to her, facing the opposite way. He wore a worried face, and now she felt his arms encircling her, keeping her from falling backward.

He was speaking softly to her. "I must hang on to you; I can't let you fall over."

She tried to talk again, but all she could manage was to move her lips.

"You can rest your head on my shoulder if you wish," he said.

She tried to nod but hadn't the strength. She didn't even have the strength to hold her head up anymore, so she let it drop against his shoulder and fell fast asleep.

Sault Sainte Marie, Ontario, Canada. October 19

Midwife Mrs. Lucille Marie Charbonneau awoke to frantic pounding on her front door. She wondered who on earth it could be. There were no expectant mothers that she knew of in town. At least none even close to going into labor.

She swung her feet out of bed and looked toward the window.

The sky was purplish.

Sunrise wasn't far off.

Dazed and dizzy from interrupted sleep, she slid her feet into her slippers. She stood up and pulled on her housecoat, drawing it around herself and tying it as she shuffled from her bedroom and into the dark hallway with its creaking floorboards. She paused halfway to the front door and listened for any strange noises.

Silence.

Continuing along the hallway, she reached up to the wall where hung the portrait of her late husband. She paused there a moment and gently touched it as she had done many times a day, every day, for the past twelve years.

When she reached the entryway to the parlor, she glanced over toward the grandfather clock in there and squinted to see the time: five thirty.

"Who on earth?"

Finally, at the front door, she stopped.

Quietly and carefully, she leaned toward it, her ear a half inch away. She held her breath and listened.

More pounding.

She jumped. *"Who's there?"* she shouted.

"Robert Proudfoot, missus. And Trevor Flood. We have the girl." She recognized the names. And she knew Robert's voice.

The girl?

She threw open the door.

It was Robert and Trevor all right, holding up a cold and wet young lady between them. She shivered and trembled and shook, appeared to be barely conscious, and was wearing a fluffy and dirty white dress and only one shoe. Her feet were black.

Mrs. Charbonneau gasped and made the sign of the cross. "My goodness gracious, look at you!" She reached out for the young lady and gently took her by the arm as the two young men walked her into the front hall.

"Where'll we take her, missus?"

"Second bedroom. Then I want you both out of there and in the kitchen starting a fire in the cookstove."

The two young men gently helped the young lady sit on the edge of the bed.

"Who is she?"

"The English girl."

"Which? Who now? *English* girl?"

"The one from the exploded ship."

"Oh, *that* English girl. Merciful heavens, you poor child. Close the door behind you, boys, so I can get her out of these wet things."

"On a raft, thirty miles up the shore, just about froze to death."

"Eight days adrift on Superior," the other one said. "And we found her."

"Yes, yes, now scoot," she said, waving them away. "Into the kitchen with you."

From the *Times*, London, England:

THANK YOU, CANADA!

Our Sussex Girl Found Alive on Superior by Hero Boatmen.

Western Union telegram received:

Delivered at Sault Sainte Marie, Ontario, Canada.

London, England, Oct 20

Departing Liverpool Oct 21 SS *Oceanic*

Arrive New York Oct 29

Arrive Sault Nov 14

Henry Eaton III

October 21

It was a small clapboard house. Well constructed. Subtle signs of postponed maintenance here and there. Whoever owned it was of modest means but proud of the place nonetheless.

The door opened, and an elderly woman appeared. Friendly smile. Kind, grandmotherly appearance.

"Mrs. Charbonneau?"

"Yes, may I help you?"

"My name is Atticus Miles. I was first mate on the steamer *Eli Greaves*. The ship that sank out on Lake

Superior a few days ago. The young lady you're caring for, ma'am. She is my fiancée."

Henry Eaton III knew only one thing right now—his daughter was alive. It had been just over a week since he'd had any news of her. He and his wife had prayed nearly non stop since learning about the sinking and had continued praying after the SS *Oceanic* departed from Liverpool several days earlier. There hadn't been enough time to learn anything about Beth's present condition after their arrival in New York because there was a river ferry to catch.

Never in his wildest dreams could he have imagined that his first trip to America would be under such circumstances as he currently faced. How strange it was, he thought, how ironic, that at the same time he was contemplating a trip to see America for himself, his daughter had endured and been rescued from a maritime catastrophe.

He knew more about American trade routes and commerce than an English textile manufacturer might be expected to have learned. From newspaper articles over recent years, he had gleaned a great deal, but it was the reports from agents with whom he'd dealt that contributed the most to his knowledge. He had agents in both North and South America, and those two continents were presently the areas of his greatest interest and, in his opinion, those that showed the greatest promise for future expansion of the Eaton family brand.

But neither expansion nor the family brand was on his mind nor his wife Margaret's mind as they made their way to the Hudson River ferry terminals. One hour later and a fifty-cent fare each, they were on a train bound for Albany, then Buffalo.

"Promise you won't wake her," Mrs. Charbonneau whispered as she slowly and quietly opened the door to the second bedroom.

"I'll be quiet," Atticus said as the two of them crossed the bedroom, then stood next to the bed.

Mrs. Charbonneau drew close to Atticus, took him by the arm, and whispered. "She's getting some color now. Beautiful girl."

Atticus nodded. "Yes, she is. Thank you for taking such good care of her."

She tugged on his sleeve and gestured that they should leave the room. They went into the kitchen.

"And how are you recovering, Mr. Miles?" She asked, pointing to the table.

He slid out a chair. "It was a rough few days for the rest of us, but we all made it. All of us who survived the explosion, that is. Fourteen men presumed lost at present. They found us on our rafts along the shore. American side. Just one raft survivor is not accounted for as of this morning. He and Maribeth and I were on rafts tied together, but we got separated."

"Maribeth," Mrs. Charbonneau said softly. "First time I've heard it. Pretty name."

"Her father is on his way over from England. Should be here by early November."

"All the way from *England?*" She shook her head in astonishment. "Oh, my word. I've never been beyond this town, Mr. Miles. Sixty-six years. Born here. And when my time comes, I'll go out my door feet first, thank you very much. If I have any say in the matter, that is. No faith in hospitals. Cream and sugar in your tea?"

Atticus smiled. "Yes please. It's nice and quiet here." He thought a moment, then asked, "Do you have any house paint, ma'am?"

"Three, four buckets in the shack. You'll see it; it's out back. A young man started doing some touch-up for me last year, but he never finished the job. Why do you ask?"

When she heard scraping outside a little later, she knew right away why he'd asked about the paint.

Beth opened her eyes in a room filled with sunlight and a lovely fragrance.

She was on a sleigh bed.

There was flowery wallpaper and a dresser with a lamp on it, along with lavender and gardenias in a white vase. The door had a nice glass doorknob, and there was a little upholstered settee along one wall.

A glass of water was on the nightstand. She picked it up and brought it to her lips. Took a few sips, then set it back down.

She rearranged the pillows, shifted and wriggled to get more comfortable; then she turned on her side, settled into the comfy pillows, and drifted softly back to sleep again.

Atticus dipped the brush into the paint while wondering what his next step ought to be. All the other survivors had hopped on board ships headed to the lower lakes.

There had been no word about Jefry. Not a good sign.

He was eager to get back to his own home in Wisconsin, but he and Beth needed to wait for her father to arrive. He was pleased that Mr. Eaton was coming and that he'd be here for the wedding. As far as wedding plans were concerned, though, that would be up to others; he knew next to nothing about that kind of thing.

He'd used up most of the first bucket of paint, and the front wall of the house and one side wall had two coats each. The paint job looked pretty nice.

When he heard the front screen door slam shut, he looked up.

Mrs. Charbonneau came around the corner of the house, walking as fast as she was able, wearing an apron and a big smile. "She's awake!"

When Atticus appeared at the bedroom door, Beth opened her arms wide. He went over to the bed, sat on the edge, and put his arms around her.

"Thank God," she said.

He said nothing as he hugged her.

"I was so afraid for you," she said.

He nodded but remained silent.

After a minute or two, he loosened his grip on her and leaned back a little. He smiled as he looked at her, liking what he saw. "Do you feel okay? Any pain at all?"

"No, but I think my feet got frostbitten."

"Shall we check?"

She nodded and threw back the covers. "Whose nightgown?"

"Mrs. Charbonneau's, I guess."

"Oh, that's the lady who's been taking care of me?"

"Yeah."

"She's quite gentle. Seems very sweet."

Atticus nodded. "Nice lady."

"They look normal. Last time I saw my feet, they were black. I thought it was gangrene from frostbite."

"Just dirty," he said, with a smile.

"So Mrs. Charbonneau even washed my feet." She looked around the room. "It was so lovely waking up here. I wasn't sure where I was, but I knew it was in somebody's nice, safe little home."

"We're on the Canadian side. Sault Sainte Marie, Ontario. They found you quite a way up the shore. Two young men did."

"I remember them. And their little boat."

They were silent for several moments, just looking into each other's eyes.

"How long have I been here?"

"Almost three days."

"The two men gave me some food, but still I should probably eat."

"The missus here, she's making something."

Beth took a deep breath and heaved a big sigh. Then she closed her eyes and shook her head. "Oh my gosh, Atticus. Everything that happened…"

"Yeah."

"I don't even know what to think about all that. I mean…"

"It just happened is all. It just happened. Now we do what needs to be done, take care of some things, all the legal matters, I guess. Then we go on and live our lives. And we must always be very thankful."

"How many were on the rafts?"

"Nine of us. All accounted for but one. And I just found out this morning they pulled one more out of the water."

"Oh my God, Atticus. Oh my God. Did she make it? Please tell me we haven't lost her."

"Some Norwegian fishermen out of Copper Harbor found somebody. That's all I've heard so far. No details yet."

Beth waited.

"There's been no sign of Jefry, darling."

She closed her eyes tight and wept silently, then seconds later, asked, "He didn't make it, did he?"

"It's not looking good. That second night was so cold. They said that on land it got down to nearly ten below zero."

"Remember when Jefry took off his sweater and put it on me?"

Atticus nodded.

"He wore no shirt underneath. And a little later he took off his cap and gave that to me as well."

"He saved you, Beth. He knew he could save your life and accepted the price."

She wept silently again. "After we left Buffalo, I think when we were on Lake Erie, he told me he was worried about something. Something that he'd felt. Something about that ship. He said he had no power, but I'm still not sure what he was talking about. And at one point, he said, 'I will help you if I can.'"

"I remember him praying over you as we put your raft together."

"In English, and some Indian words too. And even some things in Latin." She was silent for a moment. "Atticus, how could he have survived that second night?"

"It's not likely he did."

"But, honey, he kept on coming to me for two nights after that. I felt him touch my forehead and heard him saying things, praying, chanting…"

Atticus shrugged and shook his head. "Who can say what that—"

"He wouldn't let me go to sleep. In my mind, I was telling him to go away and let me sleep."

"But he wouldn't let you. He said he would help you, and he did, didn't he?"

"Yes, he never gave up. Even crazy noises would wake me up. And I knew it was him doing it."

With a soft knock on the door, Mrs. Charbonneau appeared, holding a tray. "Some food for you, dear."

Atticus was sitting on a couch in the parlor near the fireplace when Mrs. Charbonneau came in, smiling.

"Mr. Miles, she ate most of what I prepared for her. It wasn't much. She'd been mostly without food for a week, and I didn't want her to have a lot at once."

"Yes, ma'am, of course. I'm glad to hear she's had something."

"She wants to take a hot bath, so I'll ask that you stay here for a bit."

He smiled. "Of course, ma'am."

"Seeing as how you're not married yet."

"I understand. No need to expl—"

"I keep a chaste home, sir."

"Of course, missus, I respect all of that."

"Are you a religious man?"

"I was raised Protestant. Little country church in Tennessee. I haven't forgotten God, but I've been lazy about going to services these past few years."

She smiled. "He hasn't forgotten you, though. You are a good man, Mr. First Mate Miles. I can read people, and I see how much you care for that young lady and how much in love you both are. I am grateful that you're painting the place. You didn't have to do that, you know."

"Mrs. Charbonneau, I lost everything when our ship went down. Everything else I own is back in Wisconsin, and I need to repay you somehow for taking care of Beth."

She shook her head and waved off the idea. "I'd have taken care of her for free. And you're welcome to stay here as long as you need to."

"Thanks, ma'am. That's very kind of you. We've nowhere else to go right now and no funds."

"Where you're sitting. Will that be okay for sleeping, do you think?"

"I guess so; sure, why not?"

"You're tall, so your feet might hang over the arms a bit."

He smiled. "I'm sure it'll be okay. There's always the floor, up near the fire."

"My Victor. My late husband. He was a mariner too. Twenty-four years under sail. All the upper lakes. He took many naps on that couch."

"Mrs. Charbonneau, I'm not sure what's going to happen now. Beth's father is due here at the Sault in a week. In his telegram there was no mention of Mrs. Eaton, but we're hoping she's with him. After that, I don't know if he has plans, but he left England in a big hurry, of course."

She shook her head. "Don't you worry about a thing, dear." She turned to leave the room, then stopped, paused a moment, and turned to face him once again. "I feel good things about you, sir. Mr. First Mate. I feel you have a good heart and a gentle soul. And I know you will be a fine husband for that lovely girl in there."

November 4

Henry Eaton could not observe much of Buffalo, but what he saw made a good impression. Broad avenues and well-designed parks were an attractive feature, and what he could make out of the city's layout was a blend designed for both grace and efficiency.

The port facilities impressed him. He was also aware of the city's place in the movement of immigrants from New York to America's interior in the past and knew of its present importance as a terminal port for American grain shipments.

Hours later, as their passenger steamer made its way along Lake Erie, the map he'd drawn in his mind over many years was finally taking shape—this time for real.

As the thin, grayish-blue stretch of shoreline passed in the distance, names came to mind: Erie, Cleveland, Lorain, Detroit. Those places were now almost, but not yet, real in his own experience.

November 7

Even with the bedroom door closed, Beth knew when Mrs. Charbonneau was walking past the room. She knew her soft, cautious tread by now. A floorboard creaked in a certain place, just like it always did, as the lady made her way down the hall. Then the squeak of a hinge as the front door opened.

Greeting someone in her quiet voice, then speaking quickly.

Louder. Surprised.

Another voice. Higher pitched. Excited.

The person she had just let in.

A younger voice.

And then down the hall came Mrs. Charbonneau's tread, quicker now.

But ahead of her, somebody running.

Almost to the door now.

Beth closed her eyes, hoping, hoping. *"Please God. Please, please..."*

When the door flew open and Kristi appeared, she and Beth both screamed.

Kristi dove onto the bed and threw her arms around Beth, and they hugged and kissed and cried, and cried some more.

Mrs. Charbonneau and Atticus appeared and stood in the doorway. She cried too. Tears ran down Atticus's cheeks as well.

"Two fishermen guys find me! And guess what! They are speaking Norwegian to me. And they let me steer their boat and take me to their house, and I meet their wives and kids and their dogs and cats and we eat *fiskesuppe*!"

Beth hugged her even tighter.

"And Mr. Willy saves me. Made me swim to a box and push me onto it."

November 18

It was a small wedding service, hastily arranged, and it took place in Mrs. Charbonneau's own church. Mrs. Eaton wore a lovely but simple outfit, one appropriate for travel if not for grand celebrations. The bride's father wore a perfectly tailored business suit. The bride's outfit had cleaned up well, especially with the addition of some trimmings and a borrowed veil. She wore medium-heeled white shoes given to her by a friend of Mrs. Charbonneau. Mr. Eaton had a business suit tailored for the groom by a local shop. Kristi was the maid of honor and proudly wore a borrowed dress that Mrs. Charbonneau had found for her. In attendance were approximately forty residents of the Canadian Sault, all of them friends of Mrs. Charbonneau and fellow congregants of her church.

Outside the church, following the service, Mr. Henry Eaton III approached Mrs. Charbonneau. He was in his fifties, of medium height and build, clean-shaven but for thick sideburns. His hair had grayed, but his sideburns were well-groomed and snow white. He took the lady by the hand. "I am afraid words will fail me here, beautiful soul. There is so much for which I must thank you, but I'm struck speechless. We owe you everything, my dear lady. My daughter was nearly gone from this world, but your role was crucial in bringing her back."

"It was my pleasure, Mr. Eaton, sir. She is a sweet and wonderful young lady."

"And I must apologize for our haste, but a steamer will sail within the hour from the American side, and all five of us must be on board."

Mrs. Charbonneau nodded. "I understand. And I shall pray for your safe return home."

He gestured to his wife, then turned and started toward their waiting carriage.

Mrs. Eaton stepped forward. She was a handsome woman, not yet her husband's age, brunette, slender, and closely resembling her daughter in both height and facial features. She had tears in her eyes. "My dear Mrs. Charbonneau, I don't know where to begin. Just days ago, you were bringing our dear child back to health, and we hadn't yet met you." She placed her hand on Mrs. Charbonneau's arm. "We are so grateful to you for all you've done. You've arranged this lovely service, fixed the bride's dress, and included all these wonderful friends of yours in our time of joy."

Her husband came forward and stood beside her again, holding a shiny wooden box. Ten by eight inches in length and width and eight inches in height. The surface was black piano lacquer, polished to a high gloss. A plain red ribbon was around it and rendered into a bow on top.

Mrs. Eaton took the box in hand. "Please accept this small gift as a humble thank-you for how you've helped us. We are forever grateful to you. My dear, you have saved our family."

"This wasn't necessary, Mrs. Eaton. Everything I've done, as I've told Mr. Miles already, I would have done happily anyway, with no expectation of reward. I am happy for all five of you here today. It was a joy to get to know your dear girl and an even greater joy to see you all here together as a family. An even larger family than you had expected, I'm sure, now with the addition of that lovely child, Miss Kristi. And thank you for letting me be a part of it. But, of course I appreciate your generosity. I will cherish this gift. And thank you very much."

Handing over the shiny black box, Mrs. Eaton said, "I must warn you: it's quite heavy, so please be careful."

Following the wedding, Robert Proudfoot and Trevor Flood brought Mrs. Charbonneau back to her house in a borrowed carriage. Its name was painted on the side in gold leaf with flourishes. The script was rendered not professionally, but carefully and lovingly, just the same: *Miss Francine.*

Robert pulled up gently on the reins, and the horse stopped.

"Thanks for bringing me home, boys. And thanks for dressing up so nice. You two are not only heroes, like the minister said, but you are perfect gentlemen."

"Your house looks good."

"It does, doesn't it? The groom—Mr. Miles—he did that last week. Scraped off all the loose paint, put two coats on the place, and trimmed the hedges. With what paint he had left, he touched up that old toolshed."

She stepped down from the carriage, then turned around and took the black box in two hands. "My goodness, this is heavy. Weighs a ton. Thank you so much, boys. Maybe you'd like some tea before you head on to home?"

The men looked at each other and nodded.

"And bring your boxes inside," Mrs. Charbonneau said.

Several minutes later, all three of them were seated at her kitchen table with their tea in front of them. Also in front of them were their three identical wooden boxes.

They looked back and forth at one another.

"Will the table hold all this weight? What is it? Bricks?" Robert said, then laughed nervously.

"Who wants to go first?" Trevor said.

"You go," said Mrs. Charbonneau.

"I say ladies first," Robert said.

Trevor nodded, while looking at Mrs. Charbonneau.

"Okay, I'll go, but remember, Mrs. Eaton said it was humble. So don't expect much." She pulled on the ribbon and the bow came undone. After pulling away the rest of the ribbon, she folded it and gently put it aside. Lifted the lid just a bit, then leaned closer and peeked inside. Then fully opened the lid. Her jaw dropped, and her eyes went wide.

"Dear heavens," she exclaimed. She let the box lid slam shut and slumped against the back of her chair. She closed her eyes, put a hand to her chest, and took several sharp breaths while trying not to grin too much.

"Missus? You okay?"

She began to laugh and cry at the same time as she took out her handkerchief and brought it to her eyes. "Oh my word, oh my goodness gracious…"

Trevor leaned toward her, looking alarmed, and took her by the arm. "You're not gonna faint, are you?"

She shook her head and laughed some more. "Take a look. Open your boxes, boys. Go ahead."

The two young men ripped away the ribbons and threw open their boxes.

"American gold eagles," one said.

"*Double* eagles," said the other. "Lots of 'em! Must be fifteen layin' right on top. And look at all these silver coins. A whole boxful. And what the heck are all these chunks of green glass doin' in here?"

"My boys, that green glass? Those are emeralds. The most valuable precious stones there are."

"Mrs. Charbonneau, it's a whole pile of 'em. Everything's falling out of the box. What's this all mean?"

"Boys, it means we are probably the three richest people in Sault Sainte Marie. Maybe even all of Ontario."

FOURTEEN

The *Lakes Empress* steamed along the Saint Marys River on its way to DeTour Passage, bound for Milwaukee.

The *Empress* was a propeller steamer, steel-hulled, 280 feet in length, with three levels. Only two years old, her paint and trim were still fresh, and the cabin appointments and interior details rivaled those of the finest luxury hotels of the day. In the words of an enthusiastic travel magazine writer:

Upon having the good fortune to board this exquisitely-appointed Steam-Ship, one must needs be willing to transport oneself (mentally) to an era, and to a place, where grace was the rule, rather than the exception.

The Ship's Grand Salon, one is pleased to note, affords unusual space for its Passengers such that one's grasp of the physics involved in creating this cavernous room is immediately tested, in that the entire vessel—even on the outside—suddenly feels more spacious.

The ambiance is one of sophistication without pretense, grace unmarred by gaudiness, sumptuousness without ostentation and, yes, luxury without razzle-dazzle. She is warm without being stuffy, and offers friendliness that thankfully falls short of obsequiousness. The Empress is indeed royal in every sense of the word.

Amenities include Ladies' Private Salons and Gentlemen's Smoking Rooms. Her balconies and their exquisitely-crafted railings become a promenade along which gentlemen in bowler hats and ladies in voluminous skirts glide—circling around on two separate levels overhead—like angels.

Passengers amused themselves with games of whist and cribbage, or with immense jigsaw puzzles on the floor itself. There were mahogany armoires and marble statues, walls paneled in cherrywood and mahogany, crystal chandeliers overhead, and tapestries and original oil paintings adorning the walls.

Beth swung open the couple's cabin door to find her mother standing in the passageway with a large bundle wrapped in plain brown paper.

"Now that we've unpacked and with the men out on deck having a talk, it may be a good time for the bride's wedding gift," she said with a shrug and a playful smile.

"Mama, you've given us more than enough already."

"Well, a little something extra then," she added, crossing the cabin and placing the package on the bed. Then she turned around, opened her arms, and mother and daughter hugged each other.

"And thanks for letting Kristi have a cabin to herself. She and I bunked together for the past week. She didn't complain a bit, and I know she's proud right now, and thrilled that you've let her have her own room. She has never slept in such a big bed."

"Such a sweet child. And you both love each other so much. It is a wonderful thing to see. You'll replace her sad memories with joyful new ones. Not just for her but for us all. I can see already that you three will have a wonderful life together."

"Did she tell you we're Big Sister and Little Sister?"

Mrs. Eaton shook her head a little and smiled. "That's not what she calls you."

"I… What do you mean? We're—"

"She doesn't call you that anymore."

"No. No, we've been—"

Mrs. Eaton shook her head as she gently placed her hand on her daughter's arm. "Beth, honey, she calls you 'my Mama Beth.' Then Mrs. Eaton smiled tenderly at her daughter's reaction. "*Oh,* darling, I'm… I'm sorry. I am so sorry. I've made you cry, haven't I? I didn't mean to upset you. I didn't realize…"

"It's okay, Mama; I'll tell you about it later."

"To Kristi, you're her mama now."

Beth nodded, smiled through tears. "I love her so much."

"Of course you do. Of course. And now just think about the three of you starting your lives together. So, so wonderful. And what a perfect start today. Such a beautiful bride." Mrs. Eaton kissed her daughter on the cheek.

Beth held a handkerchief to her eyes. "Thank you so much for coming all this way. Halfway around the world. These have been whirlwind days, haven't they? Now I'm glad we have a little time together to talk. After seeing only Papa's name on the wire, it was such a joyous surprise to see you. I hadn't expected you."

"How could I not come, my love? But I should thank you for including us in celebrating your dashing new addition to the family."

"I couldn't have dreamed of a better husband than Atticus. He is so good to me. And such a considerate man. And he really, truly loves me. I am so lucky, Mama."

Mrs. Eaton nodded. "I realized that when I saw you two together for the first time. It was in his eyes just how much he loves you. It really was. A mother can always tell."

"He is so kind and such a protector."

"Wait till your aunts see the photographs. They'll all want to take the next liner over here and find a man like that for themselves."

"He's one of a kind," Beth said. "Not such a silly American folly anymore, is it?"

Mrs. Eaton shook her head and waved off the remark. "That was them, dear. Those chattering aunts of yours. My sisters, they'll say what they'll say. They're like magpies sitting atop a fence, squawking, commenting about everyone that passes by."

"I suppose."

"I always knew you had to find your own road, your own way. You really are so much like your father in that respect. He's always been unpredictable and unconventional, and so are you. And such an imagination he has. Always coming up with a fresh vision of something or other. Usually something to do with business, but not always. I just never know. I never know what he's going to come up with."

"He was always encouraging me to be around the animals. Remember? He knew I loved them, but also that I feared them at first."

"I remember that. Yes, absolutely, you were quite fearful of them. He said at the time that in your heart you wanted to be around them and that you shouldn't be denied your heart's desire."

"He said that?"

"Yes, he did. He wanted you to trust your heart, to follow it."

Beth smiled. "Remember how I used to love getting muddy? Especially around the goats. They were my best friends."

Her mother laughed. "I'll never forget the time when you were… let me see… maybe six years old? You showed up by the front door, ready to go outside. And you with your little bandanna all tied up and full of cakes to eat, and you informed us, quite solemnly and inarguably, I might add, that you'd decided to become a goat?"

Beth smiled. "I don't remember it, but I've heard the story a thousand times."

"You had on your little blue wool coat with the hood. Remember that one?"

"Of course."

"You said, 'I'm not running away, Mama. I'm just going to go and live with the goats. I'm gonna be a goat now.'"

"And the mama goat tolerated me."

"Yes, she did, didn't she? She actually let you cuddle up to her. It always amazes me how some animals can recognize a child for what they are and be so much more tolerant and gentler with them."

"Was I out there the entire night?"

"As a matter of fact, you were, till nearly dawn anyway. And I'm not sure if I've ever mentioned this, but your father was also out there, watching you from not too far away. All night long. He let you do what you thought you needed to do, but he wanted to make sure you'd be safe."

"He was really out there all night?"

"Mm-hmm, yes. He loves you so much."

"I know."

"Always has. As do I."

Beth reached out and gave her mother a hug. "And I love you too. And I've missed you these past months."

Half a minute later, Mrs. Eaton stood up, then picked up the package and handed it to Beth.

"What? Open it? Now?"

"Why not?"

Beth ripped the package open. "Aw, my foofie! My foofie!" she squealed, holding the little stuffed bear to her cheek.

"Miss Foo-Foo insisted on coming. How could I disappoint her?"

"This is so sweet of you."

"And Mr. Horsie is here too. But, of course, Froggy had to stay behind. Somebody had to watch the house, you know."

"Well, certainly; that goes without saying. And even my wellies. You brought them too. And some more skirts and such. Thank you so much, Mama. I can use it all. We lost everything. Well, of course you know that by now. Oh, and you've packed the sweater and cap that Mrs. Charbonneau cleaned up."

"Which belonged to that brave young deckhand, I presume," Mrs. Eaton said.

Beth nodded, holding the sweater to her chest. "I didn't even want it. I said, 'No, you keep it.' But Jefry put it on me."

"Yes, Atticus told me. He saw the young man do that. That young fellow saved your life, darling. I think he knew you had little chance of surviving, and so he passed his chance along to you. He was sacrificing everything for you. I think he realized that."

Beth nodded. "Yes, he did. I'm sure he did."

"He cared for you so much. In his own way, sweetheart… In his own way, that young man loved you. I truly believe that."

Beth nodded and dabbed at her eyes with a handkerchief. "I know."

"Always remember that, my darling. Respect it. And value it."

Beth nodded. "I will, Mama."

"Say a prayer for him every day."

Beth nodded again.

"He had his own culture, his own ways. But such greatness, such generosity, such heroism. I've never known the likes of it, and your father said the same thing. Darling, that young man gave up everything so that you could live. From now on, each day of your life is a gift from him."

Henry and Atticus stood by the rail, watching as the ship passed the woodlands along the Saint Marys River.

"It's very nice in the grand salon, beautiful, and all that sort of thing, but too noisy for me. I don't know about you, Atticus, but I can't hear myself think where it's noisy and crowded."

"Same with me, sir. Too distracting."

"And you don't need to call me sir." Henry smiled, placing a hand on his new son-in-law's shoulder.

"Thanks, Henry. I'll try to remember that."

"Have you ever gone by a nickname?"

"Not really. Maybe in school, but…" He shrugged.

"I built a little wooden sailboat when I was a boy," Henry said. "It was only a foot long. And when my father watched me launch it the first time. He called me Cap, for captain. And that nickname stuck. Other family members would call me Cap or sometimes Cappy. And I must say I always quite fancied that. No one's called me that in years."

"Shall I call you Cap? Or Cappy? I think I like Cap better."

"So do I," Henry said with a smile.

"So Cap it is. And come to think of it, just a few days ago I ran into a war veteran I'd fought alongside. He called me Attie. I had forgotten all about that nickname, and I enjoyed hearing it again."

"So there you go, Mate. It's Cap and Attie. By golly, we sound like an act from polite vaudeville."

They laughed and shook hands.

Henry was silent for several moments. "That young deckhand; I don't suppose he stands much chance of surviving now, does he?"

Atticus shook his head. "No, not much of a chance at all. There's been no trace of him up till now. I've hesitated to bring it up with Beth. I mentioned it briefly the other day, but lately I've been avoiding it."

"She knows though."

"By now yes, I think she does. There's not much hope of finding him at this point."

"He gave his own life so that my girl, my only child, could live, Attie. It comes down to that. Do you agree?"

"Oh, of course. And he knew what we were all facing. The other five and myself—we were lucky. We were spotted and got picked up after a day and a half or so; same with Kristi I gather. Beth and Jefry, they were out there alone through the worst of the cold and the squalls. Jefry had sailed for a while. He knew what it meant, being adrift on Superior, or any of these lakes."

"Attie, I am honor bound to do something in recognition of his sacrifice. Here's an idea I've been working on: I'm going to nominate this young hero for some awards for bravery and gallantry.

"In England, we have the Albert Medal for Lifesaving, the Medal for Civil Gallantry at Sea, and then we have the… um… the Sea Gallantry Medal for those who have saved the life of a British subject at sea. I am sure he'll stand a good chance of being posthumously awarded one or more of those."

"Henry, that is a very kind thought. What a wonderful idea."

"There may even be a monetary award with one or the other of those. Regardless of that, I intend to donate fifty thousand dollars to his tribe. I want to make sure his own people know what he's done. I'll have an agent pay them a visit to see what they might need. Perhaps a place of worship. Or maybe a place for a doctor to practice, or a schoolhouse.

"And back at the Sault, I asked the clergyman if he thought the town would let me purchase a small plot in the park across from his church, for having a memorial erected so the young fellow's sacrifice is always remembered."

Mother and daughter sat on the edge of the bed holding hands, with Mrs. Eaton taking nearly an hour to pass along the latest family gossip about cousins, aunts, uncles.

"You and Papa have done so much for us already, and now we've embarked on what he's calling a mystery mission. What's all that about? What's the secret?"

Mrs. Eaton chuckled and shook her head. "I really don't know, dear. I'm serious. He hasn't told me anything."

"No… really…seriously, now…"

"I *am* serious. You know how he comes up with things. Always full of surprises. It's a kind of mischievous streak he's always had; he likes to keep us guessing sometimes. Mischievous, yes, but sweet really."

"Attie, my wife and I want very much to give you the wedding celebration you deserve."

"Cap, you've done so much already. You don't need"

Henry raised his hand. "Yes, I do." He chuckled. "Mrs. Eaton would never forgive me if we returned home without celebrating the marriage of our only child."

Atticus shrugged. "I'll take my cue from you, sir. And as a prudent gentleman, I shall go into battle holding high that banner that declares: HAPPILY MARRIED."

"Smart man," Henry replied with a smile.

"Beth, I don't think your father has had a chance to tell you what happened to him in London back on… Well, let me see… Maybe three weeks or a month ago now."

Beth shook her head. "He hasn't mentioned anything."

"The strangest experience. Most peculiar. Well, our driver took him to London for a business meeting. Then, after the meeting, when he was about to step up into the carriage, someone grabbed his arm. Very strong grip.

"It was a man, apparently a local man if his accent was any indication, but not someone Henry recalled ever having seen before. He held his arm in such a tight grip that your father turned to him and was about to object when—"

"When what, Mama?"

"Something in his gaze, Henry said. He was about to speak, but suddenly he had no words when he saw the gaze of that man. Then the fellow drew closer, still gripping his arm, and said, in a quite agitated state according to your father, 'She's in grave danger, sir. This day. *This day!*'

"Well, of course your father was quite shaken by that and glanced up at our driver, who also seemed taken aback, even shocked. Then, when Henry turned around, the man was nowhere to be seen. Right away he thought it was about me, that I was in danger. But no, it was about *you* all along.

"Oh my God, Beth. The blood just drained out of your face. What's wrong, dear? What was it I said?"

"Those words. Just got a sudden chill is all." She rubbed her arms quickly, then looked toward the door.

"You're pale all of a sudden."

"I am? Oh my gosh, I'm freezing too."

Mrs. Eaton put her hand to her mouth and stood up. "My goodness, Beth! Look at you. You're white as a sheet. You look like you've seen a ghost."

Beth stood up as well. "Did you just hear something?" She took a step toward the door, then stopped.

"Beth, you're scaring me. Are you alright? What's going on?"

"I… I'm not sure."

"*Yes!* I just heard something too. *There. Again.* What was that? It sounded like a footstep, or a…a bump or something."

Beth slowly approached the door. When she got to within a foot of it, she reached for the door handle, then paused.

Her hand was shaking. She drew a deep breath, then took the handle, twisted it, and slowly, cautiously, opened the door.

She peered out onto the balcony, looked one way and then the other…

Nobody was there.

She started closing the door…

Then looked down.

And she saw, on the carpeted floor.

Inches away from her feet…

Her white glove.

Her lost right-hand glove.

FIFTEEN

Door Peninsula, Wisconsin. August. Five Years Later

Atticus leaned toward the fireplace, holding a brass-handled poker and stirring up the glowing embers. A crackling yellow tornado of sparks swirled up the chimney.

Kristi stood nearby. "*Wooooh*," she cried in awestruck glee.

Frankie crept up from behind and shook Mister Horsie in her face. She squealed—no doubt the reaction he was looking for. Then Frankie was doing the squealing as she chased him out of the parlor and into the kitchen, both of them laughing.

Beth smiled, shaking her head. She winced while struggling to get up from the couch.

Atticus looked over his shoulder. "Are you okay?"

She nodded. "I just need to get up, but it's not getting any easier." She slumped back against the cushions.

"Give me a second, dear. Let me put another one on the fire." He picked up a fresh log and lowered it onto the embers, brushed his palms together over the hearth, then turned around. "Any pain?"

She shrugged while patting her bulging belly. "Nothing more than what you'd expect at eight months."

"When did Mrs. Charbonneau say to get in touch?"

"Pretty soon. In a couple of weeks."

"That's cutting it close, isn't it?"

"She didn't seem to think so. Said the train can get her down here from the Sault pretty fast these days. It'll be okay, Atticus. You have enough to worry about as it is, what with this tug business."

He shook his head. "I keep on hearing about more harbor work coming up, but so far it's all been just words."

She moved to the edge of the couch and held out her hand. "Remember what you used to say about owning a tugboat? It's just a big hole in the water into which you throw gold coins, one after another."

He shook his head while chuckling. "Well, that turned out to be true, didn't it?"

A metallic clatter came from the kitchen.

"Be *careful*, you kids!"

"Sorry, Mama," came the reply. "Just a pot lid."

Atticus smiled while shaking his head. "Guess I should've heeded my own doubts about getting into the tugboat business, right?"

"No financial problem we face is ever an emergency," she said as he helped her up. "They really meant it when they told you that, you know."

"Yeah, I know, but I just can't let myself go crying to your father for help every time we get a little thin on cash." Atticus looked toward the front window. "Kids, go see if the paper's here yet."

Stampeding footfalls and laughter echoed from the hallway, then out the front door and onto the porch.

A minute later, the front door slammed shut. Kristi and Frankie burst into the dining room with the paper, play-fighting, competing for who would deliver the daily news to their father.

"Thank you," Atticus said as he took the paper and pulled out a chair. "And I've asked you kids before not to slam that door."

"Wash up for supper, children." Beth watched for a moment as Atticus shook out the paper, and then she started toward the kitchen. "The chicken is about ready to come out of the pot. Kristi shucked the corn and cut up the wax beans, and they ought to be about done by now. Supper's in ten minutes, darling, and just to remind you, we need more potatoes. We've already mashed up the last of what we bought from that strange man, that odd Mr. Crick. I still prefer those russets of ours, though, even with his being cheaper. But I guess it's just a matter of—"

"My God. Oh my God," Atticus said.

She stopped, then turned around. "What? What's wrong?"

"An item right here on the maritime pages. About Mr. Street."

"The same one?"

"Must be. Says here a Saint Louis shipowner, age sixty-three. Gotta be him. Same company name."

Beth slowly made her way to the dining room table, then stood behind Atticus.

"My God." He shook his head as he read the text a second time, following it with his forefinger.

She placed her hand on his shoulder. "Tell me."

"Good Lord." He shook his head some more. "Yeah. Here it is. Right here it says Joshua H. Street the second. That's the name. It's him all right. Says here, 'while performing sea trials for a newly constructed side-wheel Mississippi riverboat, Mr. Street fell into the paddles and was crushed to death.'"

He looked up. Their eyes met. They were speechless and just looked at each other, shaking their heads.

Several minutes later, Maribeth and the children were seated at the kitchen table. Atticus remained in the dining room, standing now, next to the table, his gaze fixed on the newspaper, which was still opened to the same article as before.

"Supper's getting cold," Maribeth said.

"C'mon, Papa," said Frankie.

"Mama, Mrs. Braadland asks if I can go visit them in Copper Harbor."

"I guess it'll be okay, Kristi, but we'll ask Papa when he comes to the table."

"May I please go by myself? They'll meet me at the train."

"Who's meeting who?" Atticus said, taking his place at the table.

"*Whom*, honey," said Maribeth.

"Okay…*whom* is meeting *whom?*" Atticus replied, with a smirk.

Maribeth stopped eating and tried to keep from laughing. "That family that found Kristi. The fishermen. They've invited her."

"They sent you another letter, Kristi?"

"Uh huh. And they want to show me some old stones. Some old Norse stones. With writing on them. They found one under the roots of an old, dead tree."

Atticus turned to Maribeth. "Do you know about such things?"

"A little. Runestones. Hundreds of years old. From Vikings. We have them in England and they were also found on the Isle of Man. And lots of places in Scandinavia, of course."

"May I go, Papa?"

"Maybe you could write a report about it for school in the fall."

"I can go, then? By myself on the train? *Please please please?*"

"When?"

"Next weekend. For two weeks."

"Do you think she's old enough?" said Atticus.

Maribeth shrugged, then nodded.

Atticus looked up toward the ceiling, pretending to count with his fingers. "So, let's see…nine, ten, eleven…you're what, now? Thirty years old? Something like that, right?"

All the others at the table laughed. Frankie, mimicking his papa, looked up at the ceiling and counted with his fingers, too. More laughter.

Atticus turned to Maribeth. They shared a glance. She nodded again. "Okay."

"You can go as soon as your summer reading is done," said Atticus.

"Thank you, thank you," Kristi said, then stuck out her tongue at Frankie, who returned the gesture.

"Be nice, you two," said Maribeth.

A knock at the door.

Atticus rose, headed toward the front door, then returned a minute later, holding an opened envelope and a piece of paper in his hand.

"Who was that, darling? What's that you've got?"

"Delivery boy. Telegram from England."

"Oh dear. *Now* what? What's happened?"

He turned the telegram over and looked at the backside, then the front again. Once, twice. "I'm not sure."

"What's it say?"

"Not much really. From your father."

"What do you mean, *not much?*"

"Well, it's two words. That's all. Just two words. Well, no, actually three."

She waited.

"All it says is… *Portuguese Azores.* Then…*tea.*"

Max MacCaigh

[The appearance of US Department of Defense (DoD) visual information does not imply or constitute DoD endorsement.]

Mr. MacCaigh doesn't just write sea stories; he's lived them. He enlisted in the US Navy at age seventeen and went to sea at eighteen. He served aboard a destroyer in combat, and "sailed the seven seas." His general quarters (aka battle) station on the "tin can" was *inside* the forecastle gun—directly below the author photo.

He also worked aboard a "laker," an iron-ore bulk carrier on the North American Great Lakes (photo below), and crewed on private yachts.

He has held industrial and factory jobs, authored articles in magazines and newspapers, written three novellas, and earned an honors BA degree in English literature and creative writing from the State University of New York.

This is his first full-length novel.

Lakers "threading the needle"
Detroit River, 1971
(Photo credit: Private Collection)

https://maxmaccaigh.com

 ACKNOWLEDGEMENTS

Below are listed those who helped bring this book to life:

Paul Burridge of Publishing Buddy (UK). Graphic designer. Novelist. Editor. While reading this novel, I'll often encounter a sensory detail or a turn of phrase that was inspired by Paul.

Next appeared the editing team at Victory Editing (USA): Anne, Linda, and Crystalle, editors and proofreaders extraordinaire.

Steven Grrat, formatter, at ASWebdesigner.Com for his patience, precision and professionalism.

Laine Sutherland Designs (Canada). If you have not visited my home page at https://maxmaccaigh.com you owe it to yourself to do so. The eerie, unsettling turbulence of it draws the eye like no other home page I have ever seen.

ProofreadingPal LLC (Iowa City, Iowa, USA) A special thanks to these nice folks for their detailed observations and insightful comments about all manner of mishaps. Thay are professional, laser-focused, and never let me get lazy when it came to what needed fixing. This novel is orders of magnitude better as a result of their work.

Thank you all.

 AFTERWORD

Thank you for reading *SOULS ADRIFT*. I hope you enjoyed this novel.

This is the first in my "Souls" series. It has attracted not just shipwreck, action and ghost fans, but cozy horror and suspense fans, too. Even love story fans. Welcome aboard, everyone.

Number two begins where *SOULS ADRIFT* leaves off. Most of the main characters show up in the sequel, and it's full of twists, turns, and surprises—a thrilling page-turner like no other. You're gonna love it.

Stay updated with news about my upcoming novels in the Souls series—and beyond:

Join my mailing list at: https://maxmaccaigh.com

Follow me on X (Twitter): @MaxMacCaigh

If you have a moment, please leave a review of *SOULS ADRIFT* at the store where you bought it. It would mean a great deal. Thank you in advance.

Dear reader, I look forward to meeting you again among the pages of my upcoming novels.

All the best,

Max MacCaigh

(Image Credit: Laine Sutherland Designs)
Copyright © Laine Sutherland Designs

9 798999 200580 6